W9-BVL-671

British Literature of the Blitz

British Literature of the Blitz

Fighting the People's War

Kristine A. Miller

First published 2009 by
PALGRAVE MACMILLAN

Palgrave Macmillan in the UK is an imprint of Macmillan Publishers Limited, registered in England, company number 785998, of Houndmills, Basingstoke, Hampshire RG21 6XS.

Palgrave Macmillan in the US is a division of St Martin's Press LLC, 175 Fifth Avenue, New York, NY 10010.

Palgrave Macmillan is the global academic imprint of the above companies and has companies and representatives throughout the world.

Palgrave® and Macmillan® are registered trademarks in the United States, the United Kingdom, Europe and other countries.

ISBN-13: 978–0–230–57365–9 hardback
ISBN-10: 0–230–57365–7 hardback

This book is printed on paper suitable for recycling and made from fully managed and sustained forest sources. Logging, pulping and manufacturing processes are expected to conform to the environmental regulations of the country of origin.

A catalogue record for this book is available from the British Library.

Library of Congress Cataloging-in-Publication Data

Miller, Kristine, 1966–
    British literature of the Blitz : fighting the people's war /
Kristine A. Miller.
        p. cm.
    Includes bibliographical references and index.
    ISBN-13: 978–0–230–57365–9 (alk. paper)
    ISBN-10: 0–230–57365–7 (alk. paper)
        1. English literature – 20th century – History and criticism. 2. World War, 1939–1945 – Great Britain – Literature and the war. 3. War and literature – Great Britain – History – 20th century. 4. War in literature. 5. Ideology in literature. I. Title.

PR478.W67M56 2009
820.9′358—dc22   2008029948

10 9 8 7 6 5 4 3 2 1
18 17 16 15 14 13 12 11 10 09

Printed and bound in Great Britain by
CPI Antony Rowe, Chippenham and Eastbourne

*For my family and in memory of Bette Miller,
Marian Sigler Wessell, Nils Yngve Wessell,
and James Gindin*

Contents

List of Illustrations

List of Abbreviations

AFS	Auxiliary Fire Service
ARP	Air Raid Precautions
ATS	Auxiliary Territorial Service
CEGS	Corps of Engineers Guide Specifications
CPO	Chief Petty Officer
FIL	For Intellectual Liberty, Association of Writers for Intellectual Liberty
GPO	UK General Post Office, used to describe the Film Unit subdivision
HG	Home Guard
LDV	Local Defence Volunteers, early version of the Home Guard
LFB	London Fire Brigade
MI5	Domestic Branch of the Ministry of Information
MI6	Foreign Branch of the Ministry of Information
M-O A	Mass-Observation Archive
MOI	Ministry of Information
OS	Ordinary Seaman
RAF	Royal Air Force
V-1, V-2	Vergeltunsgwaffen [retaliation weapons], unpiloted German rockets
WAAF	Women's Auxiliary Air Force
WLA	Women's Land Army
WRNS	Women's Royal Naval Service
WVS	Women's Voluntary Services

Acknowledgments

Earlier versions of some chapters have appeared as journal articles and book chapters; thanks to the editors and publishers of *Twentieth Century Literature* (45.2, 1999, Hofstra U), the *Journal of Modern Literature* (24.1, 2000, Indiana UP), *Modern Fiction Studies* (49.2, 2003, Johns Hopkins UP), and *Genre* (34.1–2, 2003, U of Oklahoma) for their publication of my articles on Elizabeth Bowen, Rosamond Lehmann, Henry Green, and Graham Greene, and to Stacy Gillis and Philippa Gates, who included my early work on Agatha Christie and Margery Allingham as a chapter in *The Devil Himself: Villainy in Detective Fiction and Film* (Westport, CT: Greenwood Publishing Group © 2002, reprinted with permission of Greenwood Publishing Group, Inc.). I am also grateful for the copyright permissions granted on behalf of the authors treated in this book. Extracts from Elizabeth Bowen's *The Heat of the Day* are reproduced with the permission of Curtis Brown Group Ltd, London, on behalf of the Estate of Elizabeth Bowen Copyright © Elizabeth Bowen, 1949. Quotation from a letter by Bowen to Charles Ritchie and a brief autobiographical note appearing in Victoria Glendinning's *Elizabeth Bowen: Portrait of a Writer* are reproduced with the permission of both Curtis Brown Group Ltd, London, on behalf of the Estate of Elizabeth Bowen Copyright © Elizabeth Bowen, 1945 and 1947, and the Orion Publishing Group Ltd on behalf of Glendinning and her publisher, Weidenfeld and Nicholson, a division of The Orion Publishing Group. The Society of Authors, as the Literary Representative of the Estate of Rosamond Lehmann, has granted permission to quote material from Lehmann's *The Echoing Grove;* the Society has also granted permission to quote briefly from personal letters between Lehmann and Bowen on 14 February and 4 March 1949. Extracts from *Back* and *Caught* by Henry Green, published by Harvill Press, are reprinted by permission of The Random House Group Ltd. Further permissions were required from Green's US publishers: extracts from *Back* by Henry Green, copyright © 1946 by Henry Green and from *Caught* by Henry Green, copyright © 1943 by Henry Green are used by permission of Viking Penguin, a division of Penguin Group (USA) Inc. For quotations from Graham Greene's *The Ministry of Fear*, permission has been granted on behalf of the author and William Heinemann/The Viking Press by David Higham Associates Ltd. I would also like to thank David Higham

Associates, as literary agents for John Lehmann's estate, for permission to quote briefly from his review under the pseudonym of Jack Marlowe in *Penguin New Writing* 17 (April–June 1943).

The book also includes illustrations and archival material for which I would like to acknowledge both the copyright holders and the archives. The Trustees of the Imperial War Museum, London, have granted permission to use the book's cover photograph (negative number D 1300) and have graciously allowed me access to material in the Films and Documents archives. Thanks to the individual copyright holders of papers held by the Department of Documents, IWM (the estates of Miss Daphne Baker, Miss Viola Bawtree, Mrs Yvonne Green, Miss Vivienne Hall, and Miss Josephine May Oakman) for permission to quote from these documents. Every effort has been made to find the copyright holders for the following collections of personal papers also held by the IWM Department of Documents: Mrs P. Bell, Mrs Elizabeth Belsey, Mr Denis Ferne, Mr F. W. Hurd, and Mr S. M. P. Woodcock; the author and the IWM would be grateful for any information which might help to trace those whose identities or addresses are not currently known. The Trustees of the Mass-Observation Archive granted me access to archival material; quotations from this material, including Occasional Papers published by the archive, are reproduced with permission of Curtis Brown Group Ltd, London, on behalf of the Trustees of the Mass-Observation Archives Copyright © Mass-Observation Archives. The British Film Institute has granted permission to quote briefly from its "Screen Dreams" website. Guardian News & Media Ltd has permitted me to quote from C. A. Lejeune's film reviews, for which they hold the copyright. *The New Statesman* has granted permission to use extracts from book reviews (by Elizabeth Bowen, Honor Tracy, and an uncredited reviewer) and an interview (by Shusha Guppy). ITV plc/Granada International has licensed me to reproduce film stills from *The Gentle Sex* (© 1943; Figure 5.1), *Millions Like Us* (© 1943; Figure 5.2), *In Which We Serve* (© 1942; Figure 5.3), and *The Life and Death of Colonel Blimp* (© 1943; Figure 5.5), and they have also allowed me to quote briefly in this book from those films. Finally, Solo Syndication/Associated Newspapers and the British Cartoon Archive at the University of Kent on behalf of David Low have given permission to reprint the cartoon "Blimp Faces the Crisis" (© 1935; Figure 5.4).

Every effort has been made to trace rights holders, but if any have been inadvertently overlooked, the publishers would be pleased to make the necessary arrangements at the first opportunity.

I also appreciate the help of the librarians, archivists, editors, and colleagues who have assisted me in my research, especially the staff at the Mass-Observation Archive, the Imperial War Museum, the British Film Institute National Library and Research Viewing Service, the British National Archives, the Berkshire Records Office, the Centre for Buckinghamshire Studies, and the British Library. I am particularly grateful to James Dean and Dean Chan for their exceptional hospitality in London. Thanks to my editor at Palgrave Macmillan, Paula Kennedy, and her assistant, Steven Hall, for their careful attention to my work. Dorothy Sheridan, head archivist at Mass-Observation, has been extremely helpful, as have colleagues at other universities – especially Penny Summerfield, Phyllis Lassner, Anthony Flinn, James Gindin, Tobin Siebers, Patricia Yaeger, Kali Israel, and Martha Vicinus – who have all thoughtfully read and commented on my work in its various stages. I would also like to express my gratitude to the English department, the College of Humanities, Arts, and Social Sciences, the ADVANCE office, and the Women and Gender Research Institute at Utah State University for their continued support of my work.

Finally, I would like to thank Brian McCuskey for tirelessly helping me and Caitlin and Dylan McCuskey for cheerfully inspiring me throughout this project. Special thanks to my grandfather, Shirley Miller, for sharing his memories of a German prisoner-of-war camp, and to my whole family – this book is dedicated to each one of you.

Introduction: Fighting the People's War

The Blitzkrieg on the United Kingdom during the Second World War was the most direct attack on civilians in British history.[1] As London and other British cities came under siege beginning in September 1940, the common cause of national defense seemed to reduce distance between soldiers and civilians, to resolve differences between men and women, and to repair divisions between leisured and working classes. Politicians and the media emphasized the unifying and leveling power of the Blitz, labeling the conflict a "People's War" and claiming that wartime changes in gender roles and class relations might lead to post-war social reform. Most literary and historical scholarship has assumed the coherence of People's War ideology and examined its effect upon British women and workers during and after the Blitz.[2] Recently, however, historians such as Angus Calder, Penny Summerfield, and Sonya Rose have begun to analyze disparities among individual accounts of the Blitz and therefore to question the assumption of a unified cultural understanding of the People's War. *British Literature of the Blitz* shifts the focus of this historical discussion to the literary imagination, arguing that tensions concerning class relations and gender roles arose not only between but also within individual representations of the People's War. The fiction, film, and personal testimonies of the Blitz emphasize the freedom to disagree with others by demonstrating the individual freedom to contradict oneself. Containing within themselves conflicted views about social upheaval during the People's War, these literary texts represent precisely that state of open-minded thought that was at stake for Britain in the fight against Nazi Germany.

The book's argument depends upon an understanding of how the ideology of a People's War developed in Britain during the Second World War. The nightly bombing of London began on 7 September 1940, a year after Britain's declaration of war, and continued until 2 November. In late October, the attack gradually shifted from London to the provinces of England: by the end of November 1940, Coventry, Merseyside, Manchester, Birmingham, Sheffield, Portsmouth, and Leicester had all been bombed. The Blitz was not limited to England: bombs also fell upon the major industrial cities of Wales (Swansea in February 1940), Scotland (Glasgow in March 1941), and Northern Ireland (Belfast in April and May 1941).[3] In 1944, the Germans developed a new kind of missile as a way of "exacting retribution for the destructive Allied bombing raids on Germany" (Dear 1249):[4] the Vergeltunsgwaffen (retaliation weapons; hereafter referred to as V-weapons) were pilot-less, robot-controlled explosives launched on Britain from bases in France or the Netherlands. The Allies called the V-weapons "doodlebugs" or "buzz bombs" because "as the doodling or buzzing grew louder, those below waited tensely in case the engine cut out," signaling its fall (Calder, *The People's War* 559; hereafter referred to as *PW*). Despite efforts by the Royal Air Force (RAF) and anti-aircraft gunners, the damage was significant: the V-weapons caused 6184 deaths and 17,981 injuries in Britain. In total, the German bombers and V-weapons damaged or destroyed over 3,500,000 homes, killed at least 60,000 civilians, and injured more than 86,000 people on the British home front.[5] Before 1943, more British civilians than soldiers had been killed or wounded;[6] by the end of the war, civilian fatalities equaled almost 25 percent of military fatalities, while the number of wounded civilians was more than 33 percent of the number of wounded soldiers.[7]

British literature of the Blitz therefore represents an altogether new type of civilian experience: the war's bullets and bombs, invasions and incendiaries, dive bombers and doodlebugs placed soldiers and civilians alike in the line of fire. Mass-Observation, a British social research organization founded in 1937, reported the following overheard conversation about the vulnerability of even specially designed bomb shelters to this barrage:

Woman, [age] 50: "Who is it?"
Man, 45: "Chap and his wife and kid, from Bermondsey Street. Shelter fell in."
Woman: "My God, even a shelter's not safe."
Another man: "Of course they ain't. Did you see that one up Walton Street? Smashed to bits it was."
Older woman: "They say eight hundred people were killed in one, Sunday."
Older man: "It's bloody awful." (Harrisson, *Living* 64)

As a result of these changing circumstances, British blitz narratives often include home-front confusion and carnage as brutal as that of any battlefield. For example, one civilian describes her bombed Stepney neighborhood as follows:

> Unexploded bomb. Building fell on a group of men and women. Screams, groans, sudden rush back of the people followed immediately by a rush forward. Women fainted, mass hysteria, men threw a fit. Men, women and children crying and sobbing. Frantic parents searching for their young. Pub near by [sic] full of casualties. Dead and dying on the pavements. (Chrisp 10)

Later, this woman recounts even more graphically another night of the Blitz: "One house fell upon a family who were sheltering in the basement. Arms and legs could be seen protruding from the debris," and she records the comment of a passerby: "It's terrible. Legs and arms of little children – all burned and scarred they are. You can see them through the bricks. Little children, no more. The Simons. Such nice people they was" (Chrisp 17). Here, life on the home front recalls life in the trenches during the Great War, when soldiers lived with the dead "underfoot; they were used to reinforce the parapets of the trenches; they were stored in trenches awaiting burial. Some turned up in bizarre places, such as in the latrine, holding up a fragile doorway, or up a tree" (Tate 66). As one working-class man exclaimed upon seeing his first blitzed home in London, "We're in the front line! Me own home – it's in the Front Line" (Harrisson, *Living* 76). Surrounded by the dead and dying, many civilians began to feel that they were fighting as soldiers in a People's War.

These changes shaped the construction of blitz narratives both during and after the war. Memoirs written and donated years later to the Imperial War Museum's Department of Documents describe the bombing in language strikingly similar to that of wartime accounts. For example, Mrs P. Bell's memoir, donated to the museum in 1985 (date of writing unknown), portrays London during the air raids with vivid detail:

> Poor old London, what a beating she took. In the confusion, the bells of the fire service, clanging, going east along the high road, the Ambulances' peals coming west, bringing the injured as far as possible from the City. It was night mare, earth quake [sic], firework show all rolled into one. It was hell let loose, men fighting fires, fear,

fatigue. Fighting for their lives and others. Carrying the mutalated [sic] bodies almost flat out on their feet, but still fighting.

Here, the image of "mutilated bodies" recalls the battlefield in much the same way as the image of "dead and dying on the pavements" does in the wartime Mass-Observation account quoted above; similarly, the use of mild profanity to describe war – the Blitz was "hell let loose" – echoes both the language of soldiers at the front and the overheard comment about the number of deaths in collapsing shelters as "bloody awful."

Penny Summerfield has written extensively about the role of memory in oral history, and her ideas help to interpret the imagery and language of postwar memoirs about the Blitz. In *Contesting Home Defence*, she and Corinna Peniston-Bird insist that "personal testimony is not simply a window on the past"; instead, "memories are formed through a complex process of interaction between an individual's experiences and publicly available constructs, including prior accounts of similar experiences" (14). I would add that this "cultural circuit" informs even contemporaneous accounts of the Blitz (14): while later memoirs and oral histories inevitably frame wartime experience within a more comprehensive set of existing narratives and images, accounts of the Blitz written in the 1940s demonstrate a keen awareness of their relationship to the dominant cultural ideology of a People's War. The diarists, letter writers, novelists, and filmmakers of the war period engage in the same "complex process of interaction" that Summerfield and Peniston-Bird describe, in this case between their personal experiences and the constructs of the People's War that were publicly available during the Blitz. As a result, many civilians not only had remarkable war stories to tell but also recorded them – a phenomenon that demands more literary critical attention than it has yet received. The collection of documents at the Imperial War Museum contains thousands of pages of Second-World-War diaries, memoirs, and letters written by civilians and demobilized soldiers, and the University of Sussex's Special Collection of Mass-Observation materials features the war writing of at least 2500 civilian volunteers. At no other moment in history have so many British citizens felt compelled to write so extensively about their daily lives and ideas. The compulsion indicates a widespread need to represent individual blitz experiences in a meaningful way, and one purpose of this book is to give these representations of the Blitz the literary critical attention that they deserve.

The extensive documentation of civilian experience during the Second World War indicates the degree to which the Blitz transformed communication between soldiers and civilians. When soldiers in foxholes received letters from home, the letters all too often described exactly that relentless, unpredictable violence from which soldiers had tried to protect civilians in the past. Mrs Elizabeth Belsey, for example, writes to her soldier husband on 3 September 1940 about "a terrific explosion somewhere around. I spilt my tea all over myself, Sally [a friend], and the tablecloth; but no harm was done. I suppose it was an unexploded bomb going off." One month later, she describes another close call: "Shortly after the all-clear, there was a sudden roar of a single plane falling on the roof, but after a minute identified as very close machine-gunfire" (7 Oct. 1940). The Belseys correspond in particular about the welfare of their six-month-old daughter: "I share all your feelings about her very poignantly," writes Mrs Belsey, "especially the feeling of thankfulness that she still knows nothing. [...] It is mostly on her account that I pray and long for this war to end: I want so much for her, and love her so much" (5 Sept. 1940).[8] The implication here is that the innocent baby cannot be protected for long; the violence of war has become terrifyingly universal.

The increasing danger to women and children on the home front became part of wartime propaganda. In April 1941, the Home Publicity Sub-committee of the Ministry of Information (MOI) decided to launch a "propaganda offensive" with the idea of the People's War as its central theme (Williams). Much of the documentary footage shot for the MOI both before and after this decision therefore includes images of falling bombs, anti-aircraft fire, and the recovery of survivors from the wreckage of the Blitz. Short films that employed this home-front footage – including "London Can Take It" (1940), "Mobile Canteen" (1941), "Post 23" (1941), "A.T.S." (1941), "WVS: Women's Voluntary Services" (1942), "Total War in Britain" (1945), and "The Eighty Days" (1945) – were screened before wartime features, like the newsreel footage of soldiers at the front. In these documentary shorts and newsreels, both soldiers and civilians could see from a distance startling representations of each other's wartime experiences. In the past, soldiers had fought and died on the battlefield, while civilians had watched and waited at home. The Blitz transformed the relationship between home front and front line by forcing civilians to fight like soldiers and soldiers to watch and wait like civilians: now everyone was fighting, and everyone knew the danger that threatened loved ones.

The increasing availability of information shaped wartime political rhetoric and literature in crucial ways. Even in early 1939, before thousands of civilians had experienced the bombing firsthand, Mass-Observation reported that the public would not tolerate rigid, controlling propaganda:

> There is great public dissatisfaction with present heavily censored newsreels. The Government's only propagandist film so far has been treated as a joke, although it was supposed to instruct people about ARP [Air Raid Precautions]. Its audience response, in terms of laughter, nearly equals an indifferent Disney. (Mass-Observation Archive: FR 1, 1939: 4; hereafter referred to as M-O A)

Once the bombing began, people stopped laughing, but they also became even more skeptical of official statements about the Blitz: "The most significant fact to emerge from the [October 1940 Mass-Observation film] survey was that those films which sought to influence people's attitudes or behaviour were conspicuously less effective than films which simply imparted facts" (Chapman 107). There was one notable exception: Mass-Observation reported that "London Can Take It" (1940) was "the most frequently commented on film, and received nothing but praise" because it illustrated so powerfully how British men, women, and children were working together to combat Nazi Germany. The fighting of a People's War, central to the film, "was to become the most important theme of British wartime propaganda" (Chapman 99). As Angus Calder observes, the idea's "influence over the press, the films and the radio was enormous; it shaped the rhetoric of five years of official and unofficial propaganda" (*PW* 138).[9] More popular than other types of propaganda because it simultaneously honored individual blitz experiences and united people in a common cause, the rhetoric of the People's War offered British citizens an idea with and against which to represent the Blitz meaningfully.[10]

Calder has analyzed the ideology behind this rhetoric in some detail and has labeled it the "myth of the Blitz" – the notion, central to British wartime propaganda, that "friendliness," "freedom," and a "Cockney spirit" united all of Britain across a "volunteers' front" during the bombing (*Myth* xiv, 195–6). He carefully explains his choice of the words "myth" and "mythology": the terms do not imply the untruth of ideas about the People's War; they suggest instead, according to an entry on "Mythology" in *Chambers Dictionary*, "an ancient traditional story of Gods or heroes, esp[ecially] one offering an explanation of some fact or phenomenon" (qtd in Calder, *Myth* 2). Calder cites Roland Barthes's idea that a myth "establishes a blissful clarity" and makes "things appear to mean something by themselves" in order to explain how particular meanings of the Blitz come to appear as truths (Barthes 143). These naturalized meanings of the Blitz constitute the political rhetoric of the People's War, which suggests, first, that the circumstances of the Blitz brought together men and women from all regions and social classes in Great Britain and, second, that the resulting feeling of gender and class equality in wartime would lead to permanent social change after the war. According to Calder, "Those who made the 'People's War' a slogan argued that the war could promote a revolution in British society" by breaking down barriers between genders and classes and thus creating new opportunities for all (*PW* 17). Victory in the People's War depended upon "British or English moral pre-eminence, buttressed by British unity," and the association of morality and unity in the rhetoric led many people to assume that wartime cooperation was inherently good and would therefore lead logically and inevitably to positive, enduring social change (*PW* 2).

Prime Minister Winston Churchill's war speeches turn People's War rhetoric to great political advantage, ensuring his own continuing popularity during the war, as S. P. MacKenzie asserts:

> The heroic imagery, the rolling prose, the absolute refusal to admit defeat, had made the Prime Minister almost the living embodiment of all that Britons felt was greatest in themselves. In an opinion poll taken in July 1940 an astonishing 88 per cent of respondents expressed confidence in his leadership – and in the face of almost unrelieved military disaster. (47)

Churchill's 1941 broadcast speech, "Westward, Look, the Land Is Bright," shows specifically how he employed the heroic imagery of the People's War. The speech praises and unites British civilians as soldiers fighting for their country:

> The sublime but also terrible and somber experiences and emotions of the battlefield which for centuries had been reserved for the soldiers and sailors, are now shared, for good or ill, by the entire population. All are proud to be under the fire of the enemy. Old men, little children, the crippled veterans of former wars, aged women, the ordinary hard-pressed citizen or subject of the King, as he likes to call himself, the sturdy workmen who swing hammers or load ships; skilful craftsmen; the members of every kind of A.R.P. service, are proud to feel that they stand in the line together with our fighting men, when one of the greatest causes is being fought out, as fought

out it will be, to the end. This is indeed the grand heroic period of our history, and the light of glory shines on all. (93)

Situating British civilians alongside soldiers and the King in this "grand heroic period of our history," Churchill unites individuals fighting for England in the People's War by shining the light of glory upon them all.

In practice the concept of the People's War was a far less coherent political idea than Churchill's conservative vision of a united national war effort implies; the idea also appealed to radicals like Tom Wintringham, who adopted the rhetoric of the People's War in order to incite local guerrilla uprisings across Europe. The rhetoric's power ultimately lay in its ability to draw together in a common cause individuals with fundamentally different points of view. Significantly, Churchill's most memorable war speeches invoke the idea of a People's War not only to draw citizens together in defense of the nation but also to suggest the more radical possibility of postwar social change. In his 1943 speech on "The Women of Britain," for example, Churchill proclaims that the war has permanently expanded the boundaries of conventional gender roles:

This war effort could not have been achieved if the women had not marched forward in millions and undertaken all kinds of tasks and work for which any generation but our own [...] would have considered them unfitted [...]. Nothing has been grudged, and the bounds of women's activities have been definitely, vastly, and permanently enlarged. (285)

Wielding the weapon of hyperbole, Churchill suggests that civilians who have demonstrated unswerving commitment to duty during the Blitz have earned the right to assume more active political roles both during and after the war. The implication here is that the common cause of national defense has not only reduced the distance between front line and home front but also broken down class boundaries and called into question the inequities of established gender roles. The prospect of a social revolution was particularly appealing in Britain during the 1940s, since the economic depression of the 1930s meant that "one million men were still unemployed as Britain went to war" in 1939 (Rose 31), and gender inequity continued, particularly in the workplace, even after the passage of British suffrage laws in 1918 and 1928.

The problem, however, was that many members of the British public actually demanded the public initiatives that Churchill's broadcasts promised but the government never offered:

> Paradoxically, Britain had found in Churchill a Conservative leader with a reactionary past who, according to his wife, knew nothing of the life and aspirations of the ordinary people, whose chauvinism and imaginative sense of British history gave the war a meaning and a political significance that struck a chord with the working class. In appealing to those great abstractions of liberty, justice and democracy, Churchill offered no proposals for change; these ideas were for him already embedded in parliamentary government and the British constitution, if not in the national character itself. Least of all did he expect his rhetoric to radicalise a popular movement for social reform. His horizons were limited by the strategic objectives of war. These objectives, however, depended upon the consent and co-operation of the ordinary people on every front. (Morgan and Evans 24)

Churchill's commitment to protecting the status quo explains his defeat in the 1945 election, which "was propelled by a tide already turned by Home-Front experience and a determination that, this time, peace would be more nearly synonymous with social justice. Labour rode in on its crest" (Hennessy 85). The 1942 Beveridge Report, however, anticipated and responded in practical terms to this changing tide by outlining a specific plan for postwar social change. Sir William Beveridge chaired "a committee which had been intended by the [wartime] government to be a relatively 'harmless' tidying-up exercise" (Hills 1). Although Churchill had not meant to give the committee much power, Beveridge "used the media of the time effectively to appeal above the heads of the Government, outflanking both the Treasury and the Prime Minister, Winston Churchill, in presenting his vision of the postwar world, and his detailed ideas for building it" (Hills 1). According to Beveridge, "the first principle" of his report was that "a revolutionary moment in the world's history is time for revolutions, not for patching" (Calder, *PW* 528), an assertion that stands in stark contrast to Churchill's belief that the ideas of the People's War were already embedded in parliamentary government, the British constitution, and even the national character itself.

The Beveridge Report therefore attempted to transform the rhetoric of revolution central to the People's War into a social reality by recommending the development of a more egalitarian social security system and welfare state. The plan offered specific benefits to the British public:

> [It] provided that all wage earners would contribute equally in weekly installments and, in return, they would receive a uniform rate of benefit. Their contributions would be supplemented by increased employer and state subsidies. National public assistance would be available for people who were not covered by the plan. Proposals for a national minimum wage with child benefits provided as a supplement for wage earners with children and the formation of a national health service were central to the plan. (Rose 65)

The plan was exactly what many civilians wanted. The 300-page report was priced at two shillings and quickly became a national bestseller that was "endlessly discussed, endlessly extolled" by civilians during the war (Ziegler 266). Every major newspaper published a summary of it, and the combined sales of the report and the brief official summary issued by the government "ran to at least 635,000 copies. Within two weeks of its publication, a Gallup Poll indicated that nineteen people out of twenty had heard of the report, and nine out of ten believed that its proposals should be adopted" (Calder, *PW* 528). Throughout the political planning and development of the welfare state, the British public therefore "remained cynical, sure that its hopes would be betrayed, certain that everything was being 'watered down' from the high Beveridge proof" (Calder, *PW* 536).

The widespread popularity of the Beveridge Report, People's War propaganda, and Churchill's war speeches indicates that the idea of the People's War captured the imaginations of many British civilians. Most current literary and cultural criticism has assumed that the phenomenon of the People's War unified the British cultural imagination and that the People's War was therefore a coherent concept. Examining the effects of the People's War on Britain, the scholarship suggests that the experience of the Blitz either did or did not transform class and gender hierarchies during and after the war. Thus, scholars such as Arthur Marwick and Phyllis Lassner have argued that the war broke down or exposed conventional boundaries within gender relations and between social classes; others, including Gill Plain and Harold Smith, have concluded that little social change occurred in wartime Britain.[11] Studies of the period tend to evaluate the impact of the People's War by considering in detail a single political issue (gender roles, class relations, propaganda production), genre (literary novels, pulp fiction, film, personal testimony), or author during the war.[12] Even Mark Rawlinson's *British Writing of the Second World War*, which spans the genres of fiction, poetry, memoir, documentary, and criticism, suggests that all of the wartime texts that he examines contributed – often unintentionally – to what he assumes to be the national mythology of a just People's War. Rawlinson argues that the literature translates the material reality of wartime death and destruction on the home front and front line into the abstract idealism of political discourse.

British Literature of the Blitz challenges the mythology that Rawlinson and others describe by approaching this literature not as a coherent collective defense of the war but as an expression of imaginative freedom to disagree about the People's War. Because People's War ideology simultaneously magnified and masked existing problems within the social system, different civilians imagined the People's War in very different ways. This book analyzes fiction, film, and personal testimony, moving from the literary fiction aimed at the middle and upper-middle classes to the pulp fiction and popular films consumed primarily by the middle and working classes conscripted into subordinate military and industrial ranks. Representations of the Blitz in both literary and popular genres expose the conflicts between social classes and within gender relations that underwrote and undercut the polished rhetoric of the People's War. Identifying in the literature a basic cultural need to imagine the paradox of a unified nation composed of individuals often at odds with one another, *British Literature of the Blitz* concludes that the imaginative representation of vastly different blitz experiences was an essential part of wartime life across social strata in British culture.

This approach to the People's War builds upon historical work by Angus Calder, Rodney Lowe, Kenneth O. Morgan, Penny Summerfield, and Sonya Rose, who have all examined the differences among individual wartime experiences in order to ground the general political ideal of the People's War in specific personal detail. Calder's books, *The People's War* and *The Myth of the Blitz*, argue that the dominant ideology of a People's War has for too long overshadowed the troublesome differences among individual lives in wartime. Lowe contends that the ideology was actually less dominant than even Calder suggests; according to Lowe, most British civilians were too "ill-informed" to demand the kinds of social welfare policies promised during the Blitz (175). Morgan and Summerfield also question the presumed power of People's War ideology, exploring records of individual experiences in order to argue that wartime rhetoric about the People's War actually had little impact on entrenched class and gender hierarchies within British culture. Most recently, Sonya Rose's *Which People's War?* has advanced the critical conversation by investigating the troublesome contradictions pervading representations of the People's War in personal testimonies and official documents. Rose explores the problem of constructing wartime national identity by examining how British citizens from various social, sexual, and racial backgrounds conceived of the People's War in conflicting and contradictory ways. Turning to People's War rhetoric itself as a literary phenomenon, *British Literature of the Blitz* sets aside the interesting question of how racial, imperial, and nationalist ideologies intersect during wartime in order to focus on the crucial interplay of class and gender ideologies in People's War rhetoric.

I argue that different understandings of the People's War arise not only between but also within individual accounts of wartime experience. Even the most apparently optimistic descriptions of the Blitz, which claim that life on the besieged home front was "extraordinary" (Bawtree, 31 Aug. 1940) or "at its best" (Bell) because the bombing broke down barriers between social classes or within gender relations, allow for this sense of conflict. For example, one middle-class diarist writes about class relations as follows:

> There is one good thing, and one only about this war – it is an instant and complete leveller of "classes." Everyone mixes and talks to anyone and I think we all find that the other is really quite a normal and interesting person and not a bit different from ourselves. (V. Hall, 4 Sept. 1939)

The rhetoric of the People's War dominates Hall's diary entry: she calls the idea of "classes" into question with protest quotes and proclaims the leveling power of the Blitz, suggesting her agreement with the propagandistic idea that "we are all 'working' class now" in wartime (M-O A: DR 1637, June 1944). However, the passage also contains a very different discourse, one that labels any person from a social stratum below one's own as "the other," even as it acknowledges that this "other" might actually be "quite a normal and interesting person." Imagining the wartime possibility of class equality as well as the persistence of class inequity, Hall employs two conflicting discourses in a narrative that seems designed only to praise the transformative social power of the People's War.

The imaginative effort required simultaneously to recognize and to bridge class differences becomes clear in Mass-Observation testimony collected after civilians had time to reflect upon the first major home-front bombing in 1940–41. One middle-class man, for example, claims in 1943 to be "as willing to make friends with people of different social classes from me as with people of my own class," and he rejoices that his experiences in the Home Guard (HG) and Army have "knocked out of me, thank heavens!" the prewar state of feeling "very shy of people in different classes to myself" (M-O A: DR 2685, Jan. 1943). Similarly, a suburban housewife asserts that the war has eliminated her class prejudice:

> The war has finally enabled me to get rid of early suburban inhibitions re[garding] meeting with supposed inferiors: I now work in a factory and like the people. I feed in British Restaurants or the Factory canteen and in public shelters during the bombing (I wasn't often in them) I saw no class distinctions. I also go to public wash-houses, so I have more acquaintances among people of different social classes than ever before. (M-O A: DR 3306, Jan. 1943)

The rhetoric of the People's War dominates both of these accounts, but a conflicting discourse subtly undercuts it by repeatedly labeling as "different" the social classes brought together in time of war. Part of the reason for this discourse of difference may have been the way in which Mass-Observation framed its question to respondents:

> Has your attitude to any of the following things changed at all since the war began, and if so in what ways has it changed: Please answer this question in some detail, and where possible trace your attitude through the war: (a) money (b) clothes (c) security (d) *people in different social classes from yourself* (e) sex (f) politics (g) conscientious objectors. (my emphasis)

Nevertheless, even the woman's testimony, which adopts the equivalent of Hall's protest quotes (*"supposed* inferiors," my emphasis) to show the impact of the People's War upon her own life, emphasizes that she has made no more than "acquaintances" among people from different social classes than her own.

The man's narrative goes on to explain why it was so difficult to move beyond acquaintance to friendship, regardless of wartime circumstances:

> I have no very close friend in a class different to my own and, if I had, I should still be chary of taking him or her home with me,

mainly, I think, because my mother and grandmother still don't like the idea of having people of lower classes as social friends, even though they are willing to meet and be friendly with them at the W.V.S. [Women's Voluntary Services], communal kitchens and so on. (M-O A: DR 2685, Jan. 1943)

Despite frequent – and usually friendly – meetings during the bombing, people from various social classes often shared only a limited range of experience. Even the experience of the Blitz itself was not the same across classes, since people had very different routines and sheltering practices depending on social background. The female Mass-Observer's testimony confirms the way that social class determined sheltering practice: although she confidently says that she finds "no class distinctions in bomb shelters," she must also admit that she "wasn't often in them."

Many working-class civilians *were* often in them, despite often unsafe and unsanitary conditions. At the beginning of the war, the British government tried to anticipate problems of public safety by distributing to every family a free, private Anderson shelter, which was "planned as a shelter for erection inside a small working-class home." However, there were ultimately "technical objections" that "ensured that it [the Anderson] had become an outdoor shelter. Unfortunately, under a quarter of the public, Mass-Observation pointed out, had gardens" (Calder, *PW* 179). As a result, many working-class people sheltered in the underground Tube stations, which were dirty and over-crowded, as this Mass-Observation report confirms:

When you get over the shock of seeing so many sprawling people, you are overcome with the smell of humanity and dirt. Dirt abounds everywhere. The floors are never swept and are filthy. People are sleeping on piles of rubbish. The passages are loaded with dirt. There is no escaping it. The arches are dank and grim. They are lighted well, until black-out time, and then all the lights on one side are put out, because the black-out arrangements are inadequate. There they sit in darkness, head of one against feet of the next. There is no room to move, hardly any room to stretch…. The sirens went at about 8 p.m. Lots of people were asleep, but in general it was too early for this. But already, at 8, people were beginning to cough, and this coughing spread, and lasted throughout the evening. I developed a cough and sore throat, in the early stages of the evening. Everyone there was working class. (M-O A: FR 431, 1940: 47–8)

Perhaps the most profound "shock" for the Observer is the stark contrast between the circumstances in the Underground and in a typical middle- or upper-middle-class home. Even Henry Moore, whose origins as an Irish coal miner's son helped him to empathize with the working classes portrayed in his famous drawings of Tube shelterers, explained that he never worked in the Underground itself because "it would have been like drawing in the hold of a slave ship" (qtd in Rawlinson 91).[13]

In contrast to the squalor of the Tube stations was the luxury of the most famous hotels in London. The hotels offered select people the chance to shelter in comfort:

> The best place to be in a raid – if one could afford it – was one of the large, steel-framed hotels. For the well-off, the Dorchester became the focal point of London after dark. The Turkish baths had been converted into a luxurious air-raid shelter, while dancing and dining went on throughout the Blitz in the downstairs grill-room. (Hewison 34)

Those with social or political power – including proponents of the People's War such as Lord Beaverbrook and Herbert Morrison, both of whom frequently sheltered at the Savoy – had more and better options than the workers who crowded into dirty public shelters to escape the massive damage to their East End homes during the Blitz.

The unequal choices available to people from different social classes in wartime exacerbated existing social tensions. Sonya Rose takes as one example the evacuation process, which should have bridged the social gap by resettling lower-class urban mothers and children with rural families in the English countryside. Instead, evacuation often did more to reinforce than to dispel "the image of two nations created nearly a hundred years previously by Benjamin Disraeli"; Rose suggests that "in place of Disraeli's industrial north and agricultural south, the two nations of the evacuation were the urban poor and country people" (58). Similar divisions plagued British industry in wartime; the fact that "unofficial strikes and the Shop Stewards Movement continued to trouble union efforts to cooperate with the Government in the name of national unity" suggests that the narrative of shared experience during the People's War told only part of the story (Rose 43). The reality was that the privileged civilians who found the myth of the Blitz most compelling often had only passing knowledge of what life was like for their working-class comrades in arms, and their knowledge was frequently based on no more than a few intense moments during the Blitz. Although People's War rhetoric built the promise of social change upon the idea that civilian men and women from all classes were "proud to feel that they stand in the line together with our fighting men" (Churchill, "Westward" 93), the differences among individual experiences paradoxically became more obvious than ever before amidst the vast destruction of the Blitz.

The destruction made visible the impact not only of social class but also of gender upon wartime civilian experience. The British government began formally registering women for war work in April 1941 and announced female conscription on 2 December 1941. By 1943, "80 per cent of married women and 90 per cent of single women were contributing to the war effort in some way, whether in full-time, part-time or voluntary job" (Hartley, *Hearts* 131). Women drove ambulances, flew airplanes, and piloted canal boats in the Auxiliary Territorial Service (ATS), the Women's Auxiliary Air Force (WAAF), and the Women's Royal Naval Service (WRNS). They joined the ARP as wardens, the Women's Land Army (WLA) as farmers, and the MOI as codebreakers. Women also worked in factories, manufacturing munitions by day after sheltering from enemy bombardment all night. These changes in conventional gender roles were particularly exciting for the privileged women who had never considered entering the workforce before the war. While working-class women remained employed in wartime because of financial need, many women from the upper classes felt "pleased at the increasing breakdown of barriers to female emancipation," as both the Blitz and female military conscription forced them out of their homes and into the political arena, often for the first time (M-O A: DR 2863, Sept. 1942).[14]

The impact of social class on women's liberation from conventional gender roles during the People's War becomes clear in wartime accounts of personal relationships between middle-class and working-class women. Penelope Barlow, a university-educated young woman working in a winding factory during the war, describes for Mass-Observation her relationship with a lower-class co-worker, Eileen Braithwaite:

> I told Eileen that I was going on Saturday; that I only came for a month to get a practical background to a theoretical education and to see how another class of people lived and worked and thought. [...] She said, "I didn't think you'd stay very long; you're too intelligent." I said, "I'm not half as intelligent as you." She said, "I've no ambition. I used to care a lot about elocution and did a lot of it, but suddenly I started to wonder what was the point of ambition and

getting on. So I followed the family into the mill." (Calder and Sheridan 156–7)

Although both women self-deprecatingly undercut their professional worth – Barlow claims that she's "not half as intelligent" as her friend, while Braithwaite asserts that she has "no ambition" – the difference in their social status guarantees very different outcomes. On the one hand, the rhetoric of the People's War aptly describes Barlow's experience: she has the wartime opportunity to live and work with another class of people and thus to add "practical background" to her "theoretical education." Braithwaite, on the other hand, finds few options for women of her class in war or in peace: despite her ambitions, she remains trapped in the winding factory. These two women must work alongside one another for the sake of the war effort, but the shared experience cannot erase the social differences that remain between them.

Yet even when women belonged to the same social class, they often disagreed about wartime gender issues much as they disagreed about changes in class relations. In the middle class, for example, some women perceived positive changes in gender roles during the war:

> I feel better pleased about the position of women in the country to day [sic] than I have ever felt before, because they are being allowed to bear their share of the burden. I feel that they should continue to have more responsibility after the war. (M-O A: DR 2973, Sept. 1942)

Others saw little or no change: "I think women are still treated disgustingly in this country, and I cannot understand how men who imagine themselves to be rational and just can go on perpetuating the constant injustices against women, nor why women accept them so patiently" (M-O A: DR 2865, Sept. 1942). Still others expressed a strong desire to return to traditional gender roles after the war:

> I feel that probably the position of women in the country at the moment is necessary because of the war – but I am not a feminist, so I don't agree with women doing men's jobs and demanding equal rights with men. I disagree especially when they demand these rights and then want to be treated as women as well. I should like to see women return to their true position – that of wives and mothers. (M-O A: DR 2873, Sept. 1942)

Although all three of these writers are middle-class women respond-ing to a Mass-Observation question in September 1942 about wartime gender roles, their conflicting opinions about the impact of the People's War on patriarchal power suggest marked differences in their personal attitudes and experiences as women at war.

Perhaps the most interesting personal testimonies about the People's War are those in which individual writers struggle to reconcile their own identities with shifting and changing ideas of the People's War. In these accounts, writers are often so emotionally fraught that they become trapped within inadequate and contradictory wartime dis-courses as they try to describe their blitz experiences. The diary of ARP warden Josephine Oakman provides one example. On duty one night early in the Blitz, Oakman is shocked to discover a warden who was a personal friend buried beneath the rubble of a bombed building:

> Thorpe was under the arch – I rolled him over and saw his face – God – he had none and what he had was a mess. All the limbs were broken and lay at horrible angles. I recognised him by his hair, uniform and ring on his hand. (14 Sept. 1940)

Over the next few weeks, Oakman uses her diary to question the ideas of the People's War that she still holds dear:

> London has now had 10 weeks of blitz and I have heard no word of complaint and saw not a single case of panic during this terrible time. London can take it! But at a cost – of lost lives, broken hearts and limbs and destroyed homes. The Lord help them – these victims of the air raids! on them the price does fall. (25 Nov. 1940)

Even as she adopts the unifying words so popular in the propaganda of 1940 – "London can take it!" – she cannot help but tally the cost of so many civilian lives lost in fighting the war.

By early 1941, Oakman herself has paid this price repeatedly:

> I've lost home and friends and very nearly blown up several times by bombs – and yet I'm still here. My time has not yet come. If it does – I hope and feel that the little bit I've done to help may not have been in vain. The man in the street has been and is my first and last con-cern – and that mere thought has kept me in Chelsea A.R.P. (12 Feb.)

As the personal toll upon Oakman gradually increases over the course of the Blitz – building upon that first discovery of Thorpe – she clings to the "mere thought" of protecting "the man in the street" as a way of giving meaning to a life that feels increasingly threatened by the nightly bombing. The diary continues in this manner, vacillating between descriptions of the noble fight for "a lasting peace – which – God willing will endure" (24 Aug. 1941), on the one hand, and Oakman's recurring and growing state of depression, on the other: "I am afraid of the goodness of our work for the future – I do not have the confidence I had" (3 Feb. 1941). Confounded by the national imperative to protect the freedom of people who seem increasingly likely to be killed, Oakman articulates a conflicted view of the People's War not uncommon among those working and fighting for their lives in the Blitz.

A similar sense of internal conflict haunts this 70-year-old working-class warden's even more personal description of his wife's death, which he communicates to a young man in the hope of recruiting him to join an ARP unit:

> He [Hitler] smashed up me home and me missus in the same night. I just went down the Post and when I come back it was as flat as this here wharfside. There was just my house like – well, part of my house. My missus were making me a cup of tea for when I come home. She were in the passage between the kitchen and the wash-house where it blowed her. She were burnt right up to her waist. Her legs were just two cinders... and her face... The only thing I could recognize her by was one of her boots. I'd have lost fifteen homes if I could have kept my missus. (Chrisp 23)

The warden begins by charging Hitler with a reckless violence that Britain must combat, and the phrase "smashed up me home and me missus in the same night" describes the resulting damage in material rather than emotional terms. The opening recruits the young man to the ARP by drawing him together with his fellow citizens against a common German enemy in the People's War. However, as the warden's personal testimony continues, his language shifts from the shocking factual description of a burned home and dead wife to an emotional portrayal of his loss: "We used to read together. I can't read mesen [sic]. She used to read to me like. We'd have our arm chairs one either side of the fire, and she read me bits of the paper. We had a paper every evening. Every evening" (Chrisp 23). The Blitz does not free this working-class man from existing social restraints, as the rhetoric of the People's War suggests it might; instead, it devastates him personally and also exposes more plainly than in peacetime an illiteracy common among people of his class. Like Josephine Oakman, this widower employs the language of the People's War to make sense of death in the Blitz, but he finds the personal details too painful to support the mythology.

The friction between a collective national identity and distinctive individual identities informs both the rhetoric of the People's War and the literature of this period. The subtitle of this book – *Fighting the People's War* – describes the way that British citizens not only cooperated to fight Nazi Germany but also questioned the nationalist ideology binding them together. The paradox of the People's War is that it counters a totalitarian threat with a potentially totalizing ideal: because it is both patriotic and utopian, the rhetoric resists critique, even though the right to question compulsory nationalism was precisely what Britain was fighting for. *British Literature of the Blitz* looks at writers who explore the disjunction between the master narrative of the People's War and the particular experiences of the people fighting that war; those experiences include the expression of doubt, confusion, and frustration about the disjunction itself. Above all else, home-front British literature values the voicing of individual opinion, even – or especially – when individuals do not agree: a utopia that denies the freedom to critique utopianism is no utopia at all.

My approach to literature of the Blitz parallels the approach that Mass-Observation took to the submissions of its volunteer writers during the war. From its inception in 1937, Mass-Observation self-consciously adopted a "religiously qualitative approach, the result of long, careful, unobserved observation. Instead of rigidly categorising people from above they would be part of the people" (Jeffrey 4). In response to a 1937 opinion letter in the *New Statesman* "suggesting that there was a need for anthropological study of British society" (Jeffrey 1), filmmaker Humphrey Jennings, poet and journalist Charles Madge, and anthropologist Tom Harrisson "founded the organisation with the desire to develop a 'science of ourselves'" (Beaven and Griffiths 3). They advertised for volunteer writers in the *New Statesmen* and other newspapers and journals, initially recruiting about 500 men and women to record their personal observations about life in a country soon to be at war. The goal was to collect and analyze a wide range of individual opinions that expressed the freedom of thought for which the Allies would eventually have to fight.

Mass-Observation's methodology had its roots in the British surrealism and documentary movements, in which its three founders shared an interest.[15] In their first published description of the organization, the founders insisted that Mass-Observation would "not set out in quest of truth or facts for their own sake, or for the sake of an intellectual minority, but aims at exposing them in simple terms to all observers, so that their environment may be understood and thus constantly transformed" (Jennings 17).[16] Their goal was much like that of the documentary movement of the 1930s, which demonstrated a "passion to present, above all to present people to themselves in wholly recognisable terms; terms which acknowledge their variety, their individuality, their representativeness, which find them 'intensely interesting'" (S. Hall 83). Documenting everyday life, Mass-Observation insisted that its "'qualitative' approach gave it special status. Mere public opinion polls and market research organisations aimed at rapid results and sought information only on particular issues; Mass-Observation studied people from all angles all the time. Hence it could spot, so the argument ran, long-term trends" (Calder, "Mass-Observation" 130; hereafter referred to as "M-O").

Skeptical of these claims to study people from all angles all the time, many scholars have criticized Mass-Observation for reaching "unscientific" conclusions based on the writing of an unrepresentative sample of volunteers (Calder, "M-O" 129).[17] Mass-Observation's self-selected panel members were generally "young-ish, left-leaning, and preponderantly [lower-] middle class" and therefore represented only a small segment of the British population during the Blitz (Calder, "M-O" 133).[18] However, defenders of Mass-Observation argue that such definitions of representation are too narrow: "Rather than conceiving of representation in terms of the individual, it is the slices of life that are viewed as representations of everyday life" (Bloome 17). The content of the writing is, of course, "individual and idiosyncratic," but it is the "obligation or desire to communicate and reveal the detail of ordinary life as something socially and historically important which frames the writing in a disciplined way" (Shaw 5). Rather than trying to quantify the views of the population at large based on a statistically representative sample, Mass-Observation aimed to qualify wartime ideas about popular thought based on an idiosyncratic group of narratives describing everyday life.

Despite its qualitative approach, Mass-Observation frequently drew conclusions about the British population, and the MOI even employed the organization to report secretly on a variety of propaganda and morale issues during the war. A Top Secret report submitted by the Director of Naval Intelligence in April 1947 summarizes Mass-Observation's work for the government:

From the end of 1939, Mass Observation was employed by the Home Intelligence Section of the Ministry of Information, to report on a wide range of subjects connected with morale, rumour, war dislocation and frustrations, industrial difficulties and general propaganda effects. In all Mass Observation made more than 400 reports for the Ministry of Information and a number for other Government Departments. (Godfrey 1)

Nevertheless, the government remained skeptical about the value of Mass-Observation's reports. A recently released file held by the British National Archives contains a "Most Secret" and highly revealing memo to Prime Minister Winston Churchill from Desmond Morton, his personal assistant and intelligence liaison. Morton claims in the 9 March 1944 memo that Mass-Observation "is an infernal nuisance and a potential danger"; he describes Mass-Observation further as "a business venture somewhat on the lines of the Gallup Poll. It was once used by the Ministry of Information, but not now. It is a dirty affair." While most scholars agree that Mass-Observation was neither making money on market research nor trying to endanger the British government, the concern here from the Prime Minister's office suggests the government's wariness regarding Mass-Observation's findings. The problem was not only that Mass-Observation was so actively seeking new projects but also that it tended to mitigate even the most general of its conclusions about the British public. When Tom Harrisson states, for example, that "these results have no *absolute* validity, but a comparative value," he confirms that Mass-Observation perceived its research as adding depth to a complicated picture of civilian attitudes about the Blitz (Richards and Sheridan 212). According to Harrisson, "There were about 45 million morales in England, not just one," and he believed that Mass-Observation should explore that plurality of morales instead of searching for the one (Harrisson, "Films" 244). Given the fact that Mass-Observation was investigating topics like hygiene, dreams, and facial hair trends as well as more official concerns about propaganda and rationing, it is perhaps unsurprising that there was never any official security protecting Mass-Observation's offices from enemy infiltration during the war, despite the ubiquitous warnings of the "Careless Talk Costs Lives" propaganda campaign.[19]

Mass-Observation's comparative approach to civilian blitz writing makes the archive a particularly important source for this book. The sample of Mass-Observation volunteers may not have been statistically representative, but it did include male and female writers from different social backgrounds who described in detail their experiences during the Blitz. Mass-Observation's imperative to study many different attitudes and views meant that the organization collected vast amounts of civilian war writing – far more than it could effectively evaluate. Between January 1939 and December 1945, at least 2500 men and women wrote monthly responses to Directive questions issued by Mass-Observation; these questions were often eclectic, particularly in the early days of the organization, when "topics ranged from such serious matters as the behaviour of people at war memorials and anti-Semitism to suggested studies of bathroom behaviour, beards, armpits and eyebrows, and the shouts and gestures of motorists" (Jeffrey 2). The archive contains 160 storage boxes of wartime diaries written by 500 volunteers and more than 1000 boxes of raw materials – including memos, questionnaires, notes, and handwritten observations – organized by topics such as "Women in Wartime," "Film," and "Men in the Forces." Despite the more than 3000 file reports that summarize research findings, the archive's strength remains the unanalyzed raw material of civilian writing, which offers a complex, often contradictory view of life on the bombed home front. This is also a strength of the Imperial War Museum's Department of Documents, which houses the largest collection of private papers (letters, memoirs, diaries) donated by British civilians and soldiers who lived through the Blitz. One goal of this book is to draw together some of these varied narratives in order to demonstrate that the freedom to represent social conflict was essential to imagining wartime Britain and therefore that imaginative representations of the Blitz almost always embed such conflict within their portrayals of the People's War.

In constructing this argument, the book places the literature of the Blitz not only at the center of British wartime experience but also at a crucial moment in British literary history. The modernist emphasis on psychological conflicts and aesthetic tensions has led critics to de-emphasize twentieth-century war writing, because its central problem is real material violence. Marina MacKay and Lyndsey Stonebridge have addressed this gap by situating writing that they define as modernist within the social and political realities of the Second World War. I take a different approach, arguing that since so many civilians endured home-front violence, representations of the Blitz occur not just among a modernist elite but at all levels of culture – from the literary novel to the hastily scrawled letter. This vast body of blitz literature engages with realistic material detail, much like the nineteenth-century novels against which modern and postmodern literatures have typically defined themselves. Examining the writing of civilians profoundly affected by the bombing of the home front, I suggest that British literature of the Blitz demands its own place within dominant narratives of modern literary history.

The book begins its investigation by analyzing in Chapters 1, 2, and 3 canonical literary representations of the Blitz, arguing that these texts self-consciously expose the conflicts inherent in the People's War. Chapter 1 examines the ways in which Elizabeth Bowen's wartime short stories, novel (*The Heat of the Day* [1949]), and memoir (*Bowen's Court* [1942]) represent the influence of social status upon the idea of the mobile woman during the People's War. Bowen represents ambivalently the social inequity that allows upper-middle-class women to opt for exciting and liberating war work during the People's War even as it confines working-class women to the same drudgery they had always endured. Chapter 2 compares Rosamond Lehmann's representation of upper-middle-class female characters in *The Ballad and the Source* (1944), *The Gipsy's Baby* (1946), and *The Echoing Grove* (1953) with Bowen's treatment of similar characters in her war writing. The chapter demonstrates how Lehmann's fiction exaggerates a problem raised by Bowen's war writing: the rhetoric of the People's War not only benefited the privileged few but also was the product of their privileged imaginations. The book's third chapter complicates the arguments about gender and class identity in Chapters 1 and 2 by examining the experience of male civilians during the Blitz. Analyzing Henry Green's *Caught* (1943) and *Back* (1946) alongside the personal testimony of men, the chapter describes the crisis of masculinity experienced by noncombatant men on the home front. As civilians, these men not only failed to live up to the masculine ideal of the soldier hero but also found themselves living alongside women who were working and fighting like heroes in the Blitz. The chapter extends the analysis of social inequity from Chapters 1 and 2 by suggesting that wartime gender relations were also more conflicted than they appeared to be within People's War ideology.

In Chapters 4 and 5, the book retraces the steps of the first three chapters in order to demonstrate how popular fiction and films of the Blitz – just as much as literary texts – represent and market the freedom to imagine the People's War in different ways. Chapter 4 challenges the dominant critical view that bestsellers and genre fiction reproduce mainstream political rhetoric uncritically in order to ensure commercial success. Instead, the chapter suggests that Agatha Christie, Margery Allingham, and Graham Greene all manipulated the conventions of detective and spy fiction in order to attract a diverse reading public desperate not for escape from the Blitz but for understanding of it. Popular detective and spy fiction of the period therefore captures the imaginations of the widest possible audience by engaging with the same wartime problems of gender identity and social difference represented by the literary fiction examined in Chapters 1, 2, and 3. Chapter 5 brings the book to a close by extending its argument to the genre of film, the most popular cultural medium during the war. The chapter analyzes four of the biggest box-office smashes of 1943 – *The Gentle Sex*, *Millions Like Us*, *In Which We Serve*, and *The Life and Death of Colonel Blimp* – films that were produced after some of the heaviest shelling on the home front in 1940–41 and at the height of civilian mobilization. Most scholars contend that the popularity of these four box-office hits was the direct result of their success as motivational wartime propaganda. However, Chapter 5 juxtaposes the features with MOI shorts and draws upon Mass-Observation cinema writing to argue that the four films simultaneously present and repress the problems of social inequity in women's war work and sexual stereotyping of men on the home front analyzed in previous chapters; the films' box-office success depends, at least in part, upon their ability to engage audiences with diverse social and political beliefs. The book concludes that the general public in Britain demanded much the same experience as wartime readers of literary and popular fiction: pitted against the Nazi threat, these British citizens especially valued the freedom to imagine the People's War in conflicting and contradictory ways.

1
Mobile Women in Elizabeth Bowen's War Writing

Elizabeth Bowen feared intensely that the Blitz would paralyze her imagination. She acknowledges this anxiety in a review of V. S. Pritchett's *In My Good Books*, which she published in 1942, the same year as her family history, *Bowen's Court*:

> These years rebuff the imagination as much by being fragmentary as by being violent. It is by dislocations, by recurrent checks to his desire for meaning, that the writer is most thrown out. The imagination cannot simply endure events; for it the passive role is impossible. Where it cannot dominate, it is put out of action. ("Contemporary" 340)

The war nearly did put Bowen's novelistic imagination out of action. Having written six novels in the 11 years between 1927 and 1938, Bowen spent the following 11 years working on one – *The Heat of the Day* – which she composed both during and after the Blitz and finally published in 1949. Not surprisingly, the time-consuming process of completing *The Heat of the Day* was unsettling for a writer who was usually so prolific. She describes her difficulty in a 1945 letter to her lover, Charles Ritchie: "Any novel I have ever written has been difficult to write and this is being far the most difficult of all. [...] It presents every possible problem in the world" (Glendinning 149–50).

These problems resulted in part from the circumstances of the Blitz, which made life "fragmentary" and therefore threatened to "rebuff" Bowen's imagination. Because her husband, Alan Cameron, worked for the BBC, the couple spent much of the war in London, where their Regent's Park flat was repeatedly bombed – once in May 1941 and again in the summer of 1944. At the same time, Bowen chose to divide her romantic attentions; although she remained with Cameron from their marriage in 1923 until his death in 1952, she also began in 1941 an intense wartime love affair with Ritchie, an Anglo-Canadian diplomat stationed in London for the duration. Furthermore, Bowen found herself juggling the various professional obligations of writing *The Heat of the Day*, volunteering nightly as an ARP warden in Marylebone, and traveling frequently to neutral Ireland, beginning in 1940, to investigate public opinion for the MOI.

Seeking to restore the dominance of her imagination at a time of so much upheaval, Bowen tried to conceive of the Blitz, on another level, as a time to expand her identity by exploring new freedoms. In the preface to *The Demon Lover*, she claims to have lived in wartime "both as a civilian and as a writer, with every pore open" (95), and looking back on the war in 1947, Bowen remembers fondly her life as a mobile woman on the home front: "I would not have missed being in London throughout the war for anything: it was the most interesting period of my life" (Glendinning 127). According to Victoria Glendinning, the Blitz revealed to Bowen how sheltered she had been before the war:

> Psychologically, one of the results of the war for Elizabeth was the breaking down of boundaries and barriers. [...] "Life with the lid on" was over for good, and a lifetime's policy of "not noticing" increasingly hard to maintain. It happened socially, as it did for all previously sheltered people, in a rather obvious way: in her neighbourhood, and in her work at the Warden's Post and on patrol, for example, she was brought into close contact with people she would not normally have become intimate with. (177–8)

One problem with choosing to write "only one book" during this People's War was that the genre of the novel forced Bowen to be a ruthless editor of her newly expanded experience: "I want my novel, which deals with this same time, to be enormously comprehensive. But a novel must have form; and, for the form's sake, one is always having to make relentless exclusions" (preface 95). These "relentless exclusions" provided material for the short stories that offered Bowen a much-needed creative outlet during the war: "Each time I sat down to write a story I opened a door; and the pressure against the other side of that door must have been very great, for things – ideas, images, emotions – came through with force and rapidity, sometimes violence" (94). Tellingly,

Bowen describes her explosive outburst of short-story writing during the Blitz with imagery of shrapnel:

> The stories had their own momentum, which I had to control. The acts in them had an authority which I could not question. Odd enough in their way – and now some seem very odd – they were flying particles of something enormous and inchoate that had been going on. (95)

Thus, even as she struggled to construct the coherent whole of *The Heat of the Day*, Bowen wrote a great deal of shorter, less comprehensive fiction, publishing several volumes of stories during the war years and returning to longer fiction in earnest only after 1945.[1]

Bowen tried to redirect and control her fear that she would never finish *The Heat of the Day* – that instead the war would force her novelistic imagination into a "passive role" – by turning not only to the more fragmentary genre of short fiction but also to the safety of Bowen's Court, the Irish family estate that she inherited on her father's death in 1930. In a general sense, Big Houses like Bowen's Court stood for the continued presence and prestige of an Anglo-Irish ascendancy in Ireland. More specifically, Bowen's Court offered Bowen an imaginative safe haven from the disjointed experiences of war – the very experiences that often inspired her short fiction. The Irish Big House became for Bowen an aestheticized "picture of peace – in the house, in the country round" – a picture distanced from the upheaval of the London Blitz (*Bowen's Court* 457; hereafter referred to as *BC*). *Bowen's Court* describes this picture in loving detail, lingering upon the battered, decaying architectural landscape of County Cork and capturing what Otto Rauchbauer calls the "aesthetic of decay" (1):

> Lordly or humble, military or domestic, standing up with furious gauntness, like Kilcolman, or shelving weakly into the soil, ruins feature the landscape – uplands or river valleys – and make a ghostly extra quarter to towns. They give clearings in woods, reaches of mountain or sudden turns of a road a meaning and pre-inhabited air. Ivy grapples them; trees grow inside their doors; enduring ruins, where they emerge from ivy, are the limestone white-grey and look like rocks. (*BC* 15)

The pleasure and meaning that Bowen finds in this "country of ruins" (15) stands in sharp contrast to the terror that she often felt living amidst the urban ruin of the London Blitz:

> We shall be due, at tonight's siren, to feel our hearts once more
> tighten and sink. Soon after black-out we keep that date with fear.
> The howling ramping over the darkness, the lurch of the barrage
> opening, the obscure throb in the air. [...] Our own "things" – tables,
> chairs, lamps – give one kind of confidence to us who stay in our
> own paper rooms. But when tonight the throb gathers over the roof
> we must not remember what we looked at this morning – these
> fuming utter glissades of ruin. No, these nights in September nowhere
> is pleasant. ("London, 1940" 23)

Nowhere in London is pleasant because everywhere are the ruined
landmarks of personal and national vulnerability.

This chapter examines Bowen's conflicting impulses in the face of a
danger that she found both fearful and compelling: on the one hand,
she longed to retreat to the safe haven of Bowen's Court away from the
London Blitz that threatened to destroy all that she held dear; on the
other, she yearned to live "with every pore open" and to write stories
about "the packed repercussions" of thousands of civilian lives "under
stress" during the bombing. As we will see, Bowen's freedom to entertain
contradictory impulses depended fundamentally upon her privileged
social standing. For now, the point is that either way, she was struggling
during the Blitz to combat the "shapelessness, lack of meaning, and
being without direction [that] is most people's nightmare" ("Why Do I
Write?" 224). A 50-year-old female diarist describes similar anxiety in
her diary written for Mass-Observation:

> I don't know whether it's the heat or I'm doing a bit too much running
> round, but today I'd a real black fit of depression – luckily rare to me. I
> felt a hood of misery over me that threatened to choke me. I felt my
> efforts were feeble and doll-eyed, and that *anything* I could possibly do
> was so futile as to be utterly *worthless*. (M-O A: FR 520, 1940: 7)

This woman feels a "hood of misery" similar to Bowen's tightening
and sinking heart, a sense that nowhere in London is pleasant because
everything one does to protect oneself and one's home ultimately seems
so "feeble." Experiencing a "black fit of depression" as dark as Bowen's
"nightmare," the diarist responds by repressing negative thoughts about
a meaningless existence. She dismisses her bout of depression as a rarity
brought on by the heat and her busy schedule.

Bowen struggled with the same tendency toward depression, and her war writing explores in detail her own conflicting desires both to experience and to escape the Blitz. Writing about the characters in her short stories, Bowen sympathizes with their need to retreat from the material and psychological horrors of the nightly London air raids: these characters often create for themselves "small worlds-within-worlds of hallucination," which Bowen describes as "those little dear saving illusory worlds" (preface 97). In the non-fictional *Bowen's Court* and the fictional *The Heat of the Day*, Bowen articulates the need for refuge in explicitly aesthetic terms, identifying Bowen's Court with "Flaubert's ideal book about nothing," which "sustains itself on itself by the inner force of its style" (*BC* 21), and describing Stella Rodney and Robert Kelway's relationship in *The Heat of the Day* as "a hermetic world, which, like the ideal book about nothing, stayed itself on itself by its inner force" (90). Flaubert's ideal book is about nothing because it tells no story other than that of its own form, creating a self-referential, self-contained fictional refuge.

The "ideal book" focuses one's attention on private or aesthetic issues, and *Bowen's Court* appears to indulge Bowen's personal desire for this form of escape. However, a closer reading reveals that the family history not only celebrates but also questions the safety that Bowen sought on the Irish estate. She describes what she found at Bowen's Court as an "intense centripetal life," a private realm "isolated by something very much more lasting than the physical fact of space: the isolation is innate; it is an affair of origin" (*BC* 20); in describing the welcome privacy of Bowen's Court (*BC* 457), the passage also suggests Bowen's keen awareness that the retreat depends upon her own social station in the Anglo-Irish ascendancy, which is certainly "innate" and "an affair of origin." Understanding that the established social hierarchy underwriting her ability to slip away to Bowen's Court was exactly what the People's War had called into question, Bowen describes the impact of wartime changes on her view of the Irish Big House in the afterword to *Bowen's Court*: "Inevitably, the ideas and emotions that were present in my initial plan of this book were challenged and sharpened by the succeeding war years in which the writing went on" (454). The narrative specifically explores the conflict between Bowen's increasing awareness of social inequity in blitzed London and her continuing reliance on established social structures as the owner of an Irish Big House.

Bowen's Court initially appears to gloss over this conflict by pitting a benevolent Irish social system against a corrupt European one. The narrative points out the relationship between Bowen's personal family history in County Cork and Irish history more generally: "Having looked back at [the Bowens] steadily, I begin to notice, if I cannot define, the pattern they unconsciously went to make. And I can see that that pattern has its relation to the outside more definite patterns of history" (452).[2] Extrapolating the political history of a whole nation from the private lives of a privileged few, this passage elides the long-standing tensions between Irish landowners and the peasant class. Bowen even goes so far as to contrast the benevolent exercise of the Irish landlord's power with the cruel exercise of Nazi power:

> I submit that the power-loving temperament is more dangerous when it either prefers or is forced to operate in what is materially a void. [...] In the area of ideas we see more menacing dominations than the landlord exercised over land. The outsize will is not necessarily evil: it is a phenomenon. It must have its outsize outlet, its big task. If the right task is not offered it, it must seize the wrong. We should be able to harness this driving force. Not the will itself but its wastefulness is the dangerous thing. (455–6)

Bowen's political interpretation of local experience is flawed; while the land might provide an appropriate "big task" for the landlord's will, one wonders what kind of "outsize outlet" could contain and neutralize the fascist will to power. The hasty parallel suggests Bowen's urgent need to explain hostilities between the Axis and Allied powers. At the same time, the hastiness reveals an equally urgent desire to maintain the illusion of Irish social harmony by contrasting fascist power with the more harmonious social relations on the site of the Big House. A comparison of the landlord's domestic power with the Nazis' political power emphasizes the landlord's benevolence and thus appears to relocate the social inequities of Ireland to Germany. The rhetorical problem here, however, is that Bowen creates a parallel in order to establish a contrast. Rather than simply convincing readers of the difference between these two types of power, the parallel reminds readers that the landlords and Nazis had something in common: Bowen's ancestors could retain social power only by continuing to exploit the Irish peasant class.

Bowen recognizes this problem, even as she struggles to sustain her hope of retreating into domestic harmony. She quite self-consciously describes "the picture of peace" at Bowen's Court as an enchanting, sustaining fantasy:

> Like all pictures, it did not quite correspond with any reality. Or, you might have called the country a magic mirror, reflecting something

that could not really exist. That illusion – peace at its most ecstatic – I held to, to sustain me throughout the war. I suppose that everyone, fighting or just enduring, carried within him one private image, one peaceful scene. Mine was Bowen's Court. War made me that image out of a house built of anxious history. (*BC* 457)

Bowen calls the house a "magic mirror," an "illusion," and a "private image" in an effort to establish its distance from the nightly bombing of the Blitz, much as she labels those "little dear saving illusory worlds" into which the characters of her short fiction escape. Although she hopes from this distance to find meaning in the nightmare of the Blitz, she also recognizes that the illusion is built upon both the chaotic experience of war and the shaky foundations of strained class relations, the "anxious history" that has always underwritten the power of the Anglo-Irish ascendancy.

Bowen's 1969 review of Angus Calder's *The People's War* demonstrates her particular facility for navigating conflicting ideas about war and social class. Bowen quotes Calder as he challenges the myth of wartime social change – "if a mythical version of the war still holds sway in school textbooks and television documentaries, every person who lived through those years knows that those parts of the myth which concern his or her activities are false" – and then takes Calder to task for creating his own myth of the Blitz, asking "*Every* person?" (181–2). She notes that Calder was only three years old when the Second World War ended and that he was the "child of a distinguished intellectual family with a political bent" and thus "grew up in what would have been an *ambiance* of discussion, re-evaluation and diagnosis" (182). Bowen suggests that this sheltered existence shaped Calder's representation of the war, which relies for its documentation on the spoken or written personal memories "invariably [...] of a left-wing élite: and this limits his field" (182). Furthermore, she concludes by asserting the legitimacy of her own response to the war:

The war on Britain was undergone by all types. Not only the People were people, so were others. For the general run of us, existence during the war had a mythical intensity, heightened for dwellers in cities under attack. The majority of us, living through those years, did not attempt to rationalize them, nor have most of us done so since. War is a prolonged passionate act, and we were involved in it. We at least knew that we only half knew what we were doing. (182)

Acknowledging the difficulty of describing without bias the "mythical intensity" of the Blitz, Bowen recognizes the limitations of her personal war stories and suggests that Calder's story is just as mythical as her own.

Bowen's self-conscious ambivalence about her war writing is what most critics miss in discussing her work. Much of the scholarship emphasizes instead her interest in the wartime relationship between "private passion" and the public "context of one's past, one's family, one's other relationships, of work, duty and society" (Coates 494).[3] According to feminist critics, Bowen is most interested in a particular aspect of that public sphere: the effect of the Blitz on conventional gender roles. These critics reach very different conclusions: on the one hand, scholars such as Patricia Coughlan and Renée Hoogland have argued that strong female relationships in Bowen's fiction replace and disrupt "male phallogocentrism" during wartime (Hoogland 6);[4] on the other hand, Harriet Chessman and Barbara Bellow Watson suggest that Bowen's fiction is more conservative: "Women, in Bowen's vision, are inherently outsiders to discourse, unless they turn traitor and defect to the other side" (Chessman 70).[5] Arguing over whether Bowen believed that the war changed everything or changed nothing for British women seeking increased social power, these critics omit the possibility of ambivalence. Deborah L. Parsons introduces this possibility in her analysis of Bowen's female flâneur, who acts as both a "metaphor for the increased freedom of women in war-time urban life" and an embodiment of the "less positive aspects of enforced war-time nomadism" (25). Extending Parsons's argument, this chapter looks beyond nomadism to Bowen's ambivalence about the People's War itself. Bowen's fiction resolutely refuses to generalize about the impact of the People's War on British women. Rather, the fiction examines critically the disparate experiences of women from various social classes even amidst wartime propaganda that promised universal social equality and gender equity.

Personal testimony of the period confirms the fact that the People's War offered far more exciting opportunities for upper- and middle-class women than for the working classes; those testimonies therefore help to situate my argument about Bowen's ambivalent rendering of the People's War. Upper-class servicewoman Diana Barnato Walker, for example, echoes Bowen's excitement about leaving behind "life with the lid on" in her statement for Mass-Observation: "We met a lot of people we wouldn't have met otherwise. In those days England was very stratified. One only met people from one's own type of upbringing. Here we were all doing the same thing, without distinction. It was wonderful" (Saywell 16).

Similarly, a middle-class homemaker writes, "Now I find I have long conversations in buses etc. about rationing, dried milk, exchanging recipes, etc. and much enjoy these whilst I am certain that before the war none of these people would have dared to speak to a stranger like me" (M-O A: DR 3002, Jan. 1943).[6] Whether these previously sheltered women were conversing about the war or mobilizing to fight it, they were excited about the possibility of crossing social barriers that had seemed impermeable in peacetime.

From the perspective of working-class women, however, the prospect was not usually so exciting or liberating. A young female pilot describes her very different perception of intensified class distinctions during the war:

> I was a working-class girl who learned to fly to make a living. There was a clique of rich girls who had all learned because it was the "in" thing to do. They owned their own planes, had their own friends, and you were never invited to their homes or parties. (Saywell 16)

The tension between the upper-class choice to follow a fashion and the working-class necessity to make a living indicates a crucial disparity in the way that women viewed their war work, a disparity that ran much deeper than the social awkwardness suggested by the pilot's comment. Unlike the well-connected, highly educated women of the upper classes, working-class women had limited options in their war work: according to Penny Summerfield, "94 per cent of women on assembly and unskilled repetitive work and 96 per cent of machinists and hand-tool operators" had received only an elementary education (*Women* 57). Uneducated and conscripted, these women were typically assigned to perform manual labor, either in the lower ranks of auxiliary military units or in the factories.

In the auxiliary services, Mass-Observation thus noted continued social stratification: "The trade division was almost identical with the social division – working-class were cooks, sparking-plug testers, general duty hands, etc. – lower middle-class were orderlies, teleprinters, clerks, etc. – middle-middle class and above were administrative workers, radio operators, plotters, etc." (M-O A: TC 32/3/E, "Letter," 1941). Analyzing a sample of 300 women, a Mass-Observation report concludes that "72% of D [working] class women said they had never thought of joining a Service" (M-O A: FR 1083, 1942: 6). Of the 28 percent of the working-class women who did consider joining the services, most were drawn to the ATS, rather than to the primarily middle- and upper-middle-class WAAF and WRNS. Social perceptions of the different branches of women's military service therefore enforced class divisions within the auxiliary armed forces. Even if a working-class woman managed to join a service typically considered above her rank, she was often snubbed; according to a Mass-Observer in the WAAFs, "Our trade employs girls of slightly superior social class, and those who manage to get into it, but don't quite come up to the accepted social standard, are liable to suffer" (M-O A: FR 757, 1941: 10).[7]

If they were not suffering in the forces, these working-class women were often doing so in the factories. Angus Calder and Dorothy Sheridan comment on a 1944 Mass-Observation report that describes the burden of factory work:

> The war may have offered adventure, travel and professional training to certain women, mainly those in the higher ranks of the Forces, but for many others, particularly women with family responsibilities, it imposed a double burden – that of combining an often strenuous job outside the home with the task of rearing children and managing housework. (176)

Mass-Observation reports confirm the strenuous nature of factory work: "Girls who are on piece work in the dogging up section are often exhausted by the end of the day; they come into the cloakroom and sit on the floor, too tired to make the effort to clean up before going home" (M-O A: FR 1390, 1942: 4). The report quotes several workers bemoaning their exhaustion; one 30-year-old woman says, "Get up, and let me have that chair for a minute so I can change my shoes; I can't bend down to them standing," while a 22-year-old co-worker comments, "Honest to god, I haven't sat down for a minute all day – he's kept me on the go all the time" (FR 1390: 4).

In addition to being strenuous, factory work was also notoriously dull. Mass-Observers stationed in war factories noted the repetitive nature of the work:

> On almost all of [the machines] the work is very simple and monotonous, involving simply placing the part in position (it is usually impossible to do this wrong) and then the raising or lowering of a handle, or some such action. With a few exceptions, the work here involved neither mental nor physical effort of any kind. It is, in fact, just the type of work one hears educated people at war work exhibitions speak of with horror: "I'd go crazy, doing that all day." (M-O, *War Factory* 26)

Part of the problem with the monotony was that it forced women to think in very narrow ways. Constance Reaveley, a lecturer in political philosophy who worked in various factories during the war, describes the work as drudgery that would cripple even the most agile and active mind:

> I realised that if you have ten hours a day for thinking of things to do and only two or three very weary ones for doing them, you either become accustomed to unfulfilled purpose [...] or else you give up making plans. Like many other people I chose the second alternative. [...] When you are tired, which is most of the time, your thoughts repeat themselves as your machine repeats its process and you can't disengage yourself from them. (Hartley, *Hearts* 149)

The repetition inevitably numbed the impulse to think creatively and independently, and as a result, women working in war factories often found it difficult to be politically engaged:

> For, paradoxical as it may seem, life in a twelve-hours-a-day war factory makes one feel further removed from the war than one could in any other type of life. [...] Is it surprising that, after a few weeks of this sort of life, a girl should begin to feel isolated from the outside world, and lose her sense of responsibility towards it? By the nature of her work and its long hours, she is cut off from the daily life of her community; she is sheltered from its day to day difficulties and problems. (M-O, *War Factory* 46–7)

The point here is not to suggest that women's war work was unimportant or to diminish its contribution to the cause of national defense but to demonstrate that middle- and upper-middle-class women tended to romanticize the idea of working in wartime because their connections and educational experiences gave them the freedom to escape the oppressive, alienating reality endured by many working-class women.

These women from different social classes had a history of vastly different kinds of work experience. In "Sisters and Brothers in Arms," Angela Woollacott explains that throughout the First World War, the established distance between working-class women who had previous contact with the public workplace and middle-class women who had always been confined within the domestic sphere remained essentially intact, despite the growing demand in Britain for women's rights and suffrage based largely on their contributions to the war effort. According to Woollacott, the upper- and middle-class women whose World-War-One writing is most familiar to contemporary readers were typically "turned into pacifists by the war" (129):

> They were thereby torn between a conviction that their brothers' and lovers' sacrifices had been pointless and the desire to empathize with and valorize those sacrifices. [...] The tension between these two conflicted views was underscored by the sense, shared by many of them, of their exclusion from the real events of the war. (129)

In contrast, working-class women played a crucial part in the real events of the First World War:

> For the million working-class women in munition factories around Britain [...] their roles in the war effort were in accord with those of their men. [...] The majority of women munition workers, by far, were from the working class; their production of the munitions of war implicated them in the making of war as much as their brothers, fiancés, husbands, or fathers in the armed services. (129)

Although work in a munitions factory was certainly as mind-numbing as – and typically more dangerous than – the work described in personal testimonies of the Second World War, Woollacott makes the important point that these working-class women were fighting alongside soldiers well before the home front came under siege in the Blitz.[8] The First World War therefore divided more than it unified various classes of British women by installing them in the conventionally distinct roles of domestic angel and menial servant.

The gap between these feminine gender roles remained wide until the ideal of the domestic angel came under direct fire in the man-power crisis of 1940–41. After the conscription of British women began on 2 December 1941, the National Service (No. 2) Act became law on 18 December 1941. The Act required all women to begin contributing to the war effort, although it "banished the idea of grandmothers firing machine guns" (Calder, *PW* 268). Britain initially conscripted unmar-ried women who were between 20 and 30 years old – 19-year-old women were added to the pool in early 1942 – giving them a choice between the auxiliary services and industrial labor.[9] Vast numbers of women from all social classes were therefore suddenly involved in essential war work, taking over jobs previously reserved for men:

> In mid-1943 [...] nearly three million married women and widows were employed, as compared with a million and a quarter before the

war. It was calculated that, among those between eighteen and forty, nine single women out of ten and eight married women out of ten were in the forces or in industry. (Calder, *PW* 331)

No longer was war work only for women who needed the money; Britain required most of its women to join in the cause of national defense.

The resulting changes of lifestyle during the Second World War were far more dramatic for upper- and middle-class than working-class women. Yet while the personal and professional possibilities of the People's War often thrilled previously sheltered women, these women were invested not only in fostering the idea of social unity in wartime but also in protecting the privileged social position that allowed them to select the kind of war work they preferred. Returning to Bowen's Court, then, we can see that this Irish Big House represented for its owner more than just a physical fortress in neutral Eire; it was also an ideological bastion protecting the class and gender hierarchies that were under siege during the People's War. *Bowen's Court* explores the writer's conflicting desires both to uphold and to overthrow the conventions: on the one hand, imagining the Blitz in detail meant destroying the "ecstatic" illusion of peace at the Irish Big House; on the other hand, protecting the security of Bowen's Court meant ignoring the anxious social history of both the house itself and the Blitz.

Phyllis Lassner has analyzed this ambivalence in Bowen's short fiction, arguing that the stories question the entrenched class hierarchy by examining critically the relationship between past and present. Lassner claims that Bowen's characters "deny historical change in order to insulate themselves from recognizing that their worlds of privilege cannot be saved because they are already in ruin" (*Elizabeth Bowen* xii; hereafter referred to as *EB*). Although Bowen shares with her characters the sense of being "both sustained and burdened" by the past as "the last and only female heir to the Anglo-Irish country estate" (*EB* 7), she recognizes what her characters deny: because the past is actually "too terrible to bear," one is tempted to replace it with "fantasies of a romantic or mythic past, 'illusions' that revise history but become self-defeating obsessions" (*EB* 6). Bowen turns the home itself into a metaphor for this nostalgic desire to conserve the past: "Bowen's houses represent codes of privilege that their occupants take as promises to fulfill the sense of purpose, order, and stability they crave" (*EB* 5). Thus, the stories repeatedly depict the traditional English household as a "fortress" ("Summer Night" 595), a "sheltered" retreat ("Sunday Afternoon" 616), a "hermetic" refuge ("Ivy Gripped the Steps" 690), or a "very strong" place without "a crack in it anywhere" ("Mysterious Kôr" 729).

Lassner's book analyzes Bowen's entire *oeuvre* of short fiction, and her brief treatment of the war stories contrasts the fantasy of an illusory past with the reality of a brutal present: she suggests that transformations of identity occur for Bowen's characters when the Blitz intrudes upon their nostalgic visions of the past. However, a closer examination of the wartime stories reveals that they are concerned not only with the contrast between a nostalgized past and an intolerable present but also with the parallel between two very different kinds of fantasy about the past and present. In the preface to *The Demon Lover*, Bowen describes the wartime search for "indestructible landmarks in a destructible world" as a struggle to "fill the vacuum for the uncertain 'I'" (97, 98). The struggle left Bowen herself conflicted about whether to retreat into the fabled safety of Bowen's Court or to embrace the mythic unity of the People's War. Rather than resolving the conflict between these equally untenable ideals, her wartime short fiction explores the problem of constructing upper-middle-class identity from the materials of fantasy. The key here is that the fantasies only work for those in a position of social privilege: a brief overview of how middle- and upper-class characters in the stories represent their conflicted identities will foreground the issues central to my subsequent interpretation of Bowen's wartime novel, *The Heat of the Day*.

Part of the conflict arises from these characters' nostalgia, and the stories critique fantasies about the past that resemble Bowen's own wish to withdraw to her own Irish estate. In "Ivy Gripped the Steps," Gavin Doddington longs to escape on leave from his wartime Ministry position to a Southstone mansion where he spent time as a boy. The mansion shows how an obsession with the past leads to the "strangulation" of the present and therefore destroys rather than defines Gavin's identity (686): an "ATS girl" now billeted nearby notices that Gavin has "the face of somebody dead who was still there – 'old' because of the presence, under an icy screen, of a whole stopped mechanism for feeling" (711). Similarly, Mary in "The Happy Autumn Fields" becomes obsessed with "a musty old leather box gaping open with God knows what – junk, illegible letters, diaries, yellow photographs" from Victorian times (677). Mary is more interested in losing herself in this box than in protecting herself from an air raid, and she therefore becomes "a person drained by a dream" (684); her identity is "irrelevant" because she has mentally "shut up shop" during the war (677, 676). Constructing characters whose retreat saps rather than strengthens their upper-middle-class identities, Bowen critiques her own temptation to search for the self within a nostalgic fantasy of an idealized past.

Yet the stories represent just as critically the utopian fantasy of a People's War. Stories such as "Careless Talk" suggest that the class hierarchy has remained intact on the home front: the wealthy civilians in the story live during the Blitz as comfortably as they lived in peacetime, lunching in fancy restaurants, paying black-market prices to avoid wartime rationing, and refusing "to bore each other" with stories of evacuees or bombs (669). The Rangerton-Karneys in "The Cheery Soul" seem different: they invite a factory worker billeted in a nearby town to their country estate for Christmas. However, they extend the invitation on false pretenses: as upper-class spies who are leaving the country at Christmastime, the Rangerton-Karneys are more interested in finding a way to "cover their tracks and divert suspicion" than in the spirit of wartime camaraderie (648). Similarly, the mistress in "Oh, Madam… " ignores the utopian rhetoric of her servant, who proclaims, "Hitler can't beat you and me, madam, can he?" (581). Leaving the servant behind as caretaker of the London home, the privileged mistress protects herself at the expense of the more patriotic servant. The repetition of the word "madam" – more than 60 times in the five pages of the story – emphasizes the enduring class divisions that undercut the utopian ideal of the People's War.

Recognizing the persistence of these social divisions, Bowen critiques her own temptation to define herself through the fantasy of a People's War. In "Sunday Afternoon," sheltered young Maria embodies part of Bowen's own wartime dilemma: she rebels against the stifling "air of being secluded behind glass" and of living in an "eternalized Sunday afternoon" in neutral Ireland by naïvely constructing a counter-fantasy of the People's War (616–17). Maria "hopes to find heroes across the sea" and therefore idolizes Henry Russel when he visits from blitzed London (618). However, Henry is no hero: although he asserts that "one cannot stay long away from wartime London" (618), he ultimately "protested against the return to the zone of death," realizing that he "still want[s] the past" safeguarded on the Irish estate (621). As a result, Maria concludes that Henry is "weak" and "half old," echoing the language of the ATS girl in "Ivy Gripped the Steps," who thinks that Gavin is "old" and "dead" because his manner continues "puzzling her somewhere outside the compass of her own youth" (711). Too inexperienced to understand that their own romantic notion of the London home front is as deluded as their elders' nostalgic longing for the past, these young women judge others without really questioning themselves.

"Mysterious Kôr" takes this idea a step further, suggesting that political idealism about the home front was often a privilege directly linked to class status. The story describes what appears to be the utopian fantasy of the People's War itself: working-class Pepita and upper-middle-class Callie perform war work together by day and share a flat in bombed London by night. For Pepita, however, the People's War offers no real social transformation: when her soldier lover returns to London on leave, she finds that she still has "not a place" to spend the night with him because it was the upper-middle-class Callie, "earning more than Pepita, who paid the greater part of the rent" (731, 732). Without a room of her own, Pepita creates an alternative fantasy to the People's War; she imagines "a completely forsaken city" called Kôr where the lovers can have privacy (729): "It's very strong; there is not a crack in it anywhere for a weed to grow in [...] and the stairs and arches are built to support themselves" (729). Callie understands neither this fantasy of self-sufficiency nor Pepita's need for it. As the "child of a sheltered middle-class household" who had "kept physical distances all her life" (733), Callie romanticizes her wartime proximity to the working class in the People's War and, more specifically, her role as hostess to Pepita's love affair: "She became the guardian of that ideality which for Pepita was constantly lost to view" (732). Dividing rather than uniting Pepita and Callie around the utopian ideal of a People's War, "Mysterious Kôr" shrewdly argues that the People's War was transformative only for those in positions of social privilege.

"In the Square" develops this argument by illustrating how the fantasy could confuse rather than clarify even upper-middle-class identity. Far more experienced than Maria in "Sunday Afternoon," Magdela lives with an odd assortment of relatives and acquaintances – including her husband's mistress – in a London house no longer her own. Together, these civilians endure the destruction of the square, on which "three of the houses had been bombed away," although "the shell of the place" in which they live remains (609). The home's "loose plumbing" and "fittings shocked from their place" by the bombing constitute a "functional anarchy" that extends to the social dislocations of privileged women like Magdela during the Blitz. She observes, "Now the place seems to belong to everyone. One has nothing except one's feelings. Sometimes I think I hardly know myself" (615). Even more than the shared experience of the bombing, the idea that Magdela's home now belongs to everyone is essential to the utopian fantasy of a People's War, which demands that the few give up ownership to the many for the benefit of the social good. The problem, however, is that the story portrays very little positive social change. Although Magdela shares her house and even asks her friend whether he thinks "we shall see a great change"

(615), the People's War remains little more than a hopeful fantasy, and Magdela, in turn, feels unsure of her own identity.

In the preface to *The Demon Lover*, Bowen describes her own similar loss of identity amidst the upheaval of the People's War:

> I felt one with, and just like, everyone else. Sometimes I hardly knew where I stopped and somebody else began. The violent dislocation of solid things, the explosion of the illusion that prestige, power and permanence attach to bulk and weight, left all of us, equally, heady and disembodied. Walls went down; and we felt, if not knew, each other. We all lived in a state of lucid abnormality. (95)

The People's War promises to incorporate individual identity into a composite whole by dislodging "prestige, power and permanence" from the trappings of material wealth. However, Bowen's word choice here suggests that the resulting "state of lucid abnormality" is an aberration from the usual state of normality that will almost inevitably return after the war. Social prestige and power are ultimately permanent, and being "one with, and just like, everyone else" is a fantasy that confuses rather than clarifies upper-middle-class identity.

Each of Bowen's wartime short stories represents a facet of the problem she describes here and in *Bowen's Court*. Read together, the stories mark the difference between nostalgic retreat and utopian engagement in wartime as a choice between competing fantasies equally dependent upon social privilege. Rather than resolving the conflict, *The Heat of the Day* examines it in more comprehensive detail: the fictional Stella Rodney faces much the same dilemma as Bowen, but distance allows Bowen the novelist to be more critical of the class hierarchy than Bowen the memoirist. Examining the experiences of upper-middle-class women like Bowen and Stella alongside the much more circumscribed lives of working-class women during the Blitz, *The Heat of the Day* calls into question social identities founded upon either the nostalgic fantasy of a remembered past or the utopian fantasy of a revolutionary present.

Stella Rodney is a character modeled upon Bowen's own experience: Stella is a prosperous woman with a flat, a job, and a lover in war-torn London, and she is legally responsible for a Big House in Ireland. Stella also shares the social privilege and freedom described by upper- and upper-middle-class women like Mass-Observers Diana Barnato Walker and Penelope Barlow – and, of course, like Bowen herself. These adventurous, well-connected young women were able to secure exciting jobs driving canal boats, piloting Tiger Moth airplanes, "smashing up motor cars, harvesting nettles, organising baths for the troops" (Hartley, *Hearts* 131) – or even, as Bowen did, writing "candid, often witty" reports for the MOI that "gauged reactions in the [Irish] republic to the mortal threat then menacing England" (George Greene 605). In *The Heat of the Day*, Stella too enjoys her undercover war work: "She was now [...] employed in an organization better called Y.X.D., in secret, exacting, not unimportant work, to which the European position since 1940 gave ever-increasing point" (26). Stella's privileged background qualifies her for this challenging war work:

> In the years between the wars she had travelled, had for intervals lived abroad; she now qualified by knowing two or three languages, two or three countries, well – having had some idea what she might most usefully do she had, still better, known whom to ask to support her application to do it. She had in her background relations, connexions, and at least former friends. (25–6)

Stella's reliance upon not only background and education but also connections was typical among women of her class. Memoirist Daphne Baker (née Humphrys), for example, describes how she landed her position as a code breaker for Naval Intelligence in the WRNS. Before the war, she had "spent six months with a charming German-Without-Tears family in Munich, studying German and music, (and skiing on the side)." Not only had Humphrys covered "the whole German grammar [...] at daily one-to-one lessons," but she also gained secretarial experience because her father, "who was then ambassador in Baghdad, wanted me to act as his Honorary Attachée." Much like Bowen, whose experience as a writer and owner of an Irish Big House qualified her to investigate public opinion in Ireland, and Stella, whose travel abroad, knowledge of languages, and social connections led to "not unimportant" war work, Humphrys was well prepared to secure a position in which she "loved the work" matching wits with enemy strategists during the war.

Socially liberated during the Blitz from the constraints of conventional class and gender roles, these women faced the dilemma that Bowen describes in *Bowen's Court*: on the one hand, they wished to safeguard the privileged backgrounds that led to stimulating war work; on the other, they enjoyed the wartime freedom to connect with people from outside the boundaries of their previously sheltered lives. In *The Heat of the Day*, Stella embodies this problem, but unlike Bowen herself, the fictional Stella is surrounded by minor characters who find it impossible either to retreat blithely into the safety of convention or to advance heedlessly toward the excitement of social change. Displacing her own wartime anxieties onto this set of characters allows Bowen to structure the problem more coherently and thus to explore it in more depth than she could in either *Bowen's Court* or the much briefer wartime stories.

Specifically, *The Heat of the Day* introduces two pairs of characters who are linked to each other by their names and to Stella by their emotional and symbolic functions. Robert Kelway and Robert Harrison embody the choice confronting privileged women like Stella in wartime: she must learn to negotiate between what appears to be an intensely private relationship with her lover, Kelway, and an exclusively political relationship with the government agent, Harrison. In a novel so focused on names, Stella is the star of her own story: she seeks a workable balance between her impulse to retreat into a private sanctuary and her obligation to engage with the political world, a balance that she eventually discovers through her relationship with the novel's two Roberts. However, *The Heat of the Day*'s other pair of supporting characters – Roderick Rodney and Louie Lewis – expose the illusions of both nostalgic regression and utopian progress upon which Stella relies so heavily during the Blitz. Like Kelway and Harrison, Roderick and Louie appear to embody two very different ideas that compete for Stella's attention: her son, Roderick, inherits along with the family's Irish Big House the problems of protecting the traditional status quo, while Stella's working-class female acquaintance, Louie, represents the radical prospect of friendship across class lines. In juxtaposing their experiences with Stella's, *The Heat of the Day* suggests that Stella's choices have more complex social ramifications than she understands. Sketching out the lives of Roderick and Louie as little more than a symbolic frame for her own experience, Stella unconsciously reveals the need to look beyond the novel's star – to see the problem of negotiating between these wartime fantasies as a social as well as a personal problem.

Like Bowen's other war writing, *The Heat of the Day* targets a middle-class audience who would tend to identify with Stella. The novel begins by describing its protagonist's personal revelations about private life and politics during the Blitz. These insights emerge from Stella's relationships with Robert Kelway and Robert Harrison, who embody the two polarized fantasies of private retreat and public engagement. On the one hand, Kelway, as Stella's lover, represents the lure of an extremely insular privacy. The couple is so focused on the love affair that it becomes their entire world; here, the metaphor of Flaubert's ideal book recalls the isolation of Bowen's Court: "The lovers had for two years possessed a hermetic world, which, like the ideal book about nothing, stayed itself on itself by its inner force" (90). On the other hand, Harrison is a British intelligence officer, a purely public figure whom Stella views not as an individual but as an agent of government action. She balks at him as at a "government order" (32) and accuses him of ringing up "like the Gestapo" (33). Stella's desire to keep these two men apart is much like Bowen's need in *Bowen's Court* to draw a line between her Irish home and the London Blitz: the idealized benefits of each – safe retreat into the status quo or exciting advance into new experience – seem impossible in the presence of the other.

However, Stella gradually comes to the realization that these two men are individuals rather than symbols and that the private and public spheres cannot be so clearly separated. Locating this conflict on the site of the wartime home, the novel shows how desperately Harrison longs to create a home life with Stella; during one of his unwanted visits to her rented flat, he even goes so far as to say, "You know, this is very nice. I so often think of this place that, if you won't mind my saying so, now I feel quite at home" (128). Perversely, the only way he can think of to establish and foster intimacy is to blackmail Stella: he suggests that if she ends her relationship with Kelway and begins one with him, he will hide from the British government the fact that Kelway is passing national secrets to Nazi Germany. Of course, Stella's flat is no home for Harrison, as she repeatedly reminds him; for her, Harrison's complete "failure to have [...] any possible place in the human scene" is the direct result of his blackmail (140). When he accuses Stella, "You talk as if there were rules" (27), he fails to realize that private life has its own rules and regulations: domestic structures such as families and relationships are not as weak as he thinks in the face of political opposition. Harrison's desire for a personal life in which intimacy and security come without effort reveals what Stella calls his "emotional idiocy" (42) – the profound inability to understand the relationship between private and public life. He breaks the rules in both parts of his life, intimidating Stella rather than loving her and betraying his political knowledge for the prospect of personal gain.

Like Harrison, Robert Kelway also radically distorts the relationship between private life and political action: while Harrison fabricates a private fantasy from his political knowledge, Kelway generates a political dream from his private experiences. Holme Dene, Kelway's childhood home, represents a miniature version of Nazi Germany and therefore provides the domestic imagery that allows Bowen to compare Kelway's and Harrison's fantasies. The home's architecture consists of "swastika-arms of passage leading to nothing" (258), and this construction denies individual privacy: the Kelway family must continually look each other "in the eye" (119). Invoking the German word for "mother," Robert calls Mrs Kelway "Muttikins," and the novel implies that she is "wicked" (110), not only because her face "showed the mute presence of an obsession" (109), but also because "she projected Holme Dene: this was a bewitched wood. If her power came to an end at the white gate, so did the world" (110). Within these gates, the fascist obsession traps little boys and turns them traitor: Kelway's young nephew, Peter, who "sported an armlet with cryptic letters" (112), plays the part of a Hitler youth in wartime, much as Robert learned to play the Nazi in this house as a child. Peter finds himself "watched with eyes like gimlets" and warned to keep the armband hidden within the walls of the home – "Peter, old man, you weren't wearing your armlet *outside* the gate?" – because "a game is a game, but this war's really rather serious" (112).

When he was a boy, Kelway too felt watched and confined by his family and their home; as he grows older, he begins to associate the social order of the family with the political order of the nation. The novel links Kelway's misguided political views to his experiences at Holme Dene, emphasizing the way in which his childhood resistance to near-fascistic authority escalates to the point of treason. When Stella asks him how he can betray England to the Nazis, he justifies himself by claiming that the concept of country is empty: "I don't see what you mean – what *do* you mean? Country? – there are no more countries left; nothing but names. What country have you and I outside this room?" (267). Kelway's political fantasy blinds him to the fact that his treason supports the very fascism he despises: he erroneously believes that he can free his private life from political control by becoming a traitorous free agent.

His mistake here is in equating his early home life with politics. Kelway lies to both his country and his lover because he believes that treason will free him from the oppression of both political ties and family life. Without these oppressive ties, he thinks that he can engage in an exclusively private relationship; he creates a sheltering "habitat" with Stella that, in his mind, can only exist in a world without national allegiance (90). However, the spy's betrayal of his country offers an escape from neither political nor familial connections: contrary to Kelway's belief, he cannot cease to be a political subject any more than he can cease to be a member of his own family. He assumes that Stella understands and approves of his political choices – "It seemed impossible that being as we were you should not know" (271) – but his assumption is false: in concealing his politics from Stella, he belies the very intimacy for which he strives. Kelway's political fantasy thus fails on two levels: first, it embeds him, ironically enough, in the political fascism of Nazi Germany rather than freeing him from the domestic fascism of Holme Dene; and second, it undermines his private relationship rather than supporting it. Kelway's simplified view of the interplay between personal and political life yields his unethical behavior, both as a dishonest lover and as a Nazi spy.

Like Harrison and Kelway, Stella is tempted to shelter herself within a fantasy. Although she wants more than anything to continue ignoring Harrison and loving Kelway, regardless of the treasonous behavior corrupting both relationships, the novel repeatedly criticizes characters who indulge their fantasies in this way and thus fail to recognize the connection between their own actions and the world around them. Kelway and Harrison exemplify this failure, but *The Heat of the Day* extends the critique through the character of Stella's cousin Nettie, who has voluntarily confined herself within a mental asylum. Wistaria Lodge tries to protect inmates like Nettie from the difficulties of an often troubled and currently war-torn world. The patients commit themselves to being locked, both literally and metaphorically, within "an indomitable surrounding wall" (218) at Wistaria Lodge, a wall that blocks out "dreadful thoughts" and appears to keep the inmates safe and happy "in a world of our own" (204). When either patients or visitors fail to keep the rest home free from negative thinking, the proprietor, Mrs Tringsby, acts as an enforcer; she scolds Stella's son, Roderick, for example, when he wears his Army uniform to his brief visit with Nettie – and thereby reminds the residents of the war.

However, even as Wistaria Lodge appears to shelter its inmates, the rest home limits their ability to be fully engaged citizens. The novel describes the lodge as a "powerhouse of nothingness, hives of lives in abeyance" (203), primarily because its residents become so isolated and self-absorbed during their time there. Mrs Tringsby censors the flow of information (such as the death of Nettie's husband, Cousin Francis) to her tenants, who thus become weak, "indecisive" prisoners within the home (218). Rather than taking an active interest in the world around them, the residents of Wistaria Lodge turn inward and away:

This was a window at the back of a home at the edge of a town; Roderick recollected that Cousin Nettie had not for years now looked out of any other. And years ago she must have ceased to look out of this, for today she sat with her back to it with finality. (206)

Although at one point, relaxing into the conversation, "Cousin Nettie, putting her cup down, glanced over her shoulder out the window," giving Roderick the impression that it had perhaps "occurred to her that the outlook might have changed" (214), there is no lasting change in Nettie: "They were back again where they had started," with Cousin Nettie "seated on the sofa with her back to what she had ascertained to be nothing," by the time that Roderick leaves (218, 215). Ultimately trapped and helpless within the voluntary prison of Wistaria Lodge, Cousin Nettie becomes a metaphor for the madness of longing to retreat completely from the war and the world around her into a fantasy of imagined shelter.

Stella learns to recognize the madness of her own fantasy of asylum with Kelway only once she begins to perceive the Blitz as a real, inescapable part of her life. Stella feels displaced in bombed London, where the flimsy walls of her rented, furnished flat "did not even look like home" (47), recalling the image of "paper rooms" that Bowen creates in her own description of the Blitz ("London, 1940" 23). Stella's displacement leads her to question the stability of the figurative wall that she has tried to erect between Kelway and Harrison. By the end of the novel, she has realized that the two men were not so different: "It seemed to her it was Robert who had been the Harrison" (275), even as "there may *have* been something between" Harrison and her (320). As a purely public figure, the lovelorn Harrison becomes "a character impossible" (140); as a strictly private lover, the treasonous Kelway is certainly "fictitious" (97). In confronting these fictions, Stella admits that the personal concerns of both men are intricately, if awkwardly, connected with their political choices.

Once she identifies this connection, Stella is ready to examine the relationship between her own private and public lives – a relationship with which Bowen herself struggles in *Bowen's Court*. Initially, Stella prefers to consign herself to "that haunted room" of her flat where "the rasping wordy battle" about her relationships with Kelway and Harrison rages, but during one night of particularly intense bombing, she suddenly realizes the value of looking out her window: "She got up and went after [Harrison] through the curtains" and to the "open window" (139). Unlike Cousin Nettie, who decisively turns her back on the outside world, Stella here discovers that it is only by "letting the curtain drop, returning to lean her forehead against the pushed up sash of the window" that "she understood, with regard to Harrison, the hopeless disparity between belief and truth" (142). In order to escape the "moral blindness" to which both Harrison and Kelway succumb (143), Stella must find a way to connect her private life meaningfully with the public world at war. This realization leads quickly to a political insight:

> To her, tonight, "outside" meant the harmless world: *the mischief was in her own and other rooms.* The grind and scream of battles, mechanized advances excoriating flesh and country, tearing through nerves and tearing up trees, were indoor-plotted; this was a war of dry cerebration inside windowless walls. (142, my emphasis)

Rejecting the idyllic safety that characterizes not only her own love affair but also the indoor-plotted strategies of war, Stella now condemns those who retreat into private strongholds to plot political violence against the harmless world. She looks out her window at the ruins of the home front and recognizes that the destruction of London has resulted from the dry cerebration that leads people to create an idealized but untenable separation between private life and public duty. If one sits inside windowless walls – or even inside Bowen's Court – it is too easy to acquiesce to the violence devastating a world of which one does not feel a part. In this scene, Stella decides to leave behind the shelter of life with the lid on, embracing instead the social unity promised by the People's War.

The novel uses the metaphor of childbirth to symbolize this change in Stella, a metaphor that marks Stella's difference from the childless, isolated Cousin Nettie even as it makes the liberation of her imagination a women's issue more generally. For Stella, the moment of metaphorical childbirth comes when she asks Kelway point-blank whether he has committed treason: she is "exhausted by having given birth to the question" (267). The birth is a long time coming; before she confronts Kelway, she sinks deep into "the birth-sleeps [...] of some profound change" (176), and she is already "two months gone" with the idea when she first mentions it to him in passing (191). The question about Kelway's espionage pointedly attacks the fantasy of keeping private life and politics separate: it is both a highly personal question, interrogating what had been their romantic habitat, and an extremely political one, probing Kelway's national allegiance and asserting Stella's roles as British citizen and government employee. In this moment, Stella herself becomes a real presence in the political world: instead of hiding within a fantasy with Kelway, she follows her initial impulse to join Harrison at the window looking out of her flat and now begins "talking and talking" to Harrison, who represents for her the public life from which she has too long been estranged (317). This is indeed a birth of imagination, for Stella must completely reconceive her relationships with the two men in order to question Kelway about his treasonous spying.

Stella's newly empowered imagination offers one form of fictional redemption for Bowen, who feared that the Blitz would paralyze her own. Ironically, however, the birth also exposes the narrow limits of Stella's insight. Although she specifically criticizes politicians unaware of the world around them, Stella focuses so intently upon her own growing self-awareness that she fails to see the price it exacts from the novel's other unlikely pair: Roderick Rodney and Louie Lewis. While Kelway and Harrison illustrate the personal dilemma facing Stella, these two younger characters embody the social consequences of that dilemma for Britain's next generation. More specifically, Roderick and Louie represent the two fantasies that compete for both Bowen's and Stella's attention: the desire to return to a protected status quo, on the one hand, and the impulse to embrace the exciting opportunities of wartime, on the other. As Stella's son and the heir to the family Big House, Roderick inherits the nostalgia for a safe private shelter; he represents the landowner's interest in protecting the traditional social hierarchy under siege during the Blitz. As Stella's working-class female acquaintance, Louie is heir to the utopian ideal of a People's War; she represents the more popular mandate to revolutionize class relations on the home front. Despite their obvious differences, Roderick and Louie occupy a similar position as Stella's literal and figurative children; they both hope that she will help them to discover who they are, beyond the limitations of the fantasies to which they are currently subject. However, Stella is so busy giving birth to her own understanding that she fails to notice these parallel struggles for Roderick and Louie. Unlocking imaginative power only for herself, Stella, like the rest of her generation, has "muffed the catch" (25); they have gained their freedom at their children's expense, a phenomenon illustrated starkly when one looks beyond the scope of Stella's rather sheltered life.

Stella's debt to her son is not immediately obvious. She is a loving mother who welcomes Roderick home when he is on leave and corresponds with him regularly while he is in Army training camp. When he inherits Mount Morris, she even attends Cousin Francis's funeral in Roderick's stead and then handles the legal transfer of the estate into his name – but Stella's interest in the Irish Big House ends there. The novel liberates Stella from the tensions that strain *Bowen's Court* by creating a convoluted inheritance story that distances her from Mount Morris: her dead ex-husband's cousin leaves the house to Roderick because he was conceived there during his parents' honeymoon. Stella must act as her 20-year-old son's legal guardian for a year, but she remains bound by neither the social conventions nor the traditional gender roles that define Mount Morris. She can therefore reap the benefits provided by her family estate without paying their price. For Stella, these benefits are substantial: she uses her social connections to secure rewarding war work and her family pedigree to arrange a postwar marriage to a "cousin of a cousin" (321).

Stella's marriage plans might seem to place her right back where she started, negating the freedoms that she has earned as a worker in wartime. However, many of the middle- and upper-middle-class women who chose interesting war work for the duration also chose marriage after the war. According to a 1944 Mass-Observation report, most middle- and upper-middle-class women looked forward "to settling down and making a home after the war" (Calder and Sheridan 180, 178).[10] In 1941, a Mass-Observer noted a similar trend, even within the high-class, "boarding school atmosphere" of the WAAF:

Few have exact plans as to what they are going to do after the war. Vaguely, "I'll get a job" seems to be the general idea. A few have their jobs to go back to; quite a few are of independent means, or can rely on their parents; a very few would like to stay on and remain in the WAAF; most hope that they'll get married. (M-O A: FR 757, 1941: 2, 11)[11]

The key for those women who married after the war was to choose actively for themselves and thus to avoid the madness of Cousin Nettie, who "had been pressed back, hour by hour, by the hours themselves, into cloudland" as an idle, isolated, and passive woman of leisure at Mount Morris (174). Unlike Nettie, who married fatalistically and lived in a home that drove her crazy – despite her conviction that "there should never have been any other story" between her and Cousin Francis (108) – Stella insists that "her prospects have alternatives" and that she has always "left things open" with regard to her upcoming marriage (322). Although she is not overjoyed at the prospect of marriage, her reasons stay ambiguous, and the choice remains her own. Stella is compelled neither to manage the affairs of the Big House nor to live as a wife within its walls, but she can nevertheless use her privileged background to create postwar opportunities for herself and thus to continue shaping her identity to her own advantage.

However, even as Stella's disengagement from Mount Morris offers her substantial benefits, it forces the inexperienced Roderick to assume full responsibility for the home with little preparation for the task. From the beginning of the novel, Stella describes Roderick as unsure of himself – "She could not believe he knew where he was himself" (51) – but she does little to help him to articulate his wartime identity: "She had, for instance, not once actually asked whether Roderick liked being in the Army" (51). Roderick himself is extremely self-conscious about his unformed identity; he is "physically at a loss" with his mother "until, by an imitation of her attitudes he supplied himself with some way to behave, look, stand – even, you might say, *be*. [...] He searched in Stella for some identity left by him in her keeping" (48). Before his first trip to Mount Morris, he even asks his mother doubtfully, "After all, who am I?" (299), and "You do really think I am a person?" (300). Increasingly sure of herself, Stella models a stable identity for Roderick: "Her clothes fitted her body, her body her self, with a general air of attractiveness and ease" (25). However, she neglects to answer his questions and then lets him travel alone when he finally secures leave from the Army "to view for the first time, and arrange for the administration of, his property" in Ireland (308–9). Although Roderick has mixed feelings about his mother's hands-off approach, Stella's attitude is clear: "Work kept his mother in London: he was sorry and not sorry, she not sorry" (309). Stella remorselessly leaves Roderick to manage alone the Big House that bolsters her identity even as it threatens to crush his own.

Once again, the novel invokes the metaphor of childbirth to describe identity construction, but in this case, childbirth describes masculine identity and property ownership rather than feminine identity. This use of the metaphor emphasizes the price that must be paid – however unnaturally – for Stella's imaginative freedom. Roderick feels the night air around the Big House "impregnating every part of his body," and then he finds himself overwhelmed by the power of the home (312):

> Nature had withdrawn, leaving everything to be nothing but the identity of Mount Morris. The place had concentrated upon Roderick its being: this was the hour of the never-before – gone were virgin dreams with anything they had had of himself in them, anything they had had of the picaresque, sweet, easy, strident. He was left possessed, oppressed and in awe. He heard the pulse in his temple beating into the pillow; he was followed by the sound of his own footsteps over his own land. The consummation woke in him, for the first time, the concept and fearful idea of death, his. Ahead were his five days more here; ahead again was the possibility of his not coming back. He had not till tonight envisaged not coming back from war. (312)

Ravished by Mount Morris, Roderick finds himself impregnated not with the possibility of imaginative transformation but with the responsibility of protecting the status quo, even at the price of his life. The images of impregnation, loss of virginity, possession, and consummation create a disturbing contrast between Stella's imaginative rebirth and Roderick's imagined death. Too involved with the figurative act of childbirth, Stella heedlessly neglects her real child's needs.

These needs are much like those of his mother: Roderick is tempted to retreat from the world at war into a completely private fantasy. The Big House is far from the front line and therefore seems to offer this young soldier an escape from the everyday grind of Army life: "By geographically standing outside war [Mount Morris] appeared to be standing outside the present. The house, non-human, became the hub of [Roderick's] imaginary life, of fancies, fantasies only so to be called because circumstance outlawed them from reality" (50). Stella knows that her own identity depends upon a refusal to retreat into nostalgic fantasy, but she does not share the insight with her son. Instead, she enjoys both the security of her social background and the freedom of her life in the Blitz, leaving Roderick to pay the price of her freedom, as both a landowner in Ireland and a soldier for England.

Stella's newfound imaginative power is the product not only of the nostalgic fantasy of past social privilege safeguarded by Roderick but also of the utopian fantasy of present social change represented by her working-class acquaintance, Louie Lewis. When Victoria Glendinning describes Bowen's enthusiasm for leaving behind life with the lid on, she notes that Bowen's war work "brought [her] into close contact with people she would not normally have become intimate with – girls like the butch Connie and feckless Louie in *The Heat of the Day*, for example" (178). On the surface, the novel seems to reinforce the ideology of the People's War by drawing a social connection between the working-class Louie and the upper-middle-class Stella. When Stella and Harrison meet Louie in a bar, for example, Stella feels profoundly war's ability to demolish not only the walls of homes, such as Louie's, but also the barriers between classes. Just as Louie hopes, "People to be friendly, that what war's for, isn't it?" (239), Stella declares, "We're all three human" (240). This moment of social affinity – the life with the lid off that Bowen found so exhilarating – suggests that both Stella and Louie enjoy and benefit from the breakdown of barriers between the classes during the People's War. At the same time, however, Bowen acknowledges and represents the tensions within this myth of the Blitz. In stories such as "Oh, Madam...," "The Cheery Soul," and "Mysterious Kôr," the working- and middle-class characters initially appear to fight alongside one another in the People's War. However, these cross-class wartime relationships are never as enduring and liberating as they promise to be; instead, they are temporary and typically controlled by the party of higher social standing. In the stories as well as in *The Heat of the Day*, Bowen exhibits a self-conscious ambivalence about the fantasy of social mobility that often delighted her in wartime. Bowen herself found "a lifetime's policy of 'not noticing' increasingly hard to maintain" during the war, not only because she noticed connections across class lines but also because she noticed the differences in social opportunity and power that continued to separate women of various classes during and after the Blitz (Glendinning 142).

The differences could be quite profound: choosing to work in a factory for the duration, upper-middle-class women like Constance Reaveley could also choose to return whenever they liked to the comfort of their peacetime lives.[12] The option of leaving drudgery behind distinguishes ladies like Stella from workers like Louie, and *The Heat of the Day* once again chooses the metaphor of childbirth to emphasize the distance. Like Roderick Rodney, Louie Lewis is a troubled, almost-grown child who looks to the more experienced, self-confident Stella as a mother figure who can help her to articulate her identity. Because "she felt she did not make sense, and still worse felt that the others knew it" (149), Louie searches rather desperately for someone to imitate, much as Roderick tries to imitate his mother: "She looked about her in vain for someone to imitate; she was ready, nay, eager to attach herself to anyone who could seem to be following any one course with certainty" (15). The danger in imitating Stella, however, is that Stella associates each of these young people with one of the class-specific fantasies that allow her to give birth to her own imaginative power. Thus, while Roderick embodies for Stella the prospect of protecting and maintaining the social status quo upon which much of her freedom rests, Louie embodies the ideal of social unity and equity during the People's War.

The rhetoric of the People's War is certainly powerful enough to inform Louie's sense of identity, just as the fantasy of protecting the status quo seems to lock young Roderick into the role of the Irish landowner. Even before she meets Stella, Louie finds great comfort in the propagandistic labels of wartime journalism: "Was she not a worker, a soldier's lonely wife, a war orphan, a pedestrian, a Londoner, a home- and animal-lover, a thinking democrat, a movie-goer, a woman of Britain, a letter writer, a fuel-saver, and a housewife?" (152). So eager to belong, Louie rather recklessly embraces the promise of the People's

War; upon first encountering Stella, she naïvely and hopefully suggests, "We women are all in the same boat" (237). Stella, however, puts Louie in her place by quickly countering, "Oh, I'm not" (237). From the safe distance of her privileged social position, Stella demonstrates that for her the myth of the Blitz is merely useful: it allows her to become "the talker" (248), unburdening herself completely and fully during a brief, intense encounter with Louie.

For Louie, however, the brief encounter is far more than a one-time affair: afterwards, "Louie dwelled on Stella with mistrust and addiction, dread and desire," believing that she had finally been "sought out exactly as she had sought to be" (248). Just as the novel describes Roderick's dream of a safe shelter impregnating and overpowering his imagination at Mount Morris, it depicts Louie's fantasy of friendship across class lines with images of sexual intimacy. Meeting Stella "overpowered Louie" (240), and in trying to understand Stella's psyche, "Louie felt herself entered by what was foreign" (247) and noticed that "her lips seemed bidden" to speak of the "soul astray" she discovers in Stella (249). The hapless Louie finds herself quite unable to defend an undefined self against the relentless power of this utopian fantasy. For Roderick, the parallel to Stella's metaphorical childbirth ends at this moment with his own figurative death. For Louie, however, the metaphor of childbirth goes a step further: not only is she entered and overpowered by a fantasy that benefits primarily privileged women like Stella, but she also becomes literally pregnant at the end of the novel. Bored with her work and lonely without her soldier husband, Louie searches for excitement and companionship in adulterous relationships – but gets only an unwanted pregnancy. Once again, Stella reaps the ideological benefits conferred by the childbirth metaphor, leaving Roderick to shoulder the economic burden and Louie to bear the biological responsibility that make Stella's rebirth possible.

Initially, the birth of Louie's son at the end of the novel seems to parallel the birth of Stella's imaginative power. Louie travels with her baby to Seale-on-Sea to visit the site of her parents' bombed-out home. Remembering her childhood in this now-absent house and wandering around the adjacent fields, Louie holds the newborn up to the sky, where British bombers are flying back from war. By connecting the birth of her son with the impending rebirth of peace in England, the novel integrates domestic life and politics on the site of a war-torn home: Louie's parents' demolished bungalow. More importantly, *The Heat of the Day* seems to frame this moment of integration as evidence of Louie's escape from the prison of conventional gender roles. Just as the birth of Stella's imaginative power frees her from Harrison's and Kelway's rigid notions of public and private space, the birth of Louie's illegitimate son should liberate her from traditional notions of marriage and fidelity. The novel's metaphors of shelter and childbirth thus appear to converge in the utopian fantasy of the People's War, universalizing the possibilities for British women during and after the Second World War.

However, a closer look at the character of Louie Lewis exposes the problem of drawing general conclusions about life on the home front from Stella's limited bourgeois experience. Like other women of her class, Stella tends to perceive the war as an equalizing force because she does not fully comprehend the complexity of female working-class experience. While Stella's metaphorical pregnancy and birth lead her toward political activism, "Louie's passiveness biggened with her [pregnant] body" (326). Louie is passive because she has little choice: a real, illegitimate baby would have made impossible for Louie the freedom that Stella experiences – even, or perhaps especially, the freedom to remarry a man of her choice. After the death of her soldier husband, a single mother like Louie would have had difficulty supporting herself and her child. According to Dorothy Sheridan, "Women with young children found it especially hard to find work which they could combine with childcare [after the war]. The nurseries were closing down and the idealised image of the mother at home dominated postwar planning" (193). This idealized image of the wife and mother was also central to moral rhetoric during this period. Despite the increase in wartime sexuality, there was a strong popular and legal bias against women who committed adultery during the war.[13] According to Sonya Rose, the "moral purity rhetoric" popular in wartime Britain "echoed the construction of the national 'we' as a society in which class was less important than virtuous behaviour in defining the members of the national community" (82). Politically, this attitude supported the publication of such documents as the White Paper "Youth Registration in 1942," which required young people to register with the government and to indicate their membership in any clubs and organizations. The purpose behind gathering this information was to "encourage young people to make good use of organized leisure activities rather than spending their time in unsupervised activities such as 'hanging about' and going to the cinema and dance halls" (90). Rose suggests that "the youth movement as it was called was created to fashion self-disciplined and responsible moral subjects. The World War II obsession with the morality and responsibility of girls and young women in Britain was thus articulated in terms that constructed moral subjects as responsible citizens" (90). When Stella chooses to remarry, she is therefore making a moral, political choice unavailable to women like Louie.

An account of a 1945 murder trial in the London *Times* illustrates the legal impact of this moral and political code:

> Cyril Patmore, 35, a private in The Royal Scots Fusiliers, father of four children, and home on compassionate leave from India, was charged at the Central Criminal Court yesterday with the murder of his wife, Kathleen Patmore, 39, by stabbing at Greenhill Road, Harlesdan, N.W. on August 4. He was found *Not Guilty* of murder; but *Guilty* of manslaughter, and he was sentenced to five years' penal servitude. It was alleged that his wife had been unfaithful while he was abroad on Army service. ("Soldier's Unfaithful Wife" 2)

The bias against adulterous women informs the legal decision to exonerate the cuckolded husband: although Cyril Patmore is punished for killing his allegedly unfaithful wife, he is convicted only of manslaughter and therefore earns a minimal sentence. For the unfaithful Louie, life in this moral climate creates a conflict: on the one hand, she longs to be a good British citizen as "a worker, a soldier's lonely wife, a war orphan, a pedestrian, a Londoner, a home- and animal-lover, a thinking democrat, a movie-goer, a woman of Britain, a letter writer, a fuel-saver, and a housewife" (Bowen, *Heat* 152); on the other hand, she is alienated by rhetoric that labels her a "good-time girl" and identifies her "moral laxity" as anti-patriotism (Rose 80).[14]

Although Louie's class position and the circumstances of her pregnancy would almost certainly have shaped her experience of motherhood in negative ways, the final scene of the novel obscures these social realities in favor of a vision of feminine rebirth and freedom. Louie's act of holding up her infant son to watch the bombers returning from war represents her "now complete life" (329). Even the baby's name – Thomas Victor – creates what appears to be a bond of shared independence between Louie and Stella: Tom and Victor are the husbands from whom Louie and Stella are now completely free. Once again, however, the freedom represented by the baby is Stella's, while the responsibility for that baby is Louie's. While Stella's life may have been symbolically completed by the birth of Louie's illegitimate son, Louie's life would almost certainly have been thrown into chaos. Like Roderick, who must manage the home that protects the fantasy of uninterrupted social power and freedom, Louie must tend the baby that represents the dream of a utopian future. In both cases, the fantasies shelter Stella from the ideological confusion unleashed by the Blitz, allowing her imaginative freedom without personal cost.

Bowen therefore examines more critically in *The Heat of the Day* the forms of shelter that she sought and found problematic in *Bowen's Court*. Just as Bowen wanted both to retreat from the war and to involve herself in it as she wrote her memoir in 1942, Stella wants to profit from two conflicting wartime fantasies: the nostalgic retreat into tradition represented by Roderick and the utopian engagement in the People's War represented by Louie. Ironically, however, the choices facing both Stella and Bowen are not between retreat and engagement but between different forms of retreat, since even their involvement in the war was circumscribed by the privileges and opportunities of their upper-middle-class status. *The Heat of the Day* counts the cost of Stella's imaginative power in the currency of other characters' lives in order to offer fictional distance from the all-too-real problems haunting *Bowen's Court*. By 1949, Bowen no longer simply wondered whether she should retreat to Ireland or entrench herself in Regent's Park; instead, she asked whether those civilians sheltered by class status were capable of abandoning a lifetime's policy of not noticing less privileged people, even after they had lived together through the horrors of the Blitz. It is this profound sense of ambivalence that characterizes much of the literary fiction of the Blitz.

2
Immobile Women in Rosamond Lehmann's War Writing

Whereas Elizabeth Bowen's wartime protagonists tend to live as dangerously as she did among the bombs and rockets of battered London, Rosamond Lehmann's characters typically live as safely as she did, evacuated to their country estates. Lehmann emphasizes their safety by setting some of her war writing in peacetime: the events of short stories such as "The Gipsy's Baby" and "The Red-Haired Miss Daintreys" and the novel *The Ballad and the Source* (1944) all occur before the Second World War, and much of the action in *The Echoing Grove* (1953) also takes place either before or after the war. This difference in distance from the Blitz shaped the two writers' fictional representations of the People's War. Bowen's upper-middle-class characters struggle to reconcile the privilege of a nostalgized past with the utopian promise of a postwar future. They therefore reveal a contradiction camouflaged by the rhetoric of the People's War: rather than changing everything for everyone, the Blitz changed only some things for some people. Lehmann's fiction more directly critiques the self-absorbed insularity of the upper-middle class. Although her characters often endorse the People's War as vehemently as Bowen's, they always do so at a safe distance from the Blitz itself; in *The Echoing Grove*, the characters think of the Blitz more as a metaphor for failed love than as a real catastrophe. Critiquing such solipsism, Lehmann insists that the ideological battles of the People's War were fought not only across class or gender lines but also within the boundaries of the upper-middle-class imagination itself.

There were times when Lehmann lived close enough to the Blitz to see its devastating impact for herself. Although she resided at her country home in Ipsden, Oxfordshire (about 50 miles west of London) during the first year of the war, often called the Phoney War because there was no bombing, she did visit London regularly during the worst months of the Blitz between September 1940 and May 1941. In March 1941, Henry Yorke (whose work, written under the pseudonym of Henry Green, is the subject of Chapter 3) offered Lehmann a room in his Kensington flat for a few nights a week so that she could more easily collaborate with her brother, John, on *Penguin New Writing*. There was some bombing in London during this time, most notably on the nights of 8 and 19 March. However, by the time Easter arrived on 13 April, Lehmann had left London for good, taking her children for a vacation to Llanstephan in western England until 1 May and then moving with them back to her family estate at Bourne End in Buckinghamshire (closer to London but still 35 miles away) in May 1941. The Buckinghamshire Records Office confirms that Bourne End itself was not targeted during this period, although on 5 May 1941, a hotel in neighboring Taplow did suffer some bomb damage.[1] In December 1941, having decided to "establish a permanent base in the country for herself and the children" (Hastings 223), Lehmann moved into Diamond Cottage at Aldworth (only seven miles southwest of Ipsden), a place that she bought before the war and then rented to tenants while she was staying at Ipsden and Bourne End. During her residence in Aldworth from 1941 until the end of the war, the only major bombing of the area occurred on 10 February 1943, when Reading town center (about 15 miles away) was hit by four enemy bombs; there were approximately 192 casualties, of which 41 were fatal.

In addition to the limited time that Lehmann spent in danger areas during the Blitz, she also did a very limited amount of war work. In his memoir, John Lehmann recalls that his sister accommodated "eleven ragamuffins" as evacuees (36), fell into "a dark state of confused anxiety and depression" just after Dunkirk (67), and endured the "ceaseless humming of aeroplanes" as "a constant reminder of the war in which we were engaged" (273), even while living in the country. Yet despite these worries, Lehmann's primary concern throughout the war remained her own writing; Wendy Pollard explains Lehmann's anxiety about completing *The Ballad and the Source*:

In the second year of the war, Lehmann was at her most distraught. [...] Despite this acute anxiety about the progress of the war, and genuine sympathy expressed elsewhere in [her] correspondence for those enduring the bombing in cities while she lived for the most part in the country, Lehmann also admitted to a selfish fear that the war and her domestic situation would seriously interfere with her work. She wrote to [Compton] Mackenzie that she had suddenly been told that she must take some evacuated children, "and oh dear! how little do I want them. It just makes my last faint hope of preserving a little leisure for writing recede altogether." (108–9)

Unlike Bowen, Lehmann thought about her wartime productivity more in terms of logistics than psychology. As a result, the two writers handled their anxieties differently: while Bowen sought inspiration amidst the London bombing, taking only occasional trips to Ireland, Lehmann sought privacy in the country, taking only occasional trips to London.

Despite this difference in distance from the Blitz, Bowen and Lehmann shared very similar social backgrounds. The solidly upper-middle-class Lehmann "was born into an unusually privileged and exceptionally talented family" (Simons 3), and she grew up in a house called Fieldhead at Bourne End, a large estate not unlike Bowen's Court. According to Judy Simons, the property "had vast gardens stretching down to the River Thames and contained room in its grounds for stables, kennels, a boathouse and even a school, erected specifically for the Lehman daughters' education and able to provide facilities for several carefully selected girls from neighboring families" (4).[2] The house was "sheltered from intrusions from the outside world" (Simons 4), and it placed the Lehmanns, like the Bowens, at a distance from others living in the area. The Lehmanns could literally look down upon these others: "On one side of the house was a row of squalid cottages, whose urchin inhabitants were to become a source of ambivalent fascination to the Lehmann children gazing down on them from the nursery windows" (Hastings 16). The shared social status that allowed both Bowen and Lehmann to live in this state of "ambivalent fascination" also underwrote their shared professional status as members of the Bloomsbury circle, an affiliation that inevitably brought about an acquaintance between the two authors in 1933. By this time, both women had married men of their own class: Bowen wed Alan Cameron in 1923, while Lehmann married first Leslie Runciman in 1923 and then Wogan Phillips in 1928, when the union with Runciman dissolved. Both of the women had unstable marriages: during her first visit to Bowen's Court in 1936, Lehmann became infatuated almost immediately with Goronwy Rees, a young man with whom the older Bowen was also smitten. The ensuing affair between Lehmann and Rees temporarily alienated her from Bowen, but the rancor between the two writers did not last: during the war, Bowen's extramarital affair with Charles Ritchie and Lehmann's relationship with poet Cecil Day-Lewis consumed their romantic attention. They resumed their friendship after the war in the late 1940s, and Lehmann visited Bowen's Court once again in 1950.

During this period of reconciliation, Lehmann wrote enthusiastic letters to Bowen in praise of *The Heat of the Day*: " 'Elizabeth, darling Elizabeth,' began one, 'I've never written this sort of letter to any writer before ... [The book] is embedded deep deep in my consciousness: an overpowering experience for which I am eternally grateful" (Hastings 268).[3] According to Selina Hastings, Lehmann responded so emotionally to the novel because she saw in it a compelling representation of her own wartime experience: "Not only did she herself identify strongly with [Bowen's] heroine, Stella, but she saw in Stella's son the double of Hugo [her own son], while [Stella's] traitor/lover, Robert, bore, she thought, a resemblance to Cecil" (268). *The Heat of the Day* describes in detail the exciting social scene in wartime London enjoyed by both its characters and women like Bowen and Lehmann:

> This was the new society of one kind of wealth, resilience, living how it liked – people whom the climate of danger suited, who began, even, all to look a little alike, as they might in the sun, snows, and altitude of the same sports station, or browning along the same beach in the south of France. [...] There was a diffused gallantry in the atmosphere, an unmarriedness: it came to be rumoured about the country, among the self-banished, the uneasy, the put-upon and the safe, that everybody in London was in love – which was true, if not in the sense the country meant. There was plenty of everything in London – attention, drink, time, taxis, most of all space. (94–5)

The passage shows how easy it was for upper-middle-class women to romanticize the new society in which they moved. In love with an exclusive society made more exclusive by the Blitz, privileged women often shared with characters like Stella the thrill of the high life in bombed London.

It was the differences, however, rather than the similarities between Bowen's and Lehmann's experiences during the Blitz that shaped their fictional representations of women in wartime. Even though Bowen could retreat when off duty into an exclusive London society where there was "plenty of everything," her ARP work nevertheless brought her into contact with others of all classes during the Blitz. The conflict between "life with the lid on" at the Savoy and life with the lid off at the warden's post was a source of tension for Bowen, one that she reconciled by using the rhetoric of the People's War to describe the opportunities of the privileged few (Glendinning 177). In contrast, Lehmann's visits to blitzed London immersed her – usually quite briefly – only in the high-society life that had "plenty of everything." When her children, Hugo and Sally, were away from Aldworth during school terms, Lehmann went to London for romantic getaways with Day-Lewis, but when the children were home, she always stayed with them in the country:

> At this period of her life [1941–43] she was settled and happy, and although the war in many ways made daily life arduous, it also intensified emotion and provided new and interesting types of experience. And unlike many of her contemporaries, she was fortunate in being able to continue in a stable and reasonably comfortable way of life. As she put it in a [1943] letter to Rayner Heppenstall, an old FIL [Association of Writers for Intellectual Liberty] colleague, "Although my life has completely changed, I am still in the country, under my own roof, with my children, within reach of my friends, and have privacy, and leisure to write." (Hastings 231)

Safely sheltered both on her country estate and within her London romance, Lehmann did not share with Bowen the fear of losing established social privileges or the thrill of proving that London could take it. Lehmann lived life with the lid on both in and out of London, and she found her upper-middle-class security confirmed rather than threatened by the distant violence of the Blitz. Her fiction allowed her the critical distance to analyze this state of privileged insularity.

The possibility that many British citizens were living such sheltered lives disturbed some members of the British government. An internal MOI memo regarding comments made by Captain L. D. Gamman, an MP in the House of Commons, suggests concern that differences in civilian experience might cause morale problems:

> Capt. Gamman's comments about apathy outside London are not far from the mark. Home Intelligence confirm that people in the Midlands are particularly apathetic to the Londoners' experiences of Fly-bombs [V-weapons]. Elsewhere there is no evidence that people have been much moved about the subject [...]. Londoners feel that there is not enough realization by the rest of the country of what they have gone through. (Briggs to Archibald, 18 August 1944)

The Director of the MOI wrote to Captain Gamman a few days later:

> I think that the main factor in all this indifference outside the flying
> bomb area is that war has taught people in the country to become a
> great deal more callous than they used to be, and people are content
> with their own troubles without troubling much about other people's.
> (Director-General MOI, 25 August 1944)

Blaming the divisions among British civilians on geographical location,
these internal government documents express concern that middle-
and upper-class insularity might undercut the unifying ideal of the
People's War.

However, Mass-Observation materials suggest that callousness was not
the issue. One report indicates that "among middle-class women there is
frequently a desire to do more than they are doing to help the war effort,
to take part in some useful, humanitarian capacity" (M-O A: FR 520,
1940: 11). Another series of observations submitted around the same
time focuses more particularly on the country living that caused so
much concern at the MOI. The report quotes a 38-year-old middle-class
woman's views about waiting for the bombing to disrupt her sheltered
life as a foreign correspondent in Scotland:

> In myself I recognise the same psychological effort that I have always
> experienced after an examination, the intense mental effort lowered
> the reservoir of nervous energy and it was days, or even weeks before
> I could take any interest at all in anything whatsoever.... I know I am
> intellectual and academic. (M-O A: FR 530, 1940: 15)

This woman feels that she "must do something active" instead of
simply waiting to be bombed, and the Mass-Observer notes that "this
is a carefully thought-out motive for doing war work, because nothing
is happening, something must be done; it is almost a physical outlet
she desires for the nervous energy and disillusion of the past weeks"
(FR 530: 15). Although the woman quoted is not "callous" toward those
more directly under siege in the Blitz – it is, after all, "almost a physical
outlet" that she desires for herself – the theoretical tone of her writing,
along with the "almost" modifying the "physical outlet," emphasizes
her safe distance from any real danger. Furthermore, the metaphor of
academic testing calls attention to her class status and magnifies the
social gap between those women who could and could not choose
where to live and work in wartime.

While Bowen's war writing struggles to bridge this gap, Lehmann's fiction explores the nature of upper-middle-class authority by focusing exclusively on the "intellectual and academic" lives of privileged characters living at a distance from the People's War. The distance is perhaps most apparent in her wartime short fiction, collected in *The Gipsy's Baby* (1946). Although Lehmann wrote and published the stories during the Blitz, they all describe the setting of her own life in wartime: a peaceful, rural England far removed from both the physical and the social upheaval of the bombing.[4] The stories illustrate so as to critique the intense self-absorption of the upper-middle-class female mind. The first two stories in the collection, "The Gipsy's Baby" (1941–42) and "The Red-Haired Miss Daintreys" (1940–41), take place before the war and represent detailed memories of a peaceful life made possible by land ownership. Young Rebecca Landon, the narrator of "The Gipsy's Baby," distinguishes between "our superior way of life" (17) and that of the working-class Wyatt children, "another species of creature, and, yes, a lower" (21). Like Lehmann and her siblings at Bourne End, the Landon children look down upon squalid cottages from the safety of their nursery window: "At the bottom of the lane that ran between our garden wall and the old row of brick cottages lived the Wyatt family. [...] It was an insanitary cottage with no damp course, mean little windows in rotting frames and discoloured patches on the walls" (9). Similarly, in "The Red-Haired Miss Daintreys," the narrator contrasts herself – "I myself have been, all my life, a privileged person with considerable leisure" (57) – with the moneyed but lowbrow Daintreys, whom she meets on holiday: Miss Mildred has a "low, harsh, cockney-genteel voice" (60) and, overall, the family's "key-note was homely simplicity, and Ma was an inveterate postage-stamp remover" (63). The protagonists of these stories exhibit an unselfconscious sense of social entitlement that distances them from the working and lower-middle classes, an attitude that seems archaic and outmoded by the time of the Second World War.

However, the stories in *The Gipsy's Baby* all show that the attitude still persists even during the People's War. In a telling echo of the two tales set in peacetime, the three war stories of the collection – "When the Waters Came" (1941), "A Dream of Winter" (1941), and "Wonderful Holidays" (1944–45) – contrast socially superior families living safely through the Blitz on their country estates with the lower classes, who remain another species of creature whether they work in the country or fight on the front lines. Introducing Mrs Ritchie, a protagonist in all three stories, "When the Waters Came" begins by emphasizing her family's comfortable distance from frontline violence:

> Nothing very disturbing was likely to happen for the present. One
> thought, of course, of sailors freezing in the unimaginable wastes of
> water, perhaps to be plunged beneath them between one violent
> moment and the next; of soldiers numb in the black-and-white
> nights on sentry duty, crammed, fireless, uncomforted on the floors
> of empty barns and disused warehouses. In her soft bed, she thought
> of them with pity – masses of young men, betrayed, helpless, and so
> much colder, more uncomfortable than human beings should be.
> But they remained unreal, as objects of pity frequently remain. (93)

Mrs Ritchie's view of soldiers as "unreal" is not possible for civilians living in major British cities during the Blitz, since they too were sleeping
crammed together in fireless shelters rather than tucked into cozy beds.
The opposition in this passage between the comforts of a rural home
and the discomforts of a dangerous front line contrasts markedly with
the rhetoric of the People's War, which emphasizes the shared experience of soldiers and civilians under enemy fire. Although the Ritchie
family has its own crisis when the young daughter, Jane, nearly drowns,
their lives mostly "waver on with only a few minor additions and sub-
tractions, in the old way," with little more than an abstract pity for
those less fortunate than themselves (93).

"A Dream of Winter" describes the resentment lurking beneath the
abstract pity for distant soldiers that Mrs Ritchie feels in "When the
Waters Came." As Mrs Ritchie lies sick with the flu in this story, two
workmen come to remove a hive of bees that has infested the Ritchies'
country home. The bedridden Mrs Ritchie's febrile, wandering thoughts
reveal that her intense desire to exterminate the bees is actually an
expression of class anxiety. She thinks of the workmen themselves as
bees: "They communicated with one another in a low drone, bee-like,
rising and sinking in a minor key, punctuated by an occasional deep-
throated 'Ah!' Knocking, hammering, wrenching developed. Somebody
should tell them she could not stand it. Nobody would" (104). This metaphor becomes political in the context of the war: the real threat to Mrs
Ritchie is not the temporary disturbance of the "bee man's" hammer
but the long-term demands of the wartime working class (103):

> What you took for the hum of growth and plenty is nothing, you see,
> but the buzz of an outworn machine running down. The workers
> have eaten up their fruits, there's nothing left for you. It's no use this

time, my girl. Supplies are getting scarce for people like you. An end, soon, of getting more than their fair share for dwellers in country houses. Ripe gifts unearned out of traditional walls, no more. All the while your roof was being sealed up patiently, cunningly, with spreading plasters and waxy shrouds. (106)

Building upon the paranoid self-interest that pervades this passage, the story turns the workman's innocent observation that "it demoralizes 'em [the bees] like when you steals their honey" into the threat of political upheaval (109). Although the rhetoric of the People's War addresses the situation of workers who have been demoralized for too long and who therefore deserve more rights and freedoms as a reward for wartime service, Mrs Ritchie is uninterested in the morale of people whom she considers to be little more than drones. Instead, she is so consumed by fever and self-pity during her illness that she perceives even this harsh reality as a dream: "It seemed to her that her passive, dreaming, leisured life was nothing, in the last analysis, but a fluid element for receiving and preserving faint paradoxical images and symbols. They were all she ultimately remembered" (110).

It is therefore ironic that Mrs Ritchie publicly commits herself to wartime community service in "Wonderful Holidays," the final story in *The Gipsy's Baby*. The story describes the elaborate planning of "Salute the Soldier" week in the Ritchies' rural village (139). Along with their wealthy neighbors, the Carmichaels, the Ritchies take charge of this fundraiser for the Armed Forces, hoping both to entertain the community and to raise money for the troops. Their efforts seem to pay off: they are pleased that the amateur theatrical performance raises "sixteen pounds eleven shillings and sixpence [...]. Really a remarkable effort for a small village. There wasn't a child who didn't put in sixpence at least; and there were a surprising number of notes. Remarkable" (180). Nevertheless, rather than unifying the members of this rural community, the event causes contention:

Nerves are getting frayed on the committee [...]. I hoped we could avoid class antagonism by having half gentry, half village, but it seems to be working out the opposite way. What it comes to is, the village feel we ought to be running it all for them. They're alarmed, I suppose, at the responsibility. If we butt in they think we're patronizing and if we retire they think we're snobbish. Both ways they're resentful. (180)

The passage describes the social tensions that arise, even in this rural village, when different classes converge in support of the war effort. Instead of uniting the village citizens in a common wartime cause, the fundraiser does little more than offer the privileged Ritchies and Carmichaels an excuse to throw themselves a private dinner party and ball celebrating the success of their play. Once again, Lehmann's characters remain at a distance from the principles of the People's War, even when they seem to be most actively engaged in fighting it. Like the other stories of *The Gipsy's Baby*, "Wonderful Holidays" critiques a sheltered British upper-middle class whose lack of interest in the rest of the world has changed little, despite the experiences of the Second World War.

Lehmann explores the extent of this social isolation more fully in *The Ballad and the Source*. Beginning as the First World War ends, the novel follows the later life of Rebecca Landon, the young narrator of the pre-war stories in *The Gipsy's Baby*. However, unlike the short fiction, *The Ballad and the Source* brings the war directly into its characters' lives by deploying a barrage of military imagery that evokes both the First and Second World Wars. The novel describes the domestic conflicts within the Jardine family as military campaigns rather than private quarrels, focusing in particular on the supremely egotistical Sibyl Jardine. When Sibyl finally reunites with her grandchildren after a long feud with her daughter, Ianthe, she fancies herself a domestic warrior and thinks of the event itself in terms of war: "She had snatched victory out of the long years of plot and counter-plot, of ambush, espionage and surprise; of mortal episodes of frontal combat. She had outwitted and outlasted. She would bring her flesh and blood back into her home" (96). Later generations remember the family in similar terms, as when Sibyl's granddaughter, Maisie, recalls her childhood:

> When I think about it now I feel as if the war started then – all roaring armies marching against one another and land mines bursting under everybody. When the real war started and every one else was in a state of chaos, it seemed to me a mere rumble on the horizon. Everything had happened for me. (253)

The metaphor of domestic warfare connects Maisie's words to both her own experience in the First World War and her grandmother's previous struggles. More importantly, however, the military language reminds readers of the context in which Lehmann wrote the novel between 1942 and 1944. As the Second World War transformed British homes into battlefields upon which civilians defended their lives, *The*

Ballad and the Source describes characters who conceive of battle only metaphorically and only in terms of themselves. The novel critiques upper-class insularity and implies that it has persisted throughout the People's War.

Phyllis Lassner is one of the few critics who have placed *The Ballad and the Source* in this embattled cultural context; she argues that the novel describes Sibyl Jardine's "futile struggle for domination" as a metaphor for the impossibility of telling a coherent story once the extreme violence of the Great War had permanently changed the world ("Timeless" 77). Ultimately unable to control either her family or her narrative, Sibyl loses substance, becoming an echo of a mythic past eradicated by trench warfare. For Lassner, *The Ballad and the Source* carefully balances the attractive and the nightmarish qualities of mythologizing: while myth may offer some comfort, it can also become totalizing. According to Lassner, Lehmann comments indirectly upon the "elusive presence" of the Second World War, a war not yet won in 1944 and not mentioned in her novel, by describing the tension between finding meaning and resisting totalitarianism within the "safe place" of the past ("Timeless" 80, 79).

However, *The Ballad and the Source* is more than just a symbolic echo of national crisis; it directly and specifically analyzes key issues of the Second World War. The novel employs echo imagery not to indicate absence but to demonstrate the continuing presence of an unchanging upper-middle class. The echoes reverberate within the Jardine family: Rebecca thinks of her present life as "somehow both graced and weakened by echoes and reflections from the prestige of that heyday" recounted by Sibyl Jardine (9); "terrible echoes" of past parental threats haunt the children of the present generation (79); and Rebecca finds in Maisie "a baffling echo of Mrs Jardine," despite the fact that "not a line, not a feature" of the girl "recalled her grandmother" (221). This echoing across generations gives the impression of a family little changed by time and experience. Even more pointed, however, is the novel's analysis of the characters' stasis: they do not change because they cannot see beyond the confines of their own experience. Sibyl is critical of her daughter, Ianthe, who ensnares herself within a trap of self-love:

> She was afraid of the world. [...] When people are afraid they dare not look outward for fear of getting too much hurt. They shut themselves up and look only at pictures of themselves, because these they can adapt and manipulate to their needs without interference, or wounding shocks. The world sets snares for their self-love. It betrays them.

> So they look in the mirrors and see only what flatters and reassures
> them; and so they imagine they are not betrayed. (115)

Yet despite her criticism, Sibyl herself remains trapped within just such
a hall of mirrors:

> From anybody else in the world [...] she gets back – *immeasurable*
> reflections of herself. It's not deliberate, so it's pointless to moralise
> about it: it's some property of her nature – some principle. Like yeast.
> She throws out all she has – her beauty, her gifts, her power over
> people – and objects – and events; and it works. Each time she tries it
> out, it works like magic. Up come all these disturbing, magnetized
> self-images. (232)

Caught within "the spell of the spell-binder" (176), locked within this
house of mirrors, the novel's narrator, Rebecca, and even her "prudent
and incorruptible" (176) mother begin to share Sibyl's "sense of the
need for family solidarity" (177). The domineering Jardine family represents synecdochically an upper-middle class so obsessed with itself that
it fails to recognize any experience but its own, a particularly jarring
image since Lehmann was writing the novel during the People's War.

Lehmann extends her critique of upper-middle-class stasis and
insularity in *The Echoing Grove*, her only depiction of the Blitz itself.
Composed between 1945 and 1952, the novel was finally published in
1953, 13 years after the first major bombing of London and nine years
after the V-1 and V-2 rocket attacks. Like Lehmann's earlier war writing, *The Echoing Grove* examines the upper-middle class from a critical
distance, this time looking back at the Blitz from a postwar perspective.
The novel tells the story of two sisters who have fought for one man's
attention throughout a four-year love affair, and it does so using metaphors of the Blitz. Because these sisters, Dinah Burkett and Madeleine
Masters, try to understand the wartime hardships endured by people
less privileged than themselves, they appear to be far more socially
engaged than the Ritchies, Landons, or Jardines of Lehmann's earlier
fiction. However, *The Echoing Grove* illustrates in more detail than any
of Lehmann's other war writing the extent to which upper-middle-class
understanding of the People's War was constrained by the boundaries
of its own experience. Even when Dinah and Madeleine seem to sym-
pathize with people from different classes, they actually do little more
than project themselves into their own preconceived notions of other
social roles. This imaginative exercise is far more aggressive than the

lack of imagination that traps Lehmann's earlier protagonists within the narrow confines of their sheltered lives. Pretending to be socially active while actually remaining selfishly complacent, the characters of *The Echoing Grove* reveal a level of class insularity at odds with the utopian fantasy of a People's War that Bowen describes.

When *The Echoing Grove* opens in 1946, the sisters' battles, like the battles of the Second World War, are finished: Rickie – Madeleine's husband and Dinah's lover – is now dead, and the affair has been over for 14 years. Moving backward and forward in time, the narrative resurrects the past in order to reconcile the sisters in the present. The fusion of a conventional romance plot with a subjective, disjointed style earned the novel what one writer called "incomprehensible reviews" (Rev. of *TEG, Nation* 441).[5] However, whether reviewers and critics thought that *The Echoing Grove* was a masterpiece, as the reviewer for the *New York Times Book Review* did, or a sentimental "sea of toasted marshmallow" (Tracy 434),[6] most of them have agreed that Lehmann's "prime interest is in personal relationships" (Sackville-West 454), much as Hastings's biography suggests.[7] Following this line of thought, criticism of *The Echoing Grove* generally either celebrates Lehmann's ability to create "an intensely personal and subjective world" (Dorosz 47) or censures her "narrow view of human life" (LeStourgeon 26).[8]

The novel's personal relationships parallel Lehmann's biography. Estranged from her second husband at the beginning of the Second World War (they would divorce in 1944), Lehmann began her nine-year affair with Cecil Day-Lewis in 1941, "after a chance reunion during one of the spring blitzes" (Day-Lewis 141).[9] Like Rickie in *The Echoing Grove*, Day-Lewis was married and unwilling to divorce; he lived a split life for years between his wife, Mary, in Devon and Lehmann in London and Aldworth. This "double marriage" took its toll: Day-Lewis began to experience severe "stomach trouble, a sure sign that his nervous system was being strained," as his relationship with Lehmann grew increasingly demanding (Day-Lewis 141, 158). Similarly, in *The Echoing Grove*, Rickie suffers from the "raw hole" of an ulcer because he is anxious about loving both his wife and his sister-in-law (297). However, unlike Rickie, who dies of the ulcer during the Second World War, Day-Lewis eventually tired of Lehmann and turned from her to yet another affair in 1950 – this time with Jill Balcon, the actress daughter of Ealing filmmaker Michael Balcon. As a newly discarded mistress, Lehmann tried to become "an ally" with Mary Day-Lewis in order to cure Cecil of his "temporary madness" with Jill (Day-Lewis 186). The combination of Lehmann's sympathy for Mary and her own experience as a jilted lover has led some critics to argue that both Madeleine and Dinah, the fictional wife and mistress of *The Echoing Grove*, are manifestations of Lehmann's "confusion at being caught up in this process of upheaval" during and between the two world wars (Simons 10).

When read only in the context of Lehmann's personal experience, *The Echoing Grove* appears to be essentially a psychological novel. In a 1953 interview with Shusha Guppy, Lehmann explicitly states her interest in personal, individual experience, and this statement seems further to support a psychological reading: "On the whole anything that becomes a cult, or a mass movement, loses its moral and spiritual value. The crusade has to be personal, individual. As soon as it becomes collective it loses its purpose" (181). Most scholars have read this statement as evidence of Lehmann's acute interest in personal, as opposed to political, experience and have therefore concluded that *The Echoing Grove* is essentially a conventional romance portraying "an intensely personal and subjective world" (Dorosz 47). However, *The Echoing Grove* offers Lehmann critical distance from a subjective view so intensely personal that it became insular. By embedding the individual psyches of its characters within the larger political unconscious, the novel invests its narrative with significance beyond the psychological without falling prey to the cults or mass movements that Lehmann so deplored.

The little cultural criticism that has been published about *The Echoing Grove* identifies this political unconscious as the ideology of the People's War, much as the scholarship on Bowen's war writing does. Critics of *The Echoing Grove* have generally represented the war as a universal experience, characterized either by radical social change or by a status quo resistant to change. Writing in support of the People's War's transformative power, feminist scholars such as Margaret Walters, Judy Simons, James M. Haule, and Sydney Janet Kaplan have claimed that the war substantially altered Lehmann's fictional representation of traditional gender roles. Gillian Tindall has pushed the argument even further by suggesting that the war "changes everything" (162). Others claim that the war conserved the status quo and made social change nearly impossible: Ruth Siegel believes that "there is a kind of existential inevitability to all that occurs" in *The Echoing Grove*, "as if the characters make choices but at the same time are caught up by larger forces" (152), while Panthea Reid Broughton indicates that the narrative's form restores a sense of previously established order to the chaos of wartime. Whether these scholars argue that the Second World War changed much or little in the lives of *The Echoing Grove*'s characters, they all assume that it affected social structures uniformly, either transforming or consolidating them on a large scale.

However, the individual disagreements about the Blitz found in personal testimony and Mass-Observation writing contradict any broad claim about the People's War. While some civilians believed that the bombing allowed greater freedom and increased opportunity for women during the war, others observed that women seemed constricted and constrained by their wartime duties. An understanding of these individual differences is as important to Lehmann's fiction as it is to Bowen's; according to Gillian Tindall, "Rosamond Lehmann's novels all display an abiding readiness to be concerned about the unfortunate individuals and a total absence of the kind of organized political thinking that can express itself as a View" (112–13). *The Echoing Grove* creates and exaggerates a View of a People's War in order to critique the cultural temptation to idealize, mythologize, and generalize social change in Britain during the Second World War. Whereas Bowen's war writing juxtaposes contradictory myths of the Blitz and asks readers to consider ambivalent representations of wartime social change, Lehmann's fiction exaggerates and amplifies the idealism of one specific type of blitz mythology in order to expose its fundamental problems.

The Echoing Grove launches its critique by connecting the social rhetoric of the People's War with the localized romantic language describing the love triangle of Dinah, Madeleine, and Rickie. Not only does the connection embed the psyches of the novel's characters within the political unconscious of the nation at war, but it also foregrounds the utopian nature of wartime political rhetoric. Thus, when the sisters meet to reconcile their differences years after the end of the affair, they portray themselves as survivors:

> This present mood in which they sat relaxed was nothing more than the relief of two people coming back to a bombed building once familiar, shared as a dwelling, and finding all over the smashed foundations a rose-ash haze of willow herb. No more, no less. It is a ruin; but suspense at least, at least the need for sterile resolution, have evaporated with the fact of the return. Terror of nothingness contracts before the contemplation of it. It is not, after all, vacancy, but space; an area razed, roped off by time; by time refertilized, sown with a transfiguration, a ruin-haunting, ghost-spun No Man's crop of grace. (8–9)

Although Dinah and Madeleine, lover and wife, were themselves neither wounded nor made homeless during the Blitz, the sisters speak with the authority of survivors, describing the affair as a "ruin" and their broken hearts as "wounds" (8, 131). Furthermore, they appropriate images of war to describe not only their present pain but also their future recovery. They hope that the "bombed building" of the affair will eventually yield a "No Man's crop of grace," a space in which desire is shared rather than contested.

Shared desire becomes in the novel a metaphor for the wartime liberation of women from conventional gender roles, a progressive ideal championed in the rhetoric of the People's War and embraced by Dinah and Madeleine. For the sisters, the war seems to herald an end of the established modes of patriarchal power embodied by their fittingly named lover and husband, Rickie Masters. Rickie is indeed one of his culture's masters: he is an aristocrat "brought up to be landed gentry" (187), a man "irrevocably out of the top drawer" (184) and conditioned by "ruling class mentality" (183). Despite his self-deprecating assertion that "my so-called background seemed to me an extremely dubious affair" (253), he nevertheless accepts his social and sexual authority as natural, with a complete "ease of mind and body" (46). Dinah notices this social entitlement and grace as Rickie skids charmingly down a staircase like a schoolboy, unconsciously doing "an upper-class thing" by "decorating bored leisure with a flourish" (46).

However, Rickie's power as a "male person of importance" gradually erodes from within over the course of the narrative (41), much as his body collapses under the strain of a duodenal ulcer. *The Echoing Grove* repeatedly connects the weakening of Rickie's body with the deterioration of his patriarchal authority. Most strikingly, the ulcer causes Rickie to regress to infancy, a state that, as a female friend reminds him, is far from masculine:

> You [men] start at a disadvantage. It *is* kind of unmanly being carried around the way you are all those nine months. And then having no choice but to submit to all those female processes – being born, fed, and all the rest. It must be a big humiliation – confusing too. No wonder you're scared you may be women in disguise. (284)

The metaphor of infantile regression recurs throughout the novel. Rickie feels that his only relief from interminable physical and emotional pain is to enter, with increasing frequency, a "state of harmless emotional regression; as indifferent to the moral challenge, or to the rudiments of etiquette, as a babe new-born" (84). He frequently bemoans the fact that, in order to soothe his ulcer, he must exchange his adult "half a tumblerful of whisky" (50) for endless glasses of the same "beastly milk" that he consumed as a child (169). Furthermore, he describes his milk consumption with a metaphor drawn from his work for the Admiralty – "My intake of milk these last seven years or so would float a battleship" (272) – indicating that the collapse of his social power extends even to his high-ranking position within the Royal Navy.

The regressive collapse of Rickie's upper-class male authority seems to allow the increasing self-confidence and freedom from patriarchal control experienced by Dinah and Madeleine during the war and after his death. For the sisters, Rickie becomes a fatality of both the affair and the Blitz: not only does his life end during the V-weapon bombings of 1944, but the Blitz also offers Dinah and Madeleine a way of describing the end of the affair. Returning to the figurative ruin of the past, they see Rickie as part of the "patch of scorched earth, black, scattered with incinerated bones" (35); maimed, burned, and destroyed, he represents for the sisters an outmoded form of male authority finally made obsolete during the war. Madeleine thus suggests that her husband "might have seen himself as a social or historical anomaly" (349), while Dinah agrees that "he was never at home in his situation, was he? – I mean the contemporary one, the crack-up" (184) and concludes, "It was a whole way of life gone – not just his own personal one: all his racial memories, you might call them" (187). Extrapolating a more general collapse of class and gender relations from Rickie's particular experiences, Dinah and Madeleine perceive the Blitz as an opportunity to redistribute the power previously reserved for upper-class men.

They hope to claim at least some of that power for themselves. Suddenly emancipated from their oppressive domestic relationships with men, the women struggle to create their own new and independent identities. For example, Dinah describes how she felt "extremely domesticated" (314) in her role as Rickie's long-time mistress, emphasizing in particular "how badly I needed authoritative protection" (41). However, over time "by dint of unremitting labour, with sweat, blood, tears – months, years of them? – I passed out of this circle; I gave birth to myself and entered into life" (40). The language in this passage echoes that of *The Heat of the Day*, where Stella gives birth to her own political imagination by destroying her lover's fantasy of complete privacy. In *The Echoing Grove*, Dinah believes that she must "die" in the role of Rickie's mistress in order to be reborn as a free, independent woman through her own effort (40). Similarly, Madeleine believes that she has become more dynamic than domestic after her relationship with her husband disintegrates. In the opening scene of the novel, Madeleine kills a rat, which most critics read as a symbol for Rickie.[10] After Dinah's own failure to destroy the rat, she tells her sister, "You know you can't," but Madeleine insists, "I can. I can and I *will*" (25). Madeleine's insistence marks a change in her self-image since Rickie's death: "I do a lot of things now I couldn't have done once" (26). Working together, the sisters do "our very, very best" (28): Madeleine kills the rat and then Dinah disposes of it. They recognize that "we must all recover" (28), not just from exterminating the rodent but, more importantly, from the affair itself. For each of these women, the break with Rickie exposes the fear of losing his protection. In this opening scene of *The Echoing Grove*, they confront and seem even to destroy their fear, creating the illusion that they can escape completely from patriarchal control and thus construct more independent, assertive female selves. Unlike Stella in *The Heat of the Day*, who cannily draws upon her social position to ensure her social mobility both during and after the war, Dinah and Madeleine in *The Echoing Grove* pretend that they can break completely free from traditional forms of patriarchal authority in their search for postwar female independence.

The problem, however, is that the structures of male authority remain, despite their apparent collapse in wartime. Even though *The Echoing Grove* takes place years after the conclusion of Dinah and Rickie's affair, the sisters' long overdue reunion is haunted by the ghosts of all the men whom they have loved. The result is insomnia and uncertainty for both women: Dinah lies "sleepless in the small hours" of the morning at the beginning of the novel (31), fearing "the shadow" of Rickie that "overtook her, accompanied her all night through labyrinths of the past and done with" (176). She hopes that her meeting with Madeleine "will bring us somehow to an extension of freedom; not end, as it still seems it might (is she thinking like thoughts, is she asleep next door?) in a place of distorting mirrors and trap doors" (32). Longing for freedom but dreading the same type of illusions that trap characters like Sibyl Jardine and her family in Lehmann's earlier fiction, Dinah worries about her own and her sister's ability to escape the labyrinth of past romantic and patriarchal relationships.

Like Dinah, Madeleine also drifts in and out of sleep in the early morning, able to imagine nothing other than the men of her life, who blend together abstractly in her mind:

Lying in the shroud of this November morning she stared at his risen image as clear to her as if she had received, suppressed it only yesterday. He [her current lover, Jocelyn] stood in his pale, silent, moon-like coldness, obscuring her potent child of light. Then they changed places, and Rob [Dinah's past lover] stood a tall shadow behind the other's shoulder. She saw his eyes, more than opaque, extinct. Jocelyn's were mobile, brimming and darting, not fixed on her. Then these eyes, both pairs, faded; and as she turned over, drowsy now, the eyes of Rickie opened on her, suspended in darkness against no background. (239)

While no single man dominates Madeleine's imagination in the passage, their collective staying power – and their disturbingly "opaque," "not fixed," and "suspended" nature – represent the inescapable and ultimately unfathomable impact that they have had upon both women's lives. Furthermore, the Easter images of the "shroud" and "his risen image," which obscure her own "potent child of light," suggest that while male authority may shift from subject to subject, it remains an undying constant in these women's lives.

Despite their crucial moments of self-doubt in the middle of the night, the sisters rather naïvely generalize in the light of day about the changes in gender identity forged in times of trauma:

It's particularly difficult to be a woman just at present. One feels so transitional and fluctuating [...]. I believe we *are* all in flux – that the difference between our grandmothers and us is far deeper than we realize – much more fundamental than the obvious social economic one. Our so-called emancipation may be a symptom, not a cause. Sometimes I think it's more than the development of a new attitude towards sex: that a new sex may be evolving – psychically new – a sort of hybrid. (363)

Here, Dinah suggests – and Madeleine agrees – that gender roles in postwar Britain have significantly changed; rather than distinct, traditional masculine and feminine roles, gender has become a hybrid of sorts. The assumption that the sisters' experiences are representative – that they can speak with some authority about the experiences of women from different classes and backgrounds – recalls the authoritative stance adopted by characters in *The Gipsy's Baby* and *The Ballad and the Source*. In *The Echoing Grove*, the Blitz itself plays a more central role, and the insularity of upper-middle-class women threatens to obscure and replace the promise of social transformation in the People's War.

The novel demonstrates this threat by emphasizing the sisters' adoption of what initially appear to be radically different gender roles and class positions. On the one hand, Madeleine assumes the gender role of the traditional housewife, who relies on "the fine codes and manners of an irremediable lady" (236) because she is "afraid – ashamed" of sex (352); on the other hand, Dinah is a "kept woman" (88), who is "curious" about sex (352), has a "free for all body" (49), and thus believes that she "couldn't have made a go of being married to [Rickie] – or to anybody else in those days" (350). Socially, Madeleine enjoys her position in the upper-middle class: she is comfortably provided for by her aristocratic husband, and she lives in the luxury of an "expensive and well chosen" household (32). Dinah, conversely, places herself within the working class as "a frugal wage-earner, managing on a few hundreds" (19) and living "in dreadful lodgings [...] in Stepney" with a "working class boy" before her eventual marriage to a Jewish Cockney soldier who is killed fighting for Communism in the Spanish Civil War (40). Styling themselves as an upper-middle-class housewife and a working-class slattern who meet on the site of a "bombed building" during the Blitz of the affair (8), Madeleine and Dinah adopt a generalized rhetoric grounded upon the range of experience implied by their social differences. Their reunion upon the "smashed foundations" of the affair thus appears to symbolize the breakdown of gender distinctions across class lines that is central to the cultural mythology of wartime social change (8).

However, *The Echoing Grove* reconstructs the People's War in this way only in order to expose the insular perspective of the sisters. Thus, even as the novel distinguishes between Dinah's and Madeleine's experiences, it insists that the differences are largely superficial. The sisters do not actually represent a broad spectrum of female experience; they share instead both a social background and a sexual history. In a discussion of Madeleine's current relationship with her working-class lover, Jocelyn, for example, Dinah and Madeleine both clearly articulate their own social position in opposition to the working class. The women know nothing of each other's past and present lovers, but they nevertheless believe that "there was a likeness" between Jocelyn and Dinah's previous lover, Rob (361), each of whom they typify as "a working class character" (217). When Jocelyn announces that he is going to marry another woman, Dinah comforts Madeleine with snobbism: "Well-developed figure, trinkets, head scarves, cheekbones, on the grubby side. *New Statesman* girl. Not *nasty*. [...] Just not our sort. [...] Oh, she's a piece of cake for a modern hero" (361–2). Although Dinah has previously defined herself by her sympathy with the working class, she now identifies with Madeleine in opposition to this presumably socialist "piece of cake" and her working-class "modern hero." Dinah even goes so far as to admit that she "couldn't be more thankful for the good sound upper-middle stock I come of. It's meant a sort of solid ground floor of family security and class confidence that's been a great stand-by" (184). Thus, as they meet to be reconciled, Madeleine and Dinah are not really a wife and a mistress from the upper and lower classes, and the connections between them do not indicate any universal social change during the war. Rather, because they are simply two sexually experienced widows from the same upper-middle stock, their reunion exposes even more fully than Stella's interaction with Louie in *The Heat of the Day* the specific class limits that circumscribe wartime freedom from established gender roles.

Once again, this freedom extends beyond the household into the professional domain. Like other women of their class, both Dinah and Madeleine have enjoyed a "ridiculous education" (18), which qualified them to select specialized forms of work during the war. Dinah volunteered "in rest centres" in Stepney, teaching drawing to homeless working-class children, while Madeleine was offered "a decent [job] in the B.B.C. – translating French" (18). Although Madeleine declined the translating position in order to care for her children, both sisters believe that their war work allowed them to cross class boundaries: Dinah brought the genteel skill of drawing to "brilliant" undiscovered artists among her group of working-class children (18), and Madeleine shared the experience of wives and mothers of all classes during the war: "I worked as hard as any working-class housewife" (18).

The truth, however, is that Madeleine and Dinah have very little idea what life is like for the working class, and the novel labels the socially delimited arena in which these women purport to enact the promise of the People's War as little more than an "echoing grove." Scholars generally agree that the novel's title refers to William Blake's poem, "My Spectre," in which the speaker tries to "root up the Infernal Grove" of "Female Love" in order to "Step into Eternity," and they tend to emphasize the relationship between Blake's poem and Lehmann's treatment of passion.[11] However, the echoing grove of the title invokes not only the "infernal grove" of the rather obscure "My Spectre," but also the "ecchoing green" of Blake's more popular *Songs of Innocence and of Experience* (1794). Blake's *Songs* examine the disjunction between individual perspectives, which are often self-centered and naïve, and the social reality in which these individuals live. Read in this context, the "echoing grove" refers to Dinah's and Madeleine's repeated insistence that their experiences have not only liberated them from patriarchal authority but have also been shared by all British women during the war. Trapped within the echoing grove of their own experience, these upper-middle-class women fail to perceive the social reality facing women less privileged than themselves.

Furthermore, Dinah and Madeleine perceive even their own situation more optimistically than realistically. Although the sisters want to believe that they can recreate themselves as strong, independent women as they emerge from the affair, the closing pages of the novel suggest that the structures of patriarchal authority are not so easily dismantled. In the final scene, Dinah decides to give back to Madeleine the cufflinks that she has kept since "the last time I saw" Rickie, when they ended the affair (370). Dinah hopes that the jewelry will forge a permanent, meaningful bond between the two sisters; however, the disturbing truth is that the real link is across generations of men. When Dinah suggests that Madeleine and Rickie's son, Colin, "ought to have them. He'd wear them, wouldn't he?" (373), Madeleine remarks, "Oh, yes, I'm sure he would. He'll be pleased. Aren't they pretty? I believe they belonged to Rickie's father. All right – I'll give them to Colin when I see him" (373). Passed down from father to son to grandson, the cufflinks gain symbolic value as Madeleine considers them in the novel's closing paragraph: "She closed her fingers over them, letting them slide into the hollow of her palm, feeling them nudge lightly, settle there; anonymous abstraction; questionable solid; cold, almost weightless weight" (373). Like the structures of patriarchal power themselves, which, though "questionable solid[s]" and "anonymous abstraction[s]," nevertheless maintain their "weightless weight," the cufflinks rest only temporarily in Madeleine's grasp. The sense here is that the power will soon enough be back in the hands of its rightful owners.

The Echoing Grove therefore calls into question both the sisters' naïveté and their insistence that their experience "echoes afterwards, backwards and forwards for ever wherever you strike it – one echo picking up another till the whole thing *sounds out*, like a fulfillment" (267). Dinah and Madeleine attend to the echoes between their past and present in order to "sound out" a personal, feminist "fulfillment" for themselves, and they believe that their personal liberation echoes beyond themselves to women more generally. However, this novel and Lehmann's other war writing demonstrate that while privileged women like Dinah and Madeleine may have generalized about others based on their own narrow range of experience, they ultimately have neither the power nor the inclination to orchestrate any substantial form of social change. Once again, the sisters emulate the behavior of many upper-middle-class British women during the war; they are like a group of WAAF recruits, whose conversation, according to a Mass-Observer stationed among them, "is always about themselves" and who "hardly ever mention or know anything about the war" because "we don't see the wood for the trees" (M-O A: TC 32/3/D, "WAAF Observations," 1941). Dinah and Madeleine suffer from a similar case of tunnel vision. Near the end of the novel, when Madeleine's lover finally leaves her for the *New Statesman* girl, the sisters unselfconsciously consolidate their upper-middle-class position by agreeing that she is "not our sort" (362). In doing so, however, they ignore the fact that this woman embodies the spirit of the People's War toward which they claim to strive: "She was – very serious, progressive... public-spirited" (361). Here, Dinah and Madeleine speak dismissively about public spirit not only because Madeleine is jealous of her romantic rival, but also because they fail throughout the novel to see past the personal to the political – to see the wood for the trees.

Rather than sounding out a fulfillment for women across class lines, Dinah's and Madeleine's experiences thus do little more than echo within the grove of their privileged class position. The echoes create the illusion that the war has brought widespread social change, when in fact the real resonance in the novel is not between women of different classes but between sisters of one class, changed little by either time or trauma. As Dinah and Madeleine come together upon the smashed foundations of the Blitz and the affair, their experiences sound out a fulfillment across Lehmann's other war writing: the sisters are as self-absorbed and isolated as all of Lehmann's other embattled women, including Mrs Ritchie, Rebecca Landon, and especially Sibyl Jardine. While Elizabeth Bowen's war writing ambivalently represents the unequal rewards of the People's War, Rosamond Lehmann's fiction more directly critiques the class insularity that causes and then obscures inequity. Although Lehmann shared with her characters both the desire and the opportunity to shelter herself from the war, she uses her fiction to get outside of her own position long enough to critique it.

In this sense, Lehmann is much like another Mass-Observer in the WAAF, who discovers not simply a homogeneous group of privileged women who cannot see the wood for the trees but rather a diverse group of women still divided by class differences during the war:

One month ago, 42 of us were called up, and met together for the first time in a large room in Victory House, Kingsway. *Immediately*, cliques were formed. The moment you entered the room, you knew exactly which group to join, almost instinctively. The noisy group in the middle was the working-class one: bar-maid, waitress, mill-girl, domestic servant, and a few others. At the side, the Colonel's daughter was surrounded by an admiring semi-circle of actresses, a dress-designer and "ladies of leisure." A hair-dresser, accountant's clerk, school-teacher and manaquin [sic] formed another group. Others paired off, skirting one or another of the main groups. (M-O A: TC 32/3/E, "Letter," 1941)

The Echoing Grove suggests how difficult it is for the upper-middle class to maintain the distance that this Mass-Observer does: she comments upon other people's class status and interaction without mentioning herself. Lehmann creates enough distance in this novel to point out the irony of selfishly taking what one can get from the People's War, suggesting that failure to perceive this irony imprisons the very people who believe themselves to be liberated. Driven not simply by revolution but also by the long-standing insularity of the privileged classes, the ideology of the People's War was potentially far more conservative than it sometimes appeared to be; Lehmann recognized how tempting and easy it often was for the upper classes to accept their insularity blindly. By challenging readers to see the social biases that shaped even their own conceptions of women's wartime liberation, *The Echoing Grove* interrogates not only the event itself but also the myth of the Blitz.

3
Real Men in Henry Green's War Writing

The civilian men in Henry Green's fiction undergo a crisis of masculinity because they are too old, too young, or too unfit to live up to the masculine ideal of the soldier hero. These noncombatant men often imagine the soldier not as he is but as an iconic standard of masculinity, a standard that civilians can necessarily never obtain. Left behind on the home front, they must therefore rethink masculinity and find other ways of being real men in wartime. The People's War compounded this crisis of masculinity by disrupting conventional gender roles on the home front: service in the People's Army instead of the military meant joining a corps of men and women functioning on increasingly equal terms. Bowen's and Lehmann's fiction investigates from a female perspective the social limits of women's freedom during the People's War; Green's war novels demonstrate from a male perspective the alarming rather than liberating prospect of changing gender roles. Examining the experiences of men across battle lines rather than those of women across class lines, the fiction describes men who either remain anxiously at home or return from combat physically and psychologically wounded. In both *Caught* (1943) and *Back* (1946), the resulting crises of masculinity force characters to become more open-minded about the possibilities for being a real man.

Green himself never saw action during the war. Born in 1905, Henry Yorke – his given name – was 34 years old at the beginning of the Second World War. He was thus within the age range of men 18–41 who were required to register for call-up, but he was significantly older than the first recruits in their early 20s. Despite the fact that "the talk then was that no man older than twenty-seven would ever be permitted in the firing line," he thought that "it did seem expedient, as it must have done to 100,000 others, to duck out into one of these non-combatant services to avoid conscription, which must mean being drafted overseas" (Green,

"Before" 268). Dodging the draft did not necessarily mean avoiding danger for men like Green: "It was widely known among those having Green's business and government connections [...] that British officials believed bombs and gas would kill some 175,000 Londoners during the war's first twenty-four hours" (Brunetta, par. 6). Deciding to stay in a London almost certain to become a battlefield in the upcoming war, Green volunteered for the Auxiliary Fire Service (AFS) in 1938.

The AFS offered Green not only the chance to serve as a noncombatant in the war but also the opportunity to continue running Pontifex, the Yorke family firm that manufactured brewery and bathroom fixtures. Green describes his experiences as a fire-fighting CEO:

> In London, for most of the war, one was kept while on duty close to the regular Fire Station of one's choice. So that when the Board of Directors agreed to my joining the AFS I was able to call in at the office every third day all through the war, for we worked two days on with one off, and if not at a fire was always available, if only in my case, to sign cheques. ("Before" 268)

Green's work at Pontifex was not only convenient but lucrative: "The company also agreed to 'make up' my wage as a fireman, to what had been my salary with the firm, which, when in another phrase 'hostilities developed', indeed made all the difference; in fact I suffered financially not at all" ("Before" 269).

Financial stability was important to Green, who was born "a mouth-breather with a silver spoon" (Green, *Pack* 1) and was thus destined to inherit a life of "rural feudalism underpinned by industrial entrepreneurism" (Treglown 16). Green's mother, Maud Wyndham, came from a family that "had figured in public life since the Middle Ages," and his father, Vincent Yorke, had "a less famous name than Wyndham, but the family was little less formidable" (Treglown 10). The family lived in an equally formidable home: like Bowen's Court and Lehmann's Fieldhead, the Yorkes' Forthampton Court was a "big old house" (Treglown 3) with "a small army of farmworkers, gardeners, grooms, and stableboys" to tend its grounds and an indoor staff of "a butler, two footmen, a hall boy, a cook, a kitchen maid, a scullery maid, five housemaids, and the personal maid of Mrs Yorke" (Treglown 14).

Green, Bowen, and Lehmann belonged together in both the upper-middle class and the same generation of literary writers. The writers were born within six years – Bowen in 1899, Lehmann in 1901, and Green in 1905 – and they met frequently within the most elite social and literary circles in wartime London. Green knew and respected Bowen and was particularly fond of Lehmann, whom he told upon the publication of *Caught* in 1943 that he "wrote for only about six people [...] and she was one of them; her approval justified everything" (Treglown 149). Eventually close platonic friends, Green and Lehmann were initially attracted to one another, and biographer Jeremy Treglown indicates that they almost certainly had a brief affair before Lehmann and Day-Lewis began their wartime relationship. In conversation with Selina Hastings, Lehmann denied this affair – "There was never any question of having an affair with Henry" (215) – but she did spend numerous nights with him at his Kensington flat during the Blitz. Alongside the jealous triangle of Bowen, Lehmann, and Goronwy Rees described in Chapter 2, this possible attraction – and definite friendship – between Lehmann and Green suggests the relatively small world in which these writers lived and worked.[1]

The temptation when examining such a close-knit social and literary community is to emphasize the connections among its writers' experiences. Like most of their social peers, Bowen, Lehmann, and Green were all free to choose interesting and compelling war work, and they thus shared the privilege of mingling selectively with the working classes during the war. However, although Green claimed to have met in the AFS "all manner of men [who] came in for training in 1938 and for a variety of reasons" ("Before" 269), he differed from Bowen and Lehmann in that he had experienced these social differences in the workplace long before the war began. Green started working at Pontifex on the factory floor in 1927 when he decided to quit his studies at Oxford, a decision that he describes in *Pack My Bag* (1940): "I had a sense of guilt whenever I spoke to someone who did manual work. As was said in those days I had a complex and in the end it drove me to go to work in a factory with my wet podgy hands" (191). Professionally and financially secure even as a young man, Green was confident about the ease with which he could move up and down the social ladder and thus gain the factory experience necessary both to run Pontifex and to write *Living* (1929), his novel about factory life: "This move was the easier because my living was to come out of the factory I worked through. It was killing two birds with one stone, which helped" (*Pack* 213). There was therefore far less novelty for Green than for women like Mass-Observer Penelope Barlow in seeing how "another class of people lived and worked and thought" during the Second World War (Calder and Sheridan 156).

Having selectively interacted with the working class in the past, Green and other men in his position were skeptical about the possibility of lasting wartime social change. Green's biography and his autobiographical war writing both describe the established social hierarchy of the Fire Service – a hierarchy that remained visible throughout the war. His "new acquaintances" in the AFS recognized the social distance between Green and themselves: "He was nicknamed 'the Honourable' by the other volunteers, some of them – because of the locality [in Westminster] – domestic servants and hotel staff intermingled [...] with occasional burglars who had joined up in the anticipation of rich pickings ahead" (Treglown 115). This motley crew took orders from newly deputized officers drawn from among the regulars of the London Fire Brigade (LFB). Mostly uneducated and working-class, the professional firemen of the LFB "were indeed fantastic men. With just over 3,000 in the Force and thirty thousand Londoners about to join the AFS, they were all shortly destined as officers to oversee the AFS" (Green, "Before" 270).[2] Green admired these men for their wartime contributions, but he hoped that what he saw as their rather crude obsession with money would end once the bombing began: "Loot and pension was all they thought of, loss of pension was the preoccupation in all their minds *until bombing started*" ("Before" 270, my emphasis).[3] However, even during the bombing, Green found that the wartime unity at his fire station was more practical than revolutionary. In *Caught*, which was based to some extent on Green's own experience, working-class Fire Station Leader Arthur Pye tries to keep the peace between the old guard of the LFB and the new recruits of the AFS by insisting to the working-class LFB officers that they "can't expect to deal with the fires that may be started as a result of war action, not on our bloody own we can't" and to the AFS men, who come from a range of social classes, that "a fireman's wage, it's not an abundance" (16). Pye's goal as a negotiator is not to fulfill the revolutionary promise of the People's War but rather to create a temporary working arrangement under which professional and volunteer firemen from all walks of life could cooperate to fight the fires of the Blitz.

The focus on cooperation for the duration was characteristic not only of men from Green's social background but of British men from all classes. Unlike the privileged women who entered the workforce only with the passage of new conscription laws, these men already knew from past experience how difficult it was to bridge the economic distance between classes, a knowledge shared by the working-class women described in Chapter 1. The men were consequently cynical about the possibility of wartime social change. Even more than Rosamond Lehmann, whose war writing critiques from a distance the exciting, if imaginary, freedom from social hierarchy during the Blitz, these more jaded social cynics often dismissed the possibility of a People's War before it even began. One 21-year-old Mass-Observer admits that despite the teamwork he witnessed in the HG, "I am afraid that after the war we shall slip back into complete class consciousness, once the voluntary organizations which brought the classes together are closed down" (M-O A: DR 2685, Jan. 1943). Another soldier more bitterly accedes, "Me! I shan't get no commission. That's for them that can afford it or have got good educations. They say it's equal for all but it isn't" (M-O A: TC 29/1/F, "The Public and Soldiers 1940–41," 1940). Recognizing that the appearance of equality was no more than a working arrangement, these men harbored little hope for – or fear of – a postwar social revolution.

What many of them did fear, however, was a sexual revolution brought on by wartime conscription legislation, which changed gender relations by drawing more women than ever before into the workforce. As Mass-Observation noted in 1942, many people had begun to think that "this is more a woman's war than a man's war on the Home Front now" (M-O A: FR 1238, 1942: 33). When asked "Would you mind if your wife joined the ATS?" one working-class soldier tellingly used the question as a chance to complain about some of his male comrades:

> War isn't the place for a woman, although I must say some women seem more suited to it than men – some of the men in our billets – they shouldn't even have been made soldiers. It's bad enough when your wife has to go out and work as some wives do – but I don't like to think of them in uniform. (M-O A: TC 32/2/E, "ATS Survey," 1941)

This kind of comment shaped the experience of not only noncombatant soldiers but also male civilians who, in contrast to the fit, virile soldiers headed to the front, were typically "too old or too young to be called up, or were 'reserved' by the state in civilian occupations deemed essential for a society at war. These tended to be unglamorous, for example, butcher, baker, mechanic and civil servant" (Summerfield and Peniston-Bird, "Women" 238–9). Mass-Observation overheard a lower-middle-class woman speaking condescendingly about her own husband: "I told him, I said if he was half the man he made himself out to be, I told him, he wouldn't be where he was" (M-O A: TC 29/1/F, "The Public and Soldiers," 1940). Thus, even if civilian men were not comparing themselves to the soldierly ideal, other men and women were clearly doing so.

However, male anxiety about a "woman's war" was largely unfounded: civilian men represented the largest group of British citizens contributing to the war effort during the Blitz. According to figures prepared by the British Central Statistical Office and published in the *Statistical Digest of the War* accompanying the "United Kingdom and Civil Series" of official histories, there were more than 11,000,000 British men in civil employment and defense in 1942, compared to only 307,000 women serving in the military auxiliary services and about 6,600,000 women working in civil employment. Thus, women made up less than eight percent of the armed forces in 1942 and only about 37 percent of the home-front workforce, and the total number of women serving in military auxiliary services and civil employment combined was still only two-thirds of the total number of men serving only on the home front in civil employment and defense. Furthermore, there were almost three times as many men serving on the home front as on the front line: 11,296,000 British men worked in civil employment, compared to only 3,784,000 serving in the military (Dear 1133).

Even the women who were working on the home front posed no financial threat to men. According to Angus Calder, most industries adopted a dilution agreement between 1940 and 1942 that stipulated that "employers could sign on women to do work previously performed by men on condition that after they had worked for thirty-two weeks they received the full man's rate for the job" (*PW* 402). However, there were many loopholes to the requirement for equal pay, and employers could easily justify unequal pay for working women and men in similar positions:

> The words which had been signed left some ground for sincere misunderstanding, and a great deal more for wilful evasion. [...] Employers could claim that the work had been "commonly performed" by women before the war, and this claim grew harder to contest as more and more skilled work was broken down by the advance of mass production. The employer could make a small alteration in the job and say that there was no pre-war precedent. He could affect to believe that the agreement applied only to skilled work, which was quite untrue, or argue more plausibly that a woman who could do only one skilled job was worth less than a fully trained man. When the eight month period when lower rates might be paid had run out, the employer could make the fact that women still needed male help occasionally in lifting heavy fixtures into a pretext for claiming that they still worked under "extra supervision."
> (*PW* 402–3)

Under similar circumstances, one female Mass-Observer claimed to be "very dissatisfied" with the position of women in Britain in 1942: "The attitude towards women especially in this rather backward rural area [Norfolk] is hostile to women in jobs. I should certainly like to see equality of pay for women as a first step" (M-O A: DR 1553, Sept. 1942). However, employers resisted taking this step: "In January 1944, women in metalwork and engineering earned on average three pounds, ten shillings a week, as compared to seven pounds for men" (*PW* 403).

Despite these economic statistics, changes in women's employment during the People's War affected home-front gender relations in profound ways. Women's war work was supposed to free men from home-front duties so that they could serve on the front line. However, men who failed medical exams, worked in reserved occupations, or fell outside of draft age limits could not enlist, no matter how many women entered the workforce. Through no fault of their own, these men found themselves blamed and accused of cowardice for staying on the home front with the women:

> There was, at this time, a resurgence of a notorious folly of the First World War. There was some pressure in the newspapers for the indiscriminate transfer of young men into the armed forces, and an epidemic of "white feathers" caused at least two suicides and forced the Government to develop a badge to identify men exempted from service on medical grounds. (Calder, *PW* 269)

The white feathers – and even the well-intentioned medical badges – labeled civilian men as noncombatants and therefore forced them to defend a masculinity called into question by their inability to serve.

Some men tried to resolve this question by identifying themselves with the soldiers typically honored as heroes by the British public. Sonya Rose has argued that wartime masculinity often seemed to depend upon visible military service, as the epidemic of white feathers suggests:

> In order for men to be judged as good citizens, they needed to demonstrate their virtue by being visibly in the military. It was only then that the components of hegemonic masculinity could cohere. It is no wonder then that male workers on the home front likened themselves to battle heroes while attempting to make the case that their contributions to the nation and those of men in the armed services were equivalent. (196)

ARP warden S. M. P. Woodcock adopts this approach in a diary entry from 13 September 1940. He chooses the term "soldiers" to describe men in both the AFS and his own ARP: "Air Raid wardens also helped to put out fires using their stirrup pumps (hand pumps). I wonder about who were considered more 'soldiers' – the AFS or the ARP – or were they on a par with each other?" Likening members of both the AFS and the ARP to battle heroes, Woodcock implies not only that the two forms of civilian defense were on a par with each other but also that they should be on a par with military service, even if the quotation marks indicate his self-consciousness about using the term "soldiers" for noncombatants.

For other men, it was more important to call the heroic standard of the soldier hero into question than it was to live up to that standard. Soldiers themselves recognized the disjunction between an idealized masculinity and the reality of military service. One soldier describes the effect of his uniform alone upon strangers: "Well, they always think you're a hero, even if you haven't *smelt* a German since you started. 'Good old Tommy' they say, as if we'd saved their lives, even when we're out on route marches" (M-O A: TC 29/1/F, "The Public," 1940). Some male civilians became so "fed up with soldiers, soldiers all the time" that they began to devalue the military work of men whom they themselves could never be (TC 29/1/F, "The Public"). When interviewed about "the crowds who usually stop to watch the soldiers drilling" in Stepney, a 25-year-old civilian tells Mass-Observation, "Oh, they had a bit of a crowd there, this morning. People stop to look at anything, really. Couple of navvies digging a hole, and the whole world comes to have a nose" (M-O A: TC 29/1/F, "The Public," 1940). Asked whether he had stopped, the man replies, "What, me? I've got better things to do than stop round schools watching a lot of young fellows stretching their arms out" (TC 29/1/F, "The Public"). Another civilian considers the ruins of his bombed Maida Vale neighborhood and suggests that Hitler has bypassed the British armed forces altogether in waging war against civilians:

> You know this sort of thing is terrible, and it'll go on until the armies come to grips. They've nothing to do now – these soldiers, and Hitler's not bombing them purposely. He knows if he wears down the civilians while the armies remain idle he can win. So he bombs London and then we bomb Berlin, more and more and more, and so the rotten old game goes on. I can't see how we're going to hold out under this sort of thing. (M-O A: TC 23/5/C, "Observations," 1940)

Undercutting the false assumption that all soldiers were heroes and thus real men, the male civilians here suggest that there might be other ways of defining masculinity in wartime.

The problem on the home front, however, was that changing gender roles and relations during the People's War complicated the crisis of masculinity for civilian men. With so many women entering the wartime workforce, noncombatant men often felt mounting pressure to enlist, since staying at home now meant engaging in war work that women could often do just as well as men. This young civilian expresses bitter frustration when asked about his attitude toward women joining the auxiliary army:

> It's very plucky of them. But I don't see why they should join up while there are still men to go – I say that although I'm still in civvies myself – I've done my best to get in the air force but they won't take me. I didn't get through the medical. But I don't like seeing all these girls go before me. It's no pleasure for me to see them. (M-O A: TC 32/2/E, "ATS Survey," 1941)

The speaker in this passage finds himself turned down by the military only to be upstaged by conscripted women. Some noncombatants tried to reassert their threatened masculinity by putting women back in their place. A 27-year-old laboratory worker, for example, declares, "It may be necessary to have women in industry, but it is unfortunate. The woman's place is in the home" (DR 2656, Sept. 1942), while a 50-year-old journalist undercuts the "extraordinary work for the war" that women are doing by insisting that ultimately, they remain "still bound up in perms and lipstick" (DR 2686, Sept. 1942). Serving alongside women in the People's Army rather than soldiers in the military, these noncombatant men express anxiety about their own ambiguous role.

Henry Green's wartime fiction takes up this problem, exposing the conflicts masked by both the masculine icon of the soldier hero and the unifying ideology of the People's War. Written during the Blitz itself and published in 1943, *Caught* is as enmeshed within the context of the People's War as Elizabeth Bowen's *The Heat of the Day*, and it therefore raises questions about the myth of the Blitz without resolving them. Exempted from conscription as a widower with a dependent child, Richard Roe finds himself caught in the no man's land between a front line where he cannot serve and a home front where his masculinity is called into question. Roe comes as close to the icon of the soldier hero as he can by joining the AFS in London, where he battles blazes to protect other civilians. Ultimately, however, he is neither soldier nor hero, and his achievements as a firefighter do not give him a strong sense of self. Describing the emotionally fraught experiences of this Auxiliary fireman during the Blitz, *Caught* rejects standard gender roles and demonstrates instead how wartime masculine identity – much like the feminine identity explored in earlier chapters – is the product of multiple, conflicting narratives about experience during the Blitz. Green's later novel, *Back*, then looks back on male experience from a postwar perspective, much as Rosamond Lehmann's *The Echoing Grove* looks back on female experience. *Back* heightens the dilemma facing Richard Roe in *Caught* by placing Charley Summers, a wounded, repatriated soldier, into that no man's land on the home front. In these circumstances, the wounded soldier becomes not an icon of heroic masculinity but a sign of instability within prevailing narratives of wartime gender identity. Even more than Roe, Charley loses his sense of self on the home front, and the extremity of his circumstances forces him to discover new ways of resolving the problem productively.

This political dimension of Green's writing has received little critical attention. Most scholars focus on linguistic and psychological rather than political and historical issues in Green's fiction, and they argue that both *Caught* and *Back* examine the protagonists' struggles with language in relation to trauma. In the 1960s, critics such as A. Kingsley Weatherhead and John Russell asserted that Charley Summers in *Back* ultimately controls both language and pain either by developing his own specific symbols for pain, according to Weatherhead, or by having "wilfully barred" the painful memories of his wartime experience, according to Russell (142). Conversely, in the poststructuralist 1980s, Michael North and Rod Mengham suggested that language inevitably escapes the characters' control: for North, language fragments the characters' conceptions of identity into a series of subjective memories, while for Mengham, it presents "anything and everything in terms of contradiction and threat" (*Idiom* 161–2).[4] Most recently, critics have analyzed not the characters' relationship with language as a whole but their position within more specific aesthetic, psychological, and social discourses, as described by genre theory (Copeland), psychoanalysis (Stonebridge), and Marxist criticism (Deeming). Yet even Deeming's Marxist analysis does not fully account for the specific historical moment of the Blitz: he argues that Green's modernist aesthetic responds "to social conditions that existed in British capitalist society anyway and were not absolutely peculiar to the conditions precipitated by the 'war effort' during the years of conflict" (877). In contrast, this chapter demonstrates that

Green's characters do struggle against two absolutely peculiar political discourses: nationalistic rhetoric about soldierly heroism, on the one hand, and the equally nationalistic rhetoric of the People's War, on the other.

Elaine Scarry has analyzed the discourse describing soldiers' heroism in *The Body in Pain*. She argues that the casualties of war become symbols co-opted by the nations for which soldiers fight: "War is relentless in taking for its own interior content the interior content of the wounded and open human body" (81). Nations must substantiate the abstract ideologies that define them through the physical reality of dead bodies:

> The dispute that leads to the war involves a process by which each side calls into question the legitimacy and thereby erodes the reality of the other country's issues, beliefs, ideas, self-conception. Dispute leads relentlessly to war not only because war is an extension and intensification of dispute but because it is a correction and reversal of it. That is, injuring not only provides a means of choosing between disputants but also provides, by its massive opening of human bodies, a way of reconnecting the derealized and disembodied beliefs with the force and power of the material world. (128)

Scarry contends that the bodies of soldiers captured, killed, or wounded in battle become material signs representing such abstract nationalist ideals as individual freedom or national sovereignty. An international dispute opens up ideological wounds by bringing two sets of national values into conflict, revealing both sets to be socially constructed rather than naturally given. During war, the nation depends upon the soldier's corpse to embody and thus to reify its threatened ideals.

Soldiers willingly sacrifice their bodies for such abstractions because nationalist ideology encourages them to place issues of national security over and above the instinct for self-preservation. In *Imagined Communities*, Benedict Anderson argues that although "the members of even the smallest nation will never know most of their fellow-members, meet them, or even hear of them" (6), soldiers experience a strong "political love" that makes them feel obligated to sacrifice themselves for their countries (143). Specifically, soldiers at war are enmeshed in a patriotic discourse that describes the nation "either in the vocabulary of kinship (motherland, *Vaterland, patria*) or that of home [...]. Both idioms denote something to which one is naturally tied" (143). The emphasis on the nation's parental or familial role subordinates the soldier's identity to that of the country, which has both produced and nurtured him. Furthermore, Anderson argues that the idea of kinship creates the feeling of brotherhood among soldiers themselves: "The nation is always conceived as a deep, horizontal comradeship. Ultimately, it is this fraternity that makes it possible, over the past two centuries, for so many millions of people, not so much to kill, as willingly to die for such limited imaginings" (7). As RAF pilot Richard Hillary concludes in *The Last Enemy*, soldiers will fight "until the ideals for which their comrades had died were stamped for ever on the future of civilization" (178) – even if those ideals are, as Anderson suggests, "limited imaginings" concerning the kinship of a nation in which most people never meet.

Ideals of kinship and brotherhood underwrite a nationalistic discourse that tells soldiers how to think about the sacrifice of their bodies during wartime. In *Fighting Fictions*, Kevin Foster argues, "When one finds oneself in a situation for which one has no script [...] the common [...] response is to neutralise one's fear of the unexpected by making use of somebody else's script" (13–14). In 1939, skeptical British soldiers were faced with the prospect of fighting a Second World War less than 25 years after the "war to end wars" (Calder, *PW* 21). Although Wilfred Owen and other writers had made it difficult to believe that *dulce et decorum est pro patria mori* in the wake of the First World War, there was no other script available to rationalize a warfare now based on massive air strikes and anti-aircraft defense. Shoring up the morale of soldiers in the Second World War with the slogans and rhetoric of the First, Britain mobilized its forces by arguing even more forcefully that the soldier was a hero bound by honor to defend his nation, home, and family.

As a master rhetorician as well as politician, Winston Churchill recognized the need for a patriotic script during the Second World War, and his war speeches exhort soldiers to understand their physical sacrifice as a heroic defense of national ideals. In a 1939 radio address to the nation, Churchill claims that British and French soldiers are fighting "to enable the peoples of Europe to preserve their independence and their liberties":

> That is what the British and French nations are fighting for. How often have we been told that we are the effete democracies whose day is done, and who must now be replaced by various forms of virile dictatorships and totalitarian despotism? No doubt at the beginning we shall have to suffer, because of having too long wished to lead a peaceful life. Our reluctance to fight was mocked at as cowardice. Our desire to see an unarmed world was proclaimed as the proof of our decay. Now we have begun. Now we are going on. Now, with the

help of God, and with the conviction that we are the defenders of civilization and freedom, we are going to persevere to the end. ("The First Month" 176)

Addressing a nation that still remembered the horrors of the last war, Churchill cannily invokes the spirit of pacifism – by arguing that British soldiers must fight and die for it. His closing lines, appealing to public belief in God, civilization, and freedom, make those deaths *dulce et decorum* once again. Furthermore, Churchill's script also rewrites the assault on Britain as an affront to British masculinity. Citing enemy comparisons of Britain's cowardice with totalitarian virility, Churchill genders both the British national body and, following Scarry's logic, the individual soldier's body that reifies national ideals. Churchill suggests that a real nation is composed of real men, and he calls for a defense of the nation's normative masculinity and heterosexuality. The speech thus motivates soldiers through the prospect of shame; soldiers who willingly sacrifice their bodies prove beyond question both the nation's virility and their own. For noncombatants, the prospect of shame is even more terrifying: unable to prove virility on the battlefield, they must prove it instead from within the home-front People's Army. It is no accident that Churchill describes the fighting nation in the iconic terms of the soldier hero, but the more he emphasizes this masculine icon during the People's War, the more difficult it becomes for civilian men to live up to that ideal.

In *Caught*, Green examines the ways in which the rhetoric of the soldier hero fails to account for masculinity on the home front. The novel tells the story of Auxiliary fireman Richard Roe, who, much like Green himself, joined the AFS "when nations were still declaring peace" in 1938 (24). On 7 September 1940, the first major Blitz on London set the docks of the East End ablaze, and the bombing over the next 76 consecutive nights was literally a trial by fire for the approximately 23,000 inexperienced Auxiliary firemen – like Green and Roe – who joined the London Fire Service at the beginning of the war. Even the core of 2500 regular firefighters had never seen anything like the destruction that swept through London in 1940–41. An Auxiliary fireman describes one such night in his memoir:

The worst blaze [...] was one which we dare not extinguish! This was caused by fractured gas-mains igniting. The alleyway was alight across its width, as also was the end of the street in which we were working. The flames issued from wide cracks in the road surface. It's pretty rotten, really, because [...] gas main fires must not be put out, as this would leave escaping gas with great risk of explosion. Actually we were working with our backs against one side of the street, aiming our jets into the warehouse, with the street alight in front of us. On top of this we were warned not to let our jets strike the brickwork of the warehouse wall as this was very shaky and the impact would probably cause it to fall. [...] And of course, if *we* didn't bring the wall down, "Jerry" might. (Hurd)

Faced with falling bombs, flying shrapnel, and gas and water main ruptures, firemen fought in the vanguard of a war waged on the British home front, and Hurd recognizes the soldierly role of the AFS when he sets the firemen in direct opposition to the enemy "Jerry." Joining the AFS was therefore as close as many civilian men could come to enlisting in the armed forces.

The home-front battle took its toll on civilians: in the 1940–41 Blitz alone, 300,000 London homes were destroyed and at least 20,000 London civilians were killed; of those, more than 1000 were firefighters (Ziegler 161). Working amidst the destruction, firemen became the indomitable "Heroes with Grimy Faces" praised by Churchill on the wireless and then honored by Humphrey Jennings onscreen in the 1943 film *Fires Were Started*, which cast real firemen in every role.[5] Firemen led the way in the People's War, working longer, more grueling hours than most to defend their burning London homes from the attacks of the German Luftwaffe. According to Angus Calder, "Firemen's hours, standardized at forty-eight hours on, twenty-four hours off, far exceeded those of other civil defenders" (*PW* 208). As one Canadian volunteer at a London fire station wrote in her wartime diary,

I tell you I take my hat off to those men, most of whom had no knowledge of a fire before except the one in their own hearth. They've had to deal with conditions of absolute frightfulness, and have come through it like heroes. I think they're magnificent. (Mrs Y. Green)

Mrs Green here pays tribute to the heroes who battled the fires of the Blitz, fires in which she herself perished shortly after writing this tribute.[6]

The sudden conversion of men with no previous knowledge of a fire into heroic firemen produces the psychological tensions explored in *Caught*. Green wrote the novel during the intense period of bombing in 1940–41, a time when the public was eager for rhetoric like Churchill's that transformed the horrors of the Blitz into a People's War. Like any myth, the myth of the Blitz offers "an ancient traditional story of Gods or heroes, esp[ecially] one offering an explanation of some fact or phenomenon" (Calder, *Myth* 2).[7] Fighting on the front lines of the People's War, firemen stood out as such gods among everyday heroes; their stories seemed to establish a sense of "blissful clarity" about the Blitz by making "things appear to mean something by themselves" (Barthes 143). As the Heroes with Grimy Faces defending the home front, the firemen appeared to embody an ideal much like that of the soldier hero: they were the civilian heroes of the People's War.

However, as a member of the AFS since 1938, Green was well aware that the public had not always conceived of firemen in such idealized terms. For the first year of the war, there were no German bomb attacks on Britain. During this Phoney War, firemen were often publicly ridiculed and scorned for drawing a salary while doing little work, and one scholar has suggested that *Caught's* title refers to being "caught in the jaws of this strange war that seemed for so long to have no teeth" (Brunetta, par. 11). An AFS volunteer recalls attitudes toward firemen in early 1940:

> So bad did the feeling become in some places [...] that Auxiliaries never wore their uniform (if they possessed one) in public, if they could avoid it. Not being thin-skinned the candid remarks so often heard about three-pounds-a-week men doing bugger-all for their money didn't worry me at all, but quite a number of competent firemen gladly got themselves into one of the services, usually the Air Force, in order to get away from the cutting remarks of ignorant members of the public. (Calder, *PW* 68)

Even Jennings's popular film, *Fires Were Started*, was criticized for its first half, which catalogs in great detail the daily routines of the fire station, culminating in a scene where the men sing together around a piano. Anxious for action, the public shared the sentiment of one reviewer, whose 1943 film review was entitled, "'Fires Were Started' – But Too Slowly." Most members of the film's audience were all too glad to hear the air-raid siren interrupt the song, prompting these domesticated firemen to become grimy-faced warriors.

Like *Fires Were Started, Caught* challenges the ideal of the fireman hero in the People's War by demonstrating how a script of macho heroics fails to account for the often conflicted identities of real men in wartime. In 1943 (the release date of both film and novel), John Lehmann, who reviewed books and films for *Penguin New Writing* under the pseudonym of Jack Marlowe, expressed a commonly held preference for novels that "perform a real service in wartime," contending that *Caught's* emphasis on its characters' anxieties "would not make anyone think the better of the British war effort" (qtd in Treglown 150–1).[8] The implication here is much like that of Churchill's speech about the first month of war: the British war effort depends upon not anxious but heroic men to uphold its ideals. *Caught* demonstrates how tempting it is for civilian men to try to play the role of hero in this propagandistic script – and how rarely the role describes the real man.

The novel's defining moment is therefore not a heroic night of firefighting but rather the day that Roe's now five-year-old son, Christopher, was kidnapped "long before the war, in the days when [Roe] was still training to become an Auxiliary" (15). The kidnapping is remembered and repressed, rather than described and discussed, because the day was so fraught with guilt and shame for the novel's fireman. Roe is ashamed of his failure to protect his son, particularly since his noncombatant status is the direct result of being widowed and becoming the sole guardian of a dependent child. Roe's inability to safeguard his son before the war makes him anxious that he might also fail to defend his nation in wartime. The novel further complicates the role of heroic firefighter with a coincidence: the kidnapper is the sister of Roe's Fire Station Leader, Arthur Pye. Struggling to find a motive for the crime, Pye is shocked to realize that his first sexual encounter – a clandestine meeting on a dark night – was perhaps not with the servant girl he remembers but with his own sister, who eventually kidnaps the boy to play the part of their unborn child. This absurd situation makes solidarity between the working-class Pye and the upper-middle-class Roe difficult and heroism nearly impossible; instead of battling the fires of the Blitz together, these men are personally at odds, consumed by their fiery emotions. Pye becomes suicidally depressed as a brother-lover who must commit his sister to a mental institution, while Roe experiences helplessness as a widowed father temporarily robbed of his son. Even their names together – Pye and Roe – suggest a personal conflagration that burns as hot as any fire in the Blitz.

Employing the metaphor of fire to underscore not the professional heroism but the emotional anxiety of its firemen, *Caught* shows that the myth of the fearless fireman in the People's War is no more than a fiction. The novel emphasizes the appeal of these fictions in wartime, even for a pragmatic businessman like Richard Roe. Roe is no writer – he vaguely refers to "days at the office" before the war (30) – but in wartime even he writes and rewrites the events of the Blitz in his imagination:

> The extraordinary thing is [...] that one's imagination is so literary. What will go on up there to-night in London, every night, is more like a film, or that's what it seems like at the time. Then afterwards, when you go over it, everything seems unreal, probably because you were so tired, as you begin building again to describe to yourself some experience you've had. (175)

Narrating his life in the Blitz, Roe becomes intensely self-aware about the literary nature of his own imagination. He wants to believe early in the novel that he can be a fireman hero in the People's War; Roe asserts that "it brings everyone together, there's that much to war" (46), and he is delighted to find that "firemen were still heroes to the public, and to women especially" in the first weeks of war before the novelty wore off and the Phoney War began (61). However, his experiences, like those of the AFS volunteer who noted "the candid remarks so often heard about three-pounds-a-week men doing bugger-all for their money," soon expose the romanticism of these dreams. Eventually, Roe concedes that all accounts of the Blitz – even the dominant ideological scripts of the People's War and the soldier hero – are equally fictional.

The novel therefore refuses to focus, as most readers at the time would have expected, on the firemen's heroic wartime service; instead, *Caught* spends so much time describing the emotional turmoil of its characters' lives that it must postpone Roe's description of the fires themselves until its final 25 pages. Even then, the narrative of the Blitz proves anticlimactic: *Caught* makes clear that Roe's story is not only extremely brief but also surprisingly boring. His sister-in-law, Dy, repeatedly marvels at "how very dull his description was" (178), and she is amazed to find that "there was nothing in what he had spoken to catch her imagination" (180). Roe begins the tale quite convention-ally: " 'The first night,' he [tells Dy], 'we were ordered to the docks. As we came over Westminster Bridge it was fantastic, the whole left side of London seemed to be alight' " (177). The East End bombing was unde-niably "fantastic," as Roe suggests here and then repeats rather help-lessly throughout his account. However, he also realizes that his vague, repetitive words fail to convey his own experiences in the London Blitz. Narrating his part in the script of the fireman hero, he discovers that he cannot tell this fictional tale with conviction, even when that is exactly what his audience wants him to do. Thus, immediately after he labels the fire "fantastic," Roe undercuts his own description: "It had not been like that at all" (177).

This moment of self-contradiction is the first in a series of parenthetical asides in the last part of the novel that show Roe thinking outside the limits of the ideological script. Repeatedly interrupting Roe's blitz narrative, the descriptions within parentheses project upon the fire the emotional anxiety that Roe typically keeps locked inside himself:

> (The firemen saw each other's faces. [...] They saw a whole fury of that conflagration in which they had to play a part. They sat very still, beneath the immensity. For, against it, warehouses, small towers, puny steeples seemed alive with sparks from the mile high pandemonium of flame reflected in the quaking sky. This fan, a roaring red gold, pulsed rose at the outside edge, the perimeter round which the heavens, set with stars before the fading into utter blackness, were for a space a trembling green.) (177–8)

Within these parentheses, Roe is no longer "putting into polite language" the terrifying experience of firefighting (178); instead, he represents the secret fear that he is more helpless than heroic. The raging fire in the passage threatens to consume the tiny, passive firemen who sit still rather than leap heroically into the fray. Unwilling for the moment either to put out the fire or to put the male anxiety that it induces back into polite language, Roe describes an experience that is far more psychologically complex than the scripted language that describes it simply as "fantastic."

The impressionistic style within these parentheses recalls the parenthetical passages describing young Christopher's abduction at the beginning of the novel. Roe remembers the kidnapping as he returns to London after spending a brief leave from the AFS with his son in the country. He has learned only the most basic facts of the abduction: "He did not know what Christopher had been through, the child was too young to tell" (14). Roe nevertheless visualizes the day in a long parenthetical section that prefigures the depiction of the unquenchable fire quoted above. Roe's vision of Christopher watching his kidnapper is as poetic and personal as his description of the firemen watching the fire:

> Dazzled by the pink neon lights beyond her features. Caught in another patch of colour, some of her chin was pillar-box red, also a part of the silver fox she wore. Furtively she glanced right, then left, but when, to make him do as she wanted, she caught full at him with

her eyes that, by the ocean in which they were steeped, were so much a part of the world his need had made, and so much more a part of it by being alive, then he felt anything must be natural, and was ready to do whatever she asked. (11)

These images mesmerize not only Christopher, who helplessly follows the stranger for a promised toy boat, but also Roe himself, who helplessly fails to protect his son. Roe fears that his passivity as a paternal guardian undermines his ability to perform heroically in civic defense.

The pressure to contain this anxiety not only inside himself but also within the parentheses of the text creates the aesthetic tension of *Caught*. The novel's firemen remain caught between the public expectation that they talk like heroes, not "cissies," as Pye calls his men at one point (79), and the private fear of helplessness that frequently overwhelms them. The conflict comes to a head in the novel's final scene, when Roe stops his blitz narrative to say how good it is to be home, an admission that makes him start to cry. His raw emotion causes his sister-in-law a discomfort characteristic of public opinion during this period: "The moment she saw these [tears] she drew away. 'Go on with what you were telling me,' she said, brisk" (190). Dy is much more comfortable when Roe claims that firemen are "absolute heroes now to everyone. Soldiers can't look us in the face even"; she responds, "Quite right too" (176). Looking to the fireman for an escape from her own wartime tears and fears, Dy wants Roe to play the part of the hero rather than the cissie. She therefore pretends that he has not wept and then demands answers: "She [...] said a very foolish thing, because it was true. 'I wonder what's the meaning of it all?'" (195). However, Roe's temper flares up against Dy's demands: "He felt a flash of anger. It spread" (196). Like the fires of the Blitz that he and his fellow firemen struggle to control, the flames of Roe's emotion flash and spread, threatening to escape from the parentheses that strain to confine them within the text. Playing with this fire, *Caught* describes a man caught between the emotional demands of his private life and the political imperative of his public image. Since the pressure to control his emotional anxiety is so great, Roe resorts to macho posturing: "'God damn you,' he shouted [at Dy], releasing everything, 'you get on my bloody nerves, all you bloody women with all your talk'" (198). Even as he releases everything here, Roe pits men against women, rebuilding the traditional gender barriers eroded by his sentimental tears only moments before. He talks like a stereotypical man, controlling and redirecting the flames of emotion in order to avoid looking like a "cissie."

Acknowledging the pressure to posture as a hero, the novel never-theless demonstrates that there is more than just this one way to talk like a man. *Caught* describes in detail how language can catch speakers up, trapping them in conventional ideas and routine phrases. Yet at the same time the novel offers an escape: through its constant revi-sion and rewriting of the Blitz, *Caught* manages itself not to become caught within any one of the several ideological scripts it describes. Thus, when Roe curses "all you bloody women with all your talk," the real problem is not the women but the talk. Roe's outburst snarls him in language so macho that it can tell only part of the story, but he almost immediately revises his point of view: he "felt a fool" for yell-ing at Dy (198). Similarly, he seems to deny his own paternal affection when, after lashing out at Dy, he snaps at his son to "get out" of the room (198); however, he softens the blow only a moment later by add-ing, "Well, anyway, leave me alone till tea, can't you?" (198). These are phrases not of indecision but of revision: using the crisis of the 1940–41 fires to expose a parallel crisis of masculinity on the home front, *Caught* rewrites the limited narratives of both the People's War and the soldier hero, narratives that threaten to extinguish Roe's private feelings. The novel demonstrates that such nationalist rhetoric is as much a product of the literary imagination as any other war story.

* * *

Having described firemen caught up in the role of the soldier hero in *Caught*, Henry Green extends his analysis of that role by turning to the soldier himself in *Back*. *Back* tells the story of Charley Summers, a British soldier just repatriated from a German prisoner-of-war camp at the end of the Second World War. The first thing we learn about Charley is that he is missing a leg: "A country bus drew up below the church and a young man got out. This he had to do carefully because he had a peg leg" (3). Charley is wounded physically because he failed to detect the German gun hiding "in that rosebush" on a French battle-field (8), and he is crippled emotionally when his lover, whose "name, of all names, was Rose" (4), unexpectedly dies while he is recovering in the prison camp. The novel thus immediately yokes physical to emotional trauma through the image of the rose, making literal the conflict between military heroics and domestic anxiety that threatens Richard Roe's masculinity in *Caught*. Charley's missing leg causes him less pain than the heartache that makes him "literally writhe while he remembered" his affair with Rose (130), yet most of the characters in the novel perceive only his peg leg, which they admire as evidence of his courage.

Charley's heroism should guarantee his sexual dominance, according to the patriotic and patriarchal discourse that valorizes his physical scars as signs of a battle-tested masculinity even as it ignores the emotional scars that might undermine that masculinity. The suggestion here is that soldiers, like Charley, who return having proven their valor on the front line can reap the benefits of a discourse that equates military power with sexual prowess. The returning hero will therefore get the girl waiting on the home front, and her kiss will then validate him as a man of action, energy, and will – both on the battlefield and in the bedroom. If, as John Costello argues in *Virtue Under Fire,* "the notion that a sexually aggressive man makes the best fighter has been universal throughout history and in all cultures," then the corollary – that the best fighters make the best lovers – is also universal (76). This symbolic logic governs many patriotic war movies of the period; however, the problem during the Second World War was that most British soldiers did not return home like John Wayne. The Introduction describes how even soldiers on active duty sometimes found themselves helplessly waiting for news of their bombed families. Those who were physically wounded in battle or captured by the enemy found it especially difficult to think of themselves as either war heroes or matinee idols upon repatriation. After all, not only did an amputated limb undercut conventional images of the desirable male body, but the prisoner of war had also spent much of the war not fighting vigorously but waiting patiently. The wounded soldier therefore returned home to find himself doubly emasculated: ironically, his symbolic castration and enforced passivity better suited him to the role of waiting girl than returning hero. Even more than the civilian men in *Caught,* wounded soldiers like Charley Summers in *Back* embody the crisis of masculinity facing men on the British home front during and immediately after the war.

One option for the wounded soldier was to combat his feelings of inadequacy by adopting and exaggerating Churchill's macho nationalistic rhetoric to showcase the war wound as proof of sexual prowess, as does Charley's fellow amputee, Arthur Middlewitch. Like Charley, Middlewitch has recently been repatriated after the amputation of a limb. However, whereas Charley awkwardly "drag[s] the aluminum leg in a pin-striped trouser" (24) and suffers from a "day-to-day sense of being injured by everyone, by life itself" (152), Middlewitch confidently carries his "chromium-plated arm under his black jacket" (24), boasting that his status as a wounded war hero ensures his sexual success on the home front. Upon repatriation, he brags, "Practically every girl I know had a go at me. Turned it to very good advantage, too, I did, on more than one occasion, I can tell you" (27). In conversation with Charley, Middlewitch repeatedly converts the physical liability of his prosthetic arm into this kind of advantage:

> But it can be a sight awkwarder at more intimate moments, eh? Lord yes. Mine squeaked the other day, just when I was putting it round her fattest bit. And a bloody sight more awkward for you I shouldn't wonder. Never fear though, they like it. (25)

Middlewitch's posturing here represents the arm that he has lost as a sign not of castration but of phallic power.

Through Middlewitch, *Back* dramatizes the coping strategies of many actual prisoners of war, whose diaries and memoirs also employ the wartime rhetoric of soldierly heroism to reaffirm their masculinity and to restore their sexual potency. For example, upon his release from a prisoner-of-war camp, British soldier Graham Palmer initially wonders at receiving "a reception worthy of conquering heroes, though I could not actually recollect having conquered anything" (204). However, he ultimately convinces himself that he has performed heroically in defending national freedom: "I began to realize that our years of suffering [in the prisoner-of-war camps] may not have been in vain" in the effort to "upset a most unpleasant invader and defend the most valuable of our assets – our freedom" (205). At the same time that he recovers a sense of his own heroism, he also recovers sexual interest and desire: before bedtime, the wounded soldiers in his Leicester hospital ward "were duly given a bath by young nurses who felt that the patients were too weak to bathe themselves, an ordeal which I in particular found hard to accept after five years of enforced celibacy" (204). To compensate for the shame of appearing too weak to bathe himself, Palmer emphasizes instead that his shrunken, asthma-stricken body still has the strength to become aroused, despite the traumatic experience of the prison camp.

Recognizing that wounded soldiers like Palmer, Middlewitch, and Charley all had to repress their sexuality in prison camps during the war, *Back* asks whether the repression produces the heightened sexual potency alluded to by Middlewitch and Palmer or whether it ultimately renders the soldier effete and powerless. Some soldiers – including Charley Summers in *Back* – responded to the "enforced celibacy" of prison camp by retreating from women. One Belgian officer, for example, remarks upon attending a strip show after his return home, "I myself was as shocked as a fifteen-year-old. Our compulsory chastity must have turned us into Puritans" (Costello 106). Similarly, in *Back*, Charley recognizes that "prison had made him very pure" (49). Whereas he had engaged in a torrid prewar sexual affair with Rose, both before and during her marriage to James Phillips, now Charley finds himself ill-equipped for either sex or marriage: "I'm not fit [...]. After those prisoner-of-war camps [...]. I can't" (153). In an effort to overcome feelings of sexual inadequacy, Charley clumsily tries to emulate Middlewitch's bravado, boasting, for example, that he has spent a recent holiday weekend with a secretary from his firm. Although Charley admits that "there's nothing doing" sexually between the secretary and him (160), he laughs knowingly when Middlewitch again invokes war rhetoric to describe the soldier's wounded body: "What, after the greatest war in history, with everyone still at it, and all we've been through? Not to speak of these secret weapons" (160). Like Middlewitch, Charley desperately wants to believe that his war experience has not undermined but enhanced his virility, that his war wound can be deployed as a sexual secret weapon.

Back compounds the soldier's problem of restoring sexual potency by connecting it to the broader postwar problem of restoring male economic power. Anxiety about changing gender dynamics in the home-front workplace was a major concern of noncombatant men during the war, and this fear continued into the postwar period. Since even conservatives like Winston Churchill recognized that "nothing has been grudged, and the bounds of women's activities have been definitely, vastly, and permanently enlarged" during the war ("Women" 285), many civilians wondered what would happen when soldiers returned home from battle. A 28-year-old army lecturer asserts both his appreciation for women's war work and his concern that this work be only for the duration; in doing so, he expresses quite plainly the male economic anxiety lurking beneath the ideal of the People's War: "They are doing a wonderful job of work, but the quicker they are back in their rightful sphere (the home) the sooner will I be pleased" (M-O A: DR 2694, Sept. 1942).[9] Women often shared this concern; a 25-year-old factory worker, for example, worries not about her own job stability but about postwar employment for repatriated men: "It's not so much what's going to happen to us, as what's going to happen to the men who come home. Will there be jobs for them?" (Calder and Sheridan 182).[10] Such anxious questions about the prospects of male breadwinners troubled British postwar gender relations, which nevertheless continued to change as a result of the economic demands of the war.

Combining these social fears with the sexual anxieties described above, *Back* explores a world that equates professional success with sexual prowess and failure with impotence; the novel's returning soldiers therefore experience the problem of getting work as the problem of getting laid. These problems are amplified for the wounded prisoner of war whose body both underwrites the war rhetoric of heroism and undercuts his ability to perform sexually. For example, although Charley himself is a well-paid production manager in a respectable manufacturing firm, he anxiously views Middlewitch as "out of my street altogether in the C.E.G.S. [Corps of Engineers Guide Specifications]" (189). Charley's unfounded feelings of professional inferiority betray his sexual jealousy about Middlewitch's love life; when Charley frets, "Got a big job there, Arthur has" (189), the subtext is that he envies the size of more than just Arthur's job. By the end of the novel, Middlewitch loses this position because of "some little disagreement at the office" (200): Middlewitch "had been betting and couldn't pay up" (238), presumably in order to support his playboy lifestyle. Cementing the association between office and bedroom, a female friend observes Middlewitch's downfall and dismisses him as a professional and sexual failure: "He's all talk and no do, that lad is" (166). Whether he is betting and losing "with someone else's money" (238) or emptily boasting about his sex life, the wounded Middlewitch rather desperately builds up his machismo until it finally causes his downfall.

Like Middlewitch, Charley initially finds that friends and colleagues watch him at work and make unwarranted assumptions about his sex life. In a private meeting, Charley's employer, Mr Mead, begins to speculate about Charley's libido:

> What I've to say isn't easy for me, Summers. [...] But I've been observing you [...]. I've a feeling I'm not getting your best at your work, not all your attention, not all of you, Summers. [...] Have women gotten hold of you, Summers? Is that it? [...]. I've been to several of their [the Reform of Prisons League] meetings [...]. It may not be a very pleasant thing to say in mixed company, Summers, but we're speaking as man to man now. It's sex is the whole trouble. There you are. Sex. (220–1)

In evaluating his employee, Mead attributes work problems to sex problems, but he assumes that Charley is promiscuous rather than celibate.

From Mead's perspective, a business manager and army veteran like Charley must be enjoying a healthy sex life; Mead's innuendo that Charley has "a little matter of account" with his secretary makes explicit the equation of sexual and professional performance (222). Charley is far from flattered by Mead's presumption, which only reminds him of how impotent he has become. The memory of just how "little" that "matter" with his secretary actually was compounds his humiliation: frustrated by Charley's diffidence, she has sex with another man instead.

Charley's humiliation is symptomatic of postwar male anxieties about sexually active and even aggressive women; once again, the experience of the wounded soldier exposes and amplifies more widespread concerns about changing gender roles on the home front. During the war, British women began enjoying not only the social and professional mobility but also the sexual freedom once afforded only to men. According to John Costello, the attitude of British women that "we were not really immoral, there was a war on" became so pervasive that "it seemed sexual restraint had been suspended for the duration as the traditional license of the battlefield invaded the home front" (7). Writing about a WAAF camp in Digby, England, a female Mass-Observer claims,

> Any comment on Digby life must have morality as its main theme. The place oozes sex. In after-duty hours it is, for the most part, one huge, casual brothel. The main subject in all conversations among women is "men": and everyone sums up members of the opposite sex in terms of sexual potentiality. (M-O A: TC 32/3/E, "Morality at Digby," 1941)

Like the men discussed at Digby, the repatriated Middlewitch and Charley find themselves sexually scrutinized and subject to "women's curiosity" about "what we did about girls all that time behind the wire" (Green, *Back* 26). In a postwar world where a secretary can quite freely judge and jilt her boss, it is no wonder that Charley feels so much anxiety.

Back demonstrates how this anxiety causes the wounded soldier to repress and deny the emotional trauma that accompanies physical trauma in time of war. Despite the intensity of the soldiers' emotional experiences, no one – including the soldiers themselves – wants to talk about emotional pain because to do so is to undermine the fragile image of the masculine war hero that the nation invests with so much political significance. Magnifying the pressure on *Caught*'s Richard Roe to contain his emotions and thus to act like a man, *Back* demonstrates how Charley Summers must literally embody national ideology, making emotional breakdown not just unpleasant but politically dangerous. For this reason, Middlewitch warns Charley against nursing his psychological wounds too openly or obviously. When Charley confesses, "My girl died while I was out there" (31), Middlewitch quickly counters,

> You see, I've kept in touch with some of the lads from our lot, and one or two have drawn their horns in, gone inside of themselves, if you follow me. Now that's dangerous. All you're doing is to perpetuate the conditions you've lived under, which weren't natural. Well, my advice to them and to you is, snap out of it. (31–2)

Civilians in the novel also expect Middlewitch and Charley to snap out of any mental anxiety caused by the war: Middlewitch's popularity immediately wanes when he becomes "worried" about his job (194) rather than garrulous about his sexual conquests, and Charley's boss is "flung off balance" and momentarily silenced when Charley confesses to him that his girlfriend has died during the war (221–2). While the public freely and openly discusses the soldier's wounded body, his wounded feelings are a taboo topic: the nationalistic discourse that defines him as a masculine hero prevents anything resembling feminine vulnerability from being expressed.

In addition to governing public conversation about the wounded soldier, this wartime discourse of the soldier hero determines and delimits Charley's ability to speak about himself. For example, when Charley finds himself trapped in a long line of people waiting to use a public telephone, he takes advantage of his physical disability to move to the front of the queue: "Excuse me won't you. A favour. Just back from Germany. Repatriated, wooden leg" (65). Once the deferential civilians allow him into the telephone booth, however, Charley "did not find himself so glib" (65). Trying to explain on the phone his anger and grief about Rose's death to her father, Mr Grant, "all Charley could get out was, 'I say,' twice" (65). Although Charley only "gaped into the receiver" while Grant was on the line (65), he finds his voice at last after Grant has hung up the phone and shouts in frustration, "You bastard, you bastard, you bastard" (66). Charley easily exploits the nationalistic discourse that defines him as a hero by jumping to the front of the line, but as soon as he tries to express his emotions, the same discourse constrains him: here and throughout the novel, Charley finds himself "tonguetied" (88), "silenced" (89), or "beyond speech" (215) whenever he attempts to convey his emotional pain. His inarticulate mumblings, his "usual state of not knowing" (6), and his tendency to be "some sentences behind" in conversations all suggest that Charley (88), like many wounded soldiers, is silenced by political rhetoric that inhibits the ability to talk about one's emotional life.

Like Charley, many British soldiers found physical trauma much easier to discuss than emotional pain. While it was often easy to make light of one's injuries publicly, it was typically much more difficult for British soldiers to find words for the emotional and psychological trauma that accompanied their wounds. According to British Army doctor George Moreton, emotional vulnerability was a primary risk of amputation, and patients required extensive counseling to cope with their psychological trauma: "It was necessary to prepare the patient for such a loss; not only the body was maimed, but also the brain [...]. He would have to reorientate his life" (165). Memoirist Denis Ferne, for example, describes the contrast between feeling comfortable amidst the "army cameraderie [sic]" on the front line and feeling "more and more conscious of the empty trouser-leg pinned up to the knee" when he returns home at the end of the war. Resigning himself at least temporarily to an uncomfortable and "unnatural" embarrassment at home, Ferne demonstrates the insufficiency of political rhetoric that can label the soldier's wounded body as the price of freedom without registering the psychic toll of war.

Despite its simplifications, nationalistic war rhetoric serves an important social function: it creates the cultural icon of the heroic soldier in which most British citizens – including Charley – desperately wanted to believe. In order to maintain this belief, Charley must suppress his emotional pain; thus, unable to emulate Middlewitch's sexual bravado, Charley plunges into deep and nearly psychotic denial of his grief over Rose's death. He constructs an elaborate fantasy in which Rose has not died but has instead staged her death and then concealed the ruse by assuming the identity of her half-sister, Nancy Whitmore. Upon meeting Nancy for the first time, Charley "pitched forward, in a dead faint, because there she stood alive, so close that he could touch, and breathing, the dead spit, the living image, herself, Rose in person" (53). Over the course of the novel, Charley tells a story about Nancy that invents a new history and personality for her to suit his needs; Charley's fantasized version of Nancy as a resurrected Rose seems to erase his grief and thus helps him to reassert a masculine identity that would otherwise be compromised by emotional vulnerability.

In forcing this narrative upon Nancy during his crisis of masculinity, Charley unwittingly adopts a variation of the rhetorical strategy that, according to Scarry, nations employ to describe the soldiers who sacrifice their lives on the battlefield. In order to shore up a national identity under siege in wartime, the nation defines a heroic masculine ideal and imposes it on soldiers like Charley. Similarly, in order to bolster a masculine identity jeopardized by his physical and emotional frailty, Charley defines a feminine ideal and imposes it on Nancy. Charley builds this feminine ideal out of his sexual memories of the dead Rose, "whom he could call to mind, though never all over at one time, or at all clearly, crying, dear Rose, laughing, mad Rose, holding her baby, or, oh Rose, best of all in bed, her glorious locks abounding" (5). The "Rose" whom Charley remembers is not Rose herself but a fantasy girl whose desire for him guarantees his virility – and promises that he, too, is best of all in bed. Like the nation that substantiates its ideologies with the bodies of dead or wounded soldiers, Charley tries to reaffirm his sexual identity by recalling the body of his dead lover.

However, Charley's idealized "Rose" represents the women in *Back* no more accurately than the idealized war hero represents the wounded soldier: neither Rose nor Nancy can possibly measure up to his fantasy. Over the course of the novel, the three Roses – the dead girlfriend, her living sister, and his sexual memory – come into conflict with one another. Although Rose herself can no longer resist Charley's fictions, Nancy refuses to be identified as his "Rose," and her resistance ignites a war of the Roses that threatens Charley's fantasy by exposing it as a lie. Charley protects the fantasy by trying to control the name "Rose," a word that defines his feminine ideal and that he then uses to define Nancy. For this reason, it is difficult for him to admit not only that the name "Rose" might not apply to Nancy but also that the word "rose" might not always mean what he intends. In the first part of the novel, Charley becomes nervous and agitated when he encounters the word "rose" used in any other context. Hearing a barmaid called "Rose" gives him "a jolt" (25); his landlady's consecutive references to the way wartime prices, his voice, and her gall all "rose" make him catch his breath (39–40). Ultimately, Charley feels guilty and confused when the word stops causing him pain, and so he remains "fastened on this word" (40), determined in the second part of the novel to reinvest "rose" with sexual significance by fastening the word as tightly as he can upon Nancy.

The problem is that Nancy will not comply. Angry that Charley has renamed and manipulated her, she accuses him of playing a "dirty trick" (62) that compromises rather than confirms his masculinity: "Why you aren't a man, a real man would never do a thing like that" (62). Ironically,

Charley's sense of self depends upon a symbolic violence that Nancy insists would be unnecessary for a "real man" who was sexually secure. Exposing Charley's masculinity as a fiction based on a self-centered fantasy about her, Nancy raises the possibility that Charley could likewise defy the nationalistic fictions imposed upon him. Furthermore, her accusation that Charley is not a "real man" demonstrates how that resistance might work. Nancy does not merely reject Charley's story; instead, she questions and revises his definition of the masculinity that he tries to defend. After Charley faints, he wakes up "to find Rose kneeling at his head, which was in her lap" (53), and he "shakily sat up to be fetched a kiss" (55). Conflated with Charley's feminine ideal, Nancy refuses to respond to him sexually, and this refusal sends Charley into a nervous collapse that makes him "tremble all over" (58). Finally, Charley manages to soothe his nerves and to explain Nancy's lack of response by convincing himself that Nancy is Rose gone "out of her mind" (55). Nancy rejects this fiction and insists that postwar masculinity must expand beyond the boundaries of prewar norms and confusions; a "real man," according to Nancy, should accept rather than deflect the burden of mental anguish that causes Charley to "tremble all over."

While Nancy is a woman who challenges the nationalist ideal of the soldier hero by claiming that Charley is not a "real man," James Phillips, Rose's widower, is a man who falls short of conventional ideas of manliness. Cuckolded by Charley and prone to speak "like a woman" (98), James is a "fat fellow" (12), a "bloody civilian" too old to fight in the war (153). Nevertheless, when Charley brings his secretary, Dot, for a holiday weekend at James's country house, "believe it or not, it was that fat James" who snuck into her bed instead of Charley (145). When Charley finally works up the nerve to visit Dot's bedroom at the end of the weekend, he finds the bed empty: "There were no pillows, for she had taken these with her. And then he heard noises next door in James's room. They were in the act" (162). Succeeding where Charley has failed, James defies the assumption that the returning war hero will always get the girl.

In challenging the ideal of the soldier hero, both Nancy and James disturb Charley by forcing him to define his masculinity in other ways. Halfway through the novel, Charley desperately demands that James confirm his fantasy that Nancy is Rose: he brings James to see Nancy and insists, "You're in this together" (104). Immediately after this encounter, the pressure to sustain a fantasy that James flatly refutes becomes too great: "Charley had gone sick. He told the office he had flu. He kept to his bed. What he thought of himself was, that he was going to lose his reason" (105). Even as Charley begins to recognize that he might be far more mad than Nancy, James clips from a magazine and sends to Charley "The Souvenirs of Madame de Créquy." James thinks that the story "seemed so close to Charley's situation that he thought he would forward it, even though he was sore at the man" for accusing him of plotting with Nancy (105). Like Charley, the story's protagonist, Septimanie de Richelieu, experiences the death of her lover and feels intense, almost physical pain every time she thinks of him: she "fainted if his name came up in conversation" (108) and "felt as though her heart were in a vice" when she discovers some of his letters (111). Charley is initially uninterested in the similarities between their stories, and he decides that "he was not even going to look through the thing" (106). However, when "his eye caught a bit about a girl fainting" (106), he decides to read the tale because he is drawn to a woman who faints, as he has recently done, at the sight of a dead lover apparently returned to life.

Charley's curiosity suggests a lingering concern about his own fainting spell, which he fears makes him seem weak and effeminate. Forced to wonder whether he is losing both his male authority and his reason, Charley begins to feel the pressure of sustaining a masculine identity so heavily reliant on the repression of emotional pain. At the moment when he begins to crack under the pressure, *Back* presents, in "The Souvenirs of Madame de Créquy," an opportunity to identify with an eighteenth-century Frenchwoman in a situation similar to his own and thus temporarily to escape the masculine identity crisis of the twentieth-century British soldier within which he is trapped. Septimanie manages her grief and emotion more efficiently than Charley does. Although she, like Charley, loses her lover and then falls for his half-sibling, Septimanie accepts the difference between her dead lover and the brother "who is his double" (112). Furthermore, she develops separate emotional relationships with them, and she publicly "cried her heart out" grieving for her dead lover (112) before she began to "cry her eyes out" over her ill-fated relationship with his brother (118). Because Septimanie distinguishes between her feelings for each brother, she is able to foster "two extraordinary passions she somehow found a way to lavish on two men who were entirely different and yet at the same time exactly similar, on the living and the dead" (120). Charley would benefit from expressing his emotions as Septimanie does: by learning to distinguish between his own "two extraordinary passions," he might also learn to escape the nationalistic discourse that narrowly defines his masculinity. Although Charley initially fails to see his connection to this French memoir, he experiences an unspoken relief at the possibilities raised by the story: "After he read right through to the end, Charley said aloud, 'Ridiculous story.' Nevertheless, when he switched out the light, he had his first good night's rest for weeks" (120). Charley sleeps well because he has confronted, albeit unconsciously, the possibility of incorporating his emotions into his masculine identity. The discovery of an alternative narrative, along with Nancy's and James's redefinitions of a "real man," offers the opportunity to escape the idealized notions of masculinity that have trapped and constrained Charley throughout the novel.

Charley realizes this opportunity only at the end of *Back*, when his relationship with Nancy finally breaks free from his fantasy of "Rose." Ultimately, Charley admits "that Rose was truly dead, that Nance was a real person" with whom he is falling in love (181). As a soldier hero, Charley should be able to get this girl and to live happily ever after. However, Charley cannot muster the courage to propose to Nancy as a real man would; instead, he miserably concludes that "a wife and kids were not for Charley Summers. He knew that. He was too slow. He'd never find a woman to put up with him" (243). Charley appears to be passive, cowardly, and effete, much as Churchill worried that the pacifist British nation would appear. However, rather than overcoming his seeming cowardice by resolving "to persevere to the end," as Churchill recommends, Charley allows Nancy to take control of their relationship; she surprises him with a marriage proposal of her own and then, even more disturbingly, imposes one condition on their union: "that they should have a trial trip" (246). Even though she desires Charley, she reserves the right to test their sexual compatibility before marriage; Nancy therefore seems to align herself with the WAAF battalion, which "sums up members of the opposite sex in terms of sexual potentiality" (M-O A: TC 32/3/E, "Morality at Digby," 1941). Her sexual assertiveness inverts the traditional gender roles of the waiting girl and the war hero and thus seems to validate male anxiety that the People's War would empower women and emasculate men.

Nancy's actions leave Charley with only two apparent options if he continues to measure himself against the standard of the soldier hero: he can either repress his emotional trauma and act like a "real man" by dominating Nancy sexually, or he can fail to be a "real man" by succumbing to the emasculating power of the British woman empowered during the People's War. However, when Charley enters Nancy's room and finds her lying naked on the bed in the final scene of the novel, he discovers that neither his masculinity nor Nancy's femininity need be so narrowly defined. As he gazes upon "the overwhelming sight of the woman he loved, for the first time without her clothes" (246), Charley sees Nancy's body lit with the colors of roses: "the pink shade seemed to spill a light of roses over her in all their summer colours, her hands that lay along her legs were red, her stomach gold, her breasts the colour of cream roses, and her neck white roses for the bride" (246). Charley watches as his "Rose" dissolves into roses, and the image suggests that Nancy's identity is more varied and complex than either the fantasy of the waiting girl or the fear of the dominating woman. Charley's vision produces an emotional outburst that unfastens him from the word "Rose": "it was too much, for he burst into tears again, he buried his face in her side just below the ribs, and bawled like a child. 'Rose,' he called out, not knowing he did so, 'Rose'" (246). Grieving for the loss of Rose as he is overwhelmed by love for Nancy, Charley expels the word "Rose" and lets go of the feminine ideal that defines neither woman. In doing so, he frees both Nancy and himself from conventional gender roles, accepting rather than fearing her sexual candor and his own emotional fragility. By the usual standards of masculinity, Charley fails sexually: his tears are the only part of him that "ran down between her legs" and "wetted her" that evening (246). However, his tears suggest a new standard that embraces emotion and celebrates its sexual function, a standard the Richard Roe has yet to discover at the end of *Caught*. According to this new standard, Charley and Nancy's intimacy lays the groundwork for success in bed; he goes to her room that night "for the first time in what was to be a happy married life" (246). Thus, even as Charley fails to live up to the masculine ideal of the hero who gets the girl, he opens up the possibility of redefining his masculinity to admit the depth of his feeling: he may lose both Rose and "Rose," but he gains Nancy.

Charley's inability to hang onto either Rose or "Rose" – and the freedom that comes from letting go of both the person and the word – follow from Henry Green's fascination throughout his work with the slipperiness of language.[11] Although critics have emphasized the philosophical and psychological aspects of Green's play with language, both *Caught* and *Back* methodically trace the connections between personal identity and political discourse in wartime and postwar Britain. Green's slippery language therefore has a radical social function: it disrupts the conventional narratives and rigid definitions that political rhetoric imposes on the self. *Caught* demonstrates Richard Roe's gradual realization that the wartime script casting him as a hero in the People's War is a fiction that fails to define him. *Back* extends the critique, not only by focusing it upon a soldier recently returned from active duty but also by exploring the attractions of such political rhetoric, even for the soldier himself. Instead of pitting individuals against an ahistorical language or discourse, *Back* presents men and women pitted against specific wartime political discourses that in turn pit them against each other. Much to his surprise, Charley Summers discovers that the warring nation cannot fasten him to its masculine ideal any more than he can fasten Nancy to his feminine ideal. The fact that Nancy can escape being called by any other name, and that Charley cannot pin a "Rose" on her, therefore helps to liberate men and women from the politically motivated fantasies of waiting girls and war heroes.

4
No Escape in the Detective and Spy Fiction of Agatha Christie, Margery Allingham, and Graham Greene

The writers we have examined so far – Elizabeth Bowen, Rosamond Lehmann, and Henry Green – all wrote literary fiction for an educated audience. Their work self-consciously represents the changing class and gender dynamics that shaped upper-middle-class experience during the People's War and critiques the limited perspective of the privileged few. This chapter turns its attention to genre fiction, arguing that wartime detective and spy novels offered readers equally complicated representations of social relations on an embattled home front. The chapter doubles back to examine how two female detection writers (Agatha Christie and Margery Allingham) and one male spy writer (Graham Greene) represented the same conflicted ideas about the myth of the Blitz that Bowen, Lehmann, and Green explored in their wartime fiction. These popular detective and spy novels experiment with generic conventions in order to market to a more diverse book-buying public the ideological conflicts central to the People's War itself.

This argument initially seems counter-intuitive, since many readers and most scholars have described genre fiction as an imaginative escape from rather than a critical engagement with the chaos of war. Mass-Observation found that "in the first week of the war there was a big drop in reading of all kinds and in nearly all districts," but the taste for genre fiction soon returned (M-O A: FR 93, 1940: 140). At the height of the London Blitz in 1940, "special 'raid libraries' were set up at the reeking entrances to underground shelters to supply, by popular demand, detective stories and nothing else" (Haycraft 536). The raid libraries aimed to provide "easy reading and harmless puzzles" as an "antidote against the blackout and shelter depression" (Robyns 117). Mass-Observation materials confirm that readers sought an antidote to wartime violence: one young working-class man says that he reads in wartime "to pass the time. That's the reason I like a good mystery," and this 35-year-old middle-class woman agrees: "Well, I used to read for all sorts of reasons – interest, following up certain lines of study, and so on. But now I'm so overworked I read hardly anything but thrillers, to get me to sleep at night" (FR 2018, 1944: 77). An older woman explains more fully how genre fiction relaxes her: "I like the detective or thriller type as, by its close-woven plot (if it is a good tale) it demands a certain amount of attention and provides as complete a break possible from the work and worries of the day" (FR 2018, 1944: 90–1). A working-class man's overheard comment makes the same point:

> This blitzing has affected people's concentration so that they can't read so well. Down where I live in Bow, we had it night after night. But you found people reading a lot in the shelters. I think they found it a good way of getting away from all the horrors. (M-O A: TC 20/4/E, "Book Reading Indirects," 1942)

Scholarship on wartime genre fiction correlates this desire to escape imaginatively from wartime violence with a desire to soothe or ignore the ideological conflicts of the People's War. The criticism attributes the immense popularity of Agatha Christie's and Margery Allingham's wartime detective fiction to the writers' masterful use of detective genre conventions to perpetuate conservative social norms. Their mysteries, the argument goes, describe the process of outwitting an evil villain – whether a private murderer or a political mastermind – in order to return the chaotic world to its more peaceful status quo. Critics of Graham Greene's wartime thriller, *The Ministry of Fear* (1943), take a slightly different approach. Suggesting that the constant risk of death in espionage had become part of everyday life on the British home front, they interpret *The Ministry of Fear*'s blitz imagery metaphorically and psychologically rather than historically and ideologically. Much like the mysteries, this "entertainment," as Greene called it, thus appears to order and clarify for readers the confusing experience of life in the Blitz. However, the assumption here is that the fiction could order all readers' wartime experiences in one coherent way. The fact that so many men and women of different classes read detective and spy fiction during the war suggests instead that the genre was flexible enough to accommodate the multiple and conflicting anxieties, desires, and perspectives of its broad audience.

According to her publisher's website, Agatha Christie is the best-selling novelist in history, and her books have sold billions of copies in English and more than 40 other languages ("Agatha Christie"). Christie's sales have extended across social as well as national boundaries. Robert Barnard refutes Edmund Wilson's 1944–45 essays "Why Do People Read Detective Stories?" and "Who Cares About Roger Ackroyd?" by insisting that "an awful lot of people" have cared about Christie's characters both during and after the war: "Agatha Christie's working-class readership was probably more numerous than that of any other popular writer, and she is said [...] to be favoured reading in Buckingham Palace" (3). Although the existence of raid libraries and the comments of many readers suggest that the public could not get enough of Christie's wartime fiction, she often wondered how much of it she could supply. Biographers tend to agree that when Christie moved to the city in 1941, after the first Blitz but before the 1944–45 V-weapon attacks, she adopted a "splendidly professional attitude to the war [...] to disregard it – or if that was impossible, to make light of it" (Murdoch 137). However, like Elizabeth Bowen, Christie worried that the war would put her imagination out of action, so much so that she wrote her final Hercule Poirot mystery, *Curtain* (1975), "as an insurance policy for her family in case she were killed in the blitz" (Hark 144). Because Christie survived the war and died much later in 1976, *Curtain* was stored unpublished in a safe-deposit box until the end of her writing career in 1975. Yet as a response to the war, the novel foregrounds Christie's valid concerns about home-front violence and mortality: in wartime London alone at least 30,000 civilians were killed, while 50,000 were admitted to hospital.[1] *Curtain* breaks all the rules of its genre: before the war, detective fiction had typically allowed an infallible detective to preside over a murder committed in a closed room. In *Curtain,* an old and dying detective Poirot commits murder himself. For Christie, murder in wartime was no longer a drawing-room puzzle; instead, it had become an institutionalized mandate that made assassins and victims of all who fought. In this sense, the genre reflects some of the central ideas of wartime and postwar espionage fiction like that of Graham Greene and John le Carré. Christie's *Curtain* recognizes that the violence of war implicates even law-abiding civilians and thus includes even Poirot in its accusation that "everyone is a potential murderer" (139).

Christie was not alone in compromising the moral and psychological integrity of her detective during the war. In Margery Allingham's *Traitor's*

Purse (1940), master sleuth Albert Campion suffers from amnesia. As he gradually regains his memory, Campion is disconcerted to find that he has been detained for "slugging a policeman" who was trying to arrest him (2), that he can pick a lock "as if he had done it a hundred times" (4), and that he is able to walk "with the sure-footed tread of a professional burglar" (49). As Campion's self-doubt grows, he trips an alarm that sounds like an air-raid siren:

> It screamed at him, sending every nerve in his body tingling to the roots of his hair. It bellowed. It raved. It shrieked, tremblingly hysterical in the night, and from every side, above him, and beneath him, other bells echoed it in a monstrous cacophony of alarum. (5)

Civilians often described "a siren's ghastly wail" (Bawtree, 20 Aug. 1940) or "the scream of the air-raid siren" as a "shriek," a "blood curdling noise" signaling the seemingly endless bombing of Britain (Harrisson, *Living* 45, 48, 46). As one woman laments, "I can't bear it. I can't *bear* it. If them sirens go again tonight, I shall die. It's me nerves, they're all used up" (Harrisson, *Living* 95). In 1940, the hysterical screaming of Campion's alarm associates his own disturbed mental state with the stress of wartime bombing. Although Allingham, like Rosamond Lehmann, lived outside of London during the Blitz, she was well aware of the city's destruction, having helped hundreds of women and children evacuees to settle temporarily in her village, Tolleshunt D'Arcy. Campion does not commit murder in *Traitor's Purse*, as Poirot does in *Curtain*; nevertheless, both detectives demonstrate how the blurring of ideological boundaries during the Blitz extended even to the lines between sanity and madness, justice and criminality.

Despite Poirot's and Campion's actions in these novels, most scholars argue that detective fiction remained popular in wartime because it refused to abandon its conservative, formulaic protection of the status quo. Critics such as Julian Symons, John Cawelti, and Robin Winks have therefore interpreted the Second World War not as a period of generic innovation but as a time of literary transition between the closed-room puzzles of classic British detective fiction and the open-ended violence of postwar American noir fiction: "The war was a watershed in the history of the crime story, separating [...] the world of reason from that of force" (Symons 151). Howard Haycraft even goes so far as to suggest that "no major developments in detective-mystery technique have distinguished the war years" (538). Given the general consensus that the Second World War was little more than a period of "static competence" in detective writing (Haycraft 537), it is perhaps unsurprising that detective genre criticism has typically focused on fiction written before or after the war.

The criticism attributes this generic paralysis to the extreme conservatism of detective fiction writers themselves. Because many of the most popular writers in the 1930s and 1940s came from "a class of society that felt it had everything to lose by social change," the argument goes, their fiction was "unquestionably Right Wing" in its concern with "exorcising the guilt of the individual or the group through ritual and symbolic sacrifice" (Symons 10, 104, 8). The sacrifice of murderers, in particular, "validates [...] visions of a safe and ordered world" (Klein 1), allowing the reader to "turn his back on the ugly reality around him and retreat into the stylized world of literary art" (Grella 48).[2] Thus, upper-class male detectives make scapegoats of social and sexual deviants who represent specific threats to established class and gender hierarchies. They do so in order to restore the status quo and therefore to manage the social anxieties of conservative writers and readers.

Such protective measures may seem an appropriate response to the material violence and ideological confusion of the Second World War. However, the Blitz also afforded significant opportunities to the privileged few, and scholarship on detective fiction has not yet accounted for the conflicted responses of the upper-middle class to the idea of a People's War. A few critics, such as Jon Thompson and M. Vipond, have identified a specific need for more cultural criticism in genre studies, recognizing that "the capacity of crime fiction to evaluate different historical moments [...] is a dominant convention of the genre" (Thompson 2). More recently, R. A. York has suggested that the act of reading itself disrupts the conservatism of the detective novel:

> The fact that the genre tends towards ironic comedy implies that the values of an established elite are not necessarily truths and that the act of reading can be an occasion for distancing oneself from the certainties which it may be necessary to live by every day. (6)

This chapter grounds the act of reading detective novels that York describes in the specific historical circumstances of the Blitz and therefore calls into question the ideological fictions about changing class and gender roles that helped civilians to make sense of the People's War.

The novels raise and emphasize these questions by experimenting with generic conventions. Both Christie and Allingham use criminal scapegoats for the unconventional purpose of presenting and managing anxieties embedded within British culture at different points of time during the war. The beginning and end of the Second World War were especially stressful political periods for civilians in Great Britain. In the early 1940s, Christie's and Allingham's novels tend to scapegoat mainstream – rather than deviant – criminals in order to condemn the abuse of established social and political power. However, later in the war, the fiction indicts and exiles deviant criminals as scapegoats – but it does so ironically, as a means of calling attention to how ruthlessly British society preserves traditional values and beliefs, even during the People's War. By selecting scapegoats from both dominant and deviant groups, the novels critique the same British social order that their detectives strive to protect. Much like the literary fiction of the period, Christie's and Allingham's war writing is thus socially and politically ambivalent, rather than unquestionably right wing, because it both upholds the British establishment and condemns it for refusing to allow social change.

The ambivalence is clear even early in the war, when Christie and Allingham wrote novels that censured respectable upper-class men for failing to lead their countries effectively. In May 1940, the year in which Allingham published *Traitor's Purse*, Prime Minister Neville Chamberlain was "told bluntly" by "men of left right and centre" in Parliament "that he must go" because he was leading the country into confusion rather than victory with his policy of appeasement (Calder, *PW* 84). In *Traitor's Purse*, Lee Aubrey is an upper-class villain who is convicted because he tries to orchestrate chaos in England. Aubrey sends a mass mailing to Britain's working class, giving them counterfeit cash from a fictitious government agency and asking them to spend it immediately. Knowing that the government will be unable to refund the money during the war, he hopes to "smash the existing economy and create a chaos," which he will then resolve with his own economic plan (178). The novel condemns Aubrey as a traitor because, unable to "provide any stretch of common ground on which to walk with normal men," he appoints himself as an economic dictator (19).

The novel's representation of criminal behavior reveals a widespread cultural fear, particularly throughout 1940, that Britain would be misruled by powerful men. Although many British citizens distrusted Neville Chamberlain's "familiar want of resolution" (Calder, *PW* 79), which led to the passive appeasement of Hitler, many of them also dreaded a more aggressive leadership, which might emulate Hitler's fascist nationalism. In answer to an April 1940 Mass-Observation interview question – "What do you think of Winston Churchill?" – some people expressed the opinion that Churchill was perhaps too aggressive: "He's an old war-monger" or "I think he's a warmonger no. 1, definitely" (TC 6/3/B, "Interviews," 1940). In Allingham's *Traitor's Purse*, Lee Aubrey's crime is defined by "his mistaken belief in his own superiority" (180) and his monomaniacal desire to implement his "drastic" and "far-reaching" plan to "put the economic life of the country on an entirely new basis" during the war (178). By representing Aubrey's economic plan in such vague, sweeping language, the novel heightens the cultural fear of reckless leadership and thus locates the threat to British national security inside rather than outside the halls of power. Instead of scapegoating a criminal who deviates from the social norm, *Traitor's Purse* convicts a villain who enforces that norm too zealously.

Even more radically, the novel implicates its detective, Albert Campion, in this web of political corruption. Campion and Aubrey are social peers, and like Aubrey, Campion is recognized not only as "a particularly brilliant man" but also as "one of the big men of our time" (13). *Traitor's Purse* compares and contrasts the detective and the villain by foregrounding the personal relationship between Albert Campion and Lee Aubrey: Aubrey is both Campion's host in the village and his rival in love. The central personal conflict in the novel is that Campion's fiancée, Amanda, threatens to leave Campion for Aubrey. Although she eventually realizes that she was "a complete mug" to fall for Aubrey (182), she strays from Campion initially because he has become an emotional tyrant, holding her with "the possessiveness of the child, the savage, of the dog, unreasonable and unanswerable" and ignoring her desire to hasten their marriage (42). Campion's mistakes are personal while Aubrey's are political, but both men represent the same basic flaw of the upper classes: they are selfishly blind to the rights, desires, and needs of others. Campion therefore treats Amanda like a possession, much as Aubrey treats the working class as an economic force in his master plan. By implicating both the detective and the villain in the same type of manipulative behavior – even though Campion finally realizes his mistake and gets the girl – *Traitor's Purse* locates corruption within the very structures of law and order that the detective presumably strives to uphold.

In 1940, the wages of a crime like Aubrey's was death. The British Parliament had just passed the 1940 Treachery Act, "providing for the use of the death penalty in grave cases of espionage and sabotage" (Calder, *PW* 107). Aubrey will hang as a traitor because he has corrupted and sabotaged the system that empowers him; however, instead of simply violating social or political norms, as most criminals do, he endorses the status quo too fully and thus poses the danger of an orthodoxy verging on fascism. Because the threat is internal rather than external, the resolution of the novel comes not simply from the execution of the traitor himself but also from the ability of Campion and the community to correct Aubrey's excesses. In contrast to Aubrey, who is convinced that "he alone was capable of directing the Empire" (180), Campion learns to see his relationships with others in a more "impersonal" way (181). The distance allows Campion to respond to Amanda as an individual, rather than merely as an object of his own desire, and this increasing ability to interact meaningfully and equally will be the foundation of their future marriage. By scapegoating Aubrey and educating Campion, *Traitor's Purse* therefore condemns *and* corrects the tendency to approach political and personal relations in a purely self-interested manner, a tendency that the British public particularly feared in its powerful leaders. The use of a scapegoat to purge extremists rather than deviants from the community of the novel demonstrates that scapegoating can serve a liberal as much as a conservative function in detective fiction.

Agatha Christie explores similar issues in *One, Two, Buckle My Shoe* (1941), but by 1941, the fear of a too-powerful leader had grown even greater. After Chamberlain's resignation in 1940, Winston Churchill assumed the role of Prime Minister. Initially perceiving Churchill as "a man of action and a man of war," the public found it "profoundly reassuring to suppose that Britain was led at this moment by a great man" (Calder, *PW* 89, 98). But by June 1941, the publication year of *One, Two, Buckle My Shoe*, the war was not going well, and Churchill took the blame. As German infantry invaded North Africa, German bombs pummeled London, and German U-boats dominated the Battle of the Atlantic, it became "much in vogue to say that Churchill is a great man and a great leader," but "if one hints that perhaps Churchill isn't all that he's supposed to be, a great many people respond immediately and will begin to tell all kinds of things that they dislike about him" (Calder, *PW* 243). Reacting to cultural anxiety about yet another Prime Minister's leadership, *One, Two, Buckle My Shoe* presents in Alistair Blunt a politically powerful villain who, like Churchill, initially appears to embody national values: he is perceived as a "most important man" who is "so essentially British" that he has become "one of the Props of Things as They Are" (Christie 11, 6, 62). Although the novel suggests that wartime political power belongs to "not Dukes, not Earls, not Prime Ministers" but financiers like Blunt (11), the narrative more broadly condemns any leader who allows a political "love of power" to grow to "overwhelming heights" (224).

This is not to say that the public feared Churchill specifically or believed him to be excessively power-hungry; rather, concern about the role of central leadership in Britain had grown with the transfer of power from Chamberlain to Churchill. Mass-Observation confirms this view, even in the month immediately following Churchill's appointment as Prime Minister:

> It should be noted that there appears to be a good deal of potential criticism of leadership in general, which is likely to increase if Churchill cannot produce some immediate achievement to contrast his activities with Chamberlain's. Now that people are gradually realising the extent to which their over-confidence has been built up in recent years, they are beginning to get more bitter, disillusion[ed] about the whole authenticity, honesty and purpose of leadership. (TC 25/6/I, "Report from Mass-Observation on Churchill's Broadcast," 1940: 6–7)

Thus, when Blunt asserts in *One, Two, Buckle My Shoe* that "the safety and happiness of the whole nation depends on me," Hercule Poirot counters, "I am not concerned with nations, Monsieur. I am concerned with the lives of private individuals who have the right not to have their lives taken from them" (224). Here, as in Allingham's *Traitor's Purse*, the villain who is condemned and banished from the wartime community is not a social misfit but a powerful mainstream figure whose self-absorption blinds him to the rights of the people whom he leads.

Furthermore, Poirot resembles Albert Campion in *Traitor's Purse* in that he must convict a representative of the same social structure that empowers him as a detective. Although Poirot convicts Blunt and tells him that he was "wrong" when he "sacrificed four human lives and thought them of no account" (224), the detective ruefully concedes that Blunt stands "for all the things that to my mind are important. For sanity and balance and stability and honest dealing" (222) – for the values that underwrite Poirot's sense of law and order. Forced to expose and arrest a villain who shares many of his own political convictions, Poirot comes to question those convictions and to indict the practice of imposing static ideas upon a changing world. As he accuses Blunt "in a tired voice" (224), Poirot sighs and enjoins the youth of the novel to construct a new, more humane world: "The world is yours. [...] In your new world, my children, let there be freedom and let there be pity.... That is all I ask" (225). Even as the novel condemns Blunt as a criminal who fails to recognize the value of individual human lives, it corrects the self-centeredness of upper-class leaders by forcing Poirot to choose humanity over ideology. The "new world" of increasing social mobility created by the war demands not the established ruthlessness of Alistair Blunt but the newfound compassion of Hercule Poirot.

Questioning government leadership in a war-wary Britain, Allingham and Christie reflect a common cultural concern of the early days of the Blitz. Their detective fiction works against generic conventions on this issue, scapegoating political extremists rather than social deviants in order to restore a degree of compassion to British conservatism. The scapegoats in both *Traitor's Purse* and *One, Two, Buckle My Shoe* are certainly criminals, and their punishment returns Britain to the status quo. However, in critiquing the bloated self-importance that leads prominent political figures to abuse their power, both of these novels represent a prevailing cultural anxiety early in the war: that Britain might be misled into betraying the fundamental principles of individuality and freedom, cooperation and fair play that should distinguish it from Nazi Germany. Scapegoating internal rather than external enemies so early in the war, the novels demonstrate a willingness to endorse the progressive values upon which the ideology of the People's War depends.

Many British citizens were eager to discover these values within their own experiences of the Blitz and thus to interpret the solidarity of a nation under siege and the cooperation of British women in the workforce as signs of impending social change. Both Christie and Allingham participated in the People's War and found it exciting. Christie volunteered to fill prescriptions at the dispensary of University College Hospital, and she was so enthusiastic about her job that she called daily to offer herself as a substitute for anyone unable to work. Allingham was enthusiastic as well, volunteering for seven different war jobs in her village, including "emergency food officer," "minder of land girls," and "evacuation officer" (Thorogood 254). In some ways, Christie's and Allingham's war work was typical of women from their social class; like their peers, Christie and Allingham enjoyed their involvement, particularly since they "met a lot of people [they] wouldn't have met otherwise" during wartime (Saywell 16). However, because both authors had already worked as primary wage-earners in their households before the war, they discovered in wartime not the thrill of entering the workforce for the first time but, more significantly, the excitement of meeting and interacting with those who had constituted a vast, faceless audience for detective fiction before the war.[3]

One effect of the novelists' immersion in the People's War was that they, like most British civilians, encountered a variety of different viewpoints that complicated the myth of the Blitz. While both Christie and Allingham enjoyed coming face to face with their previously anonymous audiences, they also recognized that as the war came to a close, there was a conservative backlash against the prospect of postwar social change outlined in the best-selling 1942 Beveridge Report.[4] One Mass-Observation writer admitted that while during the initial Blitz she had "imagined that the war had acted as a leveler in the matter of class" (M-O A: DR 2466, Jan. 1943), she had come to believe by 1944 that class divisions were "normal" and necessary: "I think my attitude to people in different social classes remains the same. They do not really mix. [...] I think that there are bound to be different social classes because tastes differ so" (DR 2466, June 1944). She continues that despite "the generally held idea that 'Jack's as good as his master,' there remains a sort of resentment that this is so, and [...] a looking forward to more 'normal' times when, presumably, everyone will return to their pre-war niches" (DR 2466, June 1944).[5] Although she uses protest quotes to indicate self-consciousness about the word "normal" here, this Mass-Observer nonetheless admits that she is "looking forward" to a return to "pre-war niches" in an established social hierarchy.

Privileged women were not alone in hoping to reinstate the prewar status quo; many men of all classes also supported a postwar re-entrenchment of patriarchal power. Among skilled male craftsmen, in particular, "Craft consciousness [...] ran high – in the sheet metal shops, for instance, the attitude of the skilled men effectively prevented dilution" (Calder, *PW* 330). Legislation such as the 1944 Reinstatement in Civil Employment Act supported the desire to protect male employment by guaranteeing that returning soldiers could reclaim the civil service jobs that they had temporarily abandoned during the war. Seeking to return women as well as men to prewar conventional gender roles, the Conservative Party even went so far as to state the value of mothers in their 1945 general election manifesto:

> Mothers must be our special care. [...] Mothers must be relieved of onerous duties which at such times so easily cause lasting injury to their health. [...] On the birth, the proper feeding and the healthy upbringing of a substantially increased number of children, depends the life of Britain and her enduring glory. (H. Smith 30–1)

Similarly, at the Conservative Party conference in 1945, politicians overwhelmingly rejected the following resolution concerning postwar gender equality:

> That with the object of maintaining in the peace the partnership between men and women as full citizens that has proved so success-ful in war, this Conference affirms its belief that it is in the interest of the nation that opportunities and rewards shall be open equally to both sexes in order to ensure that the best mind or hand shall have the same chance to excel. (H. Smith 74)

The direction of politics after the war therefore became a major source of cultural anxiety in 1945, when even right-wing backing for "power-ful private interests" was typically framed in the liberal language of nationalized health care, education, and welfare systems (Calder, *PW* 532). As the legislation (or rejection of legislation) during the period indicates, egalitarian rhetoric often aimed more to appease women and the working class than to reform a patriarchal and capitalist society. Nevertheless, the possible effects of the People's War still troubled the cultural imagination of conservative Britain. It is this deep-seated fear of social change that underwrites not only reactionary wartime legisla-tion but also conventional scapegoating in wartime detective fiction. By eliminating social and sexual miscreants, both the law and the genre appear to solidify a threatened social order.

Christie and Allingham responded to this cultural anxiety about social change, just as they addressed the public mistrust of political leaders earlier in the war. Yet despite their widely recognized political conservatism, neither of these writers simply upheld the status quo by making scapegoats out of low-life criminals who had violated established boundaries between classes or genders – even though that is what their later war fiction initially appears to do. Instead, both writers capital-ized on conflicting hopes and fears across class and gender lines, creat-ing double-edged representations of crime and punishment in wartime that appealed to readers across the political spectrum. Even as their novels punish social deviants as scapegoats, catering to an elite, con-servative audience, they mount a simultaneous critique of the compul-sion to scapegoat, appealing to disenfranchised or more liberal readers. The critique depends upon the experiences of female characters who, despite the social upheaval of wartime, find very little change in their postwar lives. Using these fictional women to expose the persistence of established class and gender hierarchies, Christie's and Allingham's later war novels suggest that the social order does not really need to be *restored* in detective fiction because it was never significantly challenged by the war. Offering up scapegoats who are as obviously unnecessary as they are obviously guilty, these novels call our attention to the ideological function of the scapegoat and therefore invite us to read their representations of scapegoats ironically.

Before the fiction can critique scapegoating, however, it must first establish how scapegoats typically operate in a detective story. In Allingham's *Pearls Before Swine* (1945, originally published as *Coroner's Pidgin*), detective Albert Campion scapegoats the criminal "swine" who try during wartime to steal "pearls" belonging to the upper class. In this case, the swine are the secretary, Dolly Chivers, and her husband, Theodore Bush. Despite his upper-class status, Bush has married beneath himself for the purposes of securing a partner in crime: Chivers is "terrified of her husband" (205), who "married her to hold her" as "part of the scheme" of stealing valuable works of art during the war (212). The marriage not only blurs class lines but also, because it is more of a business contract than a love match, undermines the conventional relationship between husband and wife. As a male detective defending the social order, Campion scapegoats these villains, whose marriage represents the wartime violation of both class and gender boundaries. He thus effectively restores order to the upper-class world of Lord Johnny Carados, the novel's protagonist, who has been wrongly accused of committing the crime. Like Allingham's earlier *Traitor's Purse*, *Pearls Before Swine* questions the integrity of upper-class authority by encouraging readers to suspect that Lord Carados is guilty of murder. However, while *Traitor's Purse* convicts the upper-class tyrant in response to cultural anxiety about political leadership early in the war, *Pearls Before Swine* exonerates him, punishing instead the deviants who embody later wartime anxieties about social upheaval.

Similarly, in Christie's *Taken at the Flood* (1948), detective Hercule Poirot exposes the guilt of David Hunter, a working-class, cross-dressing murderer. The novel's upper-middle-class protagonist, Lynn Marchmont, served in the WRNS during the war and met men much like Hunter: "Men who were reckless and slightly dangerous. Men whom you couldn't depend upon. Men who made their own laws and flouted the universe" (37). Marchmont is engaged to Rowley Cloade, a man of her own class who stayed at home to farm and thus "hadn't changed" during the war (81), but she is attracted to Hunter, for whom "everything was dangerous" (40). Hunter's world "was not the world that Lynn had been brought up in – but it was a world that held attractions for her nonetheless" (40). By contrasting these two romantic attachments, the novel emphasizes that Hunter is a social and sexual maverick who has violated class boundaries by plotting to steal the Cloades' inheritance and who has transgressed gender lines by disguising himself in women's clothing to avoid detection.

When Hunter is convicted of murder and sentenced to death at the end of the novel, he is also expelled as a scapegoat from the insular world of the Cloades. With suspicions of corruption within their own respectable families thus subdued, Lynn turns back to Rowley:

> I always wanted to marry you, didn't I? And then I got out of touch with you – you seemed to me so tame – so *meek* – I felt life would be so safe with you – so dull. I fell for David because he was dangerous and attractive – and, to be honest, because he knows women much too well. But none of that was *real*. When you caught hold of me by the throat and said if I wasn't for you, no one should have me – well – I knew then that I was *your* woman! Unfortunately it seemed that I was going to know it – just too late. [...] Luckily Hercule Poirot walked in and saved the situation. And I *am* your woman, Rowley! (190–1)

As the enfranchised male detective, Poirot succeeds not only in solving the mystery but also in restoring the status quo in class and gender relations – complete with the violence that hangs men like David even as it catches women like Lynn "by the throat" and forces them to return to their conventionally subordinate positions. The narrative circumscribes and corrects Lynn's desire to cross class and gender boundaries in her war work and love life by scapegoating David Hunter as the manifestation of that desire and then putting Lynn back in her proper place.

Most readings of wartime detective fiction stop here, having identified the conservative reaction to social change. However, because Allingham and Christie reached a market that spanned class lines and, furthermore, because both writers were sympathetic to working women, their use of scapegoats is more complicated than these readings suggest. According to Richard Martin, Allingham "lived an unconventional life for a woman; [...] she worked in order to support her small and predominantly male household," rather than relying on her wayward and unfaithful husband, Pip Carter (121). Similarly, Christie lived what M. Vipond has called "a life of ambivalences": on the one hand, she was "brought up to be a proper upper middle-class wife and mother" and believed herself to fill that role; on the other hand, she experienced a failed first marriage, led a life of professional and financial success, and enjoyed great "independence of mind" (122). Marty S. Knepper emphasizes Christie's appreciation of strong women:

> Christie, while not an avowed feminist, let her admiration for strong women, her sympathy for victimised women, and her recognition of society's discrimination against women emerge in novels written during the decades of the twentieth century more receptive to feminist ideas (such as the 1920s and World War II years). (406)

Based on their own experiences, Allingham and Christie created in their later war fiction female characters who appear to be socially mobile. However, in both *Pearls Before Swine* and *Taken at the Flood*, these women are ultimately confined and constrained by social structures that hinder any advance in women's rights. Juxtaposing representations of female war experience with the conventional scapegoating of criminals who violate class and gender norms, Allingham and Christie question the need for scapegoating in a nation that so effectively resists social and political change.

In *Pearls Before Swine*, Allingham thus scapegoats the deviant criminals, Theodore Bush and Dolly Chivers, even as she describes the apparently liberating wartime experiences of the novel's female protagonist, Susan Shering. Initially, Susan appears to embody the People's War promise of freedom from conventional gender roles. The war gives Susan a feeling that "all was fair in love and war," which leads her to commit herself rather hastily to Tom, the man who becomes her husband after she had known him "exactly six weeks. Five days after we were married he was killed" (56). This speedy wartime courtship also provides the opportunity to cross class lines. Susan describes her engagement to Lord Carados at the end of the war:

> I think Johnny decided to marry me when my husband was killed. [...] Tom was one of Johnny's pilots and he asked Johnny to look after me. When he was killed, Johnny did. It sounds very young and peculiar in this sort of atmosphere, I know, but it wouldn't on an R.A.F. station, you know. (56)

On the surface, Johnny's agreement to care for Susan seems to represent the wartime collapse of class boundaries: Tom and Johnny, pilot and officer, make a pact because they believe that despite their class differences, they are peers in wartime.

However, at the end of the war, both class barriers and patriarchal norms remain intact. Discussing her impending marriage to Johnny, Susan recognizes a postwar social resistance to the wartime transgression of class boundaries: "No one in [Johnny's] home world liked him marrying me, they're quite as insular and all-for-one and one-for-all as Tom's crowd are. I realised that as soon as I saw them. I think Johnny saw it too as soon as he got back amongst them" (57). Social insularity interferes with the marriage plans, and Susan eventually marries another man instead – but only once Johnny gives his blessing. Johnny's letter to Susan and her fiancé, American officer Don Evers, confirms that the patriarchal traffic in women continues, both during and after the war:

> You, Susan, will want to know if I love you. The answer to that is, of course I do, who could help it, but (if you don't understand this, Don will be able to explain it, I think) the feeling I had for old Tom Shering was different, but very, very much stronger. Since you're the girl I know you are, Susan, you won't think me unduly ungallant for this, and as for you, Don, you'll follow me, I fancy. (186)

While Johnny wishes the pair happiness in their marriage, he is far more interested in the wartime relationships between men. Don's comment on the letter – "It's so strong" – validates the network of male bonds that Johnny describes. While Susan finally marries the man she loves, she is not liberated from gender norms in wartime; instead, she remains a loveable object to be protected by and exchanged between men. Rather than restoring the social order by scapegoating deviant characters, the novel therefore insists that the social order was never really under threat, despite the apparent chaos of war.

Written three years after Allingham's *Pearls Before Swine*, Christie's *Taken at the Flood* illustrates even more graphically how unchanging gender roles affected mobile women when they returned home from war. Christie initially describes Lynn Marchmont as a heroine who believes that her wartime experience has significantly changed her:

> And now here she was, out of the Service, free, and back at the White House. She had been back three days. And already a curious dissatisfied restlessness was creeping over her. It was all the same – almost too much the same – the house and Mums and Rowley and the farm and the family. The thing that was different and that ought not to be different was herself. (17)

Lynn's homecoming is difficult because she perceives a postwar return in Britain to traditional gender and class relations: "That's the tragedy everywhere. People coming home changed, having to readjust themselves" to the same old domestic, upper-middle-class routines of housework, family obligations, and marriage (164). Lynn resists these routines because her "outlook has broadened" in wartime; she has "seen a lot of the world in the last three years" (34). When her mother accuses someone of not being "a lady," Lynn scoffs indignantly: "What an expression, Mums! What does that matter nowadays?" (20). Yet despite her mingling with all classes of people in the WRNS, Lynn returns to a world tragically unwilling to accommodate her newfound initiative and skills, and she begins to feel that "the thing that was different and that *ought not to be different* was herself" (my emphasis). Realizing that British women must face the same choices and restrictions after the war as they did before it began, she resigns herself to being "your woman, Rowley" because she sees no way of escaping the history of female subordination.

The novel becomes even more critical as it progresses, suggesting that women's wartime experience itself limits rather than liberates the female mind. Lynn initially believes that war work has allowed women to develop "enterprise, initiative, [and] command" that are wasted in the available jobs for "people who could cook and clean, or write decent shorthand" after the war (18). However, she eventually abandons her conviction that war has changed her:

> Was that what, ultimately, war did to you? It was not the physical dangers – the mines at sea, the bombs from the air, the crisp ping of a rifle bullet as you drove over a desert track. No, it was the spiritual danger of learning how much easier life was if you ceased to think.... She, Lynn Marchmont, was no longer the clearheaded resolute intelligent girl who had joined up. Her intelligence had been specialized, directed in well-defined channels. Now, mistress of herself and her life once more, she was appalled at the disinclination of her mind to seize and grapple with her own personal problems. (80)

Lynn is astonished to recognize not only that the war did not precipitate substantial social change but that it actually discouraged the critical thought that might have allowed women like her to escape from the "well-defined channels" of conventional behavior. Similarly, a young woman in the WAAF tells Mass-Observation that she will "never be able to settle down again after the war," not because her life was so full of excitement during the war but because "we are not having a 'lovely time,' and our life, far from 'exciting,' is more vigorously routined than ever before" (M-O A: FR 1620, 1943: 6). When Lynn Marchmont marries at the end of *Taken at the Flood*, much as Susan Shering does in *Pearls Before Swine*, the suggestion is not merely that the social order has been restored through scapegoating but also that order was more strengthened than threatened by the war.

This representation of female war experience within criminal plots creates the central problem within Christie's and Allingham's war writing. Most obviously, the expulsion of a villainous scapegoat from the confines of upper-class society soothes a conservative fear that wartime social upheaval would change traditional class and gender relations and thus unseat those in power. However, because the scapegoating in these novels is so clearly unnecessary and excessive, it invites readers instead to consider the cost of these conservative values. The scapegoats embody wartime social changes – particularly expanded freedom for women and humane treatment of the working class – that could potentially benefit British society. The blanket dismissal of any threat to established social hierarchies makes criminals not just of the murderers in these novels but also, and more importantly, of the ruling-class elite who protect a power that was never under threat in the first place. If the detective fiction at the beginning of the war critiques the egotism of right-wing leaders such as Lee Aubrey in *Traitor's Purse* and Alistair Blunt in *One, Two, Buckle My Shoe*, the later fiction questions both their political methods and its own generic conventions by exposing the scapegoat as an ideological fiction. Through this exposure, the novels criticize the conservative impulse to fear all social change even as they demonstrate how little there is to fear.

This cultural critique complicates the dominant scholarly view that detective fiction introduces and manages only upper-class anxieties. Instead, Allingham's *Pearls Before Swine* and Christie's *Taken at the Flood* reveal conflicting cultural anxieties. The novels are neither generally conservative nor specifically radical; rather, as market reflections of wartime cultural expectations, they expose specific cultural tensions about class and gender hierarchies under siege and open to question on the British home front. Furthermore, examining two particular historical moments at the beginning and the end of the war demonstrates how these cultural anxieties and tensions changed and developed over time. In a genre that is so focused upon the resolution of the particular problem of murder, it is too easy to believe that once the detective explains his deductions, the case is closed. However, by using villainous scapegoats to examine and critique the very social systems from which they are expelled, Agatha Christie's and Margery Allingham's wartime detective fiction suggests that although the case may be closed, the reader's mind should remain open.

*   *   *

Even more explicitly than Christie and Allingham, Graham Greene experiments with the conventions of genre fiction in his wartime writing. His 1943 novel, *The Ministry of Fear*, self-consciously presents itself as a spy thriller whose hero can never be the hero of a spy thriller, much as he wishes he could be. A depressed and lonely widower, Arthur Rowe wanders into a wartime charity fête, where memories of his carefree youth offer a temptingly regressive escape from the guilt and anxieties of adulthood: entering the fête, "Arthur Rowe stepped joyfully back into adolescence, into childhood" (12). More specifically, when he picks up a "dingy copy" of Charlotte M. Yonge's *The Little Duke* (1854) at the fair's white elephant booth (14), a wistful Rowe longs to step into the pages of his favorite adventure stories, where boys grow up to be heroes rather than neurotics.[6] *The Ministry of Fear* obliges almost immediately and absurdly: Rowe guesses the weight of a cake and wins not only the cake but also the roll of Nazi microfilm that has been baked inside it. The ensuing spy adventure rehearses the plots of the countless Edwardian thrillers that Rowe read as a boy; tellingly, each chapter begins with an epigraph from *The Little Duke*. However, *The Ministry of Fear* introduces a determined hero and a distressed damsel only in order to explode those stereotypes, calling into question the adolescent escapism of a genre that has become a white elephant in the context of the Second World War. Amidst the urban destruction and the social upheaval of the London Blitz, this novel asks not simply whether Rowe can shoulder the burdens of adulthood but, more pointedly, whether the spy genre itself can mature.

The Ministry of Fear begins by invoking the conventions of spy fiction, a genre that had only recently emerged around the turn of the twentieth century. The heroes of early spy novels by writers such as William Le Queux, E. Phillips Oppenheim, Erskine Childers, and John Buchan are typically Oxford- or Cambridge-educated gentlemen, "members of an élite with a traditional right to bear the burden of power and responsibility" within Britain (Stafford 45). Although a "gentleman secret agent" might publicly socialize at clubs and parties, he must privately eschew intimacy, since in these novels the future of England often depends upon the underground work of the lone spy on the run (Stafford 29).

In contrast, the villains in early spy fiction are always foreigners and often outcasts: typically, they are either alienated archenemies, marked by stereotypically German features and obvious physical deformities, or vast, faceless networks of foreign spies. Either way, the villains pose a direct threat to the British social and political institutions defended by early spy heroes, the same institutions that Christie's and Allingham's detectives appear to defend.

The opening chapter of *The Ministry of Fear* overwrites and undercuts these generic conventions by pitting Poole, a Nazi spy assigned to recapture the microfilm hidden in Rowe's prize cake, against Rowe, seemingly remade as a gentleman secret agent. Poole's physical deformity aligns him with the classic villains of early thrillers; when he appears at Rowe's flat, he is described as a "deformed figure" (24): "He was dark and dwarfish and twisted in his enormous shoulders with infantile paralysis" (22). The novel ties this physical difference between hero and villain to the class distinctions that traditionally separate them within the genre; during Poole's visit, Rowe "felt the stranger's eyes on him all the time like a starving man watching through the plate-glass window the gourmet in the restaurant" (26). A German sympathizer described as a "starving man," Poole seems to step straight from the pages of early spy fiction, in which the villains typically embody turn-of-the-century fears about changing class relations and declining imperial power in Britain. These anxieties continued through the Second World War, despite the utopianism and nationalism of the People's War. Although Britain's military strength depended upon its imperial resources and manpower, economic investment in the war necessarily weakened the nation's financial hold upon its colonies. Soon after the war ended in 1945 "came a period of decolonization, a loosening of ties" that would eventually mean the end of the British empire (Dear 1143). As a remedy for these cultural concerns, Poole should serve as a scapegoat whose vulgar manners and crippled body mark his distance from the positive social and moral values embodied by the gentleman secret agent – and who is therefore defeated in an effort to preserve the status quo.

The problem is that Rowe so clearly fails to embody those values himself. Socially and economically, Rowe holds the rank of a gentleman: he spent his childhood "with vicarage gardens and girls in white summer frocks and the smell of herbaceous borders and security" in Cambridgeshire (11), and he is now a retired journalist with "four hundred a year of his own, and as the saying goes, he didn't have to worry" (21). Morally, however, Rowe does have to worry that he cannot be counted a gentleman. A year before the war – and two years before the opening of the novel – Rowe poisoned his terminally ill wife by mixing hyoscine in her evening milk. Although he is publicly acquitted of this "mercy killing" (100), Rowe is privately ashamed of his lack of fortitude: he killed his wife because he could not bear her pain. Locked within the memories of his guilty past, Rowe wishes that the Blitz would destroy the places that remind him of his wife: "After a raid he used to sally out and note with a kind of hope that this restaurant or that shop existed no longer – it was like loosening the bars of a prison cell one by one" (22). Here, Rowe's moral guilt corrupts even his social and economic status: hoping that the Blitz will smash the restaurants and shops of his past, Rowe punishes himself by willing the destruction of the heavy plate-glass window – the protective class barrier – behind which he can afford to dine as the gourmet so envied by Poole.

Despite Rowe's obvious shortcomings as a gentleman, Poole's equally obvious qualifications as a villain tempt Rowe to play the part of the hero – and thus to redress the shortcomings of which he is all too aware. When Poole poisons him with hyoscine (not coincidentally) to get the microfilm, an outraged Rowe rises to confront the villain and, in doing so, to avoid the past: "His chief feeling was astonishment and anger, that anybody should do this to *him*. He dropped the cup on the floor and stood up" (28). Recalling the conventions of early spy fiction, both Rowe and the reader anticipate a showdown between hero and villain. At this climactic moment, however, *The Ministry of Fear* disrupts the expected plot by introducing a sudden and violent twist: "The cripple trundled away from him like something on wheels: the huge back and the long strong arms prepared themselves...and then the bomb went off" (28). Demolishing Rowe's flat, the cake, and the conflict between the would-be hero and his archenemy, the London Blitz destroys the conventional spy story before it even gets started.

Blasted out of the role of gentleman secret agent by this bomb, Rowe hastens to the Orthotex private detection agency, hoping to find the "Justice and Retribution" that a gentleman expects (33). However, all that he finds at Orthotex is Rennit, a world-weary investigator who insists that "I'm not Sherlock Holmes" (32) and prefers cases dealing in the "dull shabby human mediocrity" of marital affairs (33). Discouraged, Rowe takes matters into his own hands, visiting the agency that organized the fête, the Free Mothers, and finding there "the allies he needed" (44): the siblings and Austrian enemy-alien refugees, Anna and Willi Hilfe. At first, Rowe enjoys the brother's enthusiasm; when Willi exclaims, "I'd much rather think, until we *know*, that there's some enormous conspiracy" (45), Rowe recognizes the language of his favorite thrillers. However, he soon finds that Hilfe's "keenness was more damping than her [Anna's] scepticism," and he thus begins to acknowledge the absurdity of his situation: "The whole affair became a game one couldn't take seriously" (45).

Rowe does not laugh at this absurdity: without the game and its role-playing, he must face the depressing fact of his past, which soon leads him to contemplate suicide. Yet before he can throw himself off the Chelsea Bridge, the game begins anew: a shifty, suspicious old man who calls himself a bookseller distracts Rowe from the attempt. Rowe agrees, reluctantly at first, to carry a suitcase ostensibly full of books up to a collector's hotel room, and as the plot begins to thicken, he enjoys the return of "a forgotten sense of adventure" (96). In this excitable state of mind, Rowe discovers his new friend, Anna Hilfe, rather than the collector in the room, and he begins once again to anticipate the plot of his own story based on his knowledge of thriller conventions. Fearing that he and Anna have been targeted by an unknown spy organization, he asks her, "Who are they? I'm in a fog. Are they your people or my people?" When Anna responds that "they are the same everywhere" and that "they are the people who don't care" (100), Rowe is ready to assume a new role – no longer as a gentleman secret agent but now as a lone spy, fighting single-handedly against an anonymous, impersonal enemy. The new script allows Rowe to rewrite his social alienation as self-sufficiency and his loneliness as independence; he thus recasts himself as morally exceptional rather than exceptionable: "They've chosen the wrong man. They think they can get everything by fear. But you've checked up on me. I'm a murderer, aren't I? You know that. I'm not afraid to kill" (104). Previously, Rowe stepped into the role of the hero because he wanted to repress the memory of murder brought on by the taste of hyoscine. Now, Rowe issues himself a license to kill, validating the act of murder as a sign of courage. Yet whether Rowe represses or rationalizes his wife's euthanasia, the novel again prevents him from escaping the past through the fantasy of spying: when Rowe opens the suitcase in search of a weapon with which to fight the faceless enemy, a bomb explodes and nearly kills him. Once more at the end as well as at the beginning of Book One, *The Ministry of Fear* demolishes the conventional spy story before it can begin.

These bombs, which have now twice interrupted Rowe's nostalgic and highly literary fantasies of escape, call attention to the novel's immediate political and historical context. Greene himself spent the early part of the Blitz in London, employed in the domestic branch of the MOI (MI5) by day and serving as an ARP warden by night. While

Greene described civilians whom he saw wounded in the Blitz as "soldiers [...] in grey blood-smeared pyjamas" (*Ways* 92), he dismissed his own propaganda writing for MI5 as "all a game" (Sherry 35–6). In 1941, Greene was recruited to MI6, the foreign branch of British Intelligence, and sent to Sierra Leone to decode enemy radio messages. Reflecting on what had often been portrayed as a great adventure in the pages of spy fiction, Greene insisted that spying does not create heroes: "What I was engaged in through those war years was not genuine action – it was an escape from reality and responsibility" (*Ways* 102). Greene's disillusionment with espionage informs his novel: although Rowe wishes that he could play the part of the spy hero, *The Ministry of Fear* interrogates the conventions of a genre that evades rather than confronts the reality and responsibility of life during wartime.

In thinking about this wartime setting, critics have focused on the destruction of the Blitz, arguing that its violence has various symbolic functions in *The Ministry of Fear*. Most scholars read Rowe's statements about the Blitz – that "thrillers are like life" and that "the world has been remade by William Le Queux" (65) – as evidence that the terror of the bombing transformed the thriller genre into a mimetic genre. According to this view, "The thriller now defines (rather than offers an escape from) the structure of reality" during the war (Silverstein 27).[7] Others suggest that both the Blitz and spying become metaphors for Rowe's personal struggles with "commitment, conscience, individual will, betrayal and alienation" (Panek 112).[8] In aesthetic terms, Damon Marcel DeCoste interprets the bombing as a modernist symbol, arguing that the novel's representation of the spy genre during the Blitz illustrates the "tragic repetition" of an inescapable past (429). Even Brian Diemert, who argues that "*The Ministry of Fear* explicitly shows the failure of one kind of popular literature to remain vital in the new world of the 1940s," reads the Blitz only as a metaphor for the thriller genre's collapse (159).

The Ministry of Fear demonstrates, however, that the Blitz is the direct cause rather than the metaphorical representation of the genre's collapse. No scholarship on the novel has yet looked past the general fact of material violence during the Blitz to examine the specific types of ideological upheaval that the bombing simultaneously produced within British society, the upheaval that has been the focus of this book. While Christie's and Allingham's detective novels represent wartime class and gender hierarchies ambivalently in order to invite a variety of conflicting readings, Greene's spy novel more directly analyzes the impact of particular wartime cultural transformations upon the thriller genre itself. The novel imitates and then destroys the basic conventions of spy fiction, emphasizing in particular Rowe's discomfort with both the passive male civilians and the active female heroes who surround him during the war. In doing so, the narrative suggests that Rowe's personal guilt is symptomatic of the social anxieties experienced by many non-combatant men in wartime Britain. Rowe's escapist spy fantasies therefore offer the hope of more than a personal refuge from the guilt of killing his wife; they promise a political retreat from the larger social problem of defining masculine identity on a home front that seemed increasingly to be dominated by women. Examining the relationship between conventional gender roles and the conventions of spy fiction in the context of the Blitz, *The Ministry of Fear* addresses the gender issues that have informed the genre since its inception in the late nineteenth century.

In particular, nineteenth-century spy fiction repressed the heated debate about women's suffrage during that period by introducing spies who were lone men operating in a world of international political intrigue. David Stafford argues that the standard of the gentleman secret agent in the Edwardian period was a reactionary response to the women's suffrage movement:

> Although those professionally concerned with espionage were sometimes prepared to accept that women could act as secret agents, the novelists of the era decided otherwise. At a time when the suffragettes were stepping up their campaign for a change in the role of women, both Oppenheim and Le Queux set their faces resolutely against change. Together, they established the convention that secret agents, whether accidental or otherwise, should be single men operating in a man's world. (43)

This character type continued into the early twentieth century, when a spy's "license to kill" and ability to disguise himself for the purposes of national security offered a "controlled but total escape from the constraints of self" that typically defined masculine experience (Cawelti and Rosenberg 13–14).

Popular turn-of-the-century spy writers like Le Queux, Oppenheim, and Buchan therefore sold vast numbers of books, particularly to male readers, by creating virile heroes whose power was compromised by neither New Women nor the suffrage movement. Even after the establishment of equal voting rights for British men and women in 1928, the macho conventions of early spy fiction continued to thrive unchallenged until the Second World War.[9] The figure of the male spy operating in a masculine political arena soothed persistent cultural anxieties about female political involvement, anxieties that escalated rather than subsided with the passage of British suffrage laws. The thriller genre continued to uphold traditional boundaries between a feminine domestic sphere and a masculine political arena because many readers wanted to believe in the possibility of doing so, even – or especially – after the political enfranchisement of women.

The Blitz made it impossible to sustain these boundaries, since the bombing effectively collapsed for the duration clear distinctions between masculine and feminine spaces and roles. Mass-Observation materials indicate that regardless of whether they were excited or depressed by the bombing itself, women wanted not only to work during the Blitz, as they had done in the First World War, but also to fight. One working-class housewife declared that she would prefer to "die fighting rather than live the life of a slave" (M-O A: FR 520, 1940: 6), and this upper-middle-class woman agreed when Mass-Observation asked whether she would like to join the women's services herself:

> Yes – because it is service to your country. There are plenty wasting their time that could go in for it. It is not true that it is only for working girls or that it is too hard for the others, they are as strong as working girls, in fact stronger because they have had better food, better advantages, better everything. (M-O A: TC 32/1/E, "Women in the Forces," 1940)

Of course, by 1943, when *The Ministry of Fear* was published, most women were contributing to the war effort in some way, and as Mass-Observation noted in 1942, many people had begun to think that "This is more a woman's war than a man's war on the Home Front now" (M-O A: FR 1238, 1942: 33).

Chapter 3 argued that noncombatant men often felt particularly threatened by this notion of a "woman's war" because as long as the men were not fighting, their ability to measure up to the ideal of the soldier hero remained in question.[10] In response to this situation, some spy writers returned with renewed vigor to the generic conventions established by early spy fiction, offering an escape from wartime gender politics by pretending that the politics did not exist. This response to changing gender roles is much like the false bravado adopted by Arthur Middlewitch in Henry Green's *Back*. Within the popular genre of spy fiction, authors like Peter Cheney, whose "Dark" series of wartime thrillers includes *Dark Duet* (1942), *The Stars are Dark* (1943), *Dark Street* (1944), and *Dark Hero* (1946), created old-fashioned British spy heroes who "catch the villains, win the women, and save the country" (Stafford 157). Like his predecessors, Cheney chose to repress uncomfortable changes in traditional gender roles by creating tough male heroes who were "superior to ordinary citizens" and could thus save those citizens from evil Nazis and Communists (Panek 179). In doing so, Cheney's heroes "build a bridge to the world of [Ian] Fleming," who, like Frederick Forsyth and Ken Follett, continued the trend of focusing popular spy fiction on the male spy hero immersed in political intrigue (Stafford 157). According to Graham Dawson, postwar spies like Fleming's James Bond represented a "new breed of soldier heroes – secular, irregular, firmly distanced from the domestic" that offered a narrative model for imagining an "idealized and desirable masculinity" (190, 249). But the breed was not entirely new. Despite contemporary spy fiction's more detailed descriptions of sex, violence, and technology, these thrillers continued in the masculine tradition established in the genre's infancy.

Graham Greene's *The Ministry of Fear* responds to the gender politics of the Blitz in a very different way: the novel does not evade but rather confronts the tense wartime relationship between political and domestic space – and thus between British men and women – much as Henry Green's fiction does. Foregrounding the sexual politics that thrillers have traditionally repressed, *The Ministry of Fear* interrogates domestic as well as political issues and thus makes possible the emotionally and psychologically complex thrillers of later writers like John le Carré. Le Carré famously intertwines the domestic lives and political missions of his protagonists, reluctant spies who brood about failed relationships as much as they worry about enemy action. In *The Spy Who Came in from the Cold* (1963), Liz Gold is both Alec Leamas's lover, who teaches him the value of "caring about the little things – the faith in ordinary life" (101), and a member of the Communist Party. Similarly, in *Tinker, Tailor, Soldier, Spy* (1974), George Smiley discovers that the mole who has betrayed England to the Soviets is the same man who has previously betrayed Smiley by stealing his wife, Ann. Interrogating the personal lives of his anti-heroic spies, le Carré continues to explore the emotional and psychological territory first charted by Graham Greene.

In *The Ministry of Fear*, that territory initially seems bounded by the dark corners of Rowe's unstable mind and the ragged edges of his broken heart. Yet as the novel progresses, Rowe's inner torment becomes less idiosyncratic and more symptomatic of the wartime anxieties experienced by other men on the British home front. Rowe appears to kill his wife for benevolent reasons, and readers initially share the view of the jury that acquitted him of the mercy killing: he was justified in killing his wife because she was in too much pain to live. However, the truth eventually emerges: Rowe killed Alice not because she was too weak but because she was too strong. In contrast to Rowe, who was too young to fight in the First World War and too old and criminal to fight in the Second, the wife he deems pitifully weak actually embodies the soldier's heroic courage to confront and survive pain. Unable to endure either her pain or her pluck, Rowe poisons Alice to avoid "the agony of watching":

> It was he who had not been able to bear his wife's pain – and not she. Once, it was true, in the early days of the disease, she had broken down, said she wanted to die, not to wait: that was hysteria. Later it was her endurance and her patience which he had found most unbearable. He was trying to escape his own pain, not hers, and at the end she had guessed or half-guessed what it was he was offering her. [...] He had taken the stick and killed the rat, and saved himself the agony of watching. (89–90)

Before the war, the jury's verdict gave institutional backing to Rowe's male authority: as a husband, he had the right to decide whether his suffering wife should live or die. During the war, Rowe realizes that his wife's endurance and patience have become "almost unbearable" because she so clearly embodies the strength that he lacks. Whereas previously this dirty little secret could be covered up by a court ruling, male weakness became no longer a secret but a painfully obvious part of everyday life for civilian men like Rowe on the wartime British home front.

Rowe's cowardly act thus has public as well as private consequences: the euthanasia strips him not only of the role of husband but also of any conventional masculine role during the war:

> I'm not fit enough for the army, and as for the damned heroes of civil defence – the little clerks and prudes and what-have-yous – they didn't want me: not when they found I had done time – even time in an asylum wasn't respectable enough for Post Four or Post Two or Post any number. And now they've thrown me out of their war altogether [...]. It's not my war; I seem to have stumbled into the firing-line, that's all. (76–7)

At the beginning of the war, when many men were leaving for the front line, Rowe was leaving the asylum in which he had been confined after the death of his wife. The few posts that he manages to secure during wartime are always temporary, since the secret of his past always "came out sooner or later, like cowardice" and thus rendered him unfit for any kind of war work (40). Unlike the millions of women employed in civil and military defense during the war, Rowe, along with other, less dramatically displaced civilian men, seems to have no place in the firing line of the London Blitz.

The Ministry of Fear foregrounds the resulting wartime male anxiety about changing gender roles by surrounding Rowe with both disturbingly domesticated men and dauntingly heroic women. After his initial encounter with Poole, Rowe moves quickly from the detective agency, Orthotex, where he meets Detective Rennit, to the headquarters of the Free Mothers, where he meets Anna and Willi Hilfe. At both offices, Rowe must confront his fears of male passivity and domesticity during the war. Rennit dreads murder cases even in wartime and thus handles only "divorces and breaches of promise" at Orthotex (32). Not only does Rennit confine his cases to domestic disturbances, but he also suffers from the stereotypically feminine problem of nerves during the Blitz: "These raids are bad for the nerves. [...] One gets rattled" (32). Similarly, Willi Hilfe, the Austrian volunteer at the Free Mothers, finds that his enemy-alien status limits his options: he fights the war by "collecting woolies from charitable old dowagers" at the office (48). Although this rather passive role turns out to be the disguise of a ruthless Nazi spy, the absurdly domestic nature of Willi's war work initially aligns him with other civilian men like Rennit. Later in the novel, Rowe also encounters Johns, a near-sighted conscientious objector doubly marginalized by his ideological position and his physical condition: "Even if his views had not inclined to pacifism, his bad eyes would have prevented him from being of any active value – the poor things peered weakly and trustfully through the huge convex lenses like bottle-glass; they pleaded all the time for serious conversation" (109). Surrounded by passive men who seem to fight the war in only the most domestic and ineffectual ways, Rowe fantasizes about old-fashioned spy heroics, much like the male civilians in Chapter 3 who fantasized about a postwar return to prewar gender relations.

In contrast to the novel's passive men, its active women succeed at tasks that are both stereotypically masculine and notably difficult for Rowe to perform. For example, in the novel's first chapter, Rowe fails to maintain his own household, even as he adopts the heroic role of the spy. Although his landlady, Mrs Purvis, is essentially a servant who has "done for" him throughout the war, she does so in exchange for rent "because it was her house" in which he stayed (20). In contrast, Rowe has almost no household assets or possessions. After his wife's death, Rowe's home is no longer his castle; all familiar places now constitute for him a psychological "prison cell" from which he hopes the Blitz will spring him: "Perhaps if every street with which he had associations were destroyed, he would be free to go" (22). Passively incarcerated by guilt, Rowe forfeits his household possessions and moves into Mrs Purvis's home: "He had taken the rooms furnished and simply hadn't bothered to make any alterations. [...] The pictures were Mrs Purvis's [...]. The ugly arm-chair, the table covered with a thick woolen cloth, the fern in the window – all were Mrs Purvis's" (20–1). This furnished flat imprisons Rowe even further. Living among Mrs Purvis's possessions, Rowe finds himself complying with her will, even when it conflicts with his own desires. Her nagging "yearning" for his prize cake and her frequent, insinuating query, "Wouldn't you like the cake?" (23), lead Rowe to offer the cake to her and to Poole, even as he weakly mumbles, "I think we had better finish the biscuits first" (23). Rowe cannot assert himself as a male head of household during the war because he is confined within both his guilt and his rented room. His relationship with the mild-mannered Mrs Purvis already undermines his masculine authority even as he prepares to confront Poole – and thus gives early warning of the bomb that will explode Rowe's male fantasy at the end of this chapter. The Blitz, whether in the form of warheads or women, renders conventional gender roles and adolescent spy fantasies obsolete.

After this first bomb explodes, Rowe tries to borrow money from his friend, Henry Wilcox, and finds himself unmanned once again by a powerful woman. Doris Wilcox is Henry's "masterful wife" who has proudly displayed her many prewar field hockey trophies on the mantle in their home (81); during wartime, she starts "playing for England" instead as an ARP warden (84). When Rowe coincidentally arrives at the Wilcoxes' flat just in time for her funeral, he learns that Mrs Wilcox has died as a wartime "heroine" in a daring rescue attempt during the Blitz (85). Her husband identifies with Rowe, blaming himself for his wife's death: "I killed my wife too. I could have held her, knocked her down" (84). More than the act of murder, it is Henry's guilty passivity and his reputation around the ARP post as "a very sensitive gentleman" that connects him to Rowe (86). While Rowe asserts throughout the novel that "the army wouldn't have him" (21), Doris Wilcox has volunteered for service on the "front line" in London:

> After the ruins of St. James's Church, one passed at that early date into peaceful country. Knightsbridge and Sloane Street were not at war, but Chelsea was, and Battersea was in the front line. It was an odd front line that twisted like the track of a hurricane and left patches of peace. Battersea, Holborn, the East End, the front line curled in and out of them. (81)

Mrs Wilcox has given her life on this front line, and although her funeral initially seems to the embittered Rowe "like a parody of a State funeral," he must ultimately concede that Doris deserves to receive the George Medal for civilian heroism posthumously and that "this *was* a State funeral" (86).[11] Conspicuously alienated and denied such war work, Rowe tries to convert his liabilities into strengths: he fancies himself a lone undercover spy hero. However, Rowe's encounter with Doris Wilcox's heroics on the home front exposes once again the escapism of his wartime spy fantasy and thus leads directly to the novel's second literal explosion of spy conventions.

In each of the preceding examples, it is possible to understand these women's power as a temporary byproduct of the war: women who would in peacetime be servants or field hockey players have in wartime become householders and war heroes. However, the novel shows that the war does not produce but rather amplifies existing gender conflicts that will remain even after the war is over. Rowe's passive and anxious relationships with Mrs Purvis and Mrs Wilcox are extensions of problems he had with his wife before the war; just as his relationships with these women emphasize his wartime passivity, his prewar crime of euthanasia now prevents him from seeing either frontline or home-front action. The issue, then, is not that Rowe is weak only in wartime but that his weakness has finally become fully visible under the pressure of the Blitz.

Rowe attempts to repress the knowledge of his weakness by trying on what appears to be the courageous role of the spy hero. However, even as he becomes involved with espionage at the fête, he finds his adventure shaped more by the women surrounding him than by his own choices or actions. He enters the fortune teller's booth at the instigation of an anonymous woman: "A lady caught his arm and said, 'You must. You really must. Mrs Bellairs is quite wonderful'" (15). Rowe remains skeptical of Mrs Bellairs's powers, even if he feels compelled first to follow the woman's advice and then to repeat her description of the "wonderful Mrs Bellairs" (99, 157). As he enters the fortune-telling booth, Rowe anticipates finding no one of consequence: "He had expected the wavering tones of a lady whose other hobby was water-colours" (15). However, Mrs Bellairs is not simply a garden-party hobbyist, and her authoritative tone surprises Rowe: "He was unprepared for Mrs Bellairs's deep powerful voice: a convincing voice" (15). A powerful grip matches her deep voice; haunted by memories of his own mercy killing, Rowe tentatively holds out his hand for a palm reading and "felt it gripped firmly as though she intended to convey: expect no mercy" (16). When the novel reveals that Mrs Bellairs is a Nazi spy, her commanding voice and merciless grip begin to make sense: she mistakes Rowe for a co-conspirator, gives him the password to win the cake, and thus pulls him forcibly into the drama of wartime espionage. Even when the real Nazi courier finally arrives at the close of the fête, "He kept in the dusky background by the cake-stall and let the ladies fight for him" rather than approaching Rowe directly to claim his cake (20). From the first scene of the novel, women assume an active wartime role not simply in domestic but also in political matters, a role that suggests a change in what it means to be a "Free Mother" during the war. One might read this scene as an effort to placate patriarchal anxiety about changing gender roles by aligning politically active women with a Nazi Germany that is no match for the hero that Rowe imagines himself to be. More disturbingly, however, the contrast between the mercy killer and the merciless Nazi politicizes the home front and prepares readers for the contrast between Rowe and the many strong British women who will shape his life during the London Blitz. Although women such as Alice Rowe, Mrs Purvis, Mrs Wilcox, and even Mrs Bellairs appear to be only tangentially related to Rowe's spy adventures, they shape Rowe's identity by usurping practically every stronghold of patriarchal power and thus forcing him to define his masculinity through the nostalgic fantasy of spying. Ironically, Rowe enters the fantasy world of masculine action and heroism only when driven there by the forceful Mrs Bellairs.

Surrounded by these strong women, Rowe desperately tries to conceal a secret that can no longer be kept; he represses not only the personal memories but also the socio-political conditions that undermine his masculine identity. Early in his spy adventures, Rowe chooses to ignore a building burning in a London air raid because he is too busy thinking about his own heroics: "None of these things mattered. They were like something written; they didn't belong to his own life and he paid them no attention" (63). However, once his spy fantasy is twice exploded, it becomes clear that Rowe's storybook exploits, rather than the effects of the Blitz, "were like something written." Conveniently, Rowe loses his memory at this point, having sustained an injury in the second explosion: only amnesia could allow one to have "even forgotten the war" at the height of the Blitz (115). The novel describes the asylum in which he is confined for the treatment of memory loss as a "shell-shock clinic" because, like the soldiers of the First World War, Rowe must recover from the psychological trauma of the war by retreating into safety far away from the front line (110). In this case, however, Rowe's front line is on the home front, and the cause of his trauma is not the carnage of dead men in the trenches but the courage of living women in the Blitz.

Rowe's amnesia works much like traditional escapist spy fiction, catapulting him back into adolescence and thus allowing him to forget both personal problems and social conflicts. At the clinic, Rowe can "remember things quite clearly until say, eighteen" (110), but he recalls neither the mercy killing nor the war. Without his adult memories, Rowe embodies the condition of the ideal thriller reader, and he can therefore immerse himself fully in dreams of boyhood adventure, as he has wanted to do since the beginning of the novel. He feels "like a schoolboy" stricken by a "mood of high adventure" as he sneaks into the clinic's sick bay where his fellow inmate, Major Stone, has been unjustly confined (135, 136). Furthermore, Rowe's newfound feelings of "adolescent love" for Anna Hilfe inspire his adventure, making him try to act "heroic and worthy of someone in love" (130, 136). The problem, however, is that once he has lost his memory, Rowe is no longer trying to recapture adolescence; he is now trying to recover adulthood. As his search for memories of "the real adult life" intensifies (139), Rowe becomes increasingly dissatisfied with the conventions of adolescent spy fiction.

This change in attitude begins when Rowe first feels pity for Stone, who is locked in a straitjacket in the sick bay of the asylum: "It was horrible hearing a middle-aged man sobbing invisibly behind a locked door. [...] A terrible sense of pity moved him; he felt capable of murder for the release of that gentle tormented creature" (140–1). Rowe recalls the feeling that motivated his mercy killing, but instead of pitying his sick wife, he now pities a shell-shocked soldier confined because he "had an obsession" with combating Nazi "treachery" at the asylum (134, 141). Catching a glimpse of his own pathetic delusions in "poor imprisoned Stone" (139), Rowe hurriedly leaves the sick bay in search of the newspapers that, like his crime of euthanasia, have been hidden from him. He discovers in "these months-old newspapers" both facts about the war and the story of his own murder trial (142–3), and he resolves to leave the asylum and to stop escaping from reality: "I've escaped long enough: my brain will stand it" (148). For Rowe, the escape has largely been from the sexual politics that were sublimated by the murder and then illuminated by the Blitz: playing the part of the adolescent spy hero, he has been trying to evade the facts not only of his wife's superior courage but also of his own inferior position in wartime England. In order to recuperate his mature memory, he must confront both the personal problems and the social conflicts that threaten his masculine identity – the same difficulties from which the adolescent fantasies of spying have traditionally offered a retreat.

Rowe tries to face these difficulties when he leaves the asylum and returns to London. Seeing the ruins of the Blitz, he confesses his anxiety:

> What frightens me [...] is knowing how I came to terms with it before my memory went. When I came in to London today I hadn't realized there would be so many ruins. Nothing will seem as strange as that. God knows what kind of ruin I am myself. Perhaps I *am* a murderer? (163)

Identifying himself with the ruins and actively seeking to confront both his personal past and his political present, Rowe seems to have outgrown the boyish fantasies about wartime adventure that require him to ignore the Blitz. However, after this thoughtful look at the bombed-out buildings, he accidentally mentions Anna Hilfe's name to the police and reverts once again to his adolescent desire to defend his damsel in distress: "He was helping in a great struggle, and when he saw Anna again he could claim to have played a part against her enemies" (176). As he thinks about Anna, his view of the Blitz changes once again; rather than ignoring it or identifying with it, he now rationalizes its existence as an extension of his heroic role: "The ruins from which they emerged were only a heroic back-cloth to his personal adventure" (176). This treatment of the Blitz is much like Rowe's treatment of the murder: after failing to repress it by immersing himself in spying, he tries to rationalize it as the background of his current license to kill. Unable to ignore the Blitz any longer, Rowe makes sense of it here by claiming that it, too, is no more than a reflection of his spy heroics.

Like the murder, however, the Blitz destabilizes the gender stereotypes of male protector and female victim that underwrite the conventions of Rowe's beloved spy fiction. Enamored of the genre, he is blind to anything but the most superficial relations between Anna and himself. Thus, Rowe becomes "happily drunk with danger and action" while chasing the Nazi spies alongside a British Intelligence officer (176), primarily because he imagines dazzling Anna with stories of his adventures when he returns home: "He wanted to boast like a boy to Anna – 'I did it' " (187). Yet as Rowe's relationship with Anna intensifies, he must question those gender stereotypes that have previously allowed him both a legal escape from the murder of his wife and a literary escape from the trauma of the Blitz. Gradually learning to interrogate the conventions of both gender and genre, Rowe begins to recognize the "violent superficial chase" of the Nazi spies as a "cardboard adventure hurtling at seventy miles an hour along the edge of the profound natural common experiences of men" (178). He slows down to notice the common experiences of "a woman [...] giving birth" and "two people [...] seeing each other for the first time by the light of a lamp" (178) and feels a sudden, intense longing for adult domestic life with Anna, much as Leamas feels in le Carré's *The Spy Who Came in from the Cold* when he resolves to return to Liz with a newfound "respect for triviality" (101). Undercutting the cardboard political adventure that Rowe has so naïvely pursued, the sharp desire for a domestic relationship forces him to grow up: "The longing was like the first stirring of maturity when the rare experience suddenly ceases to be desirable" (178–9).

Rowe has desired the rare and exciting experience of living a spy thriller because it has allowed him to imagine becoming a hero within a vast political sphere reserved exclusively for men, a domain that seemed no longer to exist during the Second World War. According to his adolescent fantasy, Rowe's own spy story should climax on a grand scale with a thrilling confrontation between the heroic Rowe and the villainous Hilfe, much like the thrillers of Cheney or Fleming. However, in this wartime novel, the British hero and the Nazi villain meet not on the battlefield but in the bathroom: "The adventure he had pictured once in such heroic terms had reached its conclusion in the Gentlemen's" (214). The climactic scene is both a comic parody and a serious critique of boys' adventure fiction. Caught in the men's room during a particularly violent air raid, Rowe represents both the traditional spy and the conventional man under siege during the war. Classic spy fiction imagines a public space where heroes and villains square off man to man – and where the hero gets to plug the villain in the final scene. In contrast, *The Ministry of Fear* imagines the extremely private space of the lavatory stall where the villain retreats to shoot himself after begging a penny for the pay toilet from the hero. This parody of a heroic showdown illustrates quite graphically that the only purely masculine space remaining during the People's War is in the public toilet.

Even as conventional masculinity comes under siege in the Gentlemen's, the conventionally passive damsel in distress takes on an active role. Joining the ranks of *The Ministry of Fear*'s wartime women in action such as Alice Rowe, Mrs Purvis, Doris Wilcox, and Mrs Bellairs – and prefiguring independent women such as le Carré's Liz Gold and Ann Smiley – Anna Hilfe becomes "someone perpetually on guard to shield" Rowe from the past she believes he still cannot remember (221). Her protection forces Rowe to reassess his stereotypical views of men and women and to stop demanding that she play the victim. Furthermore, he realizes that his own desire to protect her is now much more than the immature fantasy of heroism that it once was: "He felt an enormous love for her, enormous tenderness, the need to protect her at any cost" (221). Rowe no longer feels threatened by the strength of a woman, as he did when caring for and then killing his wife. Instead, he values Anna's protection of him enough to conceal the truth from her: his memory has already returned intact. Rowe and Anna attempt a highly fraught renegotiation of masculine and feminine roles within their private relationship that corresponds to the equally fraught renegotiation of gender roles in Britain as a result of the Blitz.

Whether or not this renegotiation ends happily is far from clear at the ambivalent conclusion of the novel. Rowe and Anna must "tread carefully for a lifetime, never speak without thinking twice; they must watch each other like enemies because they loved each other so much" (221). In Greene's world, this is true love – or at least the truth about love, which cannot be sustained without deception, evasion, or pretense. But the novel's ambivalence, its refusal to provide the happy ending of conventional spy fiction, is in fact more productive than problematic; as Rowe concedes in the closing line, "After all, one could exaggerate the value of happiness" (221). More importantly, the end of the novel politicizes the private realm of sexual relations and emotional experience by positing an imaginary "Ministry of Fear" even more extensive and powerful than the actual wartime MOI: "It wasn't [a] small Ministry [...] with limited aims like winning a war or changing a constitution. It was a Ministry as large as life to which all who loved belonged. If one loved one feared" (220). The fraught sexual politics that remain either repressed or only crudely expressed in traditional spy fiction emerge explicitly here as the central concern they have always been, represented in the sophisticated terms they have always merited. By insisting that covert surveillance and political intrigue are always a part of love, *The Ministry of Fear* enlarges the scope of the spy thriller, which can now include the emotional dangers and psychological conflicts of everyday life.

Greene therefore domesticates the genre not to tame but to modernize it, exchanging high-speed chases for streams of consciousness and foreign enemies for the alienated self. Recognizing that "it was no longer a Buchan world" (*Ways* 55), Greene remakes the world of adolescent spy fantasies introduced by writers like Le Queux, Oppenheim, and Buchan and thus compels both Rowe and the genre to mature in the context of the Second World War. Offering no escape from this war, Greene's spy novel works much like Christie's and Allingham's detective fiction: it examines and critiques the cultural anxieties about social and sexual politics preoccupying the imaginations of civilians in wartime Britain. These issues also shaped the stories and novels of the Blitz by Elizabeth Bowen, Rosamond Lehmann, and Henry Green. The fact that popular genre fiction shared some of the same concerns as highly literary fiction of this period suggests a widespread cultural need to imagine the People's War not simply as an ideal that could unify the nation but also as an idea about which Britain must remain free to disagree, even – or perhaps especially – in the face of Nazi attack.

5
The Film-Minded Public

As much as pulp fiction, wartime British films appealed to the home-front popular imagination. Mass-Observation founder Tom Harrisson declared that "from the beginning film was of the highest interest to us, we were film-minded" ("Films" 235). Mass-Observation was not alone; although "the British film industry was brought practically to a stand-still by the suspension of the Quota Act" during the first three months of the war (M-O A: TC 17/2/G, "Film Report," 1940), industry leaders like Michael Balcon recognized the need for the nation itself to become "film-minded."[1] In a 22 April 1940 letter to the *Daily Telegraph*, Balcon argued "that there is only one kind of film which can properly project the British point of view, and that is the British film" (qtd in M-O A: TC 17/2/H, "Film Stars," 1940). Although audiences generally had broader tastes – enjoying MGM's *Gone With the Wind* (1939) or Disney's *Pinocchio* (1940) as much as London Film Productions' *The Lion Has Wings* (1939) or Ealing's *Let George Do It* (1940) – wartime ticket sales suggest that the British public was as film-minded as industry insiders. Mass-Observation found that "the average weekly audience at cinemas rose from 19 million in 1939 to 31.4 million in 1946, the peak year of attendance in British cinema history. Gross box office receipts trebled" (Richards and Sheridan 12). In a wartime social survey of over 5000 civilian men and women selected from a range of occupations and regions, Mass-Observation learned that "70% of adult civilians sometimes go to the cinema and 32% go once a week or more often" (M-O A: FR 1871, 1943: 1). According to Guy Morgan, "It was a phase without precedent in the history of the cinema, a phase never to be repeated, and it furnishes striking testimony of the essential part that the cinema has come to play in the life of the community at war" (10).

In 1939–40, members of the film industry eagerly forecast an essential role for cinema in the war effort: "Everyone in the cinema industry believed, and had some reason to believe, that the cinema could do big things in war and would be encouraged to do so" (M-O A: TC 17/2/G, "The Cinema," 1940). However, government bureaucracy and censorship quickly undercut these hopes, as this Mass-Observation report suggests:

> Unfortunately for the cinema elderly people took charge of the war. Many in our cabinet are far from cinema fans. The principal responsibility for the film industry in war time went to a large film department set up in the Ministry of Information [...]. The achievements of the film section as far as we can learn, from scores of interviews with people in all parts of the film industry, from our own experiences with the Ministry and our intimate contacts with people in it, are staggeringly little in the first three months of the war. The most severe restrictions prevented film units from taking films about the countryside in Britain, the most severe censorship prevented the showing of films from the front, and so every sort of film production and organization had to get sanction from the Ministry. (TC 17/2/G, "The Cinema")

No longer protected from American competition and without a government plan for wartime film distribution, British filmmakers were unsure about how to proceed during the war. A November 1939 letter from Mass-Observation concerning the MOI Films Division indicates the frustration of British directors:

> Incidentally, I had yesterday one of the GPO [General Post Office] film unit directors here, and even they, let alone the other unofficial film interests, are going nearly mad with grief and rage against the opportunities that have been wasted in this war for the intelligent use of films. (M-O A: TC 17/2/F, "Letter to Geoffrey Le Mander," 1939)

According to James Chapman, the MOI's problems resulted from poor planning before the war and inadequate policy initiatives during the short terms of the first two directors of the Films Division: Joseph Ball and Kenneth Clarke. It was not until the 1940 appointment of Jack Beddington that the division began to create specific policies guiding the production of wartime film propaganda.[2] In response to this early lack of direction, Michael Balcon wrote his impassioned letter to the *Daily Telegraph* and Mass-Observation began recruiting its wartime film panel. Both moviemakers and advocates recognized the growing need during the war for a national film industry engaged with the film-minded public.

The question, however, was what exactly this public had in mind. Previous chapters on the fiction of the Blitz have revealed tensions and disagreements within British public opinion, exploring in particular changing perceptions of class and gender identity in wartime. Juxtaposing factual and fictional accounts of individuals engaged in the People's War, these chapters have argued that British literature of the Blitz represents the People's War as a fundamentally conflicted ideal that helped to define national identity in a time of crisis. Chapter 4 took these ideas to market, analyzing how popular detective and spy novels drew wide audiences by representing both accord and discord within the myth of the Blitz. This chapter extends the line of thought about literary and pulp fiction to the movie theater, where even civilians unable or unwilling to read could find imaginative representations of the People's War. Following what Arthur Marwick has called the "law of the market," I will take four box-office smashes as case studies; Marwick argues that "the bigger its commercial success, the more a film is likely to tell us about the unvoiced assumptions of the people who watched it" (*Class* 22). However, "the people" in the audience are always individuals who have many different assumptions. The films that succeeded commercially were therefore the ones most capable of "reflecting *back* to a wide audience something of itself, whether conscious or not: a mood, conflict, need, aspiration of some kind, put into dramatic form" (Barr 8). These reflections were necessarily multifaceted, mirroring the reality of audience diversity even as they created the illusion of national unity.

Initially, many civilians treated London cinemas like bomb shelters with the added value of entertainment. In the first week of the war, all movie theaters closed temporarily, but most reopened to high demand soon thereafter: not only did people crave social interaction during the blackout, but they also enjoyed – and were willing to pay for – the distraction of films. When air raids began a year later in September 1940, many London theaters responded by remaining open 24 hours a day. Running projectors from 10:00 a.m. to 5:00 a.m. the following day, cinemas stopped their showings only for brief intervals of sleep: "By 4 a.m. or 5 a.m. most people had had enough and the auditorium and the lounges would be full of sleeping figures" (G. Morgan 32). One woman recalls working as an usher during the Blitz:

> They put a slide up on the screen during an air raid, "Those wishing to leave may do so but the programme will continue." They usually stayed and if it was still raging, the usherettes, rather than go home at half past ten at night, we used to just go down into the intake room – that's where all the light switches and knobs and things are – and we used to put palliases on the floor and just lay there until it was all over. They were given the choice of leaving or staying but the majority decided they were just as safe as walking the streets. Big pieces of shrapnel used to fall and you could get injured with shrapnel. ("Betty")

After the first week of the Blitz, however, the strain on theaters became too great. At the Granada, Tooting, the manager finally went on stage and announced that "whereas the show would go on, at its conclusion patrons not wishing to take the risk of walking home would find ample air-raid shelters outside THAT exit"; the staff were relieved to find that "when 'The King' was played, the audience moved quietly out through the exit so imperiously indicated" (G. Morgan 33). These early days of the Blitz revealed the unifying role that cinemas could play in the People's War, even within shortened hours of operation. Writing only three years after the war, Guy Morgan comments on the end of 24-hour cinema operation: "Other cinemas followed suit; the interlude of all-night entertainment was over; audiences, in a new-found spirit of comradeship and cooperation, made no complaint" (33). Morgan draws heavily on the rhetoric of the People's War, suggesting that a spirit of comradeship and cooperation united British civilians not only in the workplace and bomb shelter but also in the cinema.

However, that unity was only ever an ideal, not a reality. A letter drafted by Mass-Observation in 1939 for newspaper publication begins by acknowledging characteristic differences among British viewers:

> There is no need to go any farther than these columns to realize what wide differences there are in the tastes and ideas of cinemagoers. A word in praise of Clark Gable will bring a chorus of complaint, and one critic of Garbo or Lamarr will cause twenty to speak in her favour. Some want more war pictures or comedies or musicals; others

want less. Some like every film that is made in this country; others deride the whole British film industry. (M-O A: TC 17/2/G, "Letter from Film Observer," 1940)

The letter goes on to express Mass-Observation's desire to find consensus among potential film-panel volunteers despite variations in public taste: "Mass-Observation, an organization concerned mainly with public opinion, believes that there are fundamental points of agreement, and is trying to find out all it can about picturegoers in this country, their habits, their likes and dislikes" (TC 17/2/G, "Letter"). The government clearly needed such information, and Home Intelligence commissioned Mass-Observation to report its findings about civilian morale – including attitudes toward the cinema – to Sir John Reith, the new Minister of Information, beginning in 1940.[3]

The tasks of Mass-Observation and the MOI were difficult. In addition to sorting out differences in public taste, these agencies discovered opposing views within the industry itself about documentary and commercial filmmaking:

In formulating a film propaganda policy the MOI Films Division [...] had to deal with two different interest groups which each had its own particular agenda to pursue. The approach which was adopted was to try to incorporate both groups within official policy so that both were harnessed to the national propaganda effort. (Chapman 53)

The result, however, was not a unified film industry but a continuing, often frustrating debate about how best that industry might serve the nation at war. Initially, documentary newsreels seemed to be the best propaganda choice, since there were already five existing private newsreel companies in 1939, and the government had therefore only to begin supervising their continued production of news footage. Yet public taste once again became a factor. Some people considered the newsreels to be very informative; for example, one woman recalls, "You felt as though you really knew what was going on when you saw the newsreels. It wouldn't have been much if they'd left that out" ("Peggy"). A Deptford man emphasized the particular value of newsreels to the working class: "The news was one of the main elements of the [film] programme. It was a bit later than the newspapers, of course, but it was the only way of seeing – visually – what was going on. And most people round Deptford couldn't read!" ("Bill"). However, other audience members were more skeptical, as Mass-Observation noted in an October 1940 "Newsreel Report":

> Newsreels have lost a very considerable amount of their popularity in the last six months, and the number of those who actively dislike the reels has trebled and reached 50 per cent. In December [1939] nearly a quarter of the people questioned liked the newsreels immensely: "They are interest number one," "I go to see them." In the following August [1940] less than 10 per cent of those who like them are really enthusiastic about the reels. (Richards and Sheridan 409)

Most dissatisfied viewers expressed the opinion that "the newsreels contain no news; 35 per cent of the 50 per cent who dislike them give this as a reason, and they come from both sexes and middle and working class alike" (Richards and Sheridan 409–10).

The viewers expressed particular disdain for films "made up of reconstructed or faked news," which presented not actual footage of the reported events but recycled images from previous productions, both documentary and fictional (Richards and Sheridan 411). At times, newsreels added "a great deal of sound [...] from material in their libraries" and therefore gave audiences "a completely false interpretation of the evidence" (M-O A: FR 16, 1940: 1). Noticing this trend, Mass-Observation began investigating the use of staged footage in newsreels. In one instance, "A cameraman told an observer [...] that a regiment of soldiers had been marched backwards and forwards over a hill for a whole morning for the benefit of a newsreel"; another observer discovered that "on another occasion a tank was shot being loaded on to a ship for France, but as soon as the cameras had stopped it was taken off again as the ship was never able to carry such cargo" (M-O A: FR 16: 2). The public had very little patience for newsreels that obviously reconstructed the news or tried to manipulate the audience:

> British Paramount news (20.11.40) cut shots of crashed bombers with violent action pictures prefaced with some remarks such as "this is what it would have looked like"; at the Free News Theatre, Piccadilly Circus, an observer heard one man say "of course this isn't real" and at the Paramount Tottenham Court Road the next day, some laughed at this sequence. (M-O A: FR 16: 3)

If viewers were not laughing, they were often crying. Audiences also tended to balk at newsreels that created a "horrifying effect" by showing too much violence: "An observer in Streatham heard one elderly working-class woman say, 'Gertie and I cried all through the newsreel. Those poor boys out there in all that. The pictures were terrible'"; similarly in a Watford cinema another observer overheard two young women comment on shots of an air raid: "I don't think they should show you this, do you?" (M-O A: FR 215, 1940: 1–2). Whether the newsreels erred on the side of horrible facts or laughable lies, public dissatisfaction with them prompted the government to develop more effective forms of wartime film propaganda.

Even as newsreel popularity waned in late 1939 and early 1940, the MOI established a policy for short propaganda film production. On 3 July 1940, the Ministry announced the innovation in the London *Times*:

> Five-minute films covering food rationing, home defence, air-raid precautions, and similar subjects will soon be a feature at all the 4,000 cinemas in the country. Members of the Cinematograph Exhibitors' Association have offered to show such official films free of charge. Leading producers and directors have put their services at the disposal of the films division of the Ministry of Information for the expert and rapid production of official films. (qtd in Chapman 93)

Made in both documentary and fictional forms and designed to accompany feature films in British cinemas, these shorts not only followed the Ministry's policy of engaging its two main interest groups but also rose "very considerably higher" in public opinion than more blatant forms of propaganda (Richards and Sheridan 441).[4] The secret to the success of the shorts was their willingness to treat audiences not simply as a People's Army united in the dark of bombed theatres but as intelligent individuals entitled to their own opinions. Mass-Observation found in 1940 that

> audience response to film propaganda has been very high and very favourable except in the few cases where the propaganda has been obvious; as one worker aged 20 told an observer, "I think it un-British to shove propaganda down your throat like that; they should regard us as more intelligent than that." (M-O A: TC 17/2/G, "Film Report," 1940)

Film critic Dilys Powell also observed that wartime audiences demanded intelligent treatment:

> The British public, always a cinema-going public, has become doubly so during the war years. And with the increase in numbers, a certain

sharpening of public taste is to be observed. Themes which would once have been thought too serious or controversial for the ordinary spectator are now accepted as a matter of course. [...] There is a desire for solidity and truth, even in the sphere of entertainment. We have seen how the semi-documentary film has gained a hold over British imaginations. We have seen too how even in the film of simple fiction, the demand has grown for knowledge and understanding. The British no longer demand pure fantasy in their films; they can be receptive also to the imaginative interpretation of everyday life. (*Films* 39–40)

Audiences wanted films to give them information to evaluate; they therefore scorned both bogus newsreels and heavy-handed propaganda shorts, asking instead for more realistic and open-ended representations that allowed them to imagine their everyday lives in new and interesting ways.

For example, a 1940 Mass-Observation report contrasts audience reactions to two shorts shown at the Empire theater in Leicester Square: "Miss Grant Goes to the Door," the more popular short, "was very well received by the audience who clapped loudly at its conclusion; it was far better received than the 'Food for Thought' short" (M-O A: TC 17/4/F, "Film Reports 1938–46 – 'Miss Grant Goes to the Door,'" 1940). Mass-Observation records one lower-middle-class woman's comment:

> I like the Ministry shorts a lot but they're going off a lot. They're pure propaganda. That one last week all about your dustbins, that was obvious propaganda from beginning to end. Not like that one about the invasion. That sticks, you remember that when you forget the other. (M-O A: FR 394, 1940: 3)

"Food for Thought" follows the lead of "that one [...] all about your dustbins," explaining in detail the nutritional value of various foods and giving viewers advice about how to eat wisely. In contrast, "that one about the invasion" sticks in people's minds because it describes the crucial mistakes that Miss Grant and her spinster sister make, even as they manage to capture a German soldier at gunpoint: they turn on a light in the blackout, believe that the German parachutist is an ARP warden, and underestimate the treachery of the enemy. Mass-Observers noticed that the mistakes, in particular, drew audience commentary:

> On one occasion a woman sitting next to [Mass-]obs[erver] jumped when Miss Grant got knocked out, and turned to obs[erver] (a total

stranger) and said, "Oh, she shouldn't have done that, should she?" There was regular audible comment at the light being turned on, the church bells, the pseudo-English officer, and the useless car, these usually taking the form of one person explaining to a friend what was happening. (M-O A: TC 17/8/A, "Memo on 'Miss Grant Goes to the Door,'" 1940)

People discussed "Miss Grant" because they were trying to articulate what she should and "shouldn't have done" and "what was happening" in the short. Shot realistically and designed to present viewers with events that they might plausibly encounter themselves, the film let individuals think for themselves:

> It gave the public a chance to guess that it was wrong to put the lights on, that an invasion had started and so on; the audience saw the point each time and commented to friends to show how clever they were. People are more likely to remember what they have found out for themselves than what they have been told. (TC 17/8/A, "Memo")

Mass-Observation monitored six different showings of "Miss Grant" and noted its consistent success: "Every time it has met with excellent reception. There has been considerable applause for it in West End cinemas, and in local cinemas the degree of response has been quite exceptionally high" (TC 17/8/A, "Memo").

Viewers clearly preferred newsreels and shorts that respected rather than insulted their intelligence, but they could actually demand respect from the feature films they paid to see. Many recent film historians have identified the feature film as "the most representative example of the cultural and ideological values" of its viewers because "it is the feature which draws people into the cinemas and which appeals to the widest audiences" (Chapman 58). A 1940 Mass-Observation report on the working-class people living in London's East End identifies a widespread craving for movies even among those civilians with little time or money: "The cinema plays an important part in Stepney life. There are a lot of cinemas, and they are all full, every night – 'Standing room only, I/6 – queuing for 6d, 9d, and 1 pound'" (M-O A: TC 17/3/E, "Cinemas in Bermondsey and Stepney 1940–41," 1940). Even outside the cinemas, people were thinking about the movies: "Apart from the war, the cinema is the main theme of conversation. As soon as I entered a café (2.7.40) the proprietor wanted to know if I could tell him what was on at the Classic. (All seats one price – 6d)" (TC 17/3/E, "Cinemas"). The Wartime Social Survey of 1943 reports that "eighty percent of those who proclaimed themselves to be 'cinema enthusiasts' were from the lower economic groups" (Fox 826), and the high demand among the working classes for the cinema did not subside once the bombing began. Cinemas were often damaged or destroyed: "British cinemas had their full share of casualties. Out of 4,000 cinemas in Britain, 160 were totally destroyed, 60 of these in London" (G. Morgan 13). Nevertheless, it was the citizens engaged on the front lines of the People's War who "kept the cinemas open, even when London burned" around them during the Blitz (G. Morgan 11).

In thinking about the attraction of the cinema for so many working-class civilians, it is possible to argue, as Neil Rattigan does, that wartime British films operated primarily as propaganda created by a "ruling class" who believed in the People's War and felt "an overwhelming need to promulgate such a notion" (18). He suggests that "the ruled classes may have [had] their own view on whose Britain it was and why it should be fought for," but that view "is barely discernable in these films" (19). Rattigan acknowledges that "the way in which the carefully composed images of a certain set of perceptions of Britain are sometimes flawed, and the 'reality' of the class-ridden and class conscious British society is discerned through them" (19–20), but he is more interested in how privileged filmmakers tried to represent themselves than in how their films attracted working-class audiences. Nicholas Pronay complicates the relationship between moviemakers and audiences: while he acknowledges that the ruling classes controlled the British film industry, he explains how British wartime cinema became increasingly "conscious of being the medium of the working classes and by trial and error learned to be highly effective in that role" (176).[5] The role demanded experimentation not only because working-class tastes were difficult to discern but also because so many middle-class people were claiming that "we are all 'working' class now" during the Blitz (M-O A: DR 1637, June 1944).[6] The reality was that the war did not unite social classes in the cinema any more than it did in the workforce: just as people from various social classes had different experiences in their war work, so too did they have different experiences at the movies. Both the working-class Stepney audiences described above and their fashionable West End counterparts relied mainly upon their local theaters – and thus mixed primarily with others much like themselves. In order to succeed at the box office, feature films therefore had to reflect back to multiple, diverse audiences images of themselves engaged in the

People's War, and these images were necessarily multifaceted and often contradictory.

The following section examines three such feature films: *The Gentle Sex, Millions Like Us,* and *In Which We Serve*. These tremendously popular movies reveal the wartime British public's willingness to pay for films that were willing to question and experiment with the ideology of the People's War. While film scholarship has suggested generally that wartime feature films reflected the "cultural and ideological values" of the period (Chapman 58), the following analysis focuses specifically on the conflicted values of the People's War. The three films were all released in late 1942 and 1943, after the first London Blitz and the introduction of female conscription, and they share an interest in the problems of social and sexual identity that emerged during this period of the war. Two Cities' *The Gentle Sex* (directed by Leslie Howard) was the fifth highest-grossing British film of 1943; Gainsborough Pictures' *Millions Like Us* (directed by Sidney Gilliat and Frank Launder) earned the fifth-highest box-office income of 1944 (it was released in November 1943); Two Cities' *In Which We Serve* (directed by Noël Coward and David Lean) was the highest-grossing British film of 1943.[7] *The Gentle Sex, Millions Like Us,* and *In Which We Serve* all treat wartime experience quite realistically, not only by using black-and-white film stock and imitating documentary newsreel footage but also by reflecting back to audiences their own conflicted views about the People's War. Ultimately, these movies succeeded financially by failing ideologically; rather than trying to ignore or resolve conflicts within the ideology of the People's War, the three films emphasize the conflicts as a reflection of public opinion itself. The chapter's final section extends this argument to a more fantastic but equally popular art-house film: the Archers' *The Life and Death of Colonel Blimp* (directed by Michael Powell and Emeric Pressburger), which was the second highest-grossing film of 1943.

*   *   *

Once the British government had instituted female conscription in December 1941, the MOI Films Division began to commission titles specifically about women's war experience; *The Gentle Sex* and *Millions Like Us* were two of the most popular. Antonia Lant has examined the representation of cultural anxieties about female conscription in these films. She argues that *The Gentle Sex* has "trouble defining its target" audience (90); the movie both describes the changes in feminine gender identity during the People's War and qualifies those changes with the male narrator's repeated belief "that women really are illogical, strange, 'incalculable,' just as prewar femininity would have it" (92). Lant does not discuss *Millions Like Us* in as much detail, but she includes the film as she examines "the case of wartime cinema in Britain," which "asks us to consider how femininity might be constructed differently across different national cinemas, and indeed, how national identity might be imaged through different screen versions of femininity" in times of crisis (15). Lant is right: these two films do not have one clearly defined audience, and their contradictions suggest that conventional notions of national identity were under siege during the Blitz. However, the contradictions in films of the People's War are as often about class identity as they are about gender identity. Furthermore, *The Gentle Sex* and *Millions Like Us* do not have "trouble" defining an audience and representing gender identity to that audience. Instead, the films cannily emphasize both conservative and progressive ideas about wartime class and gender relations in order to capture the imaginations and the pocketbooks of a diverse movie-going public.

The Gentle Sex tells the story of a group of women from various social and regional backgrounds bound together by their common service in the ATS. Their unity exemplifies the ideal of the People's War, and the film heightens this effect by emphasizing from the start the social divisions among the women. For example, when the new recruits enter the noisy mess hall, the upper-middle-class officer's daughter, Anne Lawrence (Joyce Howard), declares that it is just "like school." The comment falls flat, not only because lower-middle-class Betty Miller (Joan Greenwood) immediately – and to Anne's surprise – admits that she has never been away to school but also because the working-class Gwen Hayden (Joan Gates) describes her experience as a waitress, which places her well below both Anne and Betty in the social hierarchy. Similarly, as the women discuss the bath and bed arrangements in their barracks after dinner, the working-class Scot, Maggie Fraser (Rosamund John), mentions that her family has always conserved hot bathwater by sharing it. The comment surprises several of the women and causes the middle-class dance teacher, Joan Simpson (Barbara Waring), actually to turn up her nose in disgust. These sharp social and regional distinctions not only invite viewers from various backgrounds to identify with specific characters but also encourage audience members to embrace the possibility of working alongside people completely unlike themselves.

At the ATS training center, this socially diverse group becomes a united female militia, and the recruits eventually find places within highly skilled and specialized units that transcend both class and gender differences. The footage of training drills, in particular, recalls the many propaganda newsreels – such as British Movietone News' "Britannia is a Woman" (1940) – documenting life in the women's services. The realistic style of the footage asks viewers to take the formation of a woman's auxiliary army seriously, and the emphasis in the training montage is on the increasing solidarity of a group of women who initially have little in common. By the time the recruits have learned to dress, march, and behave according to regulations, they have also been tested and placed in divisions of the ATS according to aptitude: two members of the group (lower-class beautician Dot Hopkins [Jean Gillie] and Betty) join an anti-aircraft gunner unit, while four (Czech refugee Erna Debruski [Lilli Palmer], Anne, Maggie, and Joan) become truck drivers. The film includes many scenes that demonstrate cross-class camaraderie in the People's War; one example is a scene between Anne and Maggie, a pair initially divided by regional and social differences but now united in maintaining and driving their truck. As Anne slides out from under the lorry covered with grease, Maggie fondly teases "Cinderella" about a ball scheduled for that evening. The film cements the bonds among the group's members by reuniting the drivers with their friends in the anti-aircraft unit during a particularly brutal night of the Blitz. When Dot and Betty's anti-aircraft station calls for help from the ambulance division to which Anne, Maggie, Erna, and Joan have recently transferred, the women come to each other's aid and survive the bombing together.

As the sun rises after the All-Clear and the women queue for tea, narrator and director Leslie Howard concludes the film with a final word to the audience: "Well, there they are – the women. Our sweethearts, sisters, mothers, daughters. Let's give in at last and admit that we're really proud of you, you strange, wonderful, incalculable creatures. The world you're helping to shape is going to be a better world because you're helping to make it." To appeal to as wide an audience as possible, the film holds open the question of just why that future world will be "better": is it better than the prewar world or merely better than a world at war? For liberal viewers, a better world promises a new social order, in which gender roles have expanded and class lines have blurred; for conservative viewers, a better world promises a restored social order, the one that obtained before the chaos of the Blitz. The image of the women standing together at the dawn of a new day suggests that they have built a new future; however, the film also hints that that future may look much like the past. The narrator's omniscient perspective and patronizing tone leave intact the presumption of male superiority;

Figure 5.1   The Gentle Sex, © ITV plc/Granada International, 1943

in the end, he puts the women in their place, which is still defined in relation to the men who call them "sweethearts, sisters, mothers, daughters." Furthermore, in saying goodbye to each woman in turn, sending them back to their individual lives, he effectively disbands their cross-class alliance, which diffuses the potential threat of their collective social agency:

> Goodbye, Maggie. You'll make a good wife to young Alexander.
> Sweet is revenge. You're getting what you want, Erna. But perhaps you'll soon be able to have something far sweeter: your own home and your own country.
> Well, Corporal [Joan], how nice to see a smile on your face – and such a nice smile. Who'd have thought it?
> Ah, there's that dear little thing again. Well, Half-pint [Betty], you got your gun.
> The girl who won't be left behind [Gwen].
> Well, Dot, it's a new life for you. And a happier one, we hope.

Poor Anne. Journey doesn't end in lovers meeting this time. You won't forget. But you won't go under.

In this movie, the women's journey does not end anywhere in particular – or, rather, it ends in a no man's land that can just as easily be a utopian future as a nostalgized past, both of which can be marketed with equal success.

The Gentle Sex thus accounts for middle-class disagreement about the future impact of social changes caused by the People's War; however, the film is also savvy enough to account for working-class skepticism about whether any of those changes were really happening in the first place. From the beginning, the film undercuts the unifying ideology of the People's War by consistently and deliberately leaving its Cockney waitress one step behind. In the opening scene, the narrator looks down from above a crowded railway platform and invites viewers to join him in selecting from the crowd a group of women to follow into the ATS. He singles out the first six – Betty, Anne, Maggie, Dot, Erna, and Joan – and then begins his summary once they have boarded the train: "Six women. Six lives about to be turned upside down. Six characters in search of... what?" The repetition of "six" here solidifies the group and suggests that it is complete with this number of women. However, the narrator must revise his statement to include *seven* women when the tough working-class Gwen pushes her way into both the railway carriage and the story. Laughing and calling her "the one we nearly left behind," the narrator allows Gwen to join the group, but only as the odd woman in.

At the training center, the original six women are assigned to interesting and gender-bending war work as mechanics, truck drivers, and trackers of enemy aircraft. Most of *The Gentle Sex* follows the wartime adventures of these six women as they form a cooperative cross-class unit. Yet even as the film challenges conventional gender roles and established class relations through its representation of these women, it leaves Gwen behind at the training facility. When the testing results are posted, she finds that her limited education and experience continue to restrict her options even during the People's War. Remaining essentially the same waitress in wartime as she was before the war, Gwen is assigned to work in the training facility mess hall, where she bemoans the fact that she can do no more than go "plonk, plonk, plonk all my life." Rather than quit, she seeks out additional training as a telephonist, but her character nevertheless drops out of the entire middle section of the film, which establishes the social unity of the fighting women.

Gwen finally catches up with the others at the anti-aircraft station in the final blitz scene, but it is too late. Although she shares in the fighting of the People's War for this one night, the narrator – and perhaps even the viewer – can no longer remember her name; when he says his goodbyes to the women, he calls her only "the girl who won't be left behind." Honoring each of the other women by name, nickname, or title as they pass by the camera, he offers Gwen neither name nor honor, echoing instead almost verbatim his words at the beginning of the film: "The one we nearly left behind." Thus, even as the closing scene apparently includes Gwen in the idealized promise of the People's War, it also pushes her back, however much she tries to resist, into the place where she has always been – a step behind the other women.

This ambivalent perspective regarding the wartime expansion of class and gender roles parallels Elizabeth Bowen's perspective in *The Heat of the Day*. On the one hand, *The Gentle Sex* offers the opportunity for women to unite across class lines during the People's War – and thus to challenge the stereotype that labels them as "the gentle sex." On the other hand, the film portrays more subtly the impediments blocking such change not only for working-class women but also for the privileged women who only temporarily befriend them during the Blitz. Simultaneously employing the rhetoric of the People's War and deploying examples that undermine its promise of wartime and postwar social change, *The Gentle Sex* appeals to liberal and conservative, middle- and working-class viewers alike. The film therefore ensures its own box-office success by reflecting back to audiences an image so multifaceted that every viewer can find in it a face to match his or her own.

Like *The Gentle Sex*, the 1943–44 hit *Millions Like Us* explicitly invokes the ideal of the People's War. In *The Gentle Sex*, the narrator reappears throughout the film to guide the audience's response: he speaks the rhetoric of the People's War in voiceover, drawing the women together at the beginning, evaluating their progress through training and service, and then toasting their success in the end. The narrator in *Millions Like Us* is similarly authoritative: during the opening credits, he drafts both the cast and the audience into national service, calling on "Eric Portman, Patricia Roc, and Millions Like You ... in *Millions Like Us*." Before the war, "you and millions like you swarmed to the sea" on holiday, as the Crowson family does in the first scene; the film uses stock footage of the seaside to establish this setting. In the present, "you" join the Crowsons in wartime service, marching off to the HG like Dad (Moore Marriott), to the ATS like Phyllis (Joy Shelton), or to the factory like Celia (Patricia Roc). The film follows the story of Celia, the youngest

Crowson daughter, as she enjoys a new sense of freedom during the People's War. Lant suggests that "one of the propaganda purposes of *Millions Like Us* was to counteract the impression that only Forces women were truly mobile," by showing how important and liberating factory work could be (99). *Millions Like Us* invites the audience to view it as propaganda: the establishing shots of the factory floor, for example, resemble footage in MOI shorts such as "Night Shift" (1942) or "Jane Brown Changes Her Job" (1942).

Yet although both *The Gentle Sex* and *Millions Like Us* represent increasingly mobile women, whether in the forces or in the factories, the films adopt the rhetoric of the People's War in very different ways. *The Gentle Sex* emphasizes the power of that rhetoric to mobilize and unite all citizens in defense of Britain, even if those citizens disagree about how the nation should look once the war is over. The film portrays the different experiences of women from various social classes and allows most of its women to live out the utopian fantasy of the People's War, at least for the duration. In contrast, *Millions Like Us* expresses real doubt about the possibility of living out that fantasy, even for middle-class women and even at the height of the Blitz. In this sense, *Millions Like Us* resembles Rosamond Lehmann's *The Echoing Grove* more than Elizabeth Bowen's *The Heat of the Day*: the film suggests the limited impact of the People's War by limiting its own focus to the wartime lives of two middle-class women: Celia Crowson and Jennifer Knowles (Anne Crawford). Even the slightly different social status of the two women in the film – Celia is solidly middle-class, while Jennifer is a more wealthy upper-middle-class character – emphasizes, as Madeleine's and Dinah's minor social distinctions do in *The Echoing Grove*, that the cross-class unity of the People's War is an illusion often confined to the experience of the middle class.

The film creates room for doubt by dismissing its omniscient narrator after the opening scene; without a running commentary to guide them, as in *The Gentle Sex*, viewers have more freedom to interpret and question the narrative that follows. The narrator does not even return at the end to offer a final toast; instead, *Millions Like Us* lets the People's Army speak for itself, as the film ends with a rousing chorus sung by all the women at a factory concert. Rather than focusing on the whole group, however, the film directs our attention to Celia and Jennifer, whom the song consoles as they grieve over their lost loves: Celia's soldier husband, Fred Blake (Gordon Jackson), has just died at the front, and Jennifer's working-class boyfriend, Charlie Forbes (Eric Portman), has just announced that they cannot marry in wartime. While this final scene supports the nationalistic idea of the People's War, it does so from a limited middle-class perspective: the film demonstrates the temptation for both its characters and the audience to turn even a propaganda song into a personal soundtrack.

Initially, the film extends the promise of social unity: the two middle-class protagonists join 28 other new female recruits in a factory billet like that of the ATS training center in *The Gentle Sex*. The first scenes at these lodgings suggest a similar social diversity in this group of women: Celia's working-class roommate, Gwen Price (Megs Jenkins), resembles Gwen Hayden in *The Gentle Sex*; Jennifer's Scottish roommate, Annie Earnshaw (Terry Randall), recalls *The Gentle Sex*'s Maggie Fraser. However, the audience never even meets the other members of the group; besides Celia and Jennifer, Gwen and Annie are the only factory women named and credited in the film, and they serve only as underdeveloped foils for their roommates. Rather than uniting a variety of women in the People's Army, *Millions Like Us* chooses instead to consolidate the middle-class experience of two women who "didn't ask to be sent" to the factory and who imagined that they "would hate it in a factory." In refusing to look far beyond these individual women's experiences, *Millions Like Us* suggests that the millions only look like "us" when our own middle-class experience is all that we choose to see.

These rather self-absorbed characters resemble the sisters in Lehmann's *The Echoing Grove*: they believe that the war will make them extremely mobile, even though they actually remain as firmly rooted in one place as they have ever been. For example, when Celia receives her call-up notice from the government, she thinks about it in terms of romantic possibility and social mobility, telling her father proudly, "I'm a mobile woman" and dreaming of a posting in "the WAAFs or something." When she arrives at the Labour Exchange, her fantasies about what it means to be "mobile" come to life: the posters of the WAAF, WRNS, ATS, and even WLA trigger dreams of exciting work alongside dashing young men, and her motivation for wartime service is that she might find and marry one of these men. Although Celia is disappointed to learn that the only job for her is in a factory, she soon discovers that she "likes it – she actually likes it" in the factory and that she has an aptitude for making "perfect" airplane parts. Yet just as she begins to enjoy her war work, a factory dance reclaims Celia's attention and energy. She meets an RAF air gunner named Fred, and her daydreams about him soon interfere with her factory production, recalling her earlier fantasies of finding a dashing young man during the war. Keeping her job in the factory, Celia also welcomes this happy ending to the old story that she began living before the war because it suggests that she can be fulfilled as both a wife and a worker. Playing at the People's War to get what she wants, Celia becomes a sort of poster child for the new woman of the People's War.

Similarly, Jennifer assumes that just because she now works in a factory, the rigid class barriers of prewar society are therefore breaking down. She too plays along with the utopian fantasy: her exciting romance with Charlie, the working-class factory foreman, confirms Jennifer's impression that the wartime factory enables the social equality promised by the People's War. Yet Jennifer's privileged class position is clear from the start: she arrives at the factory billet not by train and bus, as the other women do, but by taxi, inquiring about a private room and unpacking a ludicrously large wardrobe and an extensive make-up collection. When Jennifer eventually admits to Charlie that the thought of marriage "did cross my mind," he insists that she may not actually be as socially mobile as the war has made her feel; there are two types of people, he says: "You're one sort and I'm the other." He lists her "bad points": "You can't cook or sew – I doubt if you can even knit. You know nothing about life – at least not what I call life. [...] If you had to fend for yourself in the midst of plenty, you'd die of starvation," and he then concludes, "If that was all, I might take a chance." The problem for Charlie is predicting life in the postwar world: "Are we going to go on like this, or are we going to slide back, that's what I want to know. I'm not marrying you, Jenny, until I know. I'm turning you down without ever asking you." Worried that the barriers between classes have not collapsed permanently but only lowered temporarily in wartime, Charlie warily resists a marriage that depends so heavily upon that collapse. He both asks and answers the question of marriage, forcing Jennifer to acknowledge the limits of a social mobility that is possible in wartime but not necessarily afterwards.

Millions Like Us thus guarantees the possibilities of Celia's and Jennifer's lives as mobile women only for the duration – and even then only in limited ways. Although Celia can continue to do the work that she so enjoys in the home-front factory while Fred continues to fight on the front line, Fred's death means that the film never has to resolve the question of what will happen to Celia's expanded gender role once the war ends and she becomes a full-time wife and perhaps even mother. Similarly, Jennifer has fun flirting with Charlie in a cross-class romance made possible by the circumstances of the People's War, but their social mobility is never really tested; the film leaves open the question of what

Figure 5.2   *Millions Like Us*, © ITV plc/Granada International, 1943

Charlie will do once he knows whether "we are going to go on like this, or [...] slide back" into established class relations after the war. *Millions Like Us* does not rule out altogether the prospect of a more liberated future, but it makes that postwar future difficult to imagine. Unable to escape entirely or permanently from the middle-class conventions that shape their identities, Jennifer and Celia end up like Susan Shering in Allingham's *Pearls Before Swine* and Lynn Marchmont in Christie's *Taken at the Flood*: they cannot fully embrace the freedoms promised by the People's War because they cannot see beyond the war's end. The film suggests the difficulty of bridging class and gender barriers after the war if mobile women like Jennifer and Celia are never completely free from convention, even during the Blitz.

At first glance, this perspective seems different from that of *The Gentle Sex*, which represents more optimistically the possibility of life with the lid off in wartime. However, the two films achieved roughly equal box-office success, and their audiences were not necessarily distinct. One 41-year-old woman writing a 1943 Directive Reply on Favourite Films for Mass-Observation says, "I tend to like films dealing with the everyday occurrences of life in wartime; films which make the significance of our everyday lives more vivid," and she ranks *The Gentle Sex* and *Millions Like Us* as her first and second favorite films of 1943 (Richards and Sheridan 278). Both movies wrestle with the problem of how the Blitz affected – and would continue to affect – civilians' everyday lives. Although each film presents the mobile woman in a different light, both represent the future ambiguously enough for viewers to decide what to think for themselves. Like Mass-Observation itself, which recognized that there were "about 45 million morales in England, not just one" (Harrisson, "Films" 244), these box-office hits account for the tastes of as many of these millions as possible by representing the People's War in open-ended ways.

While *The Gentle Sex* and *Millions Like Us* explore various effects of the myth of the Blitz upon women's identity in wartime, *In Which We Serve* examines the mythology's impact on men at war. At the center of the film are three men – Captain Kinross (Noël Coward), Chief Petty Officer (CPO) Walter Hardy (Bernard Miles), and Ordinary Seaman (OS) Shorty Blake (John Mills) – who huddle together in the water after their ship goes down. Like the other films, *In Which We Serve* retells the basic narrative of the People's War: as Anthony Aldgate and Jeffrey Richards have argued, "The ship is clearly meant to serve as a metaphor for Britain, and the commitment to her that is expected of all in wartime" (*Britain Can Take It* 202). Noting the social distinctions between the upper-middle-class Kinross, the lower-middle-class Hardy, and the working-class Blake, James Chapman elaborates upon this point:

> The image of the men clinging to the float becomes a powerful and irresistible metaphor for class levelling: differences in background matter very little when they are up to their necks in seawater and oil. This is not to imply that the class system is swept away, but rather that there is a community of interest and a sense of comradeship between people of different backgrounds. What unites the men is devotion to their ship, and thus, by implication, to the nation. (185–6)

More than *The Gentle Sex* and *Millions Like Us*, *In Which We Serve* has inspired a great deal of biographical criticism that aims to explain the film's representation of nationalist unity as an expression of director Noël Coward's personal views. The scholarship tends to interpret the movie as propaganda designed to protect and maintain

Figure 5.3   In Which We Serve, © ITV plc/Granada International, 1942

the social status quo. Philip Hoare, for example, suggests that Captain Kinross embodies Coward's own idealized vision of the People's War: "Coward's performance is an English caricature, more theatre than film, a personal interpretation of Englishness, patriotism and the 'Britain-can-take-it' mentality in which Noël was steeped" (327). More broadly, Sheridan Morley suggests that "the ship and the crew are archetypal, and [...] they stand as obvious symbols for the eternal, indomitable fighting spirit of [Coward's] beloved navy, 'the fleet in which we serve'" (229).

These interpretations rely upon Coward's wartime autobiographical writing, in which he endorses the People's War as a patriotic but not a democratic ideal. For example, in a November 1942 diary entry, Coward describes two concerts at the "Speke [Rootes] aircraft factory. Three thousand seven hundred at each performance. Everything very well organized but the audience, as usual, stupid and dull. There can be no doubt about it, I have no real rapport with the 'workers,' in fact I actively detest them *en masse*" (19). Conversely, Coward delights in running with a high society London crowd like the one described in *The Heat of the Day*; for example, he sheltered at the Savoy on the night of 19 April 1941:

> Had a few drinks, then went to Savoy. Pretty bad blitz, but not so bad as Wednesday. A couple of bombs fell very near during dinner. Wall bulged a bit and door blew in. Orchestra went on playing, no one stopped eating or talking. Blitz continued. Carroll Gibbons [leader of the Savoy Orpheans band] played the piano, I sang, so did Judy Campbell [actress] and a couple of drunken Scots Canadians. On the whole, a strange and very amusing evening. People's behaviour absolutely magnificent. Much better than gallant. Wish the whole of America could really see and understand it. Thankful to God I came back. Would not have missed this experience for anything. (*Diaries* 6)

Coward not only marveled at the magnificent behavior of people living in luxury during the Blitz, but he also fostered wartime relationships with England's most powerful elite, including Admiral Louis Mountbatten,[8] Winston Churchill, and even the King and Queen.[9] By the end of 1943, he had learned to dine out on the growing success of *In Which We Serve*. In his diary, Coward remembers one day in which he "played croquet with Mrs Churchill all afternoon," after which "Max Beaverbrook arrived for tea and was quite amicable" (*Diaries*, 23 Oct. 1943: 22); he also recalls one of several lunches at the White House with "Mrs Roosevelt as nice as ever and the President full of vitality" (19 Dec. 1943: 23).

Despite Coward's taste for only the best society – and his corresponding distaste for the workers *en masse* – *In Which We Serve* was the most popular picture of 1943. Even more than *The Gentle Sex* and *Millions Like Us*, *In Which We Serve* succeeded in capturing the imaginations of a broad and diverse audience. Part of its appeal resulted from its frank assessment of the iconic soldier hero, an ideal that caused so much concern for civilian men on the home front. Through a series of flashbacks between frontline danger and home-front domesticity, the film shows combatants haunted by the same anxieties about masculine identity that haunted noncombatants. *In Which We Serve* therefore calls into question, this time from a soldier's perspective, the standard of military heroism that made it so difficult for the civilians in Henry Green's *Caught* and *Back* and Graham Greene's *The Ministry of Fear* to define themselves as real men.

The film opens with two montages that show men on the home front and the front line united in the common cause of national defense. After the narrator – once again Leslie Howard – initially announces that "this is the story of a ship," the first montage shows shipbuilders crafting the Torrin, fastening each rivet and painting the ship by hand; the footage here resembles the MOI short "Tyneside Story" (1943). A second montage follows captain and crew as they outfit the Torrin to sail in three days instead of the usual three weeks after the signing of the Nazi-Soviet pact in August 1939. Soon after the two montages carefully align the civilians who made the Torrin and the crew who sail it, the Germans torpedo and sink the Torrin, apparently destroying the unified nation along with it. But Britain, of course, remains united: clinging to their life raft and strafed by the Luftwaffe, the men of the Torrin recall how their families have also come under fire in wartime, and a series of flashbacks now aligns the soldiers with their families. Most disturbing is the Plymouth Blitz that kills Walter Hardy's wife, Katherine (Joyce Carey), and her mother (Dora Gregory) and causes Shorty's wife, Freda (Kay Walsh), to give birth prematurely. Alix (Celia Johnson) and Edward Kinross do not face such a direct attack; they avoid the Blitz by heading to the country, where their young son watches the sky and spots enemy aircraft. For the time being, the family is safe, but the Kinrosses are painfully aware that it is "sheer escapism" to ignore the real possibility of "all hell breaking loose immediately over our defenseless heads." In these scenes, as the Luftwaffe circles overhead at sea, on the coast, and in the countryside, the shared sense of living dangerously unites soldiers and civilians, much as the earlier montages united them in building a national defense.

Within this context, the three main characters of *In Which We Serve* all demonstrate that heroism and domesticity are not incompatible parts of masculine identity. As we have seen, many noncombatant writers for Mass-Observation described feeling trapped and emasculated on the home front, but this film appeals to those viewers by suggesting that the difference between the man of action and the man of feeling is not as great as it sometimes appears to be. For example, as Captain Kinross heroically goes down with his ship, he emotionally recalls his wife and children before the war. In the same way, when CPO Hardy nearly drowns under enemy fire, his first word upon revival is his wife's name: "Kath." OS Blake's experience is similar: despite his bravado in yelling "Missed, Butterfingers!" to Luftwaffe strafers, he is "shot through the heart" of a "Freda" arm tattoo, and the wound evokes memories of his courtship and marriage. Using wavy dissolves both to mark and to blur the boundary between the front line and the home front, the film shows the emotional vulnerability of the soldiers, even at their most heroic.

In Which We Serve stages the wartime crisis of masculinity largely in order to resolve it, as a good propaganda film would. For example, each of the three 1939 Christmas toasts at the beginning of the movie insists that sailors must always put their ship before family. Shorty Blake and his brother-in-law, Bert, argue over the relative merits of the Marines and the Navy but end by toasting both, "and the Torrin in particular," thus setting aside their family feud in favor of national cooperation. Walter Hardy's toast takes the idea further by describing the Torrin as if the ship were his wife:

> She's a creature of many moods and fads and fancies. She is, to coin a phrase, very often uncertain and coy and hard to please, but I'm devoted to her with every fiber in my being and I hereby swear to be true to her in word and deed, so help me God. Ladies and Gentlemen, HMS Torrin.

Recognizing the implications of swearing loyalty to ship rather than spouse, the captain's wife toasts a newly engaged friend, warning her against jealousy:

> Wherever she [the Naval wife] goes, there is always in her life a permanent and undefeated rival: her husband's ship. Whether it be a battleship or a sloop, a submarine or a destroyer, it holds first place in his heart. It comes before wife, home, children, everything. Some of us try to fight this and get badly mauled in the process. Others like myself resign themselves to the inevitable. That is what you will have to do, my poor, poor Maureen. That is what we all have to do if we want any peace of mind at all. Ladies and Gentlemen, I give you my rival. It's extraordinary that anyone could be so fond and so proud of their most implacable enemy. This ship – God bless this ship and all who sail her.

In each of the three toasts, the film invites viewers to follow the lead of the characters, resolving the conflict between domestic duty and military service by subordinating home to ship.

However, even as it reinforces the soldier's commitment, the analogy between ship and wife gives rise to gender trouble. The Torrin signifies both the ship itself and, metonymically, its crew: if the ship is a wife to all the men, then the men are, by implication, wives to one another, bound by emotional and domestic ties. The film nervously jokes about this feminizing effect: before the Torrin goes down, Blake serves tea on board to soldiers evacuated from Dunkirk and quips, "A woman's work is never done." However, once the men of the Torrin board a rescue ship themselves, they begin to share private feelings of weakness and vulnerability that compromise their public image as soldier heroes. Blake now confides his fears to CPO Hardy: "I'll tell you something, strictly between you and I. I'm scared stiff, and it's no good pretending I'm not." The wounded men are similarly afraid, and they need Captain Kinross not only to hold their hands but also to uphold their image: "All right – don't worry. I'll write and tell them they can be proud of you." Describing real men in ambiguous terms, this middle section of the film represents the anxieties about revealing feminine weakness that troubled not only civilians at home but also soldiers at the front.

In the end, however, *In Which We Serve* eliminates any uncertainty about what it means to be a real man by destroying the troublesome analogy between ship and wife. When the captain makes his final speech to the crew, he positions himself as the widower of "the ship we loved" as much as any wife: "Now she lies in 1500 fathoms. [...] We've lost her." Having let go of the Torrin as they all leave for other postings, the men can also let go of their spousal bond to one another. Thus, when Kinross bids goodbye to his crew, he shakes rather than holds their hands, announcing, "There isn't one of you that I wouldn't be proud and honored to serve with again. Goodbye, good luck, and thank you from the bottom of my heart." The final voiceover then reclaims the soldier as a masculine icon:

> Here ends the story of a ship, but there will always be other ships, for we are an island race. Through all our centuries, the sea has ruled our destiny. There will always be other ships and men to sail them. It is these men in peace or war to whom we owe so much. Above all victories, beyond all loss, in spite of changing values in a changing world, they give to us their countrymen eternal and indomitable pride.

On the one hand, the narrator counters the destabilizing effects of the People's War by restoring distinctions not only between men and women but also between Navy men and their countrymen, who owe the sailors so much; these distinctions make simply heroic once again the men who fight for their nation. On the other hand, however, the film has also shown that masculine identity is more complex than the icon of the soldier hero suggests, especially in a changing world. *In Which We Serve* therefore allows its audience to imagine the effects of the People's War as it chooses; the film sold tickets by marketing a mixed message about mixed-up gender roles in wartime.

* * *

The Gentle Sex, Millions Like Us, and *In Which We Serve* each exemplify the myth of the Blitz, a narrative that imposes a certain coherence even as it also allows diverse readings and conflicted meanings. However mixed the messages of these films, they all draw the nation together in the end, and their patriotic conclusions make the movies appear propagandistic. This chapter has argued that the films were more complicated than their last lines, but many reviews at the time were more interested in evaluating the movies' contributions to the war effort. In an *Observer* review, for example, C. A. Lejeune praised writer Moie Charles for her realistic portrayal of wartime women in *The Gentle Sex*, and she wrote in her *Manchester Guardian* review of *Millions Like Us*, "Nothing more clearly marks the coming of age of the British cinema than the treatment of ordinary working people [...]. In 'Millions Like Us,' they are real human beings, and the British film has reached adult maturity" ("Picture Theatres"). Similarly, Dilys Powell's *Sunday Times* review commended *In Which We Serve* for being "the best film about the war yet made in this country or America," largely because of its obviously patriotic representation of men at war. These reviews praise not only the symbolic coherence but also the visual realism of the films. Most film historians agree that "the war coincided with the era when the cinema industry was reaching the peak of its development, in terms of technique as well as popularity" (Coultass 11), and Richards and Sheridan argue that this "maturity" consists of balancing "the twin processes of documentarisation and democratisation" (13). Thus, although on the one hand, audiences expressed "a desire to see depictions of the lives of ordinary people and a willingness to accept a measure of documentary realism," on the other hand, "the pull of stars, romantic values, patriotism and glamour was just as strong as ever" (Richards and Sheridan 14–15). According to this argument, *The Gentle Sex, Millions Like Us,* and *In Which We Serve* pleased reviewers and earned box-office success by satisfying such popular demand for both documentary realism and glamorous romance. The three films' black-and-white film stock and frequent allusions to newsreels and MOI shorts effectively situated their romanticized fictional characters within the real world of wartime Britain.

Michael Powell and Emeric Pressburger's *The Life and Death of Colonel Blimp* is a different story. Although Powell insisted that *Blimp* was propaganda advocating "a realistic acceptance of things as they are, in modern Europe in Total War" (Powell and Pressburger 28),[10] the reviewers who praised *The Gentle Sex, Millions Like Us,* and *In Which We Serve* found in Powell and Pressburger's film not a familiar and coherent message but a singular ambiguity. C. A. Lejeune admits her befuddlement in a 13 June 1943 *Observer* review: "Blimp's worst fault – apart from its title and its length, which is two-and-three-quarter hours and quite absurd – is an unclarity of purpose. It is a handsome piece. It is frequently a moving piece. But what is it *about?*" (Powell and Pressburger 56). The reviewer in the *Tribune* blames the film's length on its moral indecision:

It is too long, moreover, because no one decided *exactly* what they wanted to say with it! I don't know now and I have thought about it hard, whether the point was that Old Blimp was a jolly good sort and ought to have been given a good job in *this* war, or that he was a feeble old buffer but SWEET, and good enough for the Home Guard. After all, the H. G. is not a dustbin. Or even whether David Low needs counteracting, and we can now realise that Old Blimp is a DAMN GOOD SORT and feudal England is not so bad. Or Tories are really gentlemen and sound at bottom! You can pay your money and take your choice. And all that is a grave fault in a propaganda picture, which is what "Blimp" is, or supposed to be. (Powell and Pressburger 59–60)

Dilys Powell agrees in her review of the film: "The moral of [Blimp's] career is left uncertain: with one voice the film censures his beliefs, with another protests that they are the beliefs of all upright men" (Powell and Pressburger 55). All of the critics commend *Blimp's* technical virtuosity, but they share the concern that it is just not good propaganda.

The crux of the problem is that although *The Life and Death of Colonel Blimp* was the second highest-grossing British picture of 1943 (after *In Which We Serve*), the film defies the wartime cinematic conventions that made movies like *The Gentle Sex, Millions Like Us,* and *In Which We Serve* so popular. Ian Christie describes *Blimp's* "transgression" of these conventions: not only did the picture portray German officer Theo Kretschmar-Schuldorff (Anton Walbrook) sympathetically, but also "in the context of wartime Britain, supporters of documentary-style cinema were quick to point out that *Blimp* contained no trace of 'ordinary people'; indeed, it is entirely based on 'types' drawn from the traditional characters of popular fiction and caricature" (*Arrows* 3). As an artistic fantasy film, produced in Technicolor and inspired by both David Low's Colonel Blimp cartoons and MGM's 1939 hit, *The Wizard of Oz*,[11] *Blimp* is concerned not with documenting but with caricaturing the real world at war, and it therefore works even more like wartime novels than the other films do. Rather than tease out subtle contradictions within the People's War, *The Life and Death of Colonel Blimp* inflates the myth of the Blitz until it bursts, embellishing and exaggerating its contradictions. In asking viewers to "pay your money and take your choice," the film may fail utterly as propaganda, but it succeeds wildly as a feature film.

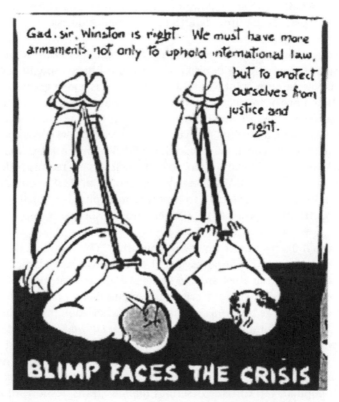

Figure 5.4   "Blimp Faces the Crisis" by David Low, © Solo Syndication/Associated Newspapers International, 1935

Blimp's over-inflation of the mythology begins with the adoption of David Low's cartoon Colonel Blimp as the film's subject.[12] From Colonel Blimp's first appearance in *The Evening Standard* in 1934, he was designed as a caricature of contradictory thinking. *Low's Autobiography* explains that the cartoonist conceived of Blimp as "a symbol of stupidity" (270), who embodied a "disposition to mixed-up thinking, to having it both ways, to dogmatic doubleness, to paradox and plain self-contradiction" (264). The cartoon reproduced here exemplifies what Low sees as the Colonel's always paradoxical point of view:

A great number of complaining people missed the point of Colonel Blimp from the start. And having done so, they imposed upon the Colonel a point of view, indifferent to the plain evidence that in his very nature he had, for himself, at least *two* points of view, mixed. (*Autobiography* 265)

Low's statement applies not just to the cartoon but also to the film, which begins by juxtaposing two very different views of how to fight a war. Powell and Pressburger's *Blimp* frames its narrative with a surprise HG attack launched by Lieutenant Spud Wilson's (James McKechnie) "B" Company against Major-General Clive Candy's (Roger Livesay) detachment. The attack triggers an extended flashback describing Candy's career and personal life. Viewers recognize in Candy's military persona one of the many paradoxes of the film: as Powell and Pressburger's script indicates, he is both the "grand old man" praised by his German friend, Theo (287), and the phony Wizard-of-Oz figure who is scorned by young Wilson because he has become a "standing joke" with the enemy (92). Candy appears to fight by highly ethical "National Sporting Club Rules" (92): after the Armistice in 1918, for example, he insists that "Right is Might" and that "clean fighting" and "honest soldiering" have won the First World War (211). However, Candy's notion of a gentleman's war sugar-coats the grim reality of battle. Candy himself unselfconsciously displays the helmet of a German "HUN, FLANDERS, 1918" alongside other hunting trophies in his den (181), and he delegates the interrogation of German prisoners to Major Van Zijl (Reginald Tate), a subordinate officer willing to practice a brutality for which Candy himself has too "tender" a heart (191).

To foreground these problems of military ethics, *Blimp* juxtaposes Candy's contradictions with those of the younger soldiers in the HG. As the neophytes storm the Turkish bath to capture Candy by surprise, their proud and foolish battle cry of "brute force and ruddy ignorance" suggests not just inexperience but irrational pride in ignorance (88). Like the American soldiers in the First-World-War scene, who insist, "Those weren't wars [before the First World War]. Those were just summer manoeuvres" (201), the younger members of the HG refuse to learn the lessons of history. Theo explains to Clive, "The enemy is different. So you have to be different too" in the Second World War, but the film insists that "different" is not necessarily better (268). Caricaturing both the idealism of the gentleman's war paradigm and the nihilism of the "brute force and ruddy ignorance" approach to battle, *The Life and Death of Colonel Blimp* considers the difficulty of resolving the ethical problem facing modern soldiers.

Within this frame story, the film further complicates soldierly experience by exploring the relationship between militarism and domesticity, much like the other fiction and film we have examined. However, whereas *Caught*'s Richard Roe, *Back*'s Charley Summers, *The Ministry of Fear*'s Arthur Rowe, and all men of the Torrin must learn to define themselves as real men in wartime, Candy never learns how to be more than a cartoon. Unselfconscious about his own masculinity and unaware of expanding roles for women, Candy becomes a caricature of old-fashioned attitudes about the rules and regulations of not only military but also domestic life. The film deepens the stolid Candy's conservatism as it traces both his lifelong friendship with German military officer Theo Kretschmar-Schuldorff and his series of romantic affairs with three women: Edith Hunter, Barbara Wynne, and Angela "Johnny" Cannon (all played by Deborah Kerr). Presenting a character cheerfully untroubled by the changing world around him, *The Life and Death of Colonel Blimp* asks audiences to consider whether Candy is a hero or a fool.

During the Boer War in 1902, a youthful Candy is briefly convinced to bend the rules. He reads a young governess's letter entreating the British military to "TELL THE TRUTH" about England in opposition to anti-British propaganda spread in Berlin by a man named Kaunitz (David Ward) (103). Deciding to investigate for himself in Germany, Candy asks the advice of Colonel Betteridge (Roland Culver) at the War Office, who warns that such undercover work is "not done" during leave and that "the way to get on in the Army" is to follow three simple rules: "Keep cool. Keep your mouth shut. Avoid politicians like the plague" (107). Candy rashly decides to go anyway, and the film rewards him for thinking independently: the letter writer, Edith Hunter, turns out to be not only beautiful and fascinating but also the love of his life. Yet although Edith's independent spirit intrigues him, Candy cannot engage with her directly; her political and social views are at odds with his own rigid conservatism. When they meet for lunch in Berlin, Candy declares with admiration that it is "a bit staggering to see a girl take such an interest in politics," particularly since he himself has been so carefully advised not to do so (124). Yet as Edith scoffs at her family belief that "the best place for a young girl is Home," Candy slips reflexively back into his patriarchal stance, responding, "Quite so!" (124). She replies by explaining the frustrations of women before suffrage: "While you've been fighting, we women have been thinking. Think for yourself, Mr Candy. What careers are there open to a woman? She can get married [...]. She can go and be a governess. But what does a governess know?" (124–5). Much as Candy would like to impress Edith, the problem is that as a soldier he has been trained not to think for himself; although she tempts him to do so, he suspects what Betteridge later confirms: "You can't afford to take a chance with your career" (172). Heeding the advice of the British embassy, Candy cautiously decides that handling the anti-British propaganda in Berlin is "a matter for careful diplomacy" (123), and he therefore refuses to help Edith in her cause. Edith's activism threatens his military career, and her liberalism jeopardizes his domestic ideal, even though he wishes he could live out that ideal together with her.

By hesitating to take either the professional or the sexual initiative, Candy leaves room for a rival: Theo becomes the third party in this love triangle, and his immediate connection with Edith soon leads to their engagement. The stark difference between Candy and Theo becomes plain during a bridge game, when Theo brings his friend, Frau von Kalteneck (Ursula Jeans), to make a foursome with Candy and Edith. The table talk reveals how little Candy and Edith have in common – and how oblivious Candy is to that fact. When Frau von Kalteneck asks him whether he likes opera, Candy replies that he prefers riding, hunting, and polo; when Theo asks Edith, who speaks German (unlike Candy), whether she likes sports, she says that she does not. As Edith falls in love with Theo, largely because he is the sort of man who asks women questions about themselves, her feelings remain obscure to Candy, even though he still believes that he loves her. Ironically enough, it is the Englishman rather than the German who is foreign to the Englishwoman; Edith and Theo are literally and figuratively speaking a language that Candy does not understand.

Candy's misunderstanding of Edith is only the beginning of the problem. As the film progresses, he begins to see all women as versions of Edith, who becomes his ideal woman despite his inability to comprehend her. Deborah Kerr's triple role in *Blimp* – as Edith Hunter ("The Governess"), Barbara Wynne ("The Nurse"), and Angela "Johnny" Cannon ("The ATS Driver") – parodies the way that films like *The Gentle Sex* and *Millions Like Us* bring together women from different backgrounds to cooperate for the duration in the common cause of national defense. *The Life and Death of Colonel Blimp* exaggerates this People's War rhetoric until it becomes ridiculous: rather than portraying women uniting in a common cause, the film shows them uniting in the shared body of Deborah Kerr. Like *The Gentle Sex* and *Millions Like Us, Blimp* brings together women from different social backgrounds: Candy's love, Edith, is a governess and political activist; his wife, Barbara, is a wealthy industrial heiress and nurse; and his driver, Angela, is a working fashion model and ATS recruit. However, these three women never cooperate in the war effort; they never even meet. Instead, they unite only in Clive's imagination, where his narrow-minded fixation upon their similarity creates a warped vision of equality. Even their surnames – Hunter, Wynne, and Cannon – suggest how difficult it is for Candy to take his mind off the battlefield for long enough to consider his personal life.

Far more than Celia and Jennifer in *Millions Like Us*, the women in *Blimp* are immobile: no matter how much they seem to enjoy the increasing independence of women over the course of the twentieth century, they remain trapped within a static male perspective from which they can never escape. Archival material from the British Film Institute shows that Emeric Pressburger considered female emancipation an important starting point for his script. In his handwritten treatment and notes, he includes a 13-page research document entitled "Emancipation of Women in England" (1942), and he even considers – and then rejects – the possibility of telling the story "from the girl's point of view" (Emeric Pressburger Collection). Yet Candy's outdated and limited point of view renders him just as immobile as the women in *The Life and Death of Colonel Blimp*, whom he both idealizes and objectifies. The film uses Candy's den full of hunting trophies to indicate symbolically the extent to which many of its characters have become trophies of what the script's stage directions call "the British acquisitive instinct" (181). When Candy returns from Berlin and moves in with his Aunt Margaret Hamilton (Muriel Aked), he momentarily forgets that he has preserved his career by losing Edith when he examines his big-game-hunter's collection of "South African heads" mounted in the den. Aunt Margaret kindly tells him, "Now, I want you to remember: wherever you go – whatever you do – you've always got a home here," suggesting for a moment that family bonds might compensate for his personal loss. However,

Aunt Margaret quickly adds, "And – whatever you shoot – there's always room here for them" (180). Unable to welcome Clive home without also welcoming his hunting trophies, Aunt Margaret unwittingly indicates the extent to which Candy's identity depends upon the "British acquisitive instinct." At this point, Candy's own shadow grows large upon the wall, placing him among the trophies and representing the fact that he has become quite literally a shadow of his previous self. In Berlin, Candy demonstrates his willingness to adhere to convention for the sake of his career, and he therefore resigns himself to becoming little more than a trophy of the British army. The army does to Candy what he does not only to his "heads" but also to his women: when he hangs his wife Barbara's portrait alongside the other hunting trophies after her death, he can only insist on "the resemblance" to Edith and assert that "all my stuff is here [in the den]. It would be an awful gap without her." Clive does not see, as Theo does, that "it's a strange place to hang such a lovely picture" (257).

This statement holds true not just for Barbara's portrait but also for *The Life and Death of Colonel Blimp* itself: the war seemed "a strange place to hang such a lovely picture." The film was certainly lovely, as critics agreed, but it was not the prize piece of propaganda that most of them had expected. Instead, the film exposes the problem of committing oneself so wholly to an irrationally fixed ideal. In the film's final scene, Candy's blitzed home represents the destruction not only of Clive's own unquestioned perspective but also of the assumption that audiences would accept propaganda without question. Candy looks at the ruined, flooded foundation of his bombed house as he discusses with Theo and Angela his embarrassing capture by Wilson's "B" Company, a military maneuver that closes the frame story opened at the beginning of the film. At the same time, he remembers a conversation with Barbara during the early days of their marriage: "Clive, you mustn't change and don't ever leave this house." "No fear," he responds. "Even if there is a second Flood, this house shall stand on its solid foundations and we'll have a private lake in the basement." Barbara replies, "That's a promise. You stay just as you are ... till the floods come ... [...] and this is a lake." Looking at his demolished home, Candy thinks, "Now here is the lake – and I still haven't changed" (287). The implication is that Candy finally recognizes here his lifelong stubbornness – or blimpishness. Although he might never actually change, he acknowledges in this final moment of insight the rigidity of his own perspective.

Most viewers and critics interpret the film's title in this manner, labeling Clive Candy as Colonel Blimp – and thus following visual cues

Figure 5.5 The Life and Death of Colonel Blimp, © ITV plc/Granada International, 1943

that align the elder Candy in the Turkish bath with Low's eponymous cartoon character. However, the Blimp here is not just the colonel but also the nation itself; *The Life and Death of Colonel Blimp* insists that it is not only Candy himself who has, as David Low says, "at least *two* points of view, mixed" but also the audience collectively. In his autobiography, Low states that he enjoyed the film for this very reason: he found the movie "extremely sentimental" in its portrayal of "a glamorous old colonel whose romantic attachments nearly – *but not quite* – obscured the conclusion that if Britain followed his out-of-date ideas in modern war, we should all be blown to blazes" (273, my emphasis). For Powell and Pressburger, the "not quite" was essential. In a letter drafted to Britain's Secretary of State, Powell insisted that the film's central theme was the paradox of modern British warfare:

> I am very much obliged for your last letter but you have misstated the theme, which is as follows: "Englishmen are by nature conservative, insular, unsuspicious, believers in good sportsmanship and

anxious to believe the best of other people. These attractive virtues, which are, we hope, unchanging, can become absolute vices unless allied to a realistic acceptance of things as they are in modern Europe and in Total War." If that isn't something worth saying I'd like to know what is! This is what the audience learns from the finished film, this is what we shall emphasise. (Powell and Pressburger 28)[13]

Powell and Pressburger's target in *The Life and Death of Colonel Blimp* is clearly not just Clive Candy himself nor "stupidity" more generally; it is a paradox at the heart of British national identity in wartime, a paradox that also informs the People's War. Even as the idealistic myth of an "insular" nation united around the values of "good sportsmanship" and social equity seemed crucial to British wartime national identity, it was equally important that the nation strive for "a realistic acceptance of things as they are in modern Europe and in Total War."

The film takes this self-reflexive insight a step further by advertising and exaggerating its own blimpish role as a caricature and cartoon. Using bright colors, character types, and extended flashbacks, *The Life and Death of Colonel Blimp* calls attention to the central role of fiction and fantasy in portraying real life in wartime Britain. The film is a fantasy about a cartoon character; it became a box-office smash not by escaping from but by engaging with the all-too-real conflicts within the myth of the Blitz. Like Powell and Pressburger's Candy and Low's Blimp, *The Life and Death of Colonel Blimp* itself mixes at least two points of view about every issue it raises. By overstating these contradictions in wartime thinking – contradictions that were present, if at times understated, in other fiction and films of the period – *The Life and Death of Colonel Blimp* points out the stupidity of pretending that the contradictions do not exist.

The film therefore provides an apt conclusion for this book not only because it caricatures the paradox at the heart of People's War ideology but also because it complicates British stereotypes about the enemy. I have argued that British literature of the Blitz represents disagreement about the People's War precisely because the freedom to disagree was at stake in the Allied fight against Nazi Germany. *The Life and Death of Colonel Blimp* does not diminish the Nazi threat, but it does insist that not all Germans were Nazis. Candy's lifelong friend, Theo, is a former German army officer who married an Englishwoman (Candy's love, Edith Hunter). After Edith's death in 1933, their sons, who are now "good Nazis – as far as any Nazi can be called good," refuse to attend her funeral, a refusal that makes Nazi politics painfully personal for Theo

(248). Thus, when Theo returns to Edith's England as an enemy alien in November 1939, he declares with conviction at a Metropolitan Police tribunal, "My outlook of life is against the Nazis" (247), and Candy, now a General in the British army who has traveled 11 hours just to see Theo, gladly stands surety for him "with everything I have, sir" (253). Humanizing Theo in this way, the film asks viewers to consider their own blimpishness: while conformist thought reached new and deadly heights in Nazi Germany, British propaganda and nationalist rhetoric encouraged citizens to pit themselves against Germany in the defense of free thought and speech. Like other narratives of the Blitz, *The Life and Death of Colonel Blimp* offers its audience the opportunity to imagine variations on the common themes of the People's War. Whether on screen or in print, the myth of the Blitz was indeed a myth – a story that could be told in a number of different ways to a number of different audiences. Wartime British literature tests out the story's full range of meanings and thus satisfies the readers and viewers who demanded imaginative interpretations of everyday life in the Blitz.

Notes

Introduction: Fighting the People's War

1. "Blitzkrieg" is a German compound meaning "lightning war." The term was typically not part of official German military terminology during the war (see Frieser and Greenwood). Instead, the word became central to Allied descriptions of German bombing, beginning with its introduction to the English-speaking world in a 25 September 1939 article in *Time* magazine describing the German invasion of Poland.
2. Some of these scholars have taken a cultural studies approach to the literature of the Second World War, although their central arguments differ substantially from mine. See in particular Hartley, Lassner, Plain, and Schneider.
3. Unlike Northern Ireland, the Irish Free State, renamed Eire in 1937, remained neutral during the Second World War. Eamon de Valera, the Prime Minister of Eire, declared a state of Emergency during the war, but he also remained firm in keeping the country neutral; Eire was the only nation in the British Empire that refused to join the Allied side. Nevertheless, 124,500 men and 58,000 women left Eire for Northern Ireland or other parts of the United Kingdom during the war. Of these, 38,544 volunteered for the British armed forces; this figure includes 7000 deserters from the Irish Army. Several thousand more already living in the United Kingdom also enlisted. In 1948, Eire became the Republic of Ireland (Dear 324–5).
4. These raids on Germany began with regular area bombing by the RAF from mid-1941 onward and intensified in January 1943 when the RAF began bombing with the goal, set at the Casablanca conference, of "weakening Germany to the point where it could not effectively repel an invasion" (Dear 20).
5. See Dear 1252 (V-weapons) and 1136 (total destruction). Estimates of civilian casualties differ depending on the source. *The Oxford Companion to World War II* draws its information from the publications of the UK Official History Series.
6. See Titmuss, who asserts, "Not until over three years had passed was it possible to say that the enemy had killed more soldiers than women and children" (335–6).
7. In all, 264,443 British soldiers were killed during the war, and 277,077 were wounded (Dear 1151).
8. The Belseys took steps to protect their daughter in mid-October when Mrs Belsey began to consider moving into a country hostel with baby Charlotte; by mid-November, they had left London and were living in Huntingdon.
9. See Chapman for a detailed description of how the MOI and the film industry in Britain struggled, particularly at the beginning of the war, to articulate the manner in which wartime propaganda should work to establish the idea of a People's War.

10. See Rose for an excellent summary of the prewar economic conditions that made promises of social equality in wartime so appealing (29–31).

11. Lassner's *British Women* and "The Timeless Elsewhere" both acknowledge that little social change actually occurred, but they do contend that "British women writers interpret their World War II experiences in ways that unsettle our conceptions of political differences, social change and gender. As they show again and again, even as 'the discourse of wartime social policy worked to limit gender disruption', their own literary discourse very often resisted traditional gender relations and expressed a yearning for social change" (*British Women* 8, quotes Higonnet 8).

12. For treatments of one or two closely related social or political issues, see in particular Bourke, Calder (*Myth*), Chapman, Dawson, Hartley (*Millions*), Lassner (*British Women*), McLaine, K. Morgan, Plain, Saywell, Schneider, and Summerfield (*Women Workers*). For treatments of one literary genre, see Aldgate and Richards, Bergonzi, Calder and Sheridan, Cawelti and Rosenberg, Gledhill and Swanson, Hewison, Klein, Lant, Mengham and Reeve, J. Palmer, Panek, Sheridan, Summerfield (*Reconstructing*), and Symons. For treatments of a single author, see Barnard, I. Christie (*Arrows*), Corcoran, Diemert, Glendinning, Jordan, Martin, Mengham (*Idiom*), Pollard, and Tindall.

13. See Chapter 3 of Stonebridge's *Writing* for a compelling psychoanalytic analysis of Henry Moore's wartime art.

14. The question for this September 1942 Directive was as follows: "What do you feel about the position of women in this country to-day? What alterations or reforms, if any, would you like to see?"

15. Harrisson was a social anthropologist who had spent the years before the war studying the "savages" in Borneo, and he returned to England wanting to study the working class in the same way. He shared with Madge and Jennings the surrealist desire to "'add to the social consciousness of the time' by presenting facts without bias and making them generally available" (Calder, "M-O" 128). The emphasis on facts and Harrisson's commitment to social anthropology are even more closely related to the documentary than to the surrealist movement.

16. Quoted from a letter written by Jennings, Charles Madge, and Tom Harrisson to the *New Statesman* on 30 January 1937.

17. For criticism of Mass-Observation, see in particular Marshall and Jahoda.

18. See Stanley for statistics about the demographic composition of the panel.

19. Mass-Observation head archivist, Dorothy Sheridan, has confirmed this fact in email correspondence and conversation (2008).

1   Mobile Women in Elizabeth Bowen's War Writing

1. The wartime stories include "Love" (1939), "No. 16" (1939), "Attractive Modern Homes" (1941), "Careless Talk" (1941), "The Easter Egg Party" (1941), "The Girl with the Stoop" (1941), "In the Square" (1941), "Look at All Those Roses" (1941), "A Love Story" (1941), "Oh, Madam..." (1941), "A Queer Heart" (1941), "Summer Night" (1941), "Sunday Afternoon" (1941), "Tears,

Idle Tears" (1941), "Unwelcome Idea" (1941), "A Walk in the Woods" (1941), "The Cheery Soul" (1942), "Green Holly" (1944), "The Happy Autumn Fields" (1944), "The Inherited Clock" (1944), "Mysterious Kôr" (1944), "The Demon Lover" (1945), "I Hear You Say So" (1945), "Ivy Gripped the Steps" (1945), "Pink May" (1945), and "Gone Away" (1946). Bowen also published the following novels before the war: *The Hotel* (1927), *The Last September* (1929), *Friends and Relations* (1931), *To the North* (1932), *The House in Paris* (1935), and *The Death of the Heart* (1938). After the war, she published three more novels between 1955 and 1969: *A World of Love* (1955), *The Little Girls* (1964), and *Eva Trout* (1969).

2. Most critics recognize Bowen's fascination with these parallels between the individual and history; *Bowen's Court*, they argue, consistently describes the public–private relationship as an issue of national identity.

3. See also Caserio, Dukes, Ellmann, Kapoor, and Mengham, "Broken Glass."

4. See also Sarisalmi, who argues, "What cannot be uttered or represented, what is left out of a story, the entailed but unknowable other of the discourse, blurs and confuses the signifying system of Bowen's text. The monolithic dominant discourse is radically transgressed by what it excludes, by the discourses of silence and madness, as is the case with Louie in *The Heat of the Day*" (153).

5. See also Watson.

6. The question asked in this January 1943 Directive was as follows: "Has your attitude to any of the following things changed at all since the war began, and if so in what ways has it changed: Please answer this question in some detail, and where possible trace your attitude through the war: (a) money (b) clothes (c) security (d) people in different social classes from yourself (e) sex (f) politics (g) conscientious objectors."

7. The women themselves often complied with these social codes and expectations. A Mass-Observer stationed in the WAAF noticed in 1941 that at a call-up meeting for 42 new WAAFs, class-based social cliques developed quickly and naturally. See M-O A: TC 32/3/E, "Letter."

8. Middle-class women certainly could and did volunteer to work in the munitions factories, but their cases were the exception to this general rule.

9. According to Calder, "Those who opted for the [auxiliary services] would not be posted to 'combatant duties' unless they volunteered for them. In any case, the tasks of the ATS and the WAAFs were clerical and culinary rather than Amazonian, though the use of women at AA [Anti-Aircraft] batteries was becoming a commonplace" (*PW* 268).

10. The quoted report is from M-O A: FR 2059: "Will the Factory Girls Want to Stay Put or Go Home?" March 1944.

11. The following year, the observer was even more explicit about the goals of the WAAFs: "And what is this thing we're all after? Obviously, a man. Preferably an officer or a sergeant-pilot. I should say that about 85% of our conversation is about men, dances (where we meet men), etc. etc.: 15% about domestic and shop matters: and a negligible percentage on other matters" (M-O A: FR 1029, 1942: 3).

12. See the description of Reaveley's circumstances in the Introduction.

13. See Saywell 13.

14. Rose describes the label of "good-time girls" more thoroughly: "The women and young girls who were perceived to be straying from convention and who were overtly seeking entertainment and pleasure were given the ironic label of 'good-time girls' or 'good timers.' The term 'good-time girl' was omnipresent in the language of moral alarm and was used to describe women who were irresponsible – who failed to consider their commitments to others" (80).

2 Immobile Women in Rosamond Lehmann's War Writing

1. Assistant Archivist Sarah Charlton from the Centre for Buckinghamshire Studies in Aylesbury, Buckinghamshire, England, helped me by searching the records of this period for evidence of bombing near Bourne End.
2. Rosamond had two sisters: the older Helen and the younger Beatrix, in addition to the youngest Lehmann child, John.
3. Excerpted from letters between Lehmann and Bowen, dated 14 February 1949 and 4 March 1949.
4. She originally published these stories in *Penguin New Writing*.
5. Walters and Broughton also discuss these issues in their criticism of the novel.
6. This was a review that particularly offended Lehmann, who usually tried not to take criticism of her work so personally.
7. See also "Cycle of Experience," the review in the *Times Literary Supplement*, and Virgilia Peterson's review in the *New York Herald Tribune Books*.
8. For other praise of Lehmann's work, see also Bowen ("Modern Novel"), Coopman, and Scott-James. For further negative criticism of the novel, see Atkins, Blodgett, and Pfaltz.
9. At the time of the affair, Day-Lewis had, "for reasons he later described as inverted snobbery [...] removed the hyphen from Day-Lewis – later restoring it as he disliked even more being addressed as 'Mr Lewis'" (Hastings 219n).
10. See, for example, Broughton 88, LeStourgeon 112, and Tindall 174.
11. See LeStourgeon and Simons. Both critics foreground the image of the grove: LeStourgeon argues that the "grove is human passion" (111), while Simons contends that the echoing "emphasises the hellish and reverberative nature of passion" (126). See also Tindall, Coopman, and Broughton for discussions of echoing. Tindall suggests that the echoing is a process involving "replications, repetitions and tricks of memory" (166); Coopman insists that the echoes represent "the persistence of the past in the present" (120–1); Broughton perceives the echoing as a symbol of how "the characters in *The Echoing Grove* have been trapped" within a "petty, jealous, contagious, possessive love" (99).

3 Real Men in Henry Green's War Writing

1. Not coincidentally, Green and Rees were also friendly with each other, meeting frequently to drink together in London pubs and clubs during the war. This was one reason that Lehmann was so eager to spend time with Green: in March 1941, her affair with Rees had just ended, and she was

eager to discuss her emotional state with interested and concerned friends.

2. Green's numbers are a little off: there were actually about 2500 men in the LFB and between 23,000 and 28,000 AFS recruits.

3. Ironically, Green is critical of an economic concern not unlike his own: the firefighters' interest in their pensions was much like Green's interest in maintaining his role as CEO of Pontifex in wartime and thus ensuring that "financially I suffered not at all" ("Before" 269). All of these men are keenly aware of the economic demands of maintaining their places within a well-established social hierarchy.

4. In his discussion of *Caught*, North recognizes a relationship between the characters and their cultural context, but his interest lies in the Phoney War's lack of impact on civilians rather than in the war's impact on both soldiers and civilians.

5. The phrase "The Heroes with Grimy Faces" also appears on John Mills's 1991 memorial to the 1051 firemen and women killed in the Blitz. The memorial now stands outside St Paul's Cathedral in London.

6. Mrs Green's daughter, Penelope Nichol, shared with me information about the memorial plaque erected in honor of her mother in 2007. The plaque was erected in Church Street, Chelsea, London, and reads, "In Memory of Auxiliary Firewoman Yvonne Green who died near this site killed by enemy action on duty with four others as Firewatchers at Chelsea Old Church on the night of 16th/17th April 1941."

7. Calder quotes the entry for "Mythology" in *Chambers Dictionary* here.

8. Treglown quotes *Penguin New Writing* 17 (April–June 1943) [this issue actually appeared in December]: 155–65.

9. The question for this September 1942 Directive was as follows: "What do you feel about the position of women in this country to-day? What alterations or reforms, if any, would you like to see?"

10. Calder and Sheridan reprint a Mass-Observation report by Diana Brinton Lee, "Will the Factory Girls Want to Stay Put or Go Home?"

11. Green's brief, usually one- or two-word titles, including *Blindness* (1926), *Living* (1929), *Party Going* (1939), *Caught* (1943), *Loving* (1945), *Back* (1946), *Concluding* (1948), *Nothing* (1950), and *Doting* (1952), particularly lend themselves to the punning and shifts in meaning throughout his fiction.

4   No Escape in the Detective and Spy Fiction of Agatha Christie, Margery Allingham, and Graham Greene

1. See Mitchell. The Introduction outlines these statistics in more detail; in the United Kingdom as a whole, more than 60,000 civilians were killed by bombing, and over 70 percent of British civilian casualties during the Blitz thus occurred in London.

2. Mandel also offers a historical analysis of how assumptions about social stability have shaped the genre of detective fiction.

3. See Christie's *An Autobiography* and Allingham's *The Oaken Heart* for detailed accounts of the writers' wartime experiences.

4. Sales of the report and/or its briefer official summary in 1942 "ran up to at least 635,000 copies," and according to a Gallup Poll, "nineteen people out of twenty had heard of the report, and nine out of ten believed that its proposals should be adopted" (Calder, *PW* 528).

5. The question that was repeated in both the January 1943 and the June 1944 Directives was as follows: "Has your attitude to any of the following things changed at all since the war began, and if so in what ways has it changed: Please answer this question in some detail, and where possible trace your attitude through the war: (a) money (b) clothes (c) security (d) people in different social classes from yourself (e) sex (f) politics (g) conscientious objectors."

6. Rowe was not alone in feeling literary nostalgia for *The Little Duke* during wartime; Jenny Hartley notes that "Charlotte Yonge [...] had a devoted following" during the war (*Millions* 4).

7. See also Adamson, Aisenberg, Gaston, R. Smith, and West for arguments about the connection between thrillers and everyday life during the war.

8. See also Hoskins, who analyzes the relationship between *The Ministry of Fear* and Wordsworth's *The Prelude,* arguing that Greene invokes Wordsworth to emphasize the absurdity rather than the sublimity of wartime fear.

9. The battle for British women's suffrage formally began in 1865 with the organization of the first National Association for Women's Suffrage, and it continued through 1918 (when women over 30 earned the right to vote) until 1928 (when women over 21 could vote, now on the same terms as men).

10. Some British men even went so far as to describe women on active duty as "unnatural": "To the soldiers, the women in their ranks seemed 'out of place somehow,' 'playing a part,' 'unnatural' – or else, a conveniently glorified brothel" (M-O A: TC 32/1/F, "Male Attitudes to Women in the Forces," 1941). Significantly, the soldiers reporting these views were typically noncombatants; one Mass-Observer notes, "In the first place, soldiers must be divided into 'combatants' and 'non-combatants.' Combatant soldiers do not now come into any more contact with the ATS than with the WAAFs or any other women's service. It is with the non-combatant corps that the ATS are principally concerned" (TC 32/1/F, "Male Attitudes," 1941). Even when men volunteered for the HG (called the Local Defence Volunteers [LDV] before Churchill changed the name in July 1940), they were often derided as unfit soldiers playing at war. A Mass-Observer overheard this 25-year-old lower-middle-class civilian man's comment about the LDV: he "said derisively, 'They look like bloody convicts'" in their inadequate uniforms (M-O A: TC 29/1/F, "The Public and Soldiers," 1940). The young woman to whom this man made his comment agreed: "They certainly don't look very smart" (TC 29/1/F, "The Public").

11. The original warrant for the George Medal, the second highest gallantry award for civilians after the George Cross, did not permit the posthumous award of the honor. It was not until November 1977 that the British government began making such posthumous awards.

5   The Film-Minded Public

1. The Quota Act is common parlance for the 1927 Cinematograph Films Act. It set a quota of British films to be distributed and exhibited in Great Britain; to

qualify as British, a film had to pay 75 percent of its salaries to British subjects. The Act was designed to increase the number of British – and to decrease the number of American – films shown in British cinemas.

2. See "The MOI Films Division," *The British at War* 13–40.

3. The Introduction describes in more detail the nature of this working relationship between the MOI and Mass-Observation.

4. From Mass-Observation's "Preliminary Report on Opinion about Ministry of Information Shorts." The GPO Film Unit typically made the documentaries, while commercial studios usually created the fictional shorts for the MOI.

5. Jo Fox argues persuasively for "the pervasive role of dialect, accent, and scripting" in establishing "the image of the collective or the ordinary" People's War in British wartime films (820). Her article is particularly interesting because it interrogates the motives of filmmakers in using accented speech in this manner.

6. The question for this Directive was the same as the question for January 1943: "Has your attitude to any of the following things changed at all since the war began, and if so in what ways has it changed: Please answer this question in some detail, and where possible trace your attitude through the war; (a) money (b) clothes (c) security (d) people in different social classes from yourself (e) sex (f) politics (g) conscientious objectors."

7. See Reid, 15–16. Lists of the top-grossing British films of the period are available in *Kinematograph Weekly*. Alongside these figures, Mass-Observation responses to a November 1943 Directive on favorite films reveal a group of extremely popular films that explore much the same problems of wartime class and gender identity examined in previous chapters on British blitz fiction. Reid's lists include American-made films; I have considered only the rankings of British-made films here. *Millions Like Us* is a special case because of its late-1943 release. Several people mentioned the film in their Directive responses to Mass-Observation, despite the fact that it was released in November 1943, the month in which the Directive was issued. That means that those who commented on the film had seen it almost immediately upon release, and its popularity continued into the following year.

8. The story of *In Which We Serve* was based on Mountbatten's experience as captain of the HMS Kelley, and when MOI Films Division director Jack Beddington "rang up [...] to say that they considered *In Which We Serve* was bad propaganda for outside England [...] because a ship was sunk in it," Coward used his connection to Mountbatten to get the film made: "Will ask Dickie [Mountbatten] to take script to Winston [Churchill]" (*Diaries*, 17 Dec. 1941: 14). The recently released volume *The Letters of Noël Coward* (ed. Barry Day) confirms the intimacy of this correspondence.

9. On 8 April 1942, Coward was delighted to receive the King, Queen, and two princesses (Elizabeth and Margaret) on the set of *In Which We Serve*: "We took them first to Stage 5, where the King took the salute. Then I did the Dunkirk speech [as Kinross]. The ship rolled, the wind machine roared, in fact everything went beautifully. All the time they were perfectly charming, easy and interested and, of course, with the most exquisite manners to everyone. The Queen is clearly the most enchanting woman. The Princesses were thrilled and beautifully behaved. Altogether it was an exhibition of unqualified

'niceness' from all concerned and I hope it impressed the studio as much as it should have" (*Diaries* 16).

10. The quote comes from an undated draft of a letter to Sir James Grigg (Secretary of State in the War Office from 1942 to 1945).

11. Ian Christie argues, in the introduction to Powell and Pressburger's script for the film, that when the young HG officer, Spud Wilson, calls Major-General Clive Wynne-Candy "Wizard" as a nickname, he "manages to combine a topical reference to the MGM musical, a reminder of that character's compensatory facade, *and* a clue to one of the films that no doubt most inspired *Blimp*'s structure" (Powell and Pressburger ix).

12. David Low and Graham Greene were "friends of 50 years standing," who met in the 1930s while Low ran an antiquarian bookshop that Greene patronized (Waterfield 5). In wartime, the two men served together as ARP wardens in Bloomsbury.

13. From an undated draft of a letter to Sir James Grigg.

Bibliography

Adamson, Judith. *Graham Greene: The Dangerous Edge: Where Art and Politics Meet.* New York: St Martin's Press, 1990.

"Agatha Christie." Author biography. 2008. *HarperCollins Authors.* HarperCollins Publishers, New York. 29 April 2008 (http://www.harpercollins.com/authors/11085/Agatha_Christie/index.aspx?authorID=11085).

Aisenberg, Nadya. *A Common Spring: Crime Novel and Classic.* Bowling Green, OH: Bowling Green Popular Press, 1979.

Aldgate, Anthony and Jeffrey Richards. *Britain Can Take It: The British Cinema in the Second World War.* 2nd ed. Edinburgh: Edinburgh UP, 1984.

Allingham, Margery. *The Oaken Heart.* Garden City: Doubleday, 1941.

——. *Pearls Before Swine.* 1945. New York: Bantam Books, 1990. Rpt of *Coroner's Pidgin.* London: Heinemann.

——. *Traitor's Purse.* 1940. New York: Bantam Books, 1983.

Anderson, Benedict. *Imagined Communities: Reflections on the Origin and Spread of Nationalism.* 1983. London: Verso, 1991.

Atkins, John. *Six Novelists Look at Society: An Enquiry into the Social Views of Elizabeth Bowen, L. P. Hartley, Rosamund Lehman* [sic], *Christopher Isherwood, Nancy Mitford, C. P. Snow.* London: John Calder, 1977.

Baker, Mrs Daphne (née Humphrys). Unpublished memoir. Department of Documents, Imperial War Museum, London.

Barnard, Robert. *A Talent to Deceive: An Appreciation of Agatha Christie.* New York: Dodd Mead, 1980.

Barr, Charles. *Ealing Studios: A Movie Book.* 1977. Berkeley: U of California Press, 1998.

Barthes, Roland. *Mythologies.* New York: Granada, 1973.

Bawtree, Miss Viola. Unpubl. diary. Dept of Docs, IWM, London.

Beaven, Brad and John Griffiths. *Mass-Observation and Civilian Morale: Working-Class Communities During the Blitz 1940–41.* Mass-Observation Occasional Papers Series, no. 8. Brighton: Mass-Observation Archive, University of Sussex, 1998.

Bell, Mrs P. Unpubl. memoir. Dept of Docs, IWM, London.

Belsey, Mrs Elizabeth. Unpubl. letter. 3 September 1940. Dept of Docs, IWM, London.

——. Unpubl. letter. 5 September 1940. Dept of Docs, IWM, London.

——. Unpubl. letter. 7 October 1940. Dept of Docs, IWM, London.

Bergonzi, Bernard. *Wartime and Aftermath: English Literature and Its Background 1939–1960.* Oxford: Oxford UP, 1993.

"Betty." Personal testimony. 7 December 2004. *British Film Institute Classroom Resources: Screen Dreams.* British Film Institute, London. 27 May 2005 (http://www.bfi.org.uk/education/resources/teaching/screendreams/resources/testimonies/wartime.html).

"Bill." Personal testimony. 7 December 2004. *British Film Institute Classroom Resources: Screen Dreams.* BFI, London. 27 May 2005 (http://www.bfi.org.uk/

education/resources/teaching/screendreams/resources/testimonies/wartime.
html).

Blodgett, Harriet. "The Feminism of Rosamond Lehmann's Novels." *University of Mississippi Studies in English* 10 (1992): 106–21.

Bloome, David, et al. *Reading Mass-Observation Writing: Theoretical and Methodological Issues in Researching the Mass-Observation Archive.* M-O Occasional Papers Series, no. 1. Brighton: M-O A, U of Sussex Library, 1996.

Bourke, Joanna. *The Second World War: A People's History.* Oxford: Oxford UP, 2001.

———. *Working-Class Cultures in Britain 1890–1960.* 1984. London; New York: Routledge, 1996.

Bowen, Elizabeth. *Bowen's Court and Seven Winters.* 1942. London: Random House, 1999.

———. "Careless Talk." *Collected Stories* 667–70.

———. "The Cheery Soul." *Collected Stories* 641–49.

———. *The Collected Stories of Elizabeth Bowen.* Ed. Angus Wilson. New York: The Ecco Press, 1989.

———. "Contemporary." Review of *In My Good Books,* by V.S. Pritchett. *New Statesman and Nation* 23 May 1942: 340.

———. *The Demon Lover and Other Stories.* London: Jonathan Cape, 1945.

———. "The Happy Autumn Fields." *Collected Stories* 671–85.

———. *The Heat of the Day.* 1949. London: Penguin, 1987.

———. "In the Square." *Collected Stories* 609–15.

———. "Ivy Gripped the Steps." *Collected Stories* 686–711.

———. "London, 1940." *The Mulberry Tree* 21–5.

———. "The Modern Novel and the Theme of Love." Review of *The Echoing Grove,* by Rosamond Lehmann. *New Republic* 11 May 1953: 18–19.

———. *The Mulberry Tree: Writings of Elizabeth Bowen.* Ed. Hermione Lee. New York; London: Harcourt Brace Jovanovich, 1987.

———. "Mysterious Kôr." *Collected Stories* 728–40.

———. "Oh, Madam...." *Collected Stories* 578–82.

———. Preface to *The Demon Lover. The Mulberry Tree* 94–9.

———. Review of *The People's War,* by Angus Calder. *Spectator* 20 September 1969. *The Mulberry Tree* 181–5.

———. "Summer Night." *Collected Stories* 583–608.

———. "Sunday Afternoon." *Collected Stories* 618–22.

———. "Why Do I Write? Part of a Correspondence with Graham Greene and V.S. Pritchett (1948)." *The Mulberry Tree* 221–9.

Briggs, Mr. Memo to Mr Archibald. Ministry of Information. 18 August 1944. HO 262/15: Morale and Flying Bombs. The National Archives, Kew, England.

Broughton, Panthea Reid. "Narrative License in *The Echoing Grove.*" *South Central Review* 1 (1984): 85–107.

Brunetta, Leslie. "England's Finest Hour and Henry Green's *Caught.*" *Sewanee Review* 100 (1992): 33 pars. *Academic Search Elite.* EBSCO. Utah State U Library. 4 June 2005 (http://web2.epnet.com). 7 pages.

Calder, Angus. "Mass-Observation 1937–49." *Essays on the History of British Sociological Research.* Ed. Martin Bulmer. Cambridge: Cambridge UP, 1985. 121–36.

———. *The Myth of the Blitz.* 1991. London: Pimlico, 1997.

———. *The People's War: Britain 1939–1945*. 1969. London: Pimlico, 1997.

——— and Dorothy Sheridan, eds. *Speak for Yourself: A Mass-Observation Anthology, 1937–49*. London: Jonathan Cape, 1984.

Caserio, Robert. "*The Heat of the Day*: Modernism and Narrative in Paul de Man and Elizabeth Bowen." *Modern Language Quarterly* 54 (1993): 263–84.

Cawelti, John. *Adventure, Mystery, and Romance: Formula Stories as Art and Popular Culture*. Chicago, IL: U of Chicago Press, 1976.

——— and Bruce Rosenberg. *The Spy Story*. Chicago, IL: U of Chicago Press, 1987.

Chapman, James. *The British at War: Cinema, State and Propaganda, 1939–1945*. New York: St Martin's Press, 1998.

Chessman, Harriet S. "Women and Language in the Fiction of Elizabeth Bowen." *Twentieth Century Literature: A Scholarly Critical Journal* 29.1 (1983): 69–85.

Chrisp, Peter, ed. *The Blitz*. Mass-Observation Teaching Booklet Series, no. 1. Brighton: M-O A, U of Sussex Library, 1982.

Christie, Agatha. *An Autobiography*. 1977. New York: Berkley, 1991.

———. *Curtain and the Mysterious Affair at Styles*. New York: Dodd, Mead and Co., 1975.

———. *One, Two, Buckle My Shoe*. 1941. New York: Berkley, 1984.

———. *Taken at the Flood*. 1948. London: Collins, 1962.

Christie, Ian. *Arrows of Desire: The Films of Michael Powell and Emeric Pressburger*. 1985. London: Faber and Faber, 1994.

———. "A Very British Epic." Introduction. Powell and Pressburger, vii–xx.

Churchill, Winston. "The First Month of War." 1 October 1939. *Blood, Sweat, and Tears*. New York: G. P. Putnam's Sons, 1941. 171–8.

———. "Westward, Look, the Land Is Bright." 27 April 1941. *The Unrelenting Struggle*. Ed. Charles Eade. Boston: Little, Brown and Co., 1942. 91–100.

———. "The Women of Britain." 29 September 1943. *Onwards to Victory*. Ed. Charles Eade. Boston: Little, Brown and Co., 1944. 283–7.

Coates, John. "The Rewards and Problems of Rootedness in Elizabeth Bowen's *The Heat of the Day*." *Renascence* 39 (1987): 484–501.

Coopman, Tony. "Symbolism in Rosamond Lehmann's *The Echoing Grove*." *Revue des Langues Vivante Tijdschrift Voor Levande Talen* 2 (1974): 116–21.

Copeland, David. "Reading and Translating Romance in Henry Green's *Back*." *Studies in the Novel* 32 (2000): 49–69.

Corcoran, Neil. *Elizabeth Bowen: The Enforced Return*. Oxford: Oxford UP, 2004.

Costello, John. *Virtue Under Fire: How World War II Changed Our Social and Sexual Attitudes*. Boston: Little, Brown and Co., 1985.

Coughlan, Patricia. "Women and Desire in the Work of Elizabeth Bowen." *Sex, Nation, and Dissent in Irish Writing*. Ed. Éibhear Walshe. New York: St Martin's, 1997. 103–34.

Coultass, Clive. *Images for Battle: British Film and the Second World War, 1939–1945*. London: Associated University Presses, 1989.

Coward, Noël. *The Noël Coward Diaries*. Ed. Graham Payn and Sheridan Morley. Boston: Little, Brown and Co., 1982.

"Cycle of Experience." Review of *The Echoing Grove*, by Rosamond Lehmann. *Times Literary Supplement* 17 April 1953: 252.

Dawson, Graham. *Soldier Heroes: British Adventure, Empire and the Imagining of Masculinities*. London; New York: Routledge, 1994.

Day, Barry, ed. *The Letters of Noël Coward*. New York: Alfred A. Knopf, 2007.

Day-Lewis, Sean. *C. Day-Lewis: An English Literary Life*. London: Weidenfeld and Nicolson, 1980.

Dear, I. C. B. and M. R. D. Foot, eds. *The Oxford Companion to World War II*. Oxford: Oxford UP, 1995.

DeCoste, Damon Marcel. "Modernism's Shell-Shocked History: Amnesia, Repetition, and War in Graham Greene's *The Ministry of Fear*." *Twentieth Century Literature* 45 (1999): 428–51.

Deeming, David. "Henry Green's War: 'The Lull' and the Postwar Demise of Green's Modernist Aesthetic." *Modern Fiction Studies* 44 (1998): 865–87.

Diemert, Brian. *Graham Greene's Thrillers and the 1930s*. Montreal; Buffalo: McGill-Queen's UP, 1996.

Director-General, Ministry of Information. Letter to Captain L. D. Gammons. 25 August 1944. HO 262/15: Morale and Flying Bombs. The National Archives, Kew.

Dorosz, Wiktoria. *Subjective Vision and Human Relationships in the Novels of Rosamond Lehmann*. Stockholm: Textgruppen, 1975.

Dukes, Thomas. "Desire Satisfied: War and Love in *The Heat of the Day* and *Moon Tiger*." *War, Literature, and the Arts* 3 (1991): 75–97.

Review of *The Echoing Grove*, by Rosamond Lehmann. *Nation* 23 May 1953: 441.

Ellmann, Maud. "Elizabeth Bowen: The Shadowy Fifth." Mengham, *Fiction* 1–25.

Emeric Pressburger Collection. Special Collections. BFI, London.

Ferne, Mr Denis. Unpubl. memoir. Dept of Docs, IWM, London.

"Fires Were Started." Dir. Humphrey Jennings. Screenplay by Humphrey Jennings. Crown Film Unit, 1943. Videocassette. Kino Video, 1992.

"Food for Thought" in "Warwork News No. 37." British Paramount News. Ministry of Supply short S15 37. Dept of Films, IWM, London, 1943.

Foster, Kevin. *Fighting Fictions: War, Narrative and National Identity*. London: Pluto, 1999.

Fox, Jo. "Millions Like Us? Accented Language and the 'Ordinary' in British Films of the Second World War." *Journal of British Studies* 45 (2006): 819–45.

Frieser, Karl-Heinz and John T. Greenwood. *The Blitzkrieg Legend: The 1940 Campaign in the West*. Annapolis, MD: Naval Institute Press, 1995.

Gaston, Georg M. A. *The Pursuit of Salvation: A Critical Guide to the Novels of Graham Greene*. Troy, NY: Whitsun Publishing Co., 1984.

The Gentle Sex. Dir. Leslie Howard. Screenplay by Moie Charles. Two Cities Films, 1943. Videocassette. Nostalgia Family Video, 1996.

Gledhill, Christine and Gillian Swanson. *Nationalising Femininity: Culture, Sexuality, and British Cinema in the Second World War*. Manchester; New York: Manchester UP; St Martin's, 1996.

Glendinning, Victoria. *Elizabeth Bowen: Portrait of a Writer*. London: Weidenfield and Nicolson, 1977.

Godfrey, Adm. John H., Director of Naval Intelligence. Top Secret Report. April 1947. ADM 223/476: Naval Intelligence Division Reports and Papers. The National Archives, Kew.

Green, Henry. *Back*. 1946. New York: New Directions, 1981.

———. "Before the Great Fire." *Surviving: The Uncollected Writings of Henry Green*. Ed. Matthew Yorke. New York: Viking, 1993. 260–79.

———. *Caught*. 1943. London: The Harvill Press, 2001.

———. *Living*. 1929. *Loving / Living / Party Going*. New York: Penguin Books, 1978.

———. *Pack My Bag: A Self-Portrait*. 1940. London: Hogarth Press, 1992.

Green, Mrs Y. Unpubl. diary. Dept of Docs, IWM, London.

Greene, George. "Elizabeth Bowen: The Sleuth Who Bugged Tea Cups." *The Virginia Quarterly Review* 67 (1991): 604–18.

Greene, Graham. *The Ministry of Fear*. 1943. New York: Penguin Books, 1978.

———. *Ways of Escape*. 1980. New York: Washington Square Press, 1982.

Grella, George. "Murder and Manners: The Formal Detective Novel." *Novel: A Forum on Fiction* 4.1 (1970): 30–48.

Guppy, Shusha. "The Art of Fiction LXXXVIII: Rosamond Lehmann." *Nation* 23 May 1953: 181.

Hall, Stuart. "The Social Eye of *Picture Post*." University of Birmingham Centre for Contemporary Cultural Studies: Working Papers in Cultural Studies. Vol. 2.

Hall, Miss Vivienne. Unpubl. diary. Dept of Docs, IWM, London.

Hark, Ina Rae. "Impossible Murderers: Agatha Christie and the Community of Readers." *Theory and Practice of Classic Detective Fiction*. Ed. Jerome H. Delamater and Ruth Prigozy. Westport, CT: Greenwood, 1997. 111–18.

Harrisson, Tom. "Films and the Home Front – the evaluation of their effectiveness by Mass-Observation." Inter-University History Film Consortium Conference. Imperial War Museum, London. 1973. Rep. in Pronay and Spring, 234–45.

———. *Living Through the Blitz*. New York: Schocken Books, 1976.

Hartley, Jenny, ed. *Hearts Undefeated: Women's Writing of the Second World War*. London: Virago, 1994.

———. *Millions Like Us: British Women's Fiction of the Second World War*. London: Virago, 1997.

Hastings, Selina. *Rosamond Lehmann*. London: Chatto and Windus, 2002.

Haule, James M. "Moral Obligation and Social Responsibility in the Novels of Rosamond Lehmann." *Critique* 26 (1985): 192–202.

Haycraft, Howard. "The Whodunit in World War II and After." *The Art of the Mystery Story*. Ed. Haycraft. 1946. New York: Carroll and Graf, 1983. 536–42.

Hennessy, Peter. *Never Again: Britain 1945–1951*. New York: Pantheon Books, 1993.

Hewison, Robert. *Under Siege: Literary Life in London 1939–45*. London: Methuen, 1988.

Higonnet, Margaret Randolph, et al., eds. *Behind the Lines: Gender and the Two World Wars*. New Haven: Yale UP, 1987.

Hillary, Richard. *The Last Enemy*. 1942. Short Hills, NJ: Burford Books, 1997.

Hills, John, et al., eds. *Beveridge and Social Security: An International Retrospective*. Oxford: Clarendon Press, 1994.

Hoare, Philip. *Noël Coward: A Biography*. New York: Simon and Schuster, 1995.

Hoogland, Renée. *Elizabeth Bowen: A Reputation in Writing*. New York: New York UP, 1994.

Hoskins, Robert. "Greene and Wordsworth: *The Ministry of Fear*." *South Atlantic Review* 48.4 (1983): 32–42.

Hurd, Mr F. W. Unpubl. memoir. Dept of Docs, IWM, London.

In Which We Serve. Dir. Noël Coward and David Lean. Screenplay by Noël Coward. Two Cities Films, 1942. DVD. Diamond Entertainment Corporation, 2003.

Jahoda, Marie. Untitled. *Sociological Review* 30 (1938): 208–9.

Jeffrey, Tom. *Mass-Observation: A Short History*. M-O Occasional Papers Series, no. 10. Brighton: M-O A, U of Sussex Library, 1999.

Jennings, Mary-Lou, ed. *Humphrey Jennings: Film-Maker, Painter, Poet*. London: British Film Institute and Riverside Studios, 1982.

Jordan, Heather Bryant. *How Will the Heart Endure: Elizabeth Bowen and the Landscape of War*. Ann Arbor, MI: U of Michigan Press, 1992.

Kaplan, Sydney Janet. "Rosamond Lehmann's *The Ballad and the Source:* A Confrontation with 'The Great Mother.'" *Twentieth Century Literature* 27 (1981): 127–45.

Kapoor, S. "Chaos and Order in Elizabeth Bowen's *The Heat of the Day*." *Punjab University Research Bulletin: Arts* 22 (1991): 119–23.

Klein, Kathleen Gregory. *The Woman Detective: Gender and Genre*. Urbana; Chicago, IL: U of Illinois Press, 1988.

Knepper, Marty S. "Agatha Christie – Feminist." *Armchair Detective: A Quarterly Journal Devoted to the Appreciation of Mystery, Detection, and Suspense Fiction* 16 (1983): 398–406.

Lant, Antonia. *Blackout: Reinventing Women for Wartime British Cinema*. Princeton, NJ: Princeton UP, 1991.

Lassner, Phyllis. *British Women Writers of World War Two: Battlegrounds of Their Own*. New York: Palgrave, 1998.

———. *Elizabeth Bowen: A Study of the Short Fiction*. Ed. Gordon Weaver. Twayne's Studies in Short Fiction Series 27. New York: Twayne Publishers, 1991.

———. "Reimagining the Arts of War: Language and History in Elizabeth Bowen's *The Heat of the Day* and Rose Macaulay's *The World My Wilderness*." *Perspectives on Contemporary Literature* 14 (1988): 30–8.

———. "The Timeless Elsewhere of the Second World War: Rosamond Lehmann's *The Ballad and the Source* and Kate O'Brien's *The Last Summer*." Mengham, *Fiction* 70–90.

le Carré, John. *The Spy Who Came in from the Cold*. 1963. New York: Ballantine Books, 1992.

———. *Tinker, Tailor, Soldier, Spy*. 1974. New York: Scribner, 2002.

Lee, Hermione. *Elizabeth Bowen: An Estimation*. London: Vision Press, 1981.

Lehmann, John. *I Am My Brother*. New York: Reynal and Co., 1960.

Lehmann, Rosamond. *The Ballad and the Source*. 1944. New York: Reynal and Hitchcock, 1945.

———. "A Dream of Winter." *Gipsy's Baby* 101–12.

———. *The Echoing Grove*. 1953. New York: Harcourt Brace Jovanovich, 1980.

———. "The Gipsy's Baby." *Gipsy's Baby* 9–54.

———. *The Gipsy's Baby and Other Stories*. 1946. London: Collins, 1954.

———. "The Red-Haired Miss Daintreys." *Gipsy's Baby* 57–90.

———. "When the Waters Came." *Gipsy's Baby* 93–8.

———. "Wonderful Holidays." *Gipsy's Baby* 115–92.

Lejeune, C. A. *Chestnuts in Her Lap 1936–1946*. London: Phoenix House, Ltd, 1947.

————. "Mädchen in Uniform." Review of *The Gentle Sex*. *Observer*, 1943. *Chestnuts* 95–6.

————. "Picture Theatres." Review of *Millions Like Us*. *Manchester Guardian* 28 December 1943.

————. Review of *The Life and Death of Colonel Blimp*. *Observer* 13 June 1943. Powell and Pressburger 55–7.

LeStourgeon, Diana. *Rosamond Lehmann*. New York: Twayne Publishers, 1965.

The Life and Death of Colonel Blimp. Dir. Michael Powell and Emeric Pressburger. Screenplay by Michael Powell and Emeric Pressburger. The Archers, 1943. DVD. Criterion, 2002.

Review of *The Life and Death of Colonel Blimp*. *Tribune* 18 June 1943. Powell and Pressburger 59–60.

"London Can Take It." Dir. Humphrey Jennings and Harry Watt. Screenplay by Quentin Reynolds. General Post Office (GPO) Film Unit, 1940. Videocassette. Kino Video, 1992.

Low, David. "Blimp Faces the Crisis." Cartoon. *Evening Standard* 5 October 1935; the British Cartoon Archive, University of Kent, catalogue record LSE5327 at ⟨http://www.kent.ac.uk/cartoons/⟩.

————. *Low's Autobiography*. New York: Simon and Schuster, 1957.

Lowe, Rodney. "The Second World War, Consensus, and the Foundation of the Welfare State." *Twentieth Century British History* 1 (1990): 152–82.

MacKay, Marina. *Modernism and World War II*. Cambridge: Cambridge UP, 2007.

MacKenzie, S. P. *The Home Guard: A Military and Political History*. Oxford: Oxford UP, 1995.

Mandel, Ernest. *Delightful Murder: A Social History of the Crime Story*. London: Pluto, 1984.

Marlowe, Jack [John Lehmann]. "A Reader's Notebook." Review of *Caught*, by Henry Green. *Penguin New Writing* 17 (April–June 1943): 155–65.

Marshall, T. H. "Is Mass-Observation Moonshine?" *Highway* December 1937: 48–50.

Martin, Richard. *Ink in Her Blood: The Life and Crime Fiction of Margery Allingham*. Ann Arbor, MI: U of Michigan Press, 1988.

Marwick, Arthur. *Class: Image and Reality in Britain, France and the USA since 1930*. New York; Oxford: Oxford UP, 1980.

————. *The Home Front: The British and the Second World War*. London; New York: Thames and Hudson, 1976.

Mass-Observation. *War Factory: A Report*. London: Gollancz, 1943.

Mass-Observation Archive: Directive Respondent 1553, reply to September 1942 Directive.

————. DR 1637, reply to June 1944 Directive.

————. DR 2466, replies to January 1943 and June 1944 Directives.

————. DR 2656, reply to September 1942 Directive.

————. DR 2685, reply to January 1943 Directive.

————. DR 2686, reply to September 1942 Directive.

————. DR 2694, reply to September 1942 Directive.

————. DR 2863, reply to September 1942 Directive.

————. DR 2865, reply to September 1942 Directive.

————. DR 2873, reply to September 1942 Directive.

———. DR 2973, reply to September 1942 Directive.

———. DR 3002, reply to January 1943 Directive.

———. DR 3306, reply to January 1943 Directive.

———. File Report 1, "Propaganda," 11 October 1939.

———. FR 16, "Faking of Newsreels," January 1940.

———. FR 93, "Us 14," May 1940.

———. FR 215, "Newsreels in Early June," June 1940.

———. FR 394, "Mass-Observation Film Work," September 1940.

———. FR 431, "Survey of the Voluntary and Official Bodies During Bombing of the East End," September 1940.

———. FR 520, "Women and Morale," December 1940.

———. FR 530, "Women and the War Effort," December 1940.

———. FR 757, "General Picture of WAAF Life," June 1941.

———. FR 1029, "WAAF Observer," January 1942.

———. FR 1083, "ATS Campaign," February 1942.

———. FR 1238, "Appeals to Women," May 1942.

———. FR 1390, "Tube Investments Ltd," August 1942.

———. FR 1620, "After the War – Feelings in the WAAF," March 1943.

———. FR 1871, "Wartime Social Survey: The Cinema Audience," June–July 1943.

———. FR 2018, "Books and the Public: Major Report on Reading Habits for the National Book Council," February 1944.

———. FR 2059, "Will the Factory Girls Want to Stay Put or Go Home?" March 1944.

———. Topic Collection 6: "Conscientious Objection and Pacifism 1939–44," 3/B, "Interviews" (Question 5: What do you think of Winston Churchill?), 5 April 1940.

———. TC 17: "Film Reports 1939–40," 2/F, "Letter to Geoffrey Le Mander re: MOI Film Department," London, 30 November 1939.

———. TC 17, 2/G, "The Cinema in the First Three Months of War," London, January 1940.

———. TC 17, 2/G, "Film Report," London, March 1940.

———. TC 17, 2/G, "Letter from Film Observer to Newspaper to Recruit Film Panel," London, 30 November 1940.

———. TC 17, 2/H, "Film Stars and the Services," London, October 1940.

———. TC 17, 3/E, "Cinemas in Bermondsey and Stepney 1940–41," Stepney, April 1940.

———. TC 17, 4/F, "Film Reports 1938–46 – 'Miss Grant Goes to the Door,'" London, August 1940.

———. TC 17, 8/A, "Memo on 'Miss Grant Goes to the Door,'" London, August 1940.

———. TC 20: "Reading Habits 1937–47," 4/E, "Book Reading Indirects," London, 2 June 1942.

———. TC 23: "Air Raids 1938–45," 5/C, "Observations Gathered in September 1940," Maida Vale, 9 September 1940.

———. TC 25: "Political Attitudes and Behaviour," 6/I, "Report from Mass-Observation on Churchill's Broadcast: 19 May 1940," London, 21 May 1940.

———. TC 29: "Forces: Men in the Forces 1939–56," 1/F, "The Public and Soldiers 1940–41," London, July–August 1940.

——. TC 32: "Women in Wartime," 1/E, "Women in the Forces," London, August 1940.

——. TC 32, 1/F, "Male Attitudes to Women in the Forces," London and Holdsworth, September and December 1941.

——. TC 32, 2/E, "ATS Survey," Hampstead, October 1941.

——. TC 32, 3/D, "WAAF Observations," Nottingham, August 1941.

——. TC 32, 3/E, "Letter to Tom Harrisson," Preston, April 1941.

——. TC 32, 3/E, "Morality at Digby," Digby, July 1941.

McLaine, Ian. *Ministry of Morale: Home Front Morale and the Ministry of Information in World War II.* London: Allen & Unwin, 1979.

Mengham, Rod. "Broken Glass." Mengham, *Fiction* 124–33.

——. *The Idiom of the Time: The Writings of Henry Green.* Cambridge: Cambridge UP, 1983.

—— and N. H. Reeve, eds. *The Fiction of the 1940s: Stories of Survival.* New York: Palgrave, 2001.

Millions Like Us. Dir. and Screenplay by Sidney Gilliat and Frank Launder. Gainsborough Pictures Ltd, 1943. Videocassette. Nostalgia Family Video, 1996.

"Miss Grant Goes to the Door." Dir. Brian Desmond Hurst. Denham and Pinewood Studios. MOI short COI 455. Dept of Films, IWM, London, 1940.

Mitchell, Ron. "The London Blitz." 3 November 2005. *WW2 People's War: An Archive of World War Two Memories.* British Broadcasting Company, London. 12 September 2007 (http://www.bbc.co.uk/ww2peopleswar/stories/47/a6655647.shtml7).

Moreton, George. *Doctor in Chains.* London: Baker, 1970.

Morgan, David and Mary Evans. *The Battle for Britain: Citizenship and Ideology in the Second World War.* London: Routledge, 1993.

Morgan, Guy. *Red Roses Every Night: An Account of London Cinemas Under Fire.* London: Quality Press, 1948.

Morgan, Kenneth O. *The People's Peace.* Oxford: Oxford UP, 1990.

Morley, Sheridan. *A Talent to Amuse: A Biography of Noël Coward.* 1969. Boston: Little, Brown and Co., 1985.

Morton, Mr. Desmond. Memo to Prime Minister Winston Churchill. 9 March 1944. PREM 3/345/6: Security Records of the Prime Minister's Office. The National Archives, Kew.

Murdoch, Derrick. *The Agatha Christie Mystery.* Toronto: Pagurian Press, 1976.

North, Michael. *Henry Green and the Writing of His Generation.* Charlottesville, VA: UP of Virginia, 1984.

Oakman, Miss Josephine May. Unpubl. diary. Dept of Docs, IWM, London.

Palmer, Graham. *Prisoner of Death: A Gripping Memoir of Courage and Survival Under the Third Reich.* Northampton, UK: Stephens, 1990.

Palmer, Jerry. *Thrillers: Genesis and Structures of a Popular Genre.* London: Edward Arnold, 1978.

Panek, LeRoy. *The Special Branch: The British Spy Novel, 1890–1980.* Bowling Green, OH: Bowling Green U Popular Press, 1981.

Parsons, Deborah L. "Souls Astray: Elizabeth Bowen's Landscape of War." *Women: A Cultural Review* 8.1 (1997): 24–32.

"Peggy." Personal testimony. 7 December 2004. *British Film Institute Classroom Resources: Screen Dreams.* BFI, London. 27 May 2005 (http://www.bfi.org.uk/education/resources/teaching/screendreams/resources/testimonies/wartime.html).

Peterson, Virgilia. "Those Experiences of the Heart." Review of *The Echoing Grove*, by Rosamond Lehmann. *New York Herald Tribune Books* 10 May 1953: 1, 8.

Pfaltz, Katherine. "The Lehmann Woman." *Études Britanniques Contemporaines: Revue de la Société d' Études Anglaises Contemporaines* 1 (1992): 99–113.

Plain, Gill. *Women's Fiction of the Second World War: Gender, Power and Resistance.* Edinburgh: Edinburgh UP, 1996.

Pollard, Wendy. *Rosamond Lehmann and Her Critics: The Vagaries of Literary Reception.* Aldershot, Hants, England: Ashgate, 2004.

Powell, Dilys. *Films Since 1939.* London: Longmans, Green, 1947.

———. Review of *In Which We Serve. Sunday Times* 29 September 1942. Clipping, file on *In Which We Serve.* BFI, London.

———. Review of *The Life and Death of Colonel Blimp. Sunday Times* 17 September 1943. Powell and Pressburger 54–5.

Powell, Michael and Emeric Pressburger. *The Life and Death of Colonel Blimp.* Ed. Ian Christie. London: Faber and Faber, 1994.

Pronay, Nicholas and D. W. Spring, eds. *Propaganda, Politics and Film, 1918–45.* 1982. London: Palgrave, 1986.

Rattigan, Neil. *This Is England: British Film and the People's War, 1939–1945.* London: Associated University Presses, 2001.

Rauchbauer, Otto. "The Big House and Irish History: An Introductory Sketch." *Ancestral Voices: The Big House in Anglo-Irish Literature.* Ed. Otto Rauchbauer. New York: Georg Olms Verlag, 1992. 1–15.

Rawlinson, Mark. *British Writing of the Second World War.* Oxford: Oxford UP, 2000.

Reid, John Howard. *Top-Grossing Pictures at the British Box-Office 1936–1970.* Original Collectors' Edition. Wyong, Australia: Reid's Film Index, 1997.

Richards, Jeffrey and Anthony Aldgate. *Best of British: Cinema and Society from 1930 to Present.* London: I.B. Taurus, 1999.

——— and Dorothy Sheridan, eds. *Mass-Observation at the Movies.* London: Routledge, 1987.

Robyns, Gwen. *The Mystery of Agatha Christie.* New York: Doubleday, 1978.

Rose, Sonya O. *Which People's War? National Identity and Citizenship in Britain 1939–1945.* Oxford: Oxford UP, 2003.

Russell, John. *Henry Green: Nine Novels and an Unpacked Bag.* New Brunswick, NJ: Rutgers UP, 1960.

Sackville-West, Vita. "The Eternal Game." Review of *The Echoing Grove*, by Rosamond Lehmann. *Spectator* 10 April 1953: 454.

Sarisalmi, Tina. "Instances of Strangeness and Disruption: Women and Language in Elizabeth Bowen's Fiction." *Voicing Gender.* Ed. Yvonne Hyrynen. Tampere, Finland: U of Tampere, 1996. 151–62.

Saywell, Shelley. *Women in War.* New York: Viking, 1985.

Scarry, Elaine. *The Body in Pain: The Making and Unmaking of the World.* 1985. New York: Oxford UP, 1987.

Schneider, Karen. *Loving Arms: British Women Writing the Second World War.* Lexington, KY: UP of Kentucky, 1997.

Scott-James, R. A. *Fifty Years of English Literature: 1900–1950.* 1951. London: Longmans, 1967.

Shaw, Jenny. *Intellectual Property, Representative Experience and Mass-Observation.* M-O Occasional Papers Series, no. 9. Brighton: M-O A, U of Sussex Library, 1998.

Sheridan, Dorothy. *Wartime Women: An Anthology of Women's Wartime Writing for Mass-Observation 1937–45.* London: Heinemann, 1990.

Sherry, Norman. *The Life of Graham Greene: Volume II: 1939–1955.* 1994. New York: Penguin Books, 1996.

Siegel, Ruth. *Rosamond Lehmann: A Thirties Writer.* New York: Peter Lang, 1989.

Silverstein, Marc. "After the Fall: The World of Graham Greene's Thrillers." *Novel* 22 (1988): 24–44.

Simons, Judy. *Modern Novelists: Rosamond Lehmann.* New York: St Martin's Press, 1992.

Smith, Harold L. *Britain in the Second World War: A Social History.* Manchester: Manchester UP, 1996.

Smith, Rowland. "A People's War in Greeneland: Heroic Virtue and Communal Effort in the Wartime Tales." *Graham Greene: A Revaluation: New Essays.* Ed. Jeffrey Meyers. New York: St Martin's Press, 1990. 104–30.

"Soldier's Unfaithful Wife." *Times* [London] 27 September 1945, late ed.: 2.

Stafford, David. *The Silent Game: The Real World of Imaginary Spies.* Athens, GA: U of Georgia Press, 1991.

Stanley, Nick. *"The Extra Dimension": A Study and Assessment of the Methods Employed by Mass-Observation in Its First Period 1937–1940.* CNAA D. Phil. Thesis, Birmingham Polytechnic.

Stonebridge, Lyndsey. "Bombs and Roses: The Writing of Anxiety in Henry Green's *Caught.*" *Diacritics* 28.4 (1998): 25–43.

———. *The Writing of Anxiety: Imagining Wartime in Mid-Century British Culture.* Language, Discourse, Society. Houndsmills, England: Palgrave Macmillan, 2007.

Summerfield, Penny. "Approaches to Women and Social Change in the Second World War." *What Difference Did the War Make?* Ed. Brian Brivati and Harriet Jones. London; New York: Leicester UP, 1993. 65–70.

———. *Reconstructing Women's Wartime Lives: Discourse and Subjectivity in Oral Histories of the Second World War.* Manchester; New York: Manchester UP; St Martin's, 1998.

———. *Women Workers in the Second World War: Production and Patriarchy in Conflict.* London; New York: Routledge, 1984.

——— and Corinna Peniston-Bird. *Contesting Home Defence: Men, Women and the Home Guard in the Second World War.* Manchester: Manchester UP, 2007.

———. "Women in the Firing Line: The Home Guard and the Defence of Gender Boundaries in Britain in the Second World War." *Women's History Review* 9 (2000): 231–55.

Symons, Julian. *Bloody Murder: From the Detective to the Crime Novel.* 1972. London: Faber and Faber, 1992.

Tate, Trudi. *Modernism, History and the First World War.* Manchester: Manchester UP, 1998.

Thompson, Jon. *Fiction, Crime, and Empire: Clues to Modernity and Postmodernism.* Urbana, IL: U of Illinois Press, 1993.

Thorogood, Julia. *Margery Allingham: A Biography.* London: Heinemann, 1991.

Tindall, Gillian. *Rosamond Lehmann: An Appreciation.* London: Chatto and Windus, 1985.

Titmuss, Richard M. *Problems of Social Policy*. Ed. W. K. Hancock. *History of the Second World War United Kingdom Civil Series*. London: Longmans, Green and Co., 1950.

Tracy, Honor. "New Novels." Review of *The Echoing Grove*, by Rosamond Lehmann. *New Statesman and Nation* 11 April 1953: 434.

Treglown, Jeremy. *Romancing: The Life and Work of Henry Green*. New York: Random House, 2000.

Vipond, M. "Agatha Christie's Women." *The International Fiction Review* 8 (1981): 119–23.

Walters, Margaret. "Romantic Pursuits: The Art of Rosamond Lehmann." *Encounter* 65.2 (1985): 44–7.

Waterfield, Robin. Foreword. *Dear David, Dear Graham, A Bibliographic Correspondence*. Oxford: The Alembic Press, 1989. 5–6.

Watson, Barbara Bellow. "Variations on an Enigma: Elizabeth Bowen's War Novel." *Southern Humanities Review* 15.2 (1981): 131–51.

Weatherhead, A. Kingsley. *A Reading of Henry Green*. Seattle, WA: U of Washington Press, 1961.

West, W. J. *The Quest for Graham Greene*. New York: St Martin's Press, 1997.

Williams, Francis. Memo to Sir Kenneth Clark. 16 April 1941. INF 1/251: Home Planning Executive Committee. The National Archives, Kew.

Winks, Robin. Introduction. *Detective Fiction: A Collection of Critical Essays*. Ed. Winks. Englewood Cliffs, NJ: Prentice-Hall, Inc., 1980. 1–14.

Wintringham, Tom. *People's War*. Harmondsworth, Middlesex, England: Penguin Books, 1942.

Woodcock, Mr S. M. P. Unpubl. diary. Dept of Docs, IWM, London.

Woollacott, Angela. "Sisters and Brothers in Arms: Family, Class, and Gendering in World War I Britain." *Gendering War Talk*. Ed. Miriam Cooke and Angela Woollacott. Princeton, NJ: Princeton UP, 1993. 28–47.

Yonge, Charlotte. *The Little Duke*. 1854. Whitefish, MT: Kessinger Publishing, 2004.

York, R. A. *Agatha Christie: Power and Illusion*. Crime Files Series. Houndsmills, Basingstoke, Hampshire, UK: Palgrave Macmillan, 2007.

Ziegler, Philip. *London at War: 1939–1945*. New York: Alfred A. Knopf, 1995.

Index